PRAISE FOR RANDAL SILVIS'S
RYAN DEMARCO SERIES

"A poignant and gritty thriller that reveals humanity's best and worst."
—Kate Kessler, bestselling author, for *No Woods So Dark as These*

"The rare crime novel infused with both darkness and light. The characters are so real I expected to meet them for a drink at the end of the day."
—Kelly Simmons, international bestselling author of *Where She Went* and *One More Day*, for *No Woods So Dark as These*

"Well-crafted prose, smart dialogue, and complex characters create a chilling thriller."
—Mary Burton, *New York Times* and *USA Today* bestselling author, for *No Woods So Dark as These*

"Silvis knows how to take you with him, how to put you in those woods right alongside DeMarco. The air is cold, the sky a blanket of gray, and an all-but-broken detective confronts a horrific new crime—even as he himself is being hunted. These woods are dark indeed."
—Joseph Schneider, author of *One Day You'll Burn*, for *No Woods So Dark as These*

"Silvis smoothly blends moments of exquisite beauty into a sea of darker emotion to create a moving story heavy with the theme of the 'past is never past.'"
—*Publishers Weekly* for *Walking the Bones*

"An absolute gem of literary suspense, pitting ordinary people in extraordinary circumstances and told in a smooth, assured, and often haunting voice, *Two Days Gone* is a terrific read."
—Michael Koryta, *New York Times* bestselling author of *Those Who Wish Me Dead*, for *Two Days Gone*

ALSO BY RANDALL SILVIS

A Ryan
DeMarco
Mystery

NO
WOODS
SO DARK
AS THESE

RANDALL SILVIS

Poisoned Pen
PRESS

Published by Poisoned Pen Press, an imprint of Sourcebooks
P.O. Box 4410, Naperville, Illinois 60567-4410
(630) 961-3900
sourcebooks.com

Library of Congress Cataloging-in-Publication Data

Names: Silvis, Randall, author.
Title: No woods so dark as these / Randall Silvis.
Description: Naperville : Poisoned Pen Press, 2020. | Series: A Ryan
    DeMarco mystery ; 4
Identifiers: LCCN 2019042453 | (trade paperback)
Subjects: LCSH: Psychological fiction. | GSAFD: Suspense fiction. | Mystery
    fiction.
Classification: LCC PS3569.I47235 N6 2020 | DDC 813/.54--dc23
LC record available at https://lccn.loc.gov/2019042453

Printed and bound in Canada.
MBP 10 9 8 7 6 5 4 3 2 1

I

Now is the winter of our discontent...
Dive, thoughts, down to my soul.

—William Shakespeare, *Richard III*

ONE

A light vapor of fog hung in the air between the trees, a subtle graying discernible only when the man looked out one of the pickup truck's windows but not when he glanced at his sons sitting beside him in the cab. By noon the fog would lift, revealing woods full of leaves startlingly golden and red and orange, but those colors were muted now, the leaves heavy with moisture that dripped onto the truck's windshield and plunked onto the metal roof like a stutter of typing from a slow-thinking writer.

A couple of times as the man drove slowly along the dirt road, he thought he detected the scent of smoke in the air, though not the sweet scent of leaf or wood smoke but with a taint of anger and bitterness, which made him wonder if the engine was overheating from being driven in low gear too long. The gauge said no, everything was fine, so he told himself that he had only imagined the unpleasant odor. The same thing happened sometimes in his home, when out of nowhere a scent of pipe smoke would be detectable, even though no one in his family smoked nor had the previous owners of the house. His father had smoked a pipe, but his father had died before the man and his family moved into that house, and sometimes at home he felt the presence of his father's spirit, a stern and watchful presence that somehow muted the still stinging grief of loss.

It was the third week of October and the kind of autumn

morning when a man remembered such things, though not unpleasantly. This was a good morning, filled with the kind of hushed excitement he had felt as a boy when alone in the woods with his own father. And now one generation had ceded and another was taking its place.

The man and his two sons, ages thirteen and nine, were having a good time cruising the unmapped roads of Otter Creek Township in the family's red Silverado. The day felt special for all of them, a rare day off from work for him and from school for the boys, and a Monday at that. The father was grateful to be able to share the woods with his sons and maybe imbue in them some of his love and respect for nature. He should have insisted on doing this years ago, should have started when his oldest boy was small. It was good for them and good for him too, rising before the sun for a change, getting away from the idiot box and the computer. He had all but forgotten the quality of light and air in the woods, the way just being there again softened his voice and slowed his movements, made him feel part of something vast and unknowable. There was no way to get that feeling in a house or office or classroom, or even, anymore, in a church. He was looking forward to getting out of the truck and walking, or just sitting on a log for a while and watching the peacefulness seep into his boys. Watching the mystery quiet their otherwise noisy, clamorous souls.

And if they were successful in their hunt next month, they would also have that story to tell and to remember always. That keenly alert elevation of their senses as they crept through the woods, as alert as the animals, sniffing and tasting the air, feeling the light and the ground and every vibration of movement.

Such mindfulness did not require the act of killing, but the prospect of killing brought it on early and gave it a fine steel point. A hunter could always decide at the last moment to lift his finger from the trigger. He had done it himself many times before he gave up hunting altogether. Yet he retained the memories of walking through the woods at sunrise in a heightened state of alertness, and they warmed him often when he found himself missing his father. He hoped now to give those moments to his sons too; they would remember them through the deadness of winter, through the dim, dreary school days after the first of the new year, those two strangulating months when the world seems not new at all but hovering close to death.

He had been told there were some big whitetails in these woods. Plus black bear, coyote, maybe some bobcats too. It was unlikely they would encounter any of those predators, and the weather was too cold for the copperheads and rattlers, but the gray and red foxes would not be as skittish, nor the wild turkey, hawks and bald eagles. He wanted his sons to learn to identify them all, learn to be comfortable in the woods, not afraid of nature as so many kids were these days. "That's what's wrong with society," his own father had told him. "You spend your whole life hiding indoors, you're going to end up with a soul the size of a raisin."

The October morning was gray and damp, with a cool mist that made the windshield wipers necessary, but the cab was warm, there was plenty of Gatorade and beef jerky to go around, and the boys, dressed in new rubber camo boots and bright orange jackets, were excited about picking out their hunting grounds for the first day of buck season. Under the Game Commission's Mentored Youth Hunting Program, the nine-year-old was of legal age to hunt, but his father disagreed, and though he would permit his youngest to accompany them into the woods in November, he did not think it rational that an instrument engineered for death should be placed in the hands of a child so young.

He considered himself a good father and believed that only

fierce love and vigilance could protect his sons from the increasing evil of the world. His single point of annoyance with his wife was that she often took her eyes off the boys at the mall and elsewhere, would try on dresses, for example, while their sons wandered off on their own. He agreed with her that boys had to be given some freedom but insisted that as parents their job was always to watch from a safe distance, to remain always alert to the possibility of harm. So when, earlier that month, the youngest boy, influenced by his classmates, had begged and begged to be allowed to hunt this year, and his mother had shrugged, his father, who had hunted with his own father from the age of twelve to twenty-three, had conceded in part, and said that he and the older son would hunt and that the younger boy would be their spotter—"an honor," he told him, "not to be taken lightly."

And now the truck moved haltingly along the muddy lane, the side windows down for a clearer view. The boys were scouring the trees and earth for "sign"—ditch and creek crossings, bedding areas, and buck rubs made on tree trunks, where an animal had scraped its head and antlers to leave scent pheromones, release sexual tension, and mark its territory.

"A mature buck can move like a ghost," the father told his boys, hearing his own father's words come alive again. "If you don't know where to look, you will never see one."

"I see a ghost down there!" the nine-year-old said a few minutes later, and leaned across his brother to point deeper into the woods.

His father slowed the truck to a halt, leaned into his son, and squinted. A wisp of smoke twisting up through the trees. "Somebody's campfire," he said.

"No it's not," the older boy told him. "There's something big down there."

"We'll have a look," his father said, and put the gearshift in

Park. Immediately the older boy sprang his door open, and he and his brother piled out, both heading into the woods. "Hold it!" their father shouted. "You boys wait for me."

The oldest pulled up short, always obedient. But the youngest broke into a run. "I'm the spotter!"

His father called him back again but to no avail, and so jogged alongside his oldest son as they followed the youngest. Soon the object in the mist became visible. A hatchback burned black, tires melted, with a thick thread of dark smoke still wafting lazily into the treetops, a stink of burned metal and rubber and meat in the air.

The father had barely enough time to recognize a mounting dread in his bones when the youngest, who had rushed up to a blasted-out window, turned to him and cried, *"Daddy!"*

The father had never seen such a look on his son's face, the disbelief and horror. Afterward, for weeks and weeks of scream-shot nights, he prayed God would wash that look and the sights and scents that triggered it from all of their dreams forever.

TWO

Jayme awoke at first light and was surprised to find DeMarco still asleep with his back to her. She thought about putting her hand against his neck and snuggling close but a part of her did not want him to awaken just yet. She eased out of bed as quietly as she could and started toward the bathroom. Along the way she glanced at the window and saw how the curtain was glowing with the first light of morning, so she crossed to the window and pulled the curtain aside and stepped up to the glass and then drew the curtain behind her so that she could hold the edge of it with her other hand and keep the light from filling the room and waking DeMarco. The curtain enclosed her and shut her off from the rest of the room. She was not ready yet to start another day or to lie down beside him again and have him open his eyes and look at her so that she had to smile and say something nice. She wanted to look out the window for a while and be left to herself.

The sun had not yet breached the horizon but the sky was glowing a lovely orange to the east and the day was going to be temperate and clear and pleasant. They would have another pleasant day and people would go about their day as usual, and all the while all around the world women would be giving birth and pushing out babies. And in some places babies were dying and in other places they were being killed before they could be born. They were being scraped out of the womb and hacked up into pieces and in some places tiny babies were starving or suffering because of their mother's habits or being abandoned or abused or being left in hot cars or being shaken or beaten or made to lie wailing all day with shitty diapers and rashes and diseases that could not be cured. All over the world babies were being born into a world of suffering and evil and it just wasn't fair. Her baby would have been loved and cherished every moment of its life; would have been taught kindness and compassion and generosity and there was not a damn thing fair about any of it. And there was nothing Jayme or anybody else could do about it now. She was supposed to be sweet and strong and to keep smiling as if nothing had ever happened. As if she had not felt that life growing inside her and had not awakened in the hospital to feel only emptiness. As if some part of her had not been irremediably ripped away leaving a hole that could never be filled or healed or sutured shut. She stood with her forehead against the cold glass and her hands pressing hard against her belly, her body convulsing with the sobs she did her best to silence and contain.

Only when DeMarco rolled onto his back and the bedsprings creaked did she draw in a long, cold breath and manage to hold herself motionless again. She waited for him to speak, but when he did not and was probably still sleeping she slipped out from under the curtain and into the bathroom without looking his way. She pulled the door shut quietly and turned on the tap and dabbed cool water against her face. She rinsed her mouth with mouthwash and then flushed the toilet, and after another long look at herself in the mirror, she opened the door and stepped out.

He was awake and lying on his side facing the bathroom now and smiling. She went to him and lay close to him and said, "Good morning, my love."

"Good morning, beauty," he said, and kissed her lightly on the lips. "We have court today. What kind of a day is it going to be?"

"Sunny and clear," she told him. "Pleasant all around."

He smiled and leaned close and kissed her again, this time holding it longer and laying his hand against her cheek.

"Are you happy, babe?" she asked, and stroked his hand with her fingertips.

"You make me very happy," he said.

"But in general are you happy? I want you to be completely happy."

"I am extraordinarily happy."

"Are you really?"

"Really? Yes, really."

"Really and *truly* happy?"

He blinked once, then stretched out his legs. "Well...I guess that depends on what you mean by 'really and truly happy.' What does that phrase mean to you?"

"To be content with your life. Exactly as it is."

"Hmm. Well, in that case, I guess I'm probably not. Not *exactly* as it is."

"To be satisfied with the way things are."

"Is that even a good thing?" he asked. "I would have to answer no, I am not satisfied with the way things are. Not everything."

"To be pleased, fulfilled, at peace with the status quo."

"None of the above. Sorry."

"Me neither," she said. The ache pinched like a claw around her heart, yet she continued to smile.

"Jesus, we're miserable people, aren't we?" he said.

THREE

"Court is now in session, the Honorable Judge Eileen Cleary presiding."

Despite its spaciousness and high ceiling and the abundant light painting the polished wood and marble with a soft glow, the courtroom seemed overheated to DeMarco. He and Jayme sat side by side behind the long counsel table and four chairs occupied by the prosecution's team. Mahoning County sheriff Ben Brinker sat beside Jayme, with Detectives Olcott and Fascetti filling out the row. Behind them, the gallery was full and hushed, the air heavy with anticipation.

"She's a good draw," Brinker had told them earlier of Judge Cleary. "Firm but fair. Law and order straight down the road, but unfortunately not a fan of capital punishment."

Nor would the prosecution be seeking the death penalty for Connor McBride. The young man had been cooperating with the DA and had agreed to plead guilty to the murders of Jerome Hufford and Justin Brenner in exchange for a recommendation of twenty years to life. The judge was not bound by that agreement, and could increase or decrease the sentence as she saw fit. McBride had turned twenty-one while in jail, and his relative youth, Brinker had said, "is likely to figure in" to the judge's deliberations. "She tends to go a little lighter on the kids. Has five of her own."

He could remember only once when she had sentenced a man

to death, and had prefaced that decision by saying, "This judgment does not weigh easily on me, nor should it. But as a shepherd of the public good, it is my responsibility to keep the flock from harm. And sometimes it is wiser to not merely chase the wolf away from the flock, but to ensure that the wolf can never return."

And now DeMarco sat motionless, hands clasped between his legs as he watched Judge Cleary at the bench. She leaned slightly forward in her seat, her eyes on a notebook laid before her. She was in her late fifties, had salt-and-pepper hair cut in a choppy shag that framed an attractive but solemn face. There was something about her that brought memories of his mother back to DeMarco. The ones from when he was small, before the weight of desperation and surrender grew too heavy in her. He remembered gathering autumn leaves with his mother. Remembered building snowmen and snow forts together in the dirty snow. In summer she would hand him a little white plastic bucket, take a bigger one in her own hand, and they would wander away from home to pick raspberries and elderberries along the roadside, or blueberries and wild apples in the woods. Those were his first excursions into the woods, the ones responsible for his love of trees and solitude and wild things. There had been lots of milkweed plants back then too, lots of caterpillars and butterflies to watch. Whatever wild fruits were in season, he and his mother would fill their buckets, then take the fruit back to the trailer, wash and boil it with sugar, make jars of jelly she would spread over slices of white Wonder Bread. Sometimes she would make french toast and spread the jelly over it too. Just thinking about it made his mouth water.

Those were all good memories. The best he had of his mother. His father was a part of none of them.

And now, as he waited for Judge Cleary to speak, he smiled to himself, and Jayme noticed that smile. She whispered, "Think of something funny?"

He shook his head. "My mother. French toast with raspberry jelly."

Before Jayme could respond, Judge Cleary looked up. Her gaze went straight to the defense table. "In the matter of the *State v. McBride*," she said, "Mr. McBride, how do you plead?"

McBride and his attorney stood, and McBride, in a neat blue suit, white shirt and plain blue tie, with his gaze aimed several feet below the judge's eyes, answered softly, "Guilty, Your Honor."

"Counsel," she asked, and turned her eyes to the prosecuting attorney, "have you reached a settlement?"

"Yes, Your Honor. The people have agreed to twenty years to life…" These words prompted a low rumble of murmurs from the gallery, which in turn prompted the young prosecutor to continue more quickly. "…contingent upon Mr. McBride's continuing cooperation in the cases pending against Professor Gillespie and Daksh Khatri."

Judge Cleary nodded. Then again shifted her gaze to the counsel table on her right. "Mr. McBride, have you been informed that by pleading guilty you forfeit the right to a jury trial?"

"Yes, Your Honor."

"I need you to look at me when you address me," she said.

He lifted his head. "Yes, Your Honor."

"And do you give up that right?"

"Yes, Your Honor."

"Do you understand what giving up that right means?"

"I do."

"Do you know that you are waiving the right to cross-examine your accusers?"

"Yes, Your Honor."

"Do you know that you are waiving your privilege against self-incrimination?"

"I do, Your Honor."

"Did anyone pressure you or force you into accepting this settlement?"

"No, Your Honor."

"Are you pleading guilty because you did in fact suffocate Justin Brenner and Jerome Hufford, and then dismember and dispose of their bodies?"

McBride's mouth twisted up at the corner, and his eyes briefly closed. "Yes, Your Honor."

In the gallery, McBride's mother moaned, and then began to sob.

The judge was quiet for a full half minute as she studied his face. Then she turned her gaze to the left again, but looked just beyond those seated at the counsel table.

"Sergeant DeMarco," she said. "I believe my deliberations would benefit from hearing from you. If you wouldn't mind."

He stood. "I am no longer with the Pennsylvania State Police, Your Honor. So the title of sergeant no longer applies."

"The respect afforded by that title still applies, sir."

"Thank you, Your Honor."

"The court would like to hear about the incident in which you and your partner were injured."

"Your Honor," McBride's attorney said, and the judge held up her hand. Then nodded for DeMarco to continue.

"Well," he answered, and paused for a moment to collect his thoughts. "After receiving a telephone call from Daksh Khatri informing us that Mr. McBride might be hiding out at the abandoned St. Margaret's Hospital in Sharpsville, Pennsylvania, and as that hospital is located only fifteen minutes or so from our home, my partner and I decided to have a look. The first floor was clear, so we proceeded to the second floor. She took the stairs on one side of the building, and I went up the other side. When I proceeded through the doors at the top of the floor, Mr. McBride jabbed at me with a stun gun. As I fell away from him, he moved toward me with a knife in his other hand. I had already drawn my sidearm, so I fired twice, striking him once in the shoulder."

"And your partner," the judge said, and offered a quick smile to Jayme, "where was she at the time?"

"At that moment, I wasn't aware of her precise location. But I had my weapon drawn as I came through the doors because I had heard her scream."

"So would it be fair to say," the judge mused, "that the only reason you weren't incapacitated and probably stabbed by the defendant was because you were moving rapidly as a result of her scream?"

"Yes, Your Honor."

"And then what happened?"

"After disabling Mr. McBride, I was fired upon from the other end of the hallway. So I returned fire."

"And who was firing at you?"

"Daksh Khatri. I recognized the report as coming from my partner's weapon, so I assumed that she had been disarmed."

"You did not yet know her condition?"

"I could see that she was supine and apparently unconscious."

"That was *all* you knew?"

"That's all, Your Honor." He had an urge to look at Jayme then, but did not. Her eyes, he knew, would be filled with tears. And so, then, would his.

"And did you proceed to advance on Mr. Khatri and to exchange fire with him?"

"I did, Your Honor. After I managed to climb over a pile of chairs and tables in the middle of the hallway."

"So from that point on, Sergeant, you had no cover whatsoever?"

"That's correct, Your Honor."

And now the judge looked at Jayme, whose eyes were lowered, her cheeks streaked by tears. To DeMarco, Judge Cleary said, "Neither you nor Mr. Khatri was struck in the exchange?"

"Well," DeMarco told her, "I had to aim high, because of Jayme. And he...he was just a lousy shot."

Judge Cleary smiled. "And all this time," she asked, "did you give any thought to the fact that the defendant might be coming at you from behind?"

"I probably should have," he answered, which elicited another smile from the judge and several people in the gallery.

She said, "The DA has chosen not to charge the defendant for that incident, Sergeant. How do you feel about that?"

Again he paused before responding. Then he answered, "I am very grateful that my partner and I are still alive, and that Mr. McBride has accepted responsibility for the deaths of three innocent people."

The judge nodded. "I understand that you were treated for a bruised coccyx sustained during that incident. That's a very painful injury, is it not?"

"It is, Your Honor. Though not fatal."

"I would also like to hear of any other harm that was done to you or your partner throughout the course of that encounter. And I encourage you to be as specific and thorough as possible."

His pause was longer this time. Then he said. "Your Honor, I consider my wound trivial compared to the physical and psychological trauma my partner suffered and is still suffering. Although the defendant did not personally inflict that damage, I believe he shares responsibility for his complicity in the ambush we were subjected to. According to two juveniles at the scene of the incident, they were paid twenty dollars by the defendant to tell us that no one else was inside the building. The ambush was obviously premeditated by the defendant and Daksh Khatri. Khatri, we believe, was hoping that the defendant would be killed in the encounter, thereby obfuscating Khatri's involvement. The defendant, according to his own admission to the DA, had been instructed by Khatri to kill both my partner and me. I believe that he fully intended to do so."

The judge closed her eyes for a moment and pinched the bridge of her nose. When she looked up, her eyes were on Jayme. "I apologize for this next question," she said. "Especially to you, Trooper Matson." She smiled briefly at Jayme—a small, commiserating smile—before addressing DeMarco again. "And do you, Sergeant, attribute the loss of your unborn child to that attack?"

A woman in the gallery gasped.

DeMarco drew in a long breath. "It does seem reasonable to do so, Your Honor."

The silence that followed was a long one, broken only when McBride's attorney stood and said, "Your Honor—"

"Sit down, Mr. Davis."

He spoke quickly. "I just wanted to ask Ms. Matson if at any time before or after the attack she saw my client anywhere in the building"

"She was unconscious, Mr. Davis. And your client has already entered his plea."

"I would also like it to be known to the court that a sizable reward of a quarter-million dollars was turned over to Mr. DeMarco and Ms. Matson. One might argue that generous reparations for their injuries have already been made."

Suddenly furious, DeMarco turned to face the attorney, but then felt Jayme's hand slip into his.

Judge Cleary asked, "Is that true, Sergeant?"

He faced her again. "Theoretically, Your Honor."

"Can you explain that, please?"

"We gave it away. Most of it to the victims' families. Mr. Hufford left a wife and two adult children behind. The rest went to the Second Harvest Food Bank and the Pediatric Care Unit at St. Elizabeth. We didn't keep a penny of it. We were paid a per diem by the county for our services."

The judge nodded. Addressed McBride's attorney. "I think it is fair to say, Mr. Davis, and I am sure you will agree, that no amount of money could compensate for the harm done by the defendant to the victims and their families. And that you, sir, cast yourself in a very dim light by even making such a suggestion."

"I apologize, Your Honor. Might I make one last statement on behalf of my client?"

"Make it brief."

"As I am sure you are aware, the deleterious effects on a fetus of a mother's use of alcohol, drugs, and even cigarettes are well-established—"

"Stop," the judge said. "Your client has pled guilty to the charges. He was fully aware of the consequences of his actions."

"It's just that there are mitigating factors that can help to account for his be—"

"Enough!" she said, and leaned forward. "Far too little and far too late, Mr. Davis. I have heard from your client, I have heard from Sergeant DeMarco, and that is all I need or intend to hear on the matter this morning."

She looked down at her desktop calendar. Flipped a page. "Sentencing is scheduled for…November 12, 9:00 a.m. This hearing is adjourned."

FOUR

Outside the courthouse, DeMarco felt as if he could breathe again, even if it was city air. Exhaust fumes, dirty sidewalks, concrete, and steel. City air always smelled dirtier when the sky was a clear, pale blue and the leaves on the few trees were full of natural color dulled by city dust. But the sky, at least, looked clean, and he tilted his head toward it as he inhaled.

They had exited on the Boardman Street side, avoiding the front lobby crammed with reporters and cameras, where Sheriff Brinker and the lawyers would be held hostage for a while. He and Jayme moved a few feet to the side of the door, heard the voices inside coming closer, Detectives Olcott and Fascetti.

DeMarco leaned close to Jayme and inconspicuously sniffed her hair. She always smelled good, no matter the season, and her scent was always revivifying, its effect like the smelling salts capsules the trainer had carried back in high school and sometimes broke open under DeMarco's nose after he had driven his helmet into a runner's chest. But sweeter. Some mornings her hair smelled like fruit, sometimes like flowers, but always the scent startled him and made him alert again to the inspiriting wonderment of life.

He wanted to hold her now and apologize for the question about their baby—for bringing her to tears. But the others were only a few steps behind. He took her hand and she looked up at him and then Olcott was coming out the door.

"Slam dunk," Olcott said, not loud, and briefly laid his hand against DeMarco's shoulder.

DeMarco answered with a small smile and nod. And now Fascetti was there too, holding out his hand. DeMarco shook it and nodded again and told himself, *Stop acting like a bobblehead.*

Olcott said, "I'm betting on an upward departure sentence. Otherwise why would she have asked you about your injuries?"

"Twenty years to life never should have been accepted in the first place," Fascetti added. "For what he did? If it were up to me, I'd bring Old Sparky out of retirement and strap McBride and Khatri in side by side."

Olcott nodded. "Our DA is such a wimp."

Fascetti raised both arms in the air and stretched his back. "So how about the Capitol? Lunch is on me."

Ever since Jayme's miscarriage the detective had been avuncular and kind, his dark eyes full of sorrow. DeMarco liked him better when he was snarky; knew better how to react to him.

Jayme gave his hand another squeeze; he looked down at her, saw the plea in her eyes. "Some other time, okay?" he told Fascetti. "I'm pretty worn-out. Neither of us got much sleep last night."

"Sure. Whatever," Fascetti said. "You guys take care." He turned to his partner. "You hungry?"

"What kind of stupid question is that?" Olcott said with a smile. He crossed in front of DeMarco and Jayme, briefly touched each on the arm in passing.

The detectives walked to the corner, turned left and crossed the street.

"Home?" DeMarco asked, and she nodded again and squeezed his hand.

FIVE

Sometimes now, two months after the loss, thoughts about the baby would leave her for a while and the fog of grief would lift away. But even on the brightest and clearest of days, a thin film of gray lay over everything, muting the pleasure she used to take in the woods and ponds and gentle hills along the two half-hour rides from Mercer to Youngstown and then back to Mercer, and the way their cell phones would say, almost simultaneously, chirping from their pockets or wherever the devices were at that moment, "Welcome to Pennsylvania" or "Welcome to Ohio." Sometimes DeMarco would answer, "Thank you very much!" It always made her smile. But he had not done that since August.

Autumn had always been her favorite season, when even a single day could bring a change in the landscape, a deepening of colors, then a gradual browning and a shedding of leaves that used to fill her with longing for her father, who had passed away at this time of year.

Too soon the trees would be bare again, the limbs turning skeletal, and then the modest homes and dilapidated sheds and barns could be seen clearly through the branches, set back from the busy interstate but not far enough away to escape the noise or dirty air. Then old cars and trucks and tractors left abandoned in somebody's field or yard would be visible. A rusting school bus parked beside a weed-filled pond with a wooden dock half-sunk in the water. A pile of rotting tires.

Too soon everything would look dirty, the algae on roofs and walls conspicuous without the leaves, the lawns getting scraggly, flower beds full of dying or dead plants, fields of brown stubble. The countryside would not look good again until snow blanketed the dirt and the trees glistened with ice. Jayme hoped that winter would come early. A few months of hibernation would be good. Quiet days and quiet nights. And then spring again. Red buds and greenery. Tulips and cherry blossoms. Delicate pinks and whites.

But now you could not drive for ten miles without seeing at least one dead deer along the road, spooked into the traffic by hunters so eager to kill that they spent nights and weekends scouting for the best sites. Even the billboards were covered with road grime. On one of them, an advertisement for a restaurant, a huge porterhouse steak had turned grayish-brown, the au jus on the plate the color of ash.

Off the exit ramp, DeMarco made a left toward home.

"Can we walk for a while?" she asked.

"Of course," he said. "Anywhere in particular?"

Both kept a pair of cross-trainers on the back seat floor, windbreakers and hoodies and fleece pullovers on the seat. They had been doing a lot of walking since the miscarriage, a lot of long, unhurried walking with little said between them. Sometimes they walked the running track at the high school, sometimes the loop around the Mercer County Courthouse. On occasion they might stop for a hot dog and root beer float in the little shop across the street. Sometimes they walked the half-mile loop that ran past the ball fields and tennis courts in Brandy Spring Park, walking uphill one-fourth of the distance, downhill another fourth.

"The park," she said. "If that's okay. It's quiet now that softball season is over."

"Anything you want is okay."

He pulled into one of the ten parking spaces across from the fenced-in dog runs. Three of the slots were occupied. In the rear-view mirror he could see part of the pond behind the equipment shed. "The geese are still hanging around, I see. A couple pairs of mallards too. Might be a warm winter after all."

She turned in her seat, reached to the back, and found her shoes. Brought them forward, dropped them at her feet, then turned and reached for his. He slid his seat back, leaned over the steering wheel, and started untying his right shoe.

She took off both of her heels, put a naked foot up on the edge of the seat, walking shoe in hand. "It's okay what you said," she told him. "I know you're still thinking about it."

"I'm sorry if it hurt you. I wish I'd kept my mouth shut."

"It's not like you reminded me or anything."

"I just never know whether to talk about it or not."

"We talk about it in group," she said. "I just assumed you wouldn't want to be hearing the same thing again and again."

"What I want to hear is any and everything you have to say."

She nodded, smiled to herself, then slipped on her shoe. Tied it, put her foot down, raised the other. Outside, five or so yards behind the car, a man's voice was growing loud. DeMarco turned to look out the rear window.

The guy was leaning down close to his dog—a shepherd mix of some type, still a puppy but already two feet tall and well over fifty pounds—screaming into its face while also pulling the leash up tight, yanking the dog's front paws off the ground. On the pavement close to the dog was a pile of fresh feces. The guy was thin and scruffy, with long greasy hair and an untrimmed beard. He wore baggy gray sweatpants and a tan, stained trench coat over a black T-shirt, looked to be in his thirties, maybe older, and wobbled unsteadily as he barked in the dog's face. The dog was making choking sounds and whimpering, its ears flattened, head turned to the side as if about to take a blow.

Then the man started jerking hard on the leash, snapping the dog up and down, his voice so loud that the four other people in the area stopped to look his way. "You think I'm picking that up, you're crazy! I oughta rub your face in it! I oughta make you eat it, that's what I oughta do."

DeMarco grabbed a fleece pullover for Jayme and laid it in her lap, then popped open his door and climbed out. "Hey!" he called. Then bent down and looked inside at Jayme. "Take out your phone and video this." Then, as he walked briskly toward the man, he yanked at the knot in his tie and opened the top button on his shirt.

The man had looked up at DeMarco's shout. Straightened. And now lessened some of the tension on the leash. "Hey what?"

DeMarco said nothing more until he was face-to-face with the man. "You need to stop abusing your dog. Right now."

Jayme climbed out and stood close to the car and watched the encounter on her screen.

"Is he *your* dog?" the man asked. "I don't think so. So maybe you need to mind your own fucking business, dude."

DeMarco looked down at the animal. Put his hand out toward it. The dog flinched. Gently then DeMarco laid his palm atop the dog's head. Rubbed his hand back and forth. The dog raised its snout to him.

"How much do you want for it?" he asked.

"Who said he's for sale?"

"He's either for sale or I report you for cruelty to an animal."

"Ha. Your word against mine."

"Look behind me. Smile for the camera."

The man squinted at Jayme, scowled, peered down at the dog.

Then turned to DeMarco again and gave him a look. As if he had peeled off his sock and saw a gangrenous foot. "Hunnerd dollars," he said.

DeMarco reached into his pocket, pulled out a wad of bills, peeled off two twenties. He said, "You get the rest when you clean up after your dog."

"In that case make it two hunnerd."

"You lost the right to negotiate. All you have now are two choices. Sell me the dog for a hundred dollars, or talk to the police."

The man breathed loudly through his nose, his mouth puckered as if he wanted to spit.

DeMarco said, "Judging from the way you smell, you do not want to talk to the police right now. I can have them here in three minutes."

They locked eyes for another fifteen seconds, DeMarco's gaze steady, the man's less so. Finally he shoved the leash toward DeMarco, who took it and let the tension fall slack. The man stepped over to the feces, scooped them up in his bare hand, carried them to a barrel in a corner of the dog run, and dropped them in. He wiped the hand on his coat as he returned to DeMarco.

By then DeMarco had five twenties in his hand. He laid them in the outstretched, dirty palm.

"Ha," the man said, and closed the bills in his fist. "I can get another mutt for free anytime I want."

DeMarco took hold of the sleeve of the man's trench coat, was careful to touch only the fabric, and pulled him close. "If you ever abuse another animal," he whispered, "I will know it. And then I will put a leash around *your* neck and pull you up on *your* toes, and we'll see how *you* like it."

Not until DeMarco released him did the man speak. He stepped away and rolled his shoulders, shook his trench coat by its lapels, and mumbled "Yeah, yeah, yeah" as he headed away.

"Hey!" DeMarco called. "What's his name?"

The man answered without turning. "Dumbfuck!"

When DeMarco returned to Jayme, with the dog trotting along beside him, she asked, "What did you whisper to him?"

"I was admiring his coat. Asked him where he bought it."

"Right," she said, then looked down at the dog, which was standing against DeMarco's leg and looking up at her with huge brown eyes.

DeMarco said, "Don't worry. I'll find it a good home."

She leaned down and held her hand in front of the snout. The dog sniffed her palm, then licked it. "I think you already did."

SIX

The first thing the dog did after DeMarco parked along the edge of his backyard, and after Jayme popped open the rear door to reach for the leash, was to leap past her and race toward the house, zigzagging from side to side to sniff at every object of interest like a perfumer turned loose in a field of exotic flowers. Jayme chased after it, shouting, "Dog! Stop! Sit, dog, sit!"

To no avail. After dragging its nose along the edge of the porch, the dog sprinted around the corner of the house and toward the street. Jayme caught up to it watering the realtor's *For Sale* sign planted near the sidewalk, and stomped her foot onto the leash. "Bad dog!" she said, but she was already falling in love with the animal, and waited patiently until it had thoroughly soaked the signpost.

DeMarco, who had hurried inside through the back door and now stood on the front threshold holding the screen door open with his body, was grinning. During Jayme's side-to-side dash after the dog, she had seemed like her old self again, brimming with energy and resolve. Now she stood with her hands on her hips, feigning disapproval.

He called, "I guess we won't need that sprinkler system after all."

The dog gave him a look, as did Jayme. She said, "Thanks for your help."

Fifteen minutes later they were about to lift the dog into the bathtub, which had been filled with six inches of warm water and three inches of fragrant, bubbly foam, when the front doorbell rang and echoed ominously through the house. Jayme flashed back to the last time she had responded to someone at the door—it had been Laraine that time, DeMarco's estranged wife.

DeMarco said, "That clown better not have followed us here."

"Who?" she said, confused.

"The guy I bought him from. That better not be him at the door."

Ten seconds later he yanked open the door to find Trooper Mason Boyd standing there, in uniform, a patrol car parked at the curb. It took DeMarco a moment to find his smile. "Trooper," he said. "How are you doing?"

Boyd held up an eight-by-ten-inch photo he had been hiding behind his back. It showed the upper half of a naked black man standing against a thick tree trunk, with what appeared to be long metal stakes driven through his neck and near the bottom of his sternum.

DeMarco winced.

"Discovered early this morning," Boyd told him. "In the woods up in Otter Creek Township."

"Is he nailed to that tree by those two pegs?"

"By three of them. Rebar rods. There's another one just above the genitals. I have a full body shot in the car if you want to see it."

DeMarco, wincing again, shook his head. "Put that away."

"It's just the tip of the iceberg, Sergeant."

"Put it away before Jayme sees it."

Boyd's gaze shifted then, went over DeMarco's left shoulder, and DeMarco felt her presence there, then her hand against his back. "What do you mean?" she asked the trooper.

"A hundred yards away was a burned-out car, an older model

Santa Fe. The remains of two bodies in the back seat. They were mostly ash by then."

DeMarco's head was already moving back and forth. "Not interested," he said. The dog squeezed into the space between his leg and Jayme's, her fingers wrapped around the collar. DeMarco let his hand drop, scratched between the dog's ears.

Boyd said, "I'm not supposed to take no for an answer."

"Fine," DeMarco told him. "Make it 'no way in hell' instead. Let's see how that works for him." He was referring to their former station commander, Captain Kyle Bowen, the man responsible for dispatching Boyd to their home.

Jayme asked, "Have they been identified?"

"We're working on it. The bodies in the car were still smoldering when a father and his two boys found them."

"*Children*?" she asked, and Boyd nodded. "How old?"

"Thirteen and nine. The youngest one saw them first."

Jayme turned, moved her eyes to DeMarco. He cocked his head, his mouth in a thin-lipped frown.

Boyd lowered the photo now, turned it against his leg.

Jayme asked, "Pennsylvania plate?"

"No plate."

"Mace, we're out," DeMarco told him. "We're taking a break. I don't care if Bowen likes it or not. Has he forgotten that we're retired?"

Trooper Mason Boyd was a slender man of medium height and had been one of DeMarco's favorite people when they worked together, principally because Boyd knew when to keep his mouth shut, which was 90 percent of the time. In terms of avoiding small talk, gossip, and all forms of idle chatter, Boyd ran a close second to DeMarco. His only answer to DeMarco now was to remain standing where he was, his face expressionless, the photo of the spiked man flattened against his leg.

To the trooper, Jayme said, "You want some coffee?"

DeMarco turned her way again. Looked at her.

"They need us," she said.

He held her gaze a moment longer, then shook his head, pivoted away from the door and crossed back into the room, shaking his head all the way.

Jayme moved aside and made room for the trooper to enter. He petted the dog's snout. "Nice dog," he said. "What's his name?"

"Nobody knows," Jayme told him. "Cream, no sugar, right?"

SEVEN

The air in the woods of Otter Creek Township sat heavily in Jayme's chest. At least the breaths of air in that particular piece of woods strung with neon yellow police tape. The stink of scorched metal and melted rubber. Burned grass and leaves and incinerated meat. It all clung to her clothing and stung her nostrils, though the torched car and the remains of its unfortunate passengers were a hundred yards to the rear. Before her was a man nailed to a tree. Black man, mid to late forties, five ten or eleven, average-to-muscular build. Naked but for several tattoos and a penis ring. One rebar stake through his neck, one through his lower sternum, one five inches below his navel. His head hung limp, arms limp at his sides. There were no signs that he had struggled while being crucified, no torn-up ground beneath his bare feet, only a wide area around the tree that appeared to have been raked clean of footprints.

Plenty of blood had spurted and oozed from each wound, painting his body and feet, indicating that he had been alive but probably unconscious during the process. His bowels had released at some point pre- or postmortem.

Jayme and DeMarco stood approximately six feet back from the body, accompanied by Joe Loughner, a member of the Evidence Recovery Team. *Seventy years old*, Jayme had guessed upon meeting him, *give or take a year*. Probably stood at least six feet tall before whatever accident gave him the limp that caused him to rest most of his weight on the good right leg. Probably close to two hundred pounds, though the white paper bodysuit might be making him appear plumper than he was. She could see enough of his gray hair to know that it was clipped almost to the scalp, which would also accentuate the fullness of his bulldog face. He seemed unperturbed by the carnage. He had lowered the face mask upon first meeting them, and now had no trouble breathing deeply, seemingly unaffected by the foul air. His blue eyes sparkled when he talked. He had probably seen and smelled it all before.

The sun was shining from the southwest through a layer of cirrus clouds, coming into their eyes soft and diffuse, so that the dead man was shaded by the tree and, had they been twenty or thirty yards farther back, would have been hard to distinguish from the oak.

DeMarco said, "Any chance of pinpointing the source of that rebar?"

"We'll try, of course," Loughner said. "But it's common stuff. Available in just about every hardware store in the country. Where I come from, people use it to stake up their tomatoes and pole beans."

He waited for another question from DeMarco, but none came.

"This looks like number four or five," Loughner told them. "No protrusions on the other side of the tree. Protrusions on this side from north to south are approximately nine, thirteen, and seven inches long. You can see where the heads have been flattened somewhat with a mallet. Entry wounds are fairly clean, not ragged as you'd expect from a blunt end being pounded in."

Jayme said, "So the other ends were sharpened first. Which means that whoever did this was in no hurry."

"Definitely not a rush job," Loughner said.

DeMarco leaned back slightly. "How long has he been here?"

"Body temp when last measured was just over fifty," said Loughner. "Air temp went down to thirty-nine last night, is currently in the high forties. Figuring a loss of one and a half degrees of body heat per hour, best guess is he died early yesterday morning."

"How early?" DeMarco asked.

Loughner shrugged. "Medical examiner thinks predawn."

Jayme kept one hand lightly covering her mouth and nose. "So they were brought here under cover of darkness. Which means the perp was familiar with this place."

"Perps," Loughner said. "No drag marks from the car. John Doe here was carried. Plus it would have taken at least one person to hold up the body while another one nailed him into place. We think we've identified at least five sets of footprints in the area, but the best of them come from the father and his kids who found the car, and they never made it this far. Thank God for small favors."

"So in terms of evidentiary value?" DeMarco asked.

"The footprints? Minimal."

"Same for vehicle treads?"

"Ditto. That light rain this morning and the harder one yesterday didn't do us any favors."

As the senior member of the Evidence Recovery Team from Erie, Loughner had introduced himself to Jayme and DeMarco upon their arrival, had stuck out his beefy hand to each of them, a quick shake, a smile, and said, "Joe Loughner. Former statie myself. Nice to meet you both. I'll be your guide for the gruesome tour."

And now, as Jayme listened and watched, she noticed some capillary damage around his nose. Cheeks flushed and dry. And he had plucked three mints out of his pocket so far and popped them into his mouth. All the signs of a lifetime of heavy drinking. Occupational medication.

The woods were full of other people too, some in uniform and some in papery white garb that made them look like the Pillsbury Doughboy's slender cousins, yellow caution tape stretching from tree to tree and surrounding both crime scenes. "No sign of John Doe's clothing?" she asked.

"We figure it got burned up with the other two victims. Or else he was brought here in the buff."

"Anything you can tell us yet about those victims?" DeMarco asked.

"Still being processed," Loughner answered. "But I can tell you this. Crematoriums burn at about 800 degrees centigrade. 1472 Fahrenheit. It takes about three hours at that temperature to reduce a body to ash. The fire in the car was almost certainly started with gasoline, and gas burns at over 1500 degrees Fahrenheit. Fortunately, not for three hours. After the initial flare-up, the temp decreases rapidly."

"So there's something left to work with?"

"We're confident the remains are of two bodies, both significantly smaller than this one. Assumed to be female. But that's not official yet."

"Not children, I hope," Jayme said.

"Not likely. But again… The good thing is, the effects of fire on a human body follow a fairly clear pattern. And some evidence, such as the type of instrument used to inflict skeletal trauma, is easier to identify *after* heat alteration. Still—and I'm sure you both know this—there's a lot of data loss from a fire that hot."

"At least we have one complete set of fingerprints," DeMarco said, and nodded toward the dead man. "If we can tie the other two to him…"

Loughner nodded. "Though why so much trouble would be taken to conceal evidence back there," he said, with a jerk of his head toward the incineration site, "yet leave us the body here… It doesn't make a whole lot of sense, does it?"

DeMarco said, "I get the feeling that the vics in the car were collateral at best. This guy was terminated with extreme prejudice."

"He could maybe be a signal to others," Jayme suggested. "Don't do what this guy did, or this is what you'll get."

DeMarco pursed his lips; Loughner's brow furrowed. Both men kept staring at the corpse as if the dead man's tattoos were hieroglyphs about to reveal their secrets. DeMarco said, "What if the perps made the other two vics watch this? Then took them back to the car and torched it?"

Loughner shrugged. "Could've gone that way. No evidence to refute it. That would explain why this one was such a production. But why teach them a lesson only to kill them?"

"Maybe the lesson wasn't for the other vics," Jayme said. "I wouldn't be surprised if there's a video of the whole thing."

DeMarco said, "I suppose it's even possible that the perp made the other two victims help carry this guy here. Made them hold him up against the tree. Maybe made them drive in the rebar. In exchange for their freedom, let's say. Which of course was a lie. But then there's still the same question…"

"Sadism," Jayme answered. "Not to teach them a lesson. But to increase their fear—for his own enjoyment"

DeMarco turned to Loughner then. "You guys are sure there was another vehicle here? Besides the one that got torched?"

"That's how it *appears*, yeah. But the ground's wet, the tread marks overlap. The first set might have been laid down a few days earlier. It's impossible to know for sure. They don't come with time stamps on them."

"So maybe there *was* only one perp," DeMarco mused. "Drove the car here with the three vics in it. Made the two back there help him with this guy. Did him, did the other two, torched the car."

"And then what?" Jayme asked. "Walked away?"

"Why not?" Again he addressed Loughner. "Think your team could do a perimeter search before you finish up? Look for signs of a foot trail of some kind?"

"Got it covered," Loughner said. Then, with a little smile on his lips, he raised his eyebrows at DeMarco, and jerked his head toward Jayme.

Only when she felt their eyes on her did she realize that she had been staring at the victim's bloated penis, the head swollen like a mushroom cap. She looked up to see both men watching her, Loughner smiling. Blushing, she said, "That's just not normal, is it?"

Loughner chuckled. "I've been waiting for you to mention that. Angel lust."

"Excuse me?"

"Postmortem erection. It's fairly common, especially in a hanging, damage to the spinal cord, or other violent death. And after it subsided, because he's standing up, the blood pooled at the lowest point. The guy looks like one of those freak porn stars. Not that he was able to enjoy any of it."

Still embarrassed, she turned to DeMarco, gave him a *help me out here* look.

"Joe," he said, "you were with the state police before this?"

The older man nodded. "Troop C, Elk County."

"God's country, huh? What took you from there to Erie?"

Loughner tapped his left leg. "Couldn't move the way I needed to anymore, but didn't want to quit working either. Plus the marriage had broken up, so there was no reason to stay where I was. Heard that retired law enforcement sometimes get work as ERTs, so I figured what the hell. I applied, got in, did some extra training in forensics, and here I am, in the woods with dead people. Better than rusting away in a beer joint in the boondocks, though, yeah?"

Broad strokes, Jayme noticed. *No details. Just being modest?* He sounded to her a lot like DeMarco. Two men who would be dangers to themselves if they had neither work nor love. One of those devices might keep them afloat, both together might actually save them. Thinking this, her opinion of Loughner as an alcoholic melted into sympathy. A man with no reason to get up in the morning and nobody to kiss him awake is a man without a purpose. And a man without a purpose is a man clinging to the precipice.

The same held true for women, of course, though women, she believed, tolerated suffering better than men did. Men turned either useless or hard or self-destructive from too much suffering, whereas women turned either useless or hard or filled with compassion. That was why she had wanted to be a part of this investigation. Her and Ryan's suffering was still fresh, plus he had an older one as a sorrowful foundation for the new one. She worried about herself and she worried about him, although, in truth, she worried more about him.

Out of the corner of her eye, she noticed a dark shape edging into her field of vision. She turned and saw a young man holding a cell phone out at chest level, making a video recording of the scene. "Hey!" she told him. "Put that away!"

Trooper Boyd, who had been standing attentively a few feet behind DeMarco, rushed forward to intercept the young man. To Jayme the kid looked no older than midtwenties. Five eight or so, lean-limbed but with broad shoulders and a solid chest. *High school wrestling*, she guessed, because he reminded her of the boy with whom she had attended the prom. This kid's dark hair was cropped close on the sides and back, but the gelled top swept in a bleached blond wave back over his head. He wore pressed khakis and a powder-blue Oxford shirt with cuffs buttoned, and brown cross-trainers. Neater than most male reporters she knew; they tended to be rushed, more than a little frenetic, and careless about their dress.

The kid lowered the phone a bit when she barked at him, but took another side step toward the impaled man, moving up against the yellow tape, his waist pushing a bulge into it. Jayme didn't know if he was trying to record their conversation or video the dead man or both, but she gave a quick nod to Trooper Boyd, who held out his hand to the kid. "Give it here," he said.

"No way. You can't confiscate private property."

"How about I arrest you for interfering with an investigation?"

"How am I interfering?"

Boyd snatched the phone from his hand. Looked at the screen. Then slipped the phone into his own pocket. "Identification," he said, and held out his hand.

"I have a right to be here. I'm with the *Record-Argus*. And you just stole my phone."

"Turn around and put your hands behind your back."

"Okay, okay. Chill, dude. I'm just doing my job, same as you."

"Identification," Boyd said again.

The young man reached into his back pocket, took out a metal credit card case, flipped it open and thumbed through till he found his driver's license, which he held out to Boyd.

Boyd looked at the card, studied it and the kid's face, then returned it. "This doesn't say anything about the *Record-Argus*."

"I'm a stringer, okay? They don't give us press credentials. Can I have my phone back now?"

"I need to check it for photos of the crime scene. Then you get it back, minus any photos or video you took, and you leave. In the meantime, you stay behind the tape." With that, Boyd walked a few feet away, turned his back to the kid, and pulled out the phone for examination.

"What's *behind* to you, Officer?" the kid asked with a grin.

Boyd half turned.

"I mean, the tape is up against my belly, right?" the kid asked. "And my belly's the front of me. That puts all of me *already* behind the tape, am I right?"

Jayme couldn't help smiling. *Cheeky kid.*

Boyd completed the turn. "Step back from the tape."

"What about freedom of the press and all that?" the kid said, still grinning.

"If you don't step back from that tape *right now*, you will forfeit your freedom."

The young man placed his right foot directly behind his left, then brought his left foot back parallel to his right. "How about my constitutional right to life, liberty, and the pursuit of happiness? I'm not happy unless I can do my job. You are depriving me of that right."

Now Jayme stepped away from DeMarco and over to the kid. "How did you manage to slip past the troopers up on the lane?"

He lifted up one mud-caked shoe. "A story like this is worth ruining several pairs of shoes."

So, he had hiked in through the woods. Which meant that he must have gotten word of the scene around the same time she and DeMarco had, or even earlier. "And how did you hear about this? Police scanner?"

He grinned. "Another good investment."

She had to admire his resourcefulness and dedication. Other reporters would be showing up soon but he would be the first to file a story. "Give us some peace until we wrap this up," she told him. "Afterward, if it's okay with Trooper Boyd, you'll maybe get a statement. Otherwise, not a word."

They held each other's gaze for a moment, and Jayme could tell that the kid was summing her up, just as she had done with him. "Finally," he said, and smiled, "a voice of reason. And a beautiful one at that." After a small bow, he took another step back from the tape.

Okay, she thought, *he's playing now*. She could play too. "Did you wrestle in high school?"

A look of surprise. "My fame precedes me! 2012 District 10 champ, 145 weight class. If you happen to have a Sharpie on you, I'll be happy to autograph your shirt. Or anything else you'd prefer."

Yes, just like the boy who took her to the prom. Full of himself, but just charming enough to get away with it. She asked, "Did you wrestle in college too?"

"First two years, yeah."

"Why did you stop? Injury?"

The kid wagged his head. "More or less. Got hit by a truck named Chloe."

And it took you a long time to recover from that, didn't it, she thought. "I hope you at least got the license number," she said.

"Ha! It was a hit-and-run with extreme prejudice. She's still running free out there somewhere, God bless her evil soul."

Okay, so he had heard DeMarco's *extreme prejudice* remark and was letting her know it. Why? So that she understood: give him the full skinny or he would run with what he had.

"Hang loose," she told him. "We'll be done here soon."

"I appreciate it." And as she turned to walk away, he added, "By the way, I think the trooper has a crush on me. You mind breaking it to him that I don't swing that way? Just in case that's of any interest to you."

EIGHT

O n the ride back to town, DeMarco, at the wheel, and Jayme, gazing out the side window, silently processed what they had learned. The crime scene was a mere eighteen miles from DeMarco's home, but most of the route was over narrow asphalt or gravel roads twisting through woods and along hay fields and wheat fields now stripped to stubby stalks. The few scattered homes were small ranchers and cottages and trailers in need of repair, or large Amish farms with dark-garbed children and adults working in the yards and fields, a few horses or head of cattle behind hand-sawed fences. Fewer than six hundred people lived in the township, in just over two hundred homes.

Jayme watched the modest homes go by and wished she had more experience in how those families lived, the way they treated one another and the dreams they shared. She had no shortage of compassion but it wasn't the same as experience. Only experience could bring true knowledge and understanding.

"It has to be somebody local," DeMarco finally said. "The ingress is little more than an old logging road."

"And not easy to see unless you know where to look."

"So maybe the thing to do is to get Boyd on a CLEAN search. See how many locals show up on it, and for what."

"I'm sure he'll run one first thing, babe."

The Commonwealth Law Enforcement Assistance Network

was used by the Pennsylvania State Police to access criminal histories and arrest records, as well as additional data, through the FBI's National Crime Information Center and other networks.

DeMarco nodded. Then continued, "And if we strike out on known criminals, we can check with the Game Commission on hunting licenses issued. There's no telling how long those bodies would have been there if that father and his kids weren't out scouting. So maybe the perp isn't a local at all but a hunter who comes back to those woods each fall."

"You still think it's just one guy did all that?"

He grimaced, cocked his head. "Just throwing spaghetti at the wall. But unlikely, I'd say."

"I'm betting on two perps minimum."

DeMarco remained silent, squinting, hands tight around the wheel. Then he shook his head and blew out a breath. "You're sure you want to do this?"

"Work this case? I'm sure. Aren't you?"

"I'm okay with it if we stick to investigation and analysis only. I will not put you in harm's way again."

She was about to say, *You didn't put me in harm's way, I did,* but decided to answer with a smile. And to change the subject. "What's your impression of Loughner?"

"Positive, I guess. He's an old salt. Seems to know his stuff. Paid his dues, that's for certain."

That was high praise coming from DeMarco. If he had any doubts he would have expressed them. She had noticed a camaraderie building between the two and was glad to see it. Loughner was old enough to be Ryan's father. It would be good for him to have a man like that as a friend.

"How do you think he got the limp?" she asked. "Line of duty?"

"Either that or something embarrassing. Like shooting himself with a nail gun."

"While three sheets to the wind," she said. Then, when he squinted a little, wished she hadn't. "I just mean he looks like a drinker to me."

"I can't disagree," DeMarco said.

He drove in silence for a minute. Then said, "You made a fan today, though. If you don't mind a little puppy love."

She smiled. "I don't mind if you don't mind."

"As long as you didn't give him your phone number."

"Name, rank, and serial number only, sir."

Before they left the crime scene, Jayme had spoken to the young man briefly. Got his name and vitals: Chase Miller, twenty-six, graduate of Allegheny College, bachelor of arts in English, lived in Greenville, was a stringer with the *Meadville Tribune* and the Greenville *Record-Argus* while also writing a biweekly blog and working two part-time jobs. In return she gave him an overview of the crime in Otter Creek Township, nothing he hadn't already seen except for her and DeMarco's names and their association with the investigation, plus the identity of "the old dude in the paper suit."

"He's harmless," she told DeMarco. They were back onto Route 258 now and headed south toward Mercer at fifty miles an hour. "He reminds me a lot of my brother Cullen."

"Cullen is the snarky one, right?"

She punched him softly in the ribs. "I think the word *irreverent* is more appropriate. Though *snarky* fits you just about perfectly."

He hadn't been snarky at all for the past few months. And she missed that side of him. Knew that he had been working hard to be nothing but kind and patient with her. Knew that he seldom smiled in her presence unless she smiled first. So she gave him another smile now and laid her hand on his thigh and tried to hide the wince of pain that struck every time she remembered their baby.

NINE

At the first traffic light in town, they turned east toward the barracks, where they spent most of an hour completing the necessary forms to work as volunteer consultants on the case, then briefed Captain Bowen and other troopers on the scene in the woods. The ERT would deliver their evidence to the lab in Erie, which would then forward their findings to Bowen, who would turn them over to Trooper Boyd to liaise with DeMarco and Jayme. Theoretically, the consultants were limited to analysis, profiling, and information gathering; any interviews would include Trooper Boyd or another trooper. DeMarco argued that having a babysitter, even one as competent as Trooper Boyd, would only slow them down.

"You either trust us or you don't," he told Bowen. "I'm not going to do this if I have to put up with Daddy looking over my shoulder all the time. Especially when Daddy is still waiting for his pubic hair to sprout."

"Get a new joke," Bowen said. "Trooper Boyd is in charge. He calls the shots. No interviews without him or Flores present."

"Who's Flores?" DeMarco asked.

"Your replacement. Younger and a lot smarter than you. You guys will meet her next time. She's busy doing her job right now." To Jayme, he asked, "Can you control him? If he colors outside the lines too far, the entire investigation could get trashed."

Before Jayme could reply, DeMarco said, "When have I ever gone too far?"

"Almost always. By the way, you understand why we can't pay you for this, right? You're both collecting pensions. So this has to be pro bono."

"I've always been pro-Bono," DeMarco told him. "Wasn't crazy about Cher, but Sonny's lyrics were infectious."

Bowen closed his eyes and shook his head. When he opened his eyes again, he looked to Jayme. "Please make him stop."

"Hey," DeMarco said, "who asked whom to join this investigation?"

"Just don't make me regret it, that's all I'm saying."

DeMarco answered with a grin.

Again Bowen turned to Jayme and raised his eyebrows in question.

She shrugged, and DeMarco chuckled under his breath; it was fun to joust with their former boss, but he had had enough human interaction for the day and was anxious to get home. He stood, laced his fingers together and cracked his knuckles, then said his goodbyes and headed for the door.

They had left their new pet in the basement. DeMarco expected to find that the dog had chewed, clawed, shat and urinated on everything within reach, all while howling to high heaven. Instead, the house, upon their return, was silent. In the kitchen, DeMarco opened the basement door, stood at the top of the stairs, peered down into the darkness, and listened. Not a sound.

"Uh-oh," he whispered to Jayme, who was pulling vegetables out of the refrigerator. "What if he choked on something?"

"Maybe you should turn on the light and go find out."

In the basement he found nothing amiss. No feces, no scent of urine, no chewed-up mess. The only thing out of place was a potato with some teeth marks in it, carried from the wooden bin against the wall and dropped near the bottom of the stairs.

DeMarco, with the dog following, carried the potato up to the kitchen and showed it to Jayme, who was washing leaves of romaine lettuce in the sink. "Five hours we've been gone, and not a thing out of place except for one potato. Good boy, Clarence. Good boy."

The dog stood with its snout against the back door. Jayme said, "He's better housebroken than you are. Apparently he has to pee. And we are not going to call him Clarence. That name is off the table."

"What do you have against Clarence?"

"It's an old man's name. You want me to start calling *you* Clarence?"

DeMarco grunted, crossed to the back door and pushed it open. He sat on the edge of the porch while the dog sniffed its way around the yard, watering six different spots. When it ventured toward the neighbor's flower beds, which she had cleaned out for the winter, DeMarco called, "Hey! Get back here!" and the dog came trotting back to him.

"I'm impressed," DeMarco said, and scratched him between the ears. "Tomorrow the vet, okay, boy? Get you some shots, get you wormed, get you snipped if you haven't been already. Not pleasant, but necessary. And I guess we have to find you a new name for you too, don't we? What do you want to be called? How about Dogstoyevsky? Salvador Doggy? How about Sniffer?"

He kept suggesting names until the dog raised a paw to DeMarco's knee. "Yeah?" DeMarco said. "You like that one? You want that to be your name?"

When they went back inside, DeMarco told Jayme, "He wants to be called Harvey Barkowitz."

She said, "How did you come up with that?"

"He picked it. After Harvey, the demon dog that told David Berkowitz to kill people."

She shook her head and sighed. "Absolutely not."

TEN

They had hoped to receive a call in the morning about the dead man's prints. No call came. That could mean a couple of things: either the tech was taking his time prepping and cleaning up the prints, or the vic had no criminal history and his prints were not among the fifty-three million in the system. To mute his restlessness, DeMarco insisted on cleaning the entire kitchen after breakfast. He could be like a pig rooting out truffles when he worked, silent but for an occasional grunt, single-minded to the point of obsession even if the work consisted of wiping down the kitchen cabinets and cleaning the dust from the plastic vent at the bottom of the refrigerator.

Jayme spent an hour outside with the dog, the leash wrapped around her wrist as she let him take the lead on an aimless and jerky meander around town. She was amazed at how many times he could urinate. By the time he was done, he had claimed half the town as his turf.

Their appointment with the vet was for 11:00 a.m. and even the dog seemed happy to finally climb into the car for the short drive. The animal clinic was in a nineteenth-century Victorian farmhouse surrounded by what appeared to be hundreds of acres of now-empty cornfields. The first floor had been remodeled to include the front desk and waiting room, a public restroom, the examination room, a storage room, and a holding room for recovering and overnight patients.

Living quarters for Dr. Lisa and her wife were on the second and third floors. "Susan's a GP in New Castle," Lisa said while delicately probing the dog's body, working backward from his neck. She was a tall, thin woman, even taller than Jayme and approximately the same age, and she spoke mainly to Jayme, who helped to keep the dog still as he lay on the padded table. DeMarco stood a few feet back from the table and would have sat had a chair been available. The only chair was at the doctor's desk and currently occupied by the young female assistant who sat poised to take notes on the examination.

"Maya's been with me for two years now," Dr. Lisa said. The young woman at the desk looked up at Jayme and smiled, and waited for something to write down.

DeMarco marveled at how quickly Dr. Lisa and Jayme had developed a rapport. Their conversation spanned the colleges they'd attended, recent Netflix movies and old series they wished would be renewed, how fascinating Lisa found Jayme's job, and how impossible it would be for Jayme to cut into an animal or God forbid have to euthanize one. Jayme moved slowly around the table to accommodate the doctor's movements, while Lisa's eyes and fingers gathered information about the dog's health, which Lisa announced and Maya silently recorded. *A well-oiled machine,* DeMarco thought. He shared a look of gratitude with his nameless pet, who seemed perfectly content to lie there grinning while four female hands stroked and explored his body.

"No skeletal problems," Dr. Lisa said when she had finished. "He seems in fairly good health, though a bit undernourished. What are you feeding him?"

"Dry kibble mostly," Jayme said. "Except for the table scraps somebody sneaks to him."

"Generally not a problem as a treat now and then. Just be careful what you give him. No fruit pits, raisins, grapes, certain nuts...no chocolate, of course. Maya will give you a list before you leave, plus some recommendations for the best puppy food. How long have you had him?"

"The day before yesterday," Jayme said.

"Rescue Center?"

"He was rescued, but...Ryan bought him from a man in the park who was abusing him."

Lisa looked away from the dog, straight at DeMarco for the first time, and gave him a warm smile. "Does he have a name yet?" she asked.

"Harvey," DeMarco said, just half of a second before Jayme said, "Rambo."

Lisa chuckled, then told them, "I wouldn't wait too long to figure it out."

"Can you tell how old he is?" DeMarco asked. "And what breed? I suspect there's some German shepherd in there."

"He's well under a year," Lisa said. "Probably half is my guess. His coloring suggests a rottweiler-shepherd mix, but the way he's just lying here enjoying this, he seems more like a Siberian husky mix. He might have a little of all that in him. He's going to get big, though. Sixty to seventy pounds or more. Are you ready for that?"

DeMarco raised his eyebrows, and deferred to Jayme, who told her, with a wink to Ryan, "I'm used to big males. Right, Sergeant?"

At the word *sergeant*, Dr. Lisa looked up again, first at Jayme, then at DeMarco. "Oh my gosh," she said.

"What?" Jayme asked.

"From this morning's paper. *That's* why your names sounded so familiar to me."

"We're in the paper?" Jayme asked.

"Maya, did you put the papers out in the waiting room?"

"I did. Would you like me to get them?"

"I'm not sure which one I saw it in…"

"*Record-Argus*," DeMarco groaned.

Dr. Lisa would keep the dog overnight, with surgery scheduled for that evening, but sent the newspaper home with Jayme and DeMarco. To their dismay, the article, read in full the moment they returned to the car, with the paper laid across the console, took up nearly half of the front page—with old photos of DeMarco and Loughner in uniform and Jayme fresh from the academy—and continued for two columns on page four. The headline read:

TWO HEROES AND FEMME FATALE SPEARHEAD TRIPLE HOMICIDE INVESTIGATION

"Somebody needs his head ripped off," DeMarco muttered, and punched a finger at the byline: *by Chase Miller*.

"Where did he get all this stuff?"

After summarizing the discovery in the Otter Creek Township woods, Miller had spent considerable ink on DeMarco's hard-scrabble youth and military history before detailing his "pivotal role" in solving not only the Huston family murder case, but also the cold case in Kentucky and the recent serial killings in Youngstown. Miller likened him to a kind of Batman/Sam Spade/Philip Marlowe—tough, taciturn, and intimidating, but ultimately a force for good. He made the same comparison between DeMarco and Loughner that Jayme had, casting them as a father-son crime-busting combo, and promising, in what struck DeMarco as comic-book prose, that with these two on the case, "the culprits who perpetrated this heinous crime will not go unpunished for long."

"Doesn't this paper have an editor?" DeMarco asked.

As annoyed as he was, he found the information about Joe Loughner illuminating. The man had put in thirty-four solid years with the Elk County State Police. Then, on a searingly cold day in January, he and his partner had responded to a disturbance outside the village of Benezette. A bearded man wearing a black hoodie, a pair of cut-off yellow sweatpants, and high black boots was reportedly screaming at and firing an automatic assault rifle over the tops of passing cars. When the patrol car approached, the shooter ran inside his trailer, locked the doors, and told the troopers that he was going to send his wife and children to heaven before sending himself to hell. He fired through the window on the front-side door, which was when Corporal Loughner heard the woman and children crying and pleading for the man to stop.

Loughner's partner assumed a safe position at the front end of the trailer and kept the man occupied at that end by screaming through the kitchen window while Loughner, fearing that the hostages were in imminent danger, crept around the home to find the second entry. At the rear end of the trailer he managed to work a pane of glass out of the lattice window, reach inside, and turn the lock. After creeping inside, he could hear the children whimpering in a locked bedroom. But the man's wife was huddled on the floor in the kitchen, her husband standing beside her, trying to get a shot at Loughner's partner outside.

Loughner crept forward as far as he dared, weapon drawn. When the woman saw him, she jerked upright and gasped in surprise. Unfortunately, this caused her husband to spin around, spraying bullets. Loughner took one in the side and one just above the kneecap, but managed to place two in the man's chest. The state police promoted Corporal Loughner to sergeant and awarded him the Medal of Honor "in recognition of personal bravery and commitment to duty despite the risk of serious bodily injury." He lost part of his liver and the ability to walk without a limp.

"He *is* a hero," DeMarco said. "Though I do have to wonder

why he was still just a corporal after thirty-four years." And asked himself, *Another way we're like each other?*

Miller saved his most flowery prose for Jayme, describing her as "a milky-skinned heartbreaker who will rip you in half if you cross the criminal line," and recounted how she had "faced down the killer of seven young women in Kentucky, dodging his bullets until she brought him to his knees with a single well-placed shot," and the bravery she had displayed just months earlier in Youngstown by helping to bring Connor McBride and Professor Gillespie to justice.

Jayme laughed when she read those lines. "Dodging bullets!" she said. "I didn't know I could move that fast."

"Few of us can," said DeMarco. "I love watching you do it, though. You're just a blur."

"The guy was firing buckshot at me, not bullets," Jayme said of the killer in Kentucky. "And I missed him with my first shot."

"Doesn't sell papers." He leaned back in his seat. "What do you say we go find the kid and turn him inside out?"

"And get sued for harassment. Or worse. There's nothing we can do about it, Ryan."

"We'll see about that."

"Stop it. We have no recourse and you know that."

"We can put the fear of God in him."

"Baby, stop," she told him. "Take a breath. We'll have a talk with him, okay? But calmly. No threats." She rubbed a hand up and down his arm as she spoke. "He's just a kid. He's trying to become a writer. He's ambitious. We can't fault him for that, can we? He didn't say anything negative about any of us. In fact, I think there's a little hero worship going on here. Half of the article is about you."

"It's you he has a hard-on for."

"That's vulgar and possibly ungrammatical," she told him. "And beneath you."

"Femme fatale."

"And don't you forget it."

DeMarco took a long, slow breath. And slowly let it out. "At least he's read Hammett and Chandler."

"And Batman."

"Which Batman is he comparing me to, I wonder. Affleck or Bale?"

"Clooney, of course."

"Now you're just trying to placate me."

"Is it working?"

"A little."

She folded up the newspaper. "We'd better call Kyle in case he hasn't seen this yet. Those woods are going to be overrun with people taking selfies, if they aren't already."

"Loughner's probably there again today. He'll keep people out. I'll call him, you call Kyle."

"Which one do you think is going to yell loudest?"

"Kyle. But his voice hasn't changed yet, so it's no big deal."

ELEVEN

Before her, he had had only an unbroken parade of days heavy with shade, nights thick with a suicidal darkness. Between the time of Ryan Jr. sleeping on his chest or laughing in his arms and painting all corners with a bright glow of meaning, between those times and his second night with Jayme, he could see nothing but soot. Not even his first night with Jayme had thrown any light into his life, only more guilt to strangle him. But that second night, years after the first, that was the night he had turned the corner. There was no accounting for something like that, no predicting when or under what configuration of circumstances such a change would happen, but from then until now she had been his lighthouse and safe harbor. His manna in a desert of sand and stone, sweet swallow of rock-cupped water.

So yes, he would throw himself into another investigation for her. He would throw himself into the pits of hell for her. If this was what she believed she needed—just as he had once believed it was what *he* needed—then of course he would go along with it. Sometimes now he fantasized about giving it all up, getting a job as a crossing guard, for example, shepherding children from one side of the road to the other, helping them remain innocent of all the carnage beneath their feet, keeping them blissfully ignorant of how red was the earth with those billions of barrels of blood spilled in anger.

He thought he could be happy as a house husband. Changing diapers, reading *Go, Dog. Go!* a hundred times, *Goodnight Moon* a thousand, sticking plastic stars to the ceiling, weaving a warm blanket of affection around his children. He could have been that kind of father. Nothing mattered more. Nothing any man or woman could do would improve the world more than being a good parent. The most original and meaningful thing anyone could do in this life was to create a child unlike any other in the world. To do that and not cherish that creation above all else struck him as a kind of deliberate insanity. He would rather raise one healthy, happy, life-affirming human being than throw a dozen murderers in jail.

But the way she had been yesterday in those blood-spattered woods. Observant. Engaged. Her mind crackling with energy. She needed that and he needed her. So once again into the killing fields. Lace up your boots, DeMarco. Keep a sharp eye out. Assume the point. And for God's sake, man, keep her safe this time. Whatever it takes, soldier, you best remember this: you are nothing without her. So you damn well better keep her safe.

TWELVE

Their evening was quiet and unhurried on the surface, the sky darkening beyond the windows. Dire Straits' "Telegraph Road" played in the living room, sending its eerie whistle out to the kitchen where Jayme and DeMarco laid out the ingredients for an early dinner. Beneath the surface, his mind was full of chatter, with fragments of worry tumbling one over another, sounding like the old transistor radio he had as a boy and whose dial he would slowly turn at night in an attempt to pick up a ball game, only to get snatches of dialogue and static, music and silence.

He wondered if Harvey, spending the night at Dr. Lisa's clinic, had been neutered yet, and if so how he was handling the pain. And every time DeMarco looked at Jayme, he thought about their baby too, that tiny sesame seed Jayme felt certain was a girl. And that, of course, made him think of Ryan Jr., which brought back the abiding ache like a ball of hot steel embedded in his chest.

With an effort he forced himself to consider the unidentified bodies incinerated in the woods. Had they been conscious when the gasoline was poured over them? Did they watch the match being struck? It was too easy to think of them only as indistinguishable bodies and not as living and feeling human beings. *Probably females*, Loughner had said. A glance at Jayme standing at the stove now with her back to him made him wince.

And with that reaction he remembered the text he had received earlier from Ben Brinker but had not yet answered. How goes it, my friend? How is our brave girl doing? The nastiness Brinker faced daily as sheriff of a county with one of the highest crime rates in the country was unrelenting, yet he always found the time to check in with DeMarco.

DeMarco pulled the phone from his pocket and responded: Doing well, brother. Day by day. Any news on the hunt?

He silenced the phone and laid it screen up on the table, then returned to building a salad in a large glass bowl. He placed the pickled beets and three pepperoncini on only one side of the salad so that the juice would not bleed onto Jayme's greens. Then cut thin slices from a seedless cucumber and placed them symmetrically atop the salad. The phone's screen lit up just as he was about to reach for the cherry tomatoes. Last sighting in Ottawa on convenience store surveillance cam. Appears to be moving east. All precautions taken. More when I get it. Good job at hearing. Let's do dinner soon. Vee sends love to all.

DeMarco responded with a smiley face. Then pocketed the phone again.

So Khatri was coming their way. It made no sense that he would be so careless as to get caught on surveillance camera time after time; he was too smart for that. Ben never suggested that Khatri wanted them to know he was coming back, but it was obvious to DeMarco.

And that knowledge always brought him right back to Jayme— Jayme looking so docile and imperturbable, inviolate in her black yoga pants and butter-yellow T-shirt, her bare feet on the kitchen floor, her pink-painted toenails. She was even tapping one heel in rhythm to Dire Straits' "Calling Elvis," her shoulders and butt rocking back and forth as she filled two long buns from a cast iron skillet—shredded chicken, sautéed onions and peppers. Then she sprinkled shredded pepper jack cheese over the meat.

DeMarco placed six cherry tomatoes atop the salad, looked down at them and blinked, and wanted to weep from the ache of loving her.

"Is it too cold to eat outside?" she asked.

He swallowed the thickness in his throat. "We can always come back inside if it is. I'll grab you a hoodie and some socks."

They sat on the edge of the back porch, their feet on the first step, plates balanced on their knees. "It's good," he said.

"I was afraid I got too much paprika on it."

"It's perfect."

Everything was perfect. Everything except for the dog with no name in a strange room and crate and maybe by now with no testicles. Everything except for three more people dead, identities unknown. Everything except for a psychopath last seen smiling at a video camera in a convenience store in Ottawa and probably headed their way. Everything except for a little unborn girl lost to that psychopath's blade, and a little boy lost to DeMarco's inattention.

Yes, everything was perfect. Except for those few things and a few billion more, all was right with the world.

THIRTEEN

S he finished the rest of her tea, set the empty glass beside the empty plate, looked out across the yard for a moment, then leaned into him. The sky was a deep gray along the horizon. She thought she could hear something labored in DeMarco's breathing. Could feel something portentous out there in the far dimness, something waiting. But waiting for what?

"I'm missing the mutt already," she said.

"Me too."

"I keep thinking how funny it is that we found him that way. One minute we're petless, two minutes later we have a dog."

"Right out of left field," he said.

She smiled but felt the fraudulence of her expression, and hoped DeMarco would not notice it. Suddenly she felt pummeled by things that had hit them right out of left field. She said, "I had a long email from my mother today."

"How is she doing?"

"Still fretting about being in Australia when I was in the hospital."

"That's what good parents do. They fret."

"I just wish she would quit apologizing for it. It's not good for either of us."

It was always with her, and she knew it always would be. *It*. The incident. The loss. Ever present, ever clear. And now she finally understood Ryan's loss too. Now she felt it. Her big, strong, silently grieving man. What would she do without him?

A sudden chill raced up her back. She said, "I don't want there to be any secrets between us."

He pulled away just far enough to look at her. "What brought that up?"

"Nothing. I was just thinking. I mean…there are things in my past I'm not particularly proud of."

"We all have them."

"I don't like keeping them from you."

"I don't need to hear them."

"But I feel like I need to tell you."

"That feeling is incorrect," he said.

"But it's like they say in group. It's good to express things. It's good to get stuff out."

He thought for a moment before responding. "I agree with the expression part. But when you express something dark to another person, a person you care about, isn't it sort of like passing some of that darkness on to them? And I don't want you carrying around any of my darkness."

"In other words, you don't want to hear mine because you don't want to tell me yours."

"Sweetheart," he said, "there is nothing to be gained by giving past sins new life."

"What if I just feel like I have to get them out? Like I'm being dishonest with you if I don't?"

He sat motionless for fifteen seconds. Then said, "Sit tight. I'll be right back." He gathered up the plates and glasses and went inside.

She heard the water running in the sink, knew he was quickly washing the dishes, using that time to think. Then the water stopped. No sounds for half a minute. What was he doing in there?

He returned carrying two of the pocket notebooks they used for field notes when working a case, two pens, and the metal trash can she had placed under the sink when she bought a new one with a lid. He handed her a pen and notebook, set the trash can on the ground between their feet, and sat.

"Write it all down," he told her. "Every secret you want to get rid of. Use a separate page for each one. I'll do the same."

Were they going to read them to each other? Or trade notebooks and read them silently? That was just like him, wasn't it?

She wrote quickly, squinting in the dimming light. When she laid her pen aside, he said, "You're done already?"

"There are really only two things. I've told you everything else already."

He nodded. Kept writing.

Finished, he tore each of the small sheets free, one at a time. Folded them once and tossed them into the trash can. She followed suit with both of her pages.

DeMarco leaned to the side and reached into a pocket. "What you really want is forgiveness," he told her. "So do I. And this is how we forgive each other."

Now she understood. "And maybe ourselves too?"

He nodded. Opened the book of matches he had taken from his pocket. Tore one match free and handed the book to her.

She tore a match free and turned to him. He tapped the tip of his match to hers and said, "Ladies first."

She struck her match, lowered it quickly to the trash can, touched the flame to one of the papers, dropped the match inside when the paper caught fire. He took the book from her and did the same.

Soon the fire grew, and for just a few moments the flame flared above the metal rim. Then it sank low. A white smoke drifted up to them. Jayme leaned close to the smoke, drew her hands through it and rubbed it over her face. Then, smiling, feeling a little bit silly but also that the impromptu ritual was justified, she drew her hands though the smoke again and rubbed them over DeMarco's face. They watched the smoke being drawn up into the sky. Watched until there was nothing left in the trash can but ashes.

He dipped a finger into the ashes, dabbed the ash on her forehead, and said, "I forgive you everything."

She dipped her finger in, traced a small cross on his forehead. "I forgive you everything."

When she looked at him smiling, his eyes as wet as hers, he told her, "We're all clean now, love. We're all washed clean."

She hoped he was right and that it was as easy as that to get clean again, and that the dog would have an easy night, and that the feeling would soon pass of a portentous something like an enormous black shark undulating toward her through its infinite sea of darkness.

FOURTEEN

Early the next morning, DeMarco took the call from Trooper Boyd while she was in the shower. Then he finished dressing, olive-green cargo pants, the thick black socks he liked for their comfort and warmth, a white Oxford shirt. Then he sat on the edge of the bed, elbows on his knees, hands clasped, until she came out naked but for the towel wrapped around her hair.

"Who was that on the phone?" she asked.

"Boyd," he said.

"Good news or bad?"

He looked away from her. "I can't think straight when you're standing there like that."

"Like what?" she asked, and grinned at his discomfort.

"See you downstairs," he told her, and stood.

She laughed. "Discipline, DeMarco. Self-discipline."

"Overrated," he answered as he went out the door.

⸺≫⸺⸺≪⸺

"So what's the news?" she asked, set down her coffee mug and reached for the banana.

He had made oatmeal for both of them, had mixed cinnamon, chopped dates, dried cranberries and raisins with the oatmeal, then laid a banana beside each bowl. While she sliced her banana, poured milk into the bowl, and ate her oatmeal, he filled her in on Trooper Boyd's report.

All VIN numbers had been removed from the torched Santa Fe, the dash plate on the bulkhead pried off, the sticker on the passenger doorpost scraped away, the number on the engine block chiseled out.

No identifying fragments of jewelry or clothing could be found among the remains in the back seat, but both skulls were intact, as well as the teeth. Examination of the dentition and recovered DNA indicated that both victims were female, one Asian, one Caucasian. Morphological changes in the teeth suggested that the women were between the ages of twenty and thirty-five. The white woman had been a heavy smoker, the Asian ground her teeth. Local dentists were being provided X-rays of all victims' teeth for comparison with their patients' records.

The male victim's fingerprints and DNA did not show up in any of the searches, which meant either no previous arrests, no past employment that would have required FBI clearance, or no arrests logged into the NCIC. His tattoos were all too generic to be of any value. One scar, three inches long, on his upper right bicep, had probably been inflicted by a jackknife. Another scar, only a half inch in length but deep enough to nick a rib, on his left side. Three toes on his right foot showed signs of old breaks, as did the pinky of his right hand. Knuckles on both hands heavily scarred. Additional scars on forehead and scalp. Blood and hair follicle analysis tested positive for both cocaine and cannabis, but registered strongest for the sedative chloral hydrate.

"Interesting," Jayme said. "We don't see much of chloral hydrate these days."

"It's easier to get in Canada and the UK."

"So we have a user, weed and coke, to whom somebody slipped a mickey."

"He's got the scars of a street fighter. The somebody didn't want to go one-on-one with him."

"And that," she said, "is all we know?"

"So far. How do you like the oatmeal?" He had made it thick, so that the layer of milk lay atop it, and the oatmeal was spooned up in chunks.

"I like it a lot. Why didn't you ever make this before?"

"Just thought of it this morning. The dried fruit makes it sweet without any sugar, especially the dates."

"So this is the first time you've had it this way?"

He shook his head no. "A long time ago I took a little camping trip by myself. Just grabbed everything from the cupboard that wouldn't spoil fast. Next morning I made some oatmeal, threw all the dried fruit in, poured in a little canned milk mixed with water, and loved it. It reminds me of my mother's bread pudding."

Camping trip? she wondered. How long ago? And why *grabbed* what he needed for the trip? It sounded as if he had been in a hurry to get away from something or someone. From his wife? Parent? Memories? God, how she wished she could see into that head of his, could turn on the faucet to his brain and let all the secrets spill out.

She said, "Isn't bread pudding usually creamier than this?"

"Not the way she made it. She wasn't much of a cook."

"Well, you are, babe. This is a healthy, stick-to-the-ribs break-fast. So how are we going to put it to use?"

"Finish up," he told her. "And put on your walking shoes."

FIFTEEN

It was after ten when DeMarco finally stepped out into the yard and saw that the sky was high and clear and cobalt blue, with only two slender streaks of white cirrus clouds above, as if a painter had used the blue canvas to clean his brush. The air was sweet and dry and the temperature more typical of May than October. With a sudden regret he realized that he had missed the morning altogether. He had been poring over property maps of Otter Creek Township, noting homes and farms and roads, then made two copies of the map and two of the satellite photo of the township, had folded them in half and slipped the copies in a canvas satchel along with bottles of water and PowerBars. But now the best part of the morning was gone and he could never get it back.

Long ago he had told himself that he would never miss the first light of morning, always the finest part of the day, and that he would always spend at least a couple of minutes outside no matter the weather, feeling and smelling and being a part of each day's birth. But he had missed this one and several others and he could never get them back.

Jayme locked the rear door and came up behind him, a tall insulated plastic cup full of coffee in each hand. "What's up?" she said.

"Beautiful morning. Except that it's almost gone."

"There's like ninety minutes of it left."

"Not the same," he said.

"Not the same as what?"

He looked at the sky a moment longer. Filled his lungs with another breath. Then turned to her and smiled and said, "Giddyup."

※————————《

In the conference room at the Troop D station house a tenth of a mile from Interstate 79, they met with Boyd and one of the new recruits, Daniella Flores. She was twenty-four years old, stood a ramrod straight five five in her shiny boots, wore her dark hair in a short shag cut that ended in line with her chin. Her large eyes were a clear, deep brown, and, when regarding DeMarco, seldom blinked.

Jayme took one look at her and remembered her own fears as a new recruit, the raw disbelief of being granted the uniform, the always alert yet nervous determination to succeed. She also recognized the look with which the younger woman regarded DeMarco.

"You look familiar," he said to Flores. "Where are you from?"

"I grew up in Farrell, sir."

"You don't need to call me sir. I'm a civilian now."

"Yes, sir."

And then he remembered. "That diner on Route 19. You used to work there."

"The Belmont. Yes, sir. I went to the same school as Meghan Fletcher, though I didn't know her personally. She was several years older than me. I worked with her mother at the diner, though."

In a rush it came back to him. A nineteen-year-old girl, her throat slit in her own bed. So long ago. So much loneliness then.

He said, "How is Mrs. Fletcher doing these days?"

"She's doing all right. She manages the diner now. Has a boy-friend who's a really good guy."

"I'm glad to hear that."

"Also, I used to play in the old St. Margaret's Hospital. I know all about what happened there last summer." She turned to Jayme. "I'm so sorry."

Jayme answered with a smile.

Flores looked to DeMarco again. "You've been an inspiration to me, sir. I applied to the academy because of you. It's an honor to work with you. With both of you. You're both just so...so..."

"Okay, enough of that stuff," DeMarco said. "Trooper Boyd is getting nauseated. Here's what I thought we could do today. If it's okay with you, Mace."

Trooper Boyd said, "It's your show, Sergeant. I mean I know what Captain Bowen said, but technically..."

"Technically," DeMarco told him, "everything I say is merely a suggestion. If you disagree, you say so."

Boyd nodded once.

DeMarco took one copy of each of the Otter Creek Township maps out of his bag and spread them open on the table. Already on the table was a short stack of papers facedown. "The X on the property map marks the approximate crime scene. Ditto the aerial view map in case you need to orient yourself. As you can see, I've divided the township into east and west of the X on the property map, one portion for each team. As per Captain Bowen's direc-tion, we need one uniform on each team. So, if it's okay with you guys, how about we put Trooper Boyd and Jayme together, and I'll work with Trooper Flores. Agreed?"

Flores began, "It would be my honor—" then stopped when DeMarco raised his eyebrows. "Agreed, sir."

"There are just shy of two hundred occupied homes in the

township. The ones marked with a yellow highlighter are, obviously, closest to the crime scene, and also those closest to a public road. In other words, home to people most likely to have seen the vehicle or the victims at one time or another. We'll focus on those today. There are more homes on the east side than on the west, but there's less territory to cover."

Jayme and Trooper Boyd shared a look and a nod. Jayme said, "We're good with that side."

"Excellent. That leaves Trooper Flores and me with the easy part."

Everybody smiled. DeMarco put his fingertip to the stack of other papers and said, "Mace, are these the photos?"

"Two of each for each team. One of each for each person, in other words."

DeMarco turned them faceup. Four photos of the dead man nailed to the tree. Four photos of the burned-out Santa Fe. He said, "Just be very careful about flashing this one," he said, his finger to a photo of the dead man. "Make sure no kids see it."

"The car too," Jayme said. "We don't want any children having nightmares about the family car burning up."

"Let's just be careful all around," DeMarco told them. "Ask before we show."

Boyd said, "We know that the vehicle was dark green. Called Black Forest Green. We're looking at 2010, 2011, 2012. If it's been around the area at all, somebody would have seen it. And, with luck, the victims."

"Any hits," DeMarco said, "Jayme, you and I will stay in touch. No call means no hits."

"Copy that," she said.

"So much for the instructions, folks. You all know what you're doing."

"If I could just add," Jayme said, and made a point of not singling out Trooper Flores by looking only at her, "nonverbal information might be our most valuable source here. Nervousness, evasiveness, hostility, even an overly zealous desire to cooperate—it all says something. Keep good, thorough notes for every house and every person canvassed."

DeMarco waited ten seconds before asking, "Any questions?"

There were none. He dug into his satchel, pulled out six Power Bars and tossed them onto the table. "Help yourselves," he said. "And stay hydrated."

Flores and Boyd each took one Power Bar. DeMarco pushed two toward Jayme, plus two bottles of water, and dropped the remaining bars back into his bag.

Outside, on the way to their vehicles, Jayme and DeMarco hung back a couple of steps. He said, "Gonna miss you, partner."

She swung her hand toward his, but the moment her fingertips touched the back of his hand, a cold shock shot up her arm, an icy, unnameable fear. She seized his hand and squeezed it. "You too, babe. Stay in touch, okay?"

"Always," he said. After a quick squeeze of his fingers, his hand fell away from hers.

SIXTEEN

Alone in the vehicle with Flores, DeMarco felt awkward and ill at ease. She kept turning her head slightly in an attempt to view him surreptitiously, and sometimes held her gaze on the side of his face so long that he felt his cheeks reddening. More than once he felt an urge to rebuke her, tell her to knock off the staring. But maybe that was why she seemed so tense and apprehensive. The guys at the barracks had probably painted him as an ogre who would bite her in half at the first wrong word. Plus there was the whole thing about her following his career, about joining up because she used to serve him his breakfast. He had never thought of himself as a role model for anybody. Didn't even want to model himself after himself, let alone have an impressionable young woman do so.

He let out a long breath, tried to blow some of the stiffness out of his neck. It was too early in the day for a stiff neck.

He turned his head away from her. Glanced out the side window. They were coming up now on a long hay field he liked, especially in the early evening when the sun was below the horizon. The field rose up from the highway in a long, gentle incline, so that the slope crested a couple of hundred yards beyond and above the car. Right now the sun was above Flores's side of the car, not yet at solar noon, so the huge cylindrical bales of hay, all wrapped in sleeves of white plastic, resembled monstrous white maggots. In the early evening, with the sun at their back, they would look like great shaggy-headed bison asleep across the horizon.

To Flores he said, "What do you think bison dream about?"

The question startled her at first, but then she smiled. "Other bison?"

"There were thirty million of them in North America before the white man came along."

She was silent for a few moments, seemed unsure of how to answer. But after he looked at her and smiled, she said, "Stupid white man."

He grinned, nodded, and kept driving.

He liked her. She was just a kid to him but she was alert and eager and she would do fine. Today should be simple. Knock on a door, ask a few questions, move on and repeat. Nothing to worry about.

"Listen," he told her. "Chances are, today will be a cakewalk. But there's always that one chance in a million it won't. That's the one you always have to be expecting."

She nodded. "The murderer might be in one of the houses. Might open the door. And might do something stupid when he sees my uniform. Don't worry; I'll be ready."

"Good," he said. He slowed to make a left off Folk Road, a two-laner, and onto Donation Road, a narrower asphalt road with no lane markings. Soon they would be in Otter Creek Township.

"What made you think of bison?" she asked.

"I'll show you later. On the way back."

"Oh. Okay."

"We have bison here too. But they're always sleeping."

She cocked her head, gave him a quizzical look.

"Better cap your water bottle," he told her. "The road gets fairly bumpy from here."

SEVENTEEN

Lots of maybes. Lots of *yeah, I think I did but I have no idea when*. DeMarco handed out a card at every stop, said, "If you remember anything or hear anything, please give me a call." Flores carried her own cards, which included only the state police contact information, unlike DeMarco's or Jayme's, which included their names, *Private Investigations*, and the number for their landline.

Flores noted that DeMarco's introduction was always the same: "I'm Detective DeMarco and this is Trooper Flores; we're with the state police." *With the state police*. Technically correct, but prone to misinterpretation. Only she was *of* the state police. She knew that he was too smart not to have chosen his words deliberately.

Most people wanted to be helpful. After the initial stops, the residents seemed to be expecting the knock and showed no surprise to find a detective and state trooper on the other side of the door. *The cell phone towers are getting a good workout*, Flores thought.

At fourteen homes, nobody answered the door. She wrote *Please call ASAP* on a card and stuck it between the door and the jamb. Only a few people were hostile, answered brusquely, and slammed the door. Two men said, "I wouldn't tell you anything even if I did know."

Through it all, Flores stood a long stride behind DeMarco at the door, off to his right, her hand open against her hip, thumb touching the holster. *Please God*, she prayed each time DeMarco knocked. *Please Blessed Mother of Jesus Christ, please.*

Only twice during the day was she frightened enough to slide her hand over the holster. An older man stinking so strongly of beer and old sweat that she could smell him from six feet away. Average height, maybe sixty years old, dirty white whiskers, tufts of white hair in his ears. Face like dried-out leather. Small squinting eyes as gray as river ice. He kept his right shoulder and arm behind the doorjamb, spoke loudly through the screen, swore at DeMarco for waking him up, lobbed one f-bomb after another. DeMarco spoke calmly, evenly, told him how important it was that he and his neighbors assist them in finding the people responsible for this crime. How grateful he was for the man's cooperation. And in the end the man took the card DeMarco held out to him, pulled it away clamped between his tobacco-stained fingers, said, "Yeah all right, I hear what you're saying," before he closed and locked the door.

The other man was all cooperation, all smiles and soft voice. But he was huge. At least six four, over two hundred pounds, mid to late forties, cleanly shaved skull and face. Dressed in pressed blue jeans and a clean white T-shirt and Nike suede-and-mesh slip-on sneakers. He had the look of a former weight lifter going paunchy. But he oozed something negative, had that imperious air she had experienced from a couple of lawyers, a Lexus salesman, several married businessmen, and most of the boyfriends she had been too young and stupid to avoid. They thought they were smarter than you and better than you and could talk you into anything. There was a quiet intensity to everything they said, as their eyes never strayed from yours and they leaned close as if sharing a secret. They gave her the creeps. *Like a white Cory Booker*, she told herself. *Or Mitt Romney without hair.* At the end of the day, these were the two she remembered most vividly, the ones who made her skin feel dirty.

DeMarco parked the car at a pullout beside an oil holding tank. Finished up his notes, then waited for her to finish. When she looked up from her notes, he asked, "So what do you think?"

She didn't need to consult her notes but pretended to anyway. "The older man in the trailer with the ratty old sofa and other stuff in his yard. And the bald weight lifter guy in that beautiful old farmhouse. I got bad vibes from both of them."

"Read me your notes," he said.

"All of them?"

"Just those two."

"Edson Wetzel, 148 Kitch Road. Sixtyish, smelly, cranky old man. Retired logger. Says two unemployed sons live with him, come and go. Neither currently present. Angry and evasive. Never showed his right arm or hand. Probably not strong enough to overpower or move male victim on his own, but with sons' help?"

"Okay; good. Who else?"

"Luther Reddick, 379 Linn Tyro Road. Online dealer, antiques and collectibles. Late forties, clean-cut, soft-spoken, well-dressed. Single, lives alone. Is certain he's seen the Santa Fe several times but doesn't remember where, probably somewhere in town, doesn't remember noticing the plate. Doesn't remember ever seeing the vic. Uber cooperative. *Asked* for a card. Shook Sergeant's hand. Winked at me when saying goodbye. Feels skeevy. Ugh. Made me want to spit."

She looked up at DeMarco then and said, "Sorry about that last part."

"Don't apologize. Half of this job is trusting your instincts. The other half is in knowing when to follow up on them."

"Some men just rub me the wrong way. But it doesn't mean they're murderers."

He nodded. "Did you notice anything else of interest in Wetzel's yard?"

"Mmm...just a lot of junk, as far as I recall."

"I saw two red plastic fuel containers. One gallon and five gallons."

"How did I miss that?"

"They were halfway buried under other stuff. Still...you have to notice *everything*."

"But wasn't there evidence of a melted container inside the Santa Fe?"

"And...?"

"Okay. Maybe that one was burned up, but the presence of the other two...it means he uses them. Maybe the two with the junk have holes in them."

"How far is his trailer from the crime scene?"

She looked at the property map. "Maybe two and a half miles?"

"How much does a five-gallon container of gas weigh?"

"Over thirty pounds."

"So?" he said.

"So if it was Wetzel...he either had help, such as his two sons, or he drove there. Which is unlikely because one of the vics would have had to drive the Santa Fe."

"Or maybe they all drove to the crime scene, and he walked home alone afterward, empty-handed."

"Yeah, that works," she said sheepishly. "Except if they all drove there in one car ... how did he initially get to where their car was? Unless the vics were at his place to begin with." She paused, thought a moment longer, then said, "I guess I just don't see him, all by himself, handling three other people. And didn't the lab say that the chloral hydrate in the male victim was administered orally? Why would a big guy like him not resist and fight back? For my money, if Wetzel's involved, he isn't in it alone."

DeMarco smiled. "And Reddick?"

"He's big and strong. Even without a gun in his hand, he could be intimidating."

"And you think there's something fishy about him?"

"How many square feet in a house like that? Maybe three thousand? And he lives there alone? I don't know. Yeah, something smells fishy to me. Maybe the house is filled with antiques and that's why he lives alone. Maybe he just likes the extra space. Maybe he inherited the place. But I guess those are things I would want to look into."

"Why don't you do that," he told her with a smile.

"Yes, sir," she said.

He laid his notepad aside and started the engine. "The sun's going down. Want to go see those bison now?"

"Absolutely, sir. Is it a big herd? And what did you mean that they're always sleeping?"

He answered with a smile. "Buckle up, Trooper."

EIGHTEEN

At approximately 6:30 p.m. DeMarco dropped Flores off at the station house. Boyd's patrol car was already parked and empty. Flores climbed out of DeMarco's car, put her hand to the door, but paused. Then she bent down to look across the seat at him. "Thanks for being patient with me today," she said.

"Patience is my middle name. Didn't anybody tell you that?"

The way she smiled, making her eyes crinkle a little, he knew she had been warned just the opposite. Had probably been holding her breath all day, waiting for him to blow up.

She said, "And thanks for showing me your bison."

"Now they're your bison too."

Her face did something funny then, the tiniest quiver in her mouth, a glimmer of dampness in her eyes. He looked away quickly, stared out the windshield and said, "Let Jayme know I'm out here waiting, okay?"

"Will do," she said, then closed the door softly and strode toward the building.

A little sun of warmth radiated from his chest as he watched her go, and his cheeks warmed too. That his few words of kindness had nearly brought her to tears—it was an embarrassing thing. Who was he to have such power? He was nobody. Certainly not a role model. Well, okay, he was a work in progress. Anyhow it was a nice way to end a frustrating day of work, giving an earnest young woman a little boost of confidence. And he had done it without thinking, without having to plan it out. What could be wrong with that?

The dusky light of evening was quickly graduating to darkness, and with his window down DeMarco could feel the temperature cooling. A dull rumble emanated from Interstate 79. It was louder than he remembered it, always a muted thrum from his former desk inside the building, now a throbbing, palpable growl as the endless caravan of eighteen wheelers sped by, each truck spewing diesel fumes and as much nitrogen oxide and particulates as 150 cars. Interstate 80 five miles south was even busier and noisier. He wondered if living between those two concrete trails, being caught in their unabating slipstream of noise and stink, could account for his many years of insomnia and constant state of agitation. How could it not be unhealthy?

Nearly all cities were now virtually wrapped inside such growling, vibrating ribbons of concrete, especially in the eastern half of the country. Could that proximity to superhighways be to blame, at least in part, for the alarming increase in incivility? And how about the rise in digestive disorders? He had read that gut problems had risen by over 200 percent in the past twenty years. Also the use of antidepressants, up at least 65 percent. He hadn't seen any studies that compared the incidence of those problems in cities and rural areas, but he was willing to bet that—

"Hey," Jayme said after popping open the passenger door. She climbed in and asked, "Who were you dreaming about?"

"Peace and quiet," he said. "How would you feel about checking out Wyoming or Montana when this case is wrapped up?"

"Another road trip? Sure; why not?" She pulled her seat belt and harness on. "By the way, I had a text from Dr. Lisa a while back. Rambo pulled through and is ready to come home. Do you think he'll be mad at us?"

"I would be. And since when did he become Rambo?"

"Since I thought of it last night."

"You dream of Sylvester Stallone often?"

"Depends on what you call often," she said with a smile.

He drove out to the road, checked to his right, then made a left.

She said, "I didn't hear from you out there today, so I guess you and Flores struck out too?"

"A couple of suspicious characters, but that's it."

"That's what she said. Same here. She and Boyd will run them through the databases and get back to us tomorrow. Which leaves what for us to do?"

"Tonight? Pick up Harvey, grab some chow, hit the sack."

"He's not a Harvey, babe."

"He's not a Rambo either."

Neither of them spoke for a while. When he glanced her way again and saw her head turned, her gaze going miles and miles away out the side window, he knew that they had been lost in the same fantasy, imagining a child playing with the dog. The only difference was that the child in his fantasy was a boy, and in hers a little girl.

NINETEEN

Forty minutes later they returned home with a pepperoni and mushroom pizza and a morose puppy of undefined breed, the pizza in a cardboard box, the dog in a metal crate loaned by Dr. Lisa. They carried both into the house, set the pizza box on the kitchen counter, set the crate on the living room floor. Jayme opened the crate and reached inside but she could not coax Rambo to crawl out. He lay there with his chin on the floor of the crate, his sad eyes on Jayme.

"I feel so bad," she said as she stroked his head. "We're awful parents, aren't we?"

The remark stung DeMarco more than it should have, so that he turned away, went back to the kitchen for the pizza and napkins. From there he said, "Should I make a salad?"

"Whatever you want. I don't know if I can eat anything or not."

"She said to expect him to be a little blasé for a while."

"He knows what we did to him. I can see it in his eyes."

DeMarco put four slices of pizza on a plate and carried it to the living room, placed it on the coffee table. Jayme was sitting cross-legged in front of the crate now, with the dog's head resting over her foot. She told DeMarco, "Go ahead and eat. Don't wait for me."

He sat on the sofa but did not reach for the pizza. Watched

Jayme and the dog for a while. *Definitely a Harvey*, he thought. *Rambo wouldn't pout. He would rip our throats out.*

DeMarco leaned back and rested his neck against the cushion, slowly rolled his head back and forth. When he sat erect again he noticed the red light blinking on the landline phone. "We have a message," he said, stood and crossed to the phone, looked down at the readout. "Unknown."

"Maybe it's from one of the people we talked to today."

He punched the Play button but kept his fingertip poised above Delete.

"Greetings!" a young male voice said. "Hey, guys, it's Chase Miller here, your biggest fan. Just wondering how you felt about the piece I did. I hope I didn't get anything wrong. I pride myself on accuracy! Anyway, I hope you don't mind my calling you at this number. It's in the book, so, you know…public information and all that. So anyway, the actual reason I called was to offer a proposal. I mean, you've probably researched me by now as much as I've researched you, so I'm sure you know that this stringer gig is just for the experience and to help pay the bills. What I'd really love is to maybe hook up with you guys in a learning capacity, you know? I'm a whiz at research! I can dig up anything about anybody. And for the honor of working with you two, I'd do it all for peanuts. Expenses, that's it. The only thing I'd ask in return is the right to tell the story. In print, of course. Like maybe for *GQ*, *Playboy*, any of the big glossies. Some place where I can maybe get some recognition. Like Sebastian Junger, you know? *The Perfect Storm*? Or Jon Krakauer. Even Norman Mailer, *The Executioner's Song*. I'm not saying I'm as good as any of those guys but I think maybe I can be, you know, with the right kind of tutelage. And who better to learn from than the two most famous PIs in the tristate area?"

Miller paused for a breath. DeMarco rolled his eyes at Jayme; she smiled and stroked the dog's head.

"Anyway," Miller continued, "I believe I can actually make a contribution. And please don't tell me to take some classes. Classes are bullshit. I've had a couple and I know. How many writing classes did Hemingway take? And Norman Mailer. Yeah, he studied at Harvard and the Sorbonne a little but where did he actually earn his chops? On the job! There's no other way to really and truly learn anything. And I know you agree with me, Sergeant DeMarco. I know you do. And that's why I'm asking you now… that's why I'm *begging* you…please let me contribute. When am I ever going to get another chance like this? Never! Not in this nowhere land."

There was another brief pause, then Miller continued, his voice softer now and more than a little plaintive. "So that's it, I guess. That's my pitch. I hope it wasn't for nothing. I'm at your mercy here." He ended with his cell phone number, and the promise, "Just give me a shot, that's all I'm asking. I swear you won't regret it."

When the recorded voice on the landline said, "End of message," DeMarco raised his hand to hit Delete. But Jayme said, "Wait!"

He cocked his head and looked at her sideways. "No way," he said.

"What's it going to hurt?"

"What's it going to hurt? We already have one puppy to babysit. We don't need another one."

"And we've already cut off one pair of balls today. Do you really want to cut off another pair?"

TWENTY

S he could not convince DeMarco to commit to giving Miller the chance he sought, but he did agree to "look into it." They would do the research Miller expected they already had; they would check out his background, his history. And then make a decision.

DeMarco did not fail to notice how the prospect of helping a young man launch his career buoyed Jayme's spirits and brought back her appetite. She warmed up the pizza in the microwave and opened a bottle of merlot rosé. She and DeMarco sat together on the sofa, with the twice-named dog asleep at Jayme's feet, and watched the movie *Turistas*.

Not long after the first hour of the movie, Jayme was asleep too, now with her head in DeMarco's lap, her long legs folded up close. He kept his eyes open until the movie was nearly over, then drifted off until after midnight. When he woke and saw the time in blue numbers on the cable box, he whispered to her until she awoke and looked at him.

"Let's go to bed, baby," he said, and she groaned "Okay" and slid her feet to the floor and started, wobbly, toward the stairs. He carried Harvey out through the back door and set him on the grass. At first the dog did not seem to know what to do, only stood there looking either drunk or suicidal until DeMarco told him, "Pee now or hold it until morning."

Finally Harvey turned away and, like an old drunk locked out of his favorite saloon, wobbled over to the corner of the porch, where he lifted his leg and urinated against the wood.

Finished after little more than a trickle, he turned at the neck to look back. "Good enough," DeMarco said.

Inside, cradling the dog in his arms, he hurried through his routine of checking the lock on the back door, checking that the coffee maker and oven were turned off, checking the front door, and turning off all the lights as he moved through the house.

The whole process took only a minute and a half, but by the time he reached the bedroom, Jayme was asleep with her clothes in a pile beside the bed. *Why not*, he thought, and laid the dog on the floor. He took off everything but his boxers and T-shirt and, skipping the usual brush and gargle, slid in beside her. Within minutes he was asleep too.

The dream was brief and vivid and startling. Two gray aliens leaning over him as he lay on his back, paralyzed beside a soundly sleeping Jayme. The taller of the two aliens used what looked like a crystal knife to slice him open from his neck to his penis, then pulled back the layers of skin and fat to peer inside. DeMarco felt no pain, only shock and fear. But he could not move, could not speak. The only thing that kept him from screaming inside his head was the knowledge that the tall gray was his father and the smaller one was Ryan Jr. They looked nothing like those two, had pear-shaped heads and huge black eyes, spindly bodies and elongated fingers, but he knew them all the same. Both grays had their fingers inside him now, probing, and he could hear their thoughts.

I can't find it anywhere, the small one said.

Neither can I.

I don't think he has one.

Probably never did.

We're wasting our time here.

Should we close him up?

Why bother? He's empty.

Just as he knew that the grays were his father and Ryan Jr., DeMarco knew they were talking about his soul. He didn't have one. Probably never did.

He awoke with a strangled scream in his throat and his body hot with fear.

TWENTY-ONE

Shaken by his dream, DeMarco reached for his cell phone on the bed table, crept out of bed and into the hallway, where he sat against the wall and telephoned Dr. Hoyle in Kentucky. Hoyle answered with a sleepy, "It is 3:23 a.m. where you are, is it not, Sergeant?"

"I guess so," DeMarco said. "Why do you ask?"

"Because it is 2:23 a.m. here."

"Oh. Right. I'm sorry if I woke you."

"I will assume a good reason. Which is?"

"I wanted to get your take on something."

"Proceed," Hoyle said.

"Because you're a scientist," DeMarco said, "but also because you've said other things that imply, or make me think that maybe you're not locked into that particular way of, I don't know—"

"Sir," Hoyle interrupted. "I was in the middle of a wholly comfortable slumber, to which I would prefer to return while that possibility remains. So if you please…"

"Do you believe in the soul?" DeMarco asked. "Do you believe that we have one?"

So much silence passed that DeMarco began to suspect that the call had dropped. Then Hoyle said, "Have you ever seen frog eggs, Sergeant?"

"As a boy I did. Several times. But, uh…"

"Unfertilized frog eggs are round, simple, undifferentiated things. But the moment the egg is fertilized—the very moment, Sergeant—the egg begins to produce an electromagnetic field. And as the egg develops, the electromagnetic field adheres precisely to the developing spine."

"Well," DeMarco said, "that's interesting, I guess. Are you saying that the electromagnetic field is the soul?"

"Are you familiar with the word *kundalini*?"

"It has something to do with yoga, doesn't it?"

"Kundalini is the life force. The chi, the prana, the Great Mother who gives birth to all that is."

"Life force being equivalent to soul?"

"The caduceus of Hermes," Hoyle said. "Adopted by some as the emblem of the medical profession. But is in fact an ancient Greek alchemical symbol denoting the spine, with the pine cone–shaped top representing the pineal gland, and the two serpents, the life force, entwined around the staff, which represents the spine."

"So...like with the frogs? The life force entwined around the spine?"

"The chi rests in the first chakra at the base of the spine. If awakened, it moves up the spine and into the pineal gland. The awakening of kundalini is the awakening of the self to the knower. To the knowledge that the true self *is* the knower."

"In other words," DeMarco said, becoming confused, "you believe that the soul is real. Is that what you're telling me?"

"I have sliced open human brains," Hoyle told him. "Examined them under the microscope. I understand neurons, brain chemicals, synapses. I have *seen* them. I understand how they behave. But do you know what I do not understand, nor does anyone else?"

"No, sir, I don't."

"Consciousness, young man. Nobody understands consciousness. It is clear that the physical brain is somehow related to consciousness, is perhaps a kind of receiver, but there is not a speck of evidence that the brain is capable of *producing* consciousness."

"And this is related to...?"

"Everything," Hoyle said. "To every question that has haunted you ever since you were a boy. And to the questions that haunt you now."

DeMarco found himself short of breath. He did not fully comprehend what Hoyle was saying in his disjointed, cryptic way, but some part of it had stolen his breath, had bent him over his knees in the darkness, his left hand against his chest as he spoke into the phone. "Thank you, Dr. Hoyle. I, uh...I'm sorry I called so late."

"Melatonin," Hoyle told him. "Five milligrams to start. And now I have a question for you, if I may."

"Of course. Go ahead."

"There is no one in Pennsylvania with whom you can discuss matters such as these?"

"I called you because you might be the smartest man I know."

"Might be?" Hoyle said.

"*May* be?"

"I wasn't questioning your grammar, sir. Good night."

And the line went dead.

TWENTY-TWO

At breakfast Jayme sensed a disquietude in DeMarco, suggested by his relative silence and slower-than-usual movements. Most mornings he was a bundle of energy, ready to take on the world. She had made coffee and a large bowl of sliced strawberries, mango, and melon chunks in vanilla Greek yogurt, and he now sat at the table staring down into his bowl, using the tip of his spoon to push around a chunk of melon as if it were an unexpected specimen in a petri dish. Rambo lay on the floor between them, Jayme's stockinged feet against the dog's spine, DeMarco's against the belly.

"A dollar for your thoughts," she said.

He lifted his eyes to her and smiled. "The price has gone up."

"Inflation."

Again he smiled. But said nothing.

"Control to Sergeant Ryan," she said.

"Sorry." He released his spoon, leaned back in his chair. "I had a restless night. Dreamed a couple of aliens had cut me open and were looking for my soul. They couldn't find one."

"Oh my God," she said. "And then what?"

"And then I woke up or...I think I did. Went out in the hall and called Hoyle. Asked if he believed in the existence of the soul."

"You didn't. What time was it?"

"Almost three thirty here."

"Seriously? And what did he say?"

"Yes, I think. Though it took him a long time to say it. I'm hoping I only dreamed I called him."

"Check your phone."

For a few seconds he made no move to do so, then, almost fearfully, reached into his pocket, pulled out the phone and opened his call log. "Shoot," he said. "I didn't dream it."

She tried to hold back a laugh but in doing so made a quick snorting sound. When he raised his eyebrows, she sobered up and said, "You know dreams never mean what they seem to mean. They're always symbolic of something else."

"The aliens were my dad and Ryan Jr."

"Ooh, that's interesting, isn't it? They were obviously trying to tell you something. Did you ask Dr. Hoyle about it?"

"About my dream? He already thought I was an idiot. I wasn't about to confirm it for him."

Again she laughed. "I'm sorry, babe. I can tell it's bothering you but... Trust me, you have a soul. A big, beautiful, healthy one."

"That's not what the aliens said." But he had to smile too. And she recognized that sheepish look of embarrassment. Time to change the subject.

She said, "I was thinking we should invite Dr. Lisa and her partner over for dinner some night. How would you feel about that?"

"Me and three females sitting around the table together?"

"You could invite Joe Loughner to keep you company."

"I don't know about that. It's an hour down here from Erie. Long way to drive home, especially if you'd be serving wine with dinner."

"You could suggest that he bring a date."

"And what if he doesn't? Or what if he does and she drinks even more than he does?"

"Ugh. I hadn't considered that."

"We could invite Ben and Vee," he said.

"Oh, I would like that. How about Mason and Daniella too?"

"He'll think we're trying to set them up together."

"How do you know he would be against that?"

"Do you know something I don't?"

She smiled. "He was very complimentary of her yesterday. I sensed something there."

DeMarco thought about it, wagged his head a little. "Tricky situation," he said. "We invite two troopers but not the rest of them?"

"Right again," she said with a frown.

"Look," he told her. "I know you hit it off with Dr. Lisa. And I *want* you to have friends. So maybe you could invite her and, what's her wife's name? Susan? Maybe you could take Lisa and Susan to lunch someday."

"That'll work," she said.

She was disappointed not to be having a dinner party, especially now that Ryan was coming out of his hermit crab shell. She remembered how Trooper Flores had looked yesterday evening when she returned to the station house. The girl had been *glowing*. And when Jayme had asked, "Did he behave himself?" the young woman had blushed and answered, "Perfectly."

So Jayme knew that he had been kind and warm and considerate of the greenhorn. He was certainly capable of those qualities, but, around people he did not know well, he tended more toward a reserved civility. Yet ever since the miscarriage, he had been showing a more open side to his personality. Lathea had told her, only a few days before the miscarriage, "Everything happens for a reason." She had even insisted that Jayme repeat the phrase, almost as if she had known what was about to befall them.

What if Lathea were right? What if that tiny little soul had come into their lives too briefly only so that Jayme could not merely understand but *feel* Ryan's grief for his lost son, and so that Ryan could learn to step out of his own misery so as to comfort her in hers? It seemed too much of a sacrifice, and too cruel a lesson.

She tried not to let the tears come again but there was no stopping them.

He looked up from the bowl of fruit, saw the streaks down her cheeks and the wide, confusing smile. "Baby," he said. "What's wrong?"

"I'm just crying because I love you."

TWENTY-THREE

"L uthor Reddick, with an o" was the first thing Joe Loughner said after DeMarco tapped the phone icon and said hello. "You got the spelling wrong."

"Hey, Joe. How's it going?"

"You spelled Luthor with an e-r. He spells it o-r. After Lex Luthor, Superman's archrival. His real name is Thomas. Thomas Reddick Jr."

"He does sort of resemble Lex Luthor, I guess. How do you know him?"

"Him, not so much. But if he's anything like his old man, and I'm betting he is, he's our guy. I'd bet my life on it."

"How do you know his father?"

"He was my number one pain in the ass back in Elk County. A small-time drug dealer, though we could never nail him for that. Had him before the court on at least five different assault charges, though. He liked to beat people up, especially his wife and kid. Put him away for three years, which was about one one-hundredth of what he deserved."

DeMarco needed a moment to process the information.

Fifteen seconds later, Loughner said, "You still there?"

"Still here. How did you hear that we were looking at Reddick?"

"I checked in with Trooper Boyd this morning to see if you had any leads. He told me the five persons of interest your team came up with. And the moment I heard Reddick's name, my radar went crazy. I'm telling you, DeMarco, this guy is bad news. You need to get him behind bars ASAP. Frankly, I'm surprised somebody hasn't put him there already. Surprised and more than a little disappointed it wasn't *him* nailed to that tree."

All this from knowing the father? DeMarco thought.

DeMarco glanced at the time. "Any chance you'd be free for lunch? Meet you halfway? In Meadville, say?"

"I could use some eggplant parm, sure. Chovy's at...let's make it one. Give the business crowd time to thin out."

"See you there," DeMarco said.

He ended the call, then placed a call to Trooper Boyd, from whom he learned that several of the individuals canvassed the previous afternoon had rap sheets, but mostly for misdemeanors such as driving under the influence, domestic abuse, drunk and disorderly, simple possession. Nothing suggesting an individual who could drug and crucify a man and torch two females.

"So they are definitely female?" DeMarco asked.

"Skulls and femurs say so, yes. Ages early to late twenties. Cranium morphology confirms one Asian, one white."

"That young? Any chance the male could be their father?"

"No, sir. Unrelated."

"Dental records?"

"That's going to take a while. Especially since the vics don't appear to be local. No outstanding missing person reports."

"Hmm," DeMarco grunted. "So we still have two Jane Does and one John Doe."

"Yes, sir. I have the male's photo out nationwide. No hits yet."

"Flores and I both got bad vibes from a Wetzel and a Reddick yesterday. She was going to look into both of them."

"Yes, sir, she did. Wetzel is unemployed, was a janitor for GE a while back but got fired for coming to work drunk. Now apparently subsisting on welfare. His two sons, though, bear looking into some more if we can track them down. Apparently a couple of bad characters, starting when they were still in their teens."

"Bad how?" DeMarco asked.

"Shoplifting, breaking and entering, assault—the usual progression. They both spent several months in the county jail last year for burglarizing summer homes at Lake Latonka. They were released within a couple of weeks of each other. Haven't been seen around here since. The old man claims he has no idea where they are."

"They have cell phones, don't they?"

"The old man has a landline. I'm hoping to get his records today."

"Let me know if anything turns up."

"Will do."

"I'll be having lunch with Joe Loughner today. He has some strong suspicions concerning one of the men Flores and I spoke to yesterday."

"Yes, sir, he shared those suspicions with me. I ran Reddick and he came up clean. Though not sparkling clean."

"Meaning what?"

"Other than a less than honorable discharge from the army. For homicidal tendencies."

"You're kidding me."

"No, sir. That's how it reads. I got in touch with his former squad leader, who said it's not as bad as it sounds. Says Reddick was just too gung ho for their comfort. Kept begging to get sent to a war zone. They were afraid his 'undue ferocity and zeal' would endanger others."

"That's what they called it? Undue ferocity and zeal?"

"Exact words, sir."

"I thought the army wanted gung ho soldiers."

"Different times, I guess."

"And now he sells antiques online. Undue ferocity in an antique dealer. Does that jibe for you, Trooper?"

"Depends. Twenty years and modern medicine can work wonders."

"You have been of no help whatsoever today, Mace."

"Sorry, sir. I will try to do better."

"As will we all," DeMarco said. "You're welcome to join me and Joe for lunch if you'd like."

"I'll have to take a rain check on that. Going to work the computer all day, see if I can dig up something shiny."

"Good luck with that. And hey, how's Flores today?"

"Confidentially?"

"If that's how you want it, sure."

"Confidentially, I think you're lucky to be spoken for. Else you might be having some girl trouble right now."

"Oh boy," DeMarco said. "Do we have a young trooper with daddy issues?"

"You might say that. When the captain asked how you two got along, she called you *a very sweet man*."

"What's so surprising about that? Haven't I always been sweet to you?"

"I'm going to take the fifth on that one, sir."

DeMarco chuckled. "Have a good day, Mace. Either Joe or I will be in touch."

"Ten-four, Sergeant. Oh, by the way, Captain wanted me to let you know he got approval to reimburse your expenses. One meal per day each for you and Jayme, plus mileage."

"Tell him for me that we didn't ask him to reimburse our expenses. And that he should put the money toward those testosterone injections he needs."

The call ended with both men chuckling.

In the kitchen, where Jayme was plugging in her laptop, he filled her in on the context of both calls and invited her to join him for lunch in Meadville.

She pulled out a chair, sat, and flipped up the screen. "Thanks for the invite, babe, but next time maybe. I'm still full from breakfast. I think I'll stay here and see what I can learn about our young Norman Mailer."

"He strikes me as more like a preppy Jack Kerouac. Shy on self-discipline. Anyway that's what Mailer said about him. 'Kerouac lacks discipline, intelligence, honesty and…' something else I can't remember. 'His rhythms are erratic,' he's blah blah blah something else, and oh yeah, yeah, this is the good part. He's 'as pretentious as a rich whore, as sentimental as a lollypop.'"

She laughed. "As sentimental as a lollypop?"

"Good stuff, huh?"

She couldn't stop laughing. "Go see Joe. Enjoy yourself."

"Want me to bring something home for dinner? How about that pasta Michelangelo you like?"

"Ooh, yeah. But what was that tortiglioni you had last time? That was really good too."

"The all'arrabbiata. I'll bring home one of each. I'll just have the bruschetta for lunch. That way I'll be hungry with you."

"Lollypops for dessert?" she asked.

He leaned down to kiss her cheek. "Research Mr. Miller, my love. And don't be a sucker."

TWENTY-FOUR

The truth was, she could not stop thinking about her baby. Still wondering about the goodness of a God that would allow a pregnancy to begin, only to end it a few weeks later. Such events were a good argument *against* the existence of a God. And Jayme didn't want to agree with that argument. More than anything, she needed to disagree with it. If only it weren't so difficult to do.

It was a good thing she had work to distract her, or else she would sit there brooding and drive herself crazy. Into the Google search box she typed *Chase Miller*.

Darn, not an uncommon name. Chase Miller the country singer. The model. The race car driver. The golfer, the hockey player, the soccer player, the police officer, the infant murdered by his brother, the lawyer, the actor, the Chase Miller dead at twenty-seven, dead at fourteen, dead at forty-six, dead at eighteen months... And that didn't include the Chases who weren't Millers or the Millers who weren't Chases.

She sat back and took a few breaths. Then leaned forward and typed *"Chase Miller" Facebook*.

Okay, that was encouraging. Only 614 Chase Millers on Facebook to sift through.

She pushed back her chair and stood. Went to the refrigerator, opened it and stood there looking inside.

No, not hungry. Not thirsty.

She glanced under the kitchen table. Rambo was awake, lying there as before, chin to the floor, eyes raised to hers. "You want anything?" she asked. His tail flicked once, then lay still.

She closed the refrigerator door and went to the sink. Looked out the window at the backyard. Empty. "Need to go pee?" she asked.

That was usually enough to get him racing to the back door. But not today.

She sat down at the laptop again, slid her feet forward until they touched a warm body. There was something about the contact that made her feel better. She hoped it had the same effect on him.

She sat with fingers poised over the keys. What to type? She had done hundreds of name searches on criminal and military databases, knew how to search court dockets and outstanding warrants, sexual predator and deadbeat dad lists, but a law-abiding citizen? Her brain was full of fog, full of thoughts she wished would go away for a while.

She typed *"Chase Miller" writer "Greenville Tribune PA."*

Here we go. His most recent article, the embarrassing one. Byline at the top, and…bingo. At the end of the article: *Follow Chase on Twitter @ChasetheACE.*

He had 2611 followers, fewer than a hundred tweets. Not much of a bio. *Ace reporter, blogger, social critic, boat rocker. Have pen, will scribble.*

His tweets were mostly statistics, intended, she assumed, to rock the boat:

> Over ONE-THIRD of the total US population is on WELFARE! Read about it at DireWireFunFACTS .com

US Taxpayers fund secret BLACK OPS to the tune of $81 BILLION this year! Read about it at DireWireFunFACTS.com

The sordid tale of the Birmingham CANNIBAL! Read my latest blog post at DireWireFunFACTS.com

MASSIVE Global Pedophile Ring linked to Washington ELITES! Read about it at DireWireFunFACTS .com

Average American family shells out $6000/year to subsidize giant transnational corporations already making BILLIONS in profit! Read about it at DireWireFunFACTS.com

US taxpayers soaked TWO BILLION $$ every year to pay for anchor babies born to illegal aliens! Read about it at DireWireFunFACTS.com

Miller's blog, *Dire Wire Fun Facts*, expanded on such tweets, providing information from not only legitimate sources but also questionable ones. His favorite targets appeared to be welfare fraud and the United States government in general:

Mr. H's tenant weighs, by his estimate, at least 400 pounds. She has difficulty walking from the bedroom to her living room sofa. Yet she is paid $16 per hour, for 60 hours per week, to be the "caretaker" of another tenant in the same building who weighs over 600 pounds. Her check comes from an agency that subcontracts from the state, which pays that agency $32 per hour. Both tenants receive free housing through HUD, plus Medicaid, food stamps, Meals on Wheels, and other subsidies. Would exercise classes be cheaper? You figure it out.

When Donna went to prison for cooking meth in her kitchen, the county placed her two children with Donna's mother, who was paid approximately $600 per month per child. Twenty-eight months later, Donna was released from prison and regained custody of her children *and* the $600 per month per child subsidy, as well as collecting social security disability for diabetes, food stamps, rent support, utility bill support, and free medical care for the family. At this point Donna's 16-year-old son, who had been living with his father, moved back in with his mother, who was then paid an additional $16 per hour FOR TAKING CARE OF HER OWN SON!!!!

Do you know where the swamp begins in Washington DC? It's called CONGRESS.

Are you aware that every member of Congress works an average of 2.7 days a week and gets a salary THREE TIMES that of the average American, and CAN VOTE RAISES FOR THEMSELVES IN ADDITION TO the annual Congressional cost-of-living adjustment?

They ALSO receive a $900,000 ANNUAL ALLOWANCE for a staff, a QUARTER OF A MILLION $$ expense budget, FREE parking at the office and at airports, FREE meals at the legislative dining hall, GENEROUS healthcare and retirement packages, FREE travel between DC and their home districts AS OFTEN AS THEY LIKE, and FREE "business" travel vacations to OTHER COUNTRIES!

If a member of Congress dies in office (AND NOT

ENOUGH OF THEM DO!), their families receive DEATH
BENEFITS 75% HIGHER than those awarded to families of
SOLDIERS KILLED IN BATTLE!

Members of Congress undergo NO PERFORMANCE
REVIEWS, and the ONLY way to get rid of an INCOMPETENT
is at the voting booth!

Who is stupid enough to pay for all this without demand-
ing accountability?

THE AMERICAN TAXPAYERS!!!

Members of Congress are supposed to be serving YOU
but they take the biggest servings FOR THEMSELVES and
give you THE CRUMBS!

Other blog posts were graphic recreations of violent crimes
committed throughout the world, which Miller had read about
and researched online. He called these pieces "fictionalized true
stories in the manner of *In Cold Blood* and *The Executioner's Song*":

How long Freddy Sheffeld simmered in rage before decid-
ing to act upon his cannibalistic fantasies is unknown.
But what else does a lifelong doper and welfare parasite
have to do? His days were filled with the trailer trash cir-
cuses of Maury Povich and Jerry Springer, and his nights
with shambling along the mean streets, doing his best to
mooch a joint or a hit from the pipe. He even leeched off
the leeches. The wonder is that he was ever able to muster
the initiative for his first kill. But once he got a taste of firm,
ripe flesh, nothing else could set his perverted taste buds
to singing...

Jayme read three of these crime blogs, then did her own research to verify that the crimes had actually occurred. Miller frequently took liberties with the details, and his prose was too often florid and sensationalistic, but the gist of each story was true. Despite her training and experience, every tale sickened her a little more. Yet she read on, mesmerized by the duplicity, stupidity, and depravity of which human beings are capable.

Over two hours passed before she decided that she'd had all the dire fun facts she could stand for one day. Most fascinating and confusing of all was that the narratives had been rendered by such an attractive and clean-cut young man. She knew enough about human behavior to know that one's outward appearance can be either a mirror of the inner self or a cloak concealing it, but she did not feel up to the task of plumbing deeper into yet another labyrinthine psyche.

She cut and pasted excerpts from a half dozen blogs into one document and printed it out for DeMarco to assess. Then she took her throbbing headache to a kitchen cabinet, shook two Advils into her palm, and chased them down with a mouthful of tepid water.

She turned away from the sink and looked again at the dog. "I need to lie down for a while. I could use some company."

But he wasn't interested. He looked at her—admonishingly, she thought—but made no move to rise.

In the bedroom she stripped off her jeans and put some soft music on the CD player, the Eagles' *Long Road Out of Eden*, disc 2, a CD she listened to only when DeMarco wasn't home. He wouldn't have complained but she knew that the Eagles weren't his kind of music. She liked the CD because it took her back to high school and community dances, to a time before she felt bad about anything, to when her body had become her own and she could do anything with it that she wanted and not hate herself the next day.

But that was twenty years ago. Now, as she lay with the comforter pulled to her neck, she was able to hold back the tears only until "I Dreamed There Was No War." Then she let them flow. Let the sobs rack her body, let the grief excoriate her throat. Because that was okay too. A good cry now would give her strength to hide the tears when Ryan came home again and kissed her cheek, looked at her for any signs of collapse, and asked, in his own voice wearied by too much dire news, his own voice steadied only for her, always for her, "How was your day, baby?"

TWENTY-FIVE

J oe Loughner was staring at his last swallow of beer from a
twenty-ounce schooner when DeMarco came up to the bar.
"Good timing," Loughner said, and motioned for the bartender.
"What are you having?"

DeMarco smiled at the young woman tending bar. "Water
with lemon, please."

"Are you sick?" Loughner asked. "You can't even join me for
a beer?"

"Maybe later, Joe. After I get some food in my stomach."

"Beer *is* food." Loughner drained his glass, waited until the new
one was set before him, then took a long drink. "It's not healthy to
eat on an empty stomach," he said.

DeMarco swung a leg over the adjacent stool, looked over the
eight other patrons at the bar, made a half turn and surveyed the
dining room. Most of the tables were occupied. "This place never
changes," he said.

"The prices do. Eight dollars for a draft beer now. Can you
believe that?"

DeMarco turned a few degrees back toward Joe. "Did you get
us on the list for a table?"

"What's wrong with here? I always eat at the bar."

DeMarco winced a little at this reminder of his own drinking
days. Though he had never been a public drinker. And never a
happy drunk. Thank God those days were in the past.

"Would you gentlemen care to see a menu?" the bartender asked.

Joe said, "He might. I know what I want. Steak Milanese, rare. French fries, no salad."

"Would you care to choose another side dish in place of the salad?"

"Extra fries," he said.

Whoa, too familiar, DeMarco thought. "I'll have the bruschetta," he said. "Plus one pasta Michelangelo dinner, and one tortiglioni all'arrabbiata to go. No dressing on the salads. Please ask the chef to have them ready in…forty-five minutes or so, Joe?"

"Suit yourself, pal. I have nothing else to do today."

"I promised Jayme I'd bring home dinner."

The bartender moved away from them to enter the order in her point of sale terminal.

"Both of you take your rabbit food without any dressing?" Joe asked. "I don't know how you do that."

"We'll put dressing on it at home. Otherwise it gets too soggy."

"Aren't you the domesticated one."

DeMarco smiled. Wondered how long Joe had been sitting at the bar, how many schooners had sailed by. He said, "So Luthor Reddick."

Joe nodded. "Thomas Reddick Jr., spawn of Thomas Reddick Sr., lowest rat bastard I ever had the pleasure of arresting. May he rest in pieces."

"How did he die?"

"Blunt trauma to the punkin. We never could catch a break on who did it. Found a few grams of coke sprayed all over the floor, like he and somebody else had a wrestling match over it. Couldn't lift any prints but his, unfortunately. Not that anybody was going to shed any tears over it."

"So it's still an open case?"

Loughner waggled his hand. "Officially, sure. I doubt a single man-hour has been wasted on solving it, though. It's all about heroin up there now."

"Up there and everywhere," DeMarco said.

"My old troop seized thirty-eight bricks in St. Marys last week. Plus I don't know how many kilos of meth. If it was up to me I'd dig a fifty-foot-deep moat from the Gulf Coast to the Pacific, fill it with monster crocs and sharks and welcome anybody who wanted to cross to come on over. Except that they have to swim."

"That would slow down the drugs, wouldn't it?"

"Would slow down a lot of things."

The bartender set place mats, cutlery and napkins in front of them.

"So Reddick Jr.," DeMarco said after she moved away. "Was he involved in his father's business?"

Joe shook his head, took a sip of beer. He talked slowly, with frequent pauses and sips. Both men kept their voices low, though as the conversation progressed, Joe seemed less aware of the other customers.

"The kid dropped out of school at sixteen or so," he said. "Was pretty much a punching bag for the old man till then. His mother was glad to sign the papers to get him into the army."

"Trooper Boyd said he received a less than honorable discharge."

"Yeah, but later. Sapper Leader Course. He'd only just got started with it."

"He was in training to be a combat engineer?"

"Till he came back from his old man's funeral. Actually the army had to track him down. He went AWOL, something like two and a half weeks. They found him with a couple of women— girls, really—in an old cabin in the eastern part of the Quehanna Wild Area. Army took him back to Fort Leonard Wood, where he sobered up and begged them not to discharge him. Claimed he'd gone crazy with grief. Some of the people who knew him well claimed he'd been celebrating."

"Getting welcomed back after being AWOL wouldn't have flown in my day," DeMarco said.

"Nor in mine. But it's not the army it used to be. Thing is, he came back wanting out of sapper school. Shaved his head completely bald and told everybody to call him Luthor. Said' he was the anti-Superman. Anybody who laughed or made some kind of remark got the shit beat out of him. He bloodied something like nine of his buddies before they tossed him with the discharge."

"For homicidal tendencies, Boyd said."

"Yep. Far as I'm concerned, his old man's genes finally kicked in."

Their lunches, carried by the bartender and a male server, arrived. Joe picked up a knife and fork and sawed into his steak. DeMarco, on the other hand, found himself no longer hungry. He had a hard time tuning out the ambient noise, the other patrons' chatter, the movement of chairs and the clink of silverware, the annoying Muzak drifting down from the ceiling. When had all this started to bother him? His bruschetta plate held a six-inch baguette sliced in half, each half toasted and covered with tomato chunks, olive oil, spices, and Romano cheese. Were Jayme there, each would take half. He was keenly aware of her absence. Hoped she and the mutt had made up.

Only because he didn't want the bartender inquiring if something was wrong with his meal, he picked up one piece of the bruschetta and took a bite, careful to keep the tenuous layering of ingredients on the level. The tomatoes tasted bitter.

"After the discharge," he said, "did Reddick go back to Elk County to live?"

Joe jabbed his fork into the pile of french fries, which he had doused with ketchup. "Not back to Benezette, no. Thank God for little favors. Last I heard before retiring was that he was living with some woman up in Potter County. Never once heard his name mentioned after that until Trooper Boyd said it this morning."

For a while, then, they ate without talking, DeMarco taking one bite to every four by Joe, one sip of water to every three gulps of beer. He wished there were a way to gently broach the subject of Joe's drinking. But where did DeMarco get off thinking he had the right to do so? He heard his father's voice in his head then: *The only thing worse than a priest is a reformed drunk.*

When had his father said that? He couldn't remember. Maybe during one of those times when his mother started attending church. She would go to Mass two or three times a week, always during the day when Ryan was at school, but then, after a month or so, would stop altogether, and he would come home to find her not nicely dressed and made-up and filled with kind words and smiles, but still lying on her bed in her house robe, often with an open wine bottle on the headboard. This back-and-forth from churchgoing teetotaler to wino, how many times had he seen it play out?

He shook away the memory, saw that Joe's plate was nearly empty. DeMarco took two quick bites from his bruschetta. Thought about texting Jayme. He could ask, *How's the pup?* Then decided against it. "So when did Reddick Sr. die?" he asked.

"That was...let's see. Honestly, I can't remember. Too long ago to give a shit."

DeMarco considered what else he might ask. "And you have no idea where Reddick Jr. spent those years? Between his discharge and now?"

"Like I said, somewhere in Potter County. Not my jurisdiction, not my concern."

"Other than the discharge, he has no criminal record. Maybe he straightened himself out."

Joe shook his head. "Sometimes the absence of evidence *is* the evidence."

"How does that work?"

"You'd have to have known the old man. Scum of the earth. Doper, dealer, thief, liar—if it was dirty, he was doing it. But he was smart too, knew how to cover his tracks. He'd beat up his wife and kid on a regular basis, but there was always an excuse for the marks he left on them. Now imagine all that seeping down to the boy. And I remember him at sixteen—scrawny piece of work. Tall but skinny as a rail. Looked like he'd been put together with twigs and string. He goes into the army weighing maybe one-fifty soaking wet, and within a year he's all bulked up and three inches taller. We had a unit there when the army picked him up in Quehanna. Two-thirty minimum, every ounce of it muscle. And if that wasn't steroid muscle, I don't know what is. Plus nobody gets into sapper school without plenty of brain power under the lid. He's his old man's son, all right, rotten to the core. Just a medically enhanced version of it."

DeMarco pressed his lips together, sucked air through his teeth.

Loughner said, "You talked to the guy. He make you feel all warm and fuzzy inside?"

Joe was right. Reddick's smile had radiated vibes that both Flores and he had felt. So okay, he was worth more time. What could it hurt? DeMarco wasn't about to make the same mistake with Reddick that he had made with Khatri. Maybe a total lack of evidence *could* be the evidence. At least enough to get the ball rolling.

DeMarco caught the bartender's eye and signaled with a nod. When she came over, he said, "Could you put in my takeout order now? And I'll need a box for this bruschetta, if you don't mind."

"I'll need another beer," Loughner told her.

To DeMarco, the server said, "Was there something wrong with the bruschetta, sir?"

"Not a thing," he told her, "or I wouldn't be taking it home with me." She smiled and turned away.

When she was gone, Loughner said, "Your girl's got you pretty well trained, I see. According to Boyd, it's a fairly recent development."

"Best thing that ever happened to me." DeMarco sensed the opening he had been waiting for. "I'd been on a downhill slide for a long time, Joe. Drank myself to sleep every night, gulped coffee all day just to stay awake. Hated myself and life in general. Thanks to Jayme, I'm as healthy now as I was at thirty. Wake up every morning grateful to be alive."

"Whoopee for you," Loughner said, and clinked his empty schooner against DeMarco's water glass. "Let's hope it lasts."

Time to wrap this up, DeMarco told himself. He wasn't going to hold the older man's insensitivity against him. Knew from whence it came. Loughner was a painful reminder of where DeMarco had been headed. He said, "So you're convinced Reddick Jr. could be involved with what happened in Otter Creek Township?"

"Could be?" Loughner said. With the tip of his fork he speared the last french fry, dragged it through the last smear of meat juice and ketchup, and said, before shoving the fry into his mouth, "That crime has Reddick written all over it. If you don't make him suspect numero uno, you're a bigger fool than I think you are."

TWENTY-SIX

Over dinner, warmed in the oven while DeMarco took a quick cold shower in hopes of waking himself up, he and Jayme filled each other in on information gleaned from their afternoon's work. Jayme admitted that her time reading Miller's tweets and blogs had worn her out too, just as DeMarco's time with Loughner had depleted him.

"He's passionate," she said of the young journalist. "But geez. I wish I'd seen a little more compassion and empathy in what he writes."

"What I'm wondering is why we're even considering taking him on. Since when have we needed an assistant of any kind?"

"We do have a tendency to work ourselves to the bone, don't we? And to get a little myopic at times?" She refilled his glass of iced tea from the glass pitcher. "And I guess I just want to help him out a little. He wants to be useful, do something meaningful. Doesn't that appeal to you at all?"

He thought of Flores and of how satisfying it had been to watch the light in her eyes when they parked along the road looking at the shadowy straw bison asleep on the hill. He never would have admitted it to anybody, but he'd felt like a kind of Zen master then, a Morpheus to Flores's Neo.

"But what kind of work would he do for us?" he asked.

"The least we can do is to talk with him, right? Let's not just dismiss him out of hand. That wouldn't be very compassionate of *us*."

Instead of replying, he nodded at her plate. He had filled each of their plates with a serving from both dishes. "Which do you prefer?"

"Well, my first bite was the fettuccine. And I thought to myself, this is wonderful. But then I tasted the tortiglioni. Its flavor is so much stronger, in a good way, that it sort of wiped out the Alfredo sauce."

He reached for her plate. "I'll take the fettucine. You can have my—"

"No," she said. "I want them both. Keep your greedy hands to yourself."

He smiled and lifted his hand away.

"So Joe," she said. "Do you think he's right about Reddick Jr.?"

"I plan to find out. We can start digging in the morning."

"Sounds like a plan. And what about the kid?"

He gave her a long look. Before he could speak, she asked, "Didn't you ever have a mentor?"

"No," he said. Then allowed himself to remember. "Kyle's dad, I guess."

"Our Captain Kyle?"

DeMarco nodded. "William, but he went by Will. He was always a rank or two ahead of me. Cut me a lot of breaks when he was station commander. Breaks I didn't deserve. Especially after I got kicked back down to sergeant."

She hesitated before asking, "Why did you get kicked back down?"

He forced himself to return her gaze. "Dereliction of duty, basically. Though he never really called it that. This was right after the baby died. I was a zombie. Hated everybody and everything, most of all myself. And I refused to talk to anybody about it. Just wanted to stew in my misery, I guess."

"You wanted to punish yourself."

"Later on, before Will retired, he tried to promote me again, but I declined. I never wanted to be in charge of anybody else. Not ever again."

"I always wondered about that," she said.

"You never asked any of the guys?"

"Oh, I asked. But nobody would ever say a word against you."

"Hmm," he said, but allowed himself a smile, and returned to eating.

After a while, she stood and recovered the foam boxes that had held their dinners, and returned the remainder of hers to a box. "Are you going to finish yours?" she asked.

"Naw, too much food." He reached for the other box.

Just then the dog came shuffling into the kitchen, paused at the threshold to look at them, then lay down without moving any closer.

DeMarco said, "When was the last time he peed?"

"Just a little tinkle before you got home."

He pushed back his chair. "You need to go out, mutt?"

One ear twitched. Then nothing.

"We really need to decide on a name," Jayme said.

"Harvey is a name."

"Not for him it's not. And Rambo isn't completely right either. The right name is important."

DeMarco said, "Native Americans used to change their names to reflect significant experiences in their lives. Some of them also had secret sacred names."

"The truth is, we don't really know much about him. Except

for the last couple of days. And we're not going to name him for that." She pushed back her chair. "I'll put the food away. If you want to grab the leash, maybe we can coax him into a walk."

He regarded the dog. Then stood, but did not yet move toward the doorway. He said, "I don't care how useful and so-called responsible neutering is. There's something barbaric about cutting off an animal's testicles."

Jayme frowned. "Poor puppy. We have a lot to make up for, don't we?"

"Seems like that's pretty much what life is, doesn't it? An endless process of making up for our mistakes."

"Hey," Jayme said. "Don't go all maudlin and melancholy on me, DeMarco."

He shrugged. "What are we going to call him until he has a better experience?"

"How about Buddy?" she asked after a few moments. "That's what he is right now, right? He's our buddy."

DeMarco looked into the dog's soulful eyes. He remembered the puppy he'd brought home for a few hours as a boy. He had called it Buddy. Then his father had found the pup and killed it.

DeMarco crossed to the doorway. The big brown eyes followed him and looked up from the floor. "Let's go, Buddy," DeMarco said. "Time for a walk."

TWENTY-SEVEN

In the morning, DeMarco was awakened by wet, warm breath on his face. With eyes closed, he reached out for Jayme… and touched fur. He was lying on the edge of the bed, his back to Jayme, the dog standing with his nose only six inches from DeMarco's.

He was glad to see Buddy standing. Apparently he needed to go outside. DeMarco looked down across the bed. Pale gray light in the windows. In the third week of October, the sun would not peek over the horizon until 7:30 or so, first light a half hour earlier. He had overslept.

As quietly as he could, he slipped out of bed. His movement woke Jayme. "Where you going?" she mumbled.

"Buddy and I have to pee."

"He walked upstairs?"

"Unless you installed an elevator last night."

She smiled, mumbled, "Have fun," and closed her eyes again.

Downstairs, still in only his boxers and T-shirt, DeMarco followed Buddy to the back door and then outside. The animal was in no way frisky but walked the way DeMarco felt, old and heavy and missing the warmth of his bed. The grass was chilly with dew and the air made DeMarco's leg hairs stand up.

Buddy stood in place a few feet to the right of the unfinished brick path. Lifted his head and sniffed the air. "My toes are getting numb here," DeMarco said. But the dog showed no interest in lifting a leg.

DeMarco shivered awhile longer and considered showing Buddy how to pee in Mrs. Craig's forsythias, which were now only clumps of naked branches, the younger ones tall and spindly, the thicker branches mere stumps pruned early last summer. But a soft yellow light shone in the old woman's kitchen window. So he led the dog to the bushes, said, "You figure it out," and hustled back onto the porch with his toes stinging and his bladder full.

A few minutes later, as he watched Buddy from the threshold, Jayme padded up behind him. "How's he doing?" she asked.

"Number two," he said. "And you can't have two without one."

She rubbed a hand against his back. "I didn't smell any coffee brewing, did I?"

"Flip you for brew or doggie doo retrieval."

"I'm on the coffee," she said, and turned away. A minute later she returned to hand him an empty plastic sandwich bag. "How about Max for his permanent name? It means *the greatest*."

"Too much pressure to put on a guy," DeMarco said. "How about Draco?"

"That makes no sense at all," she said, and pushed him toward the steps.

≫———————≪

At exactly 9:00 a.m. Jayme's cell phone rang. Dr. Lisa inquiring of her patient's status. After the call, Jayme joined DeMarco in the dining room, where he was seated with the case notes spread before him, the dog at his feet.

"She says it might be two weeks before he's back to his old self. We shouldn't expect much until he's finished the antibiotics. Until then keep him clean, don't let him lick himself, and keep an eye out for infection."

"Don't let him lick himself? That's like telling a goose not to honk."

"We could call him Goose," she said. "That's a cute name for a dog."

"He doesn't poop enough to be a goose."

She sat down across from him, pulled her laptop close but did not open it. "We should get back to Chase Miller today."

"Okay. Let me know how he takes the news."

"We haven't made that decision yet."

He pretended to be engrossed in his notes, then felt her eyes on him and lifted his head. "He's your project, not mine," he told her. "You clean up his messes, I'll clean up Buddy's."

She flashed him a scowl, then stood and went into the living room to collect Miller's phone number from the landline.

He could hear her talking as he worked, but could not follow the conversation. A few minutes later she returned to stand beside him. Laid a hand on his shoulder. "I'm meeting him in an hour at the Gallery Grille. I think you should go too."

He looked up from his papers. "You're driving to Greenville?"

"He works there. It opens for lunch at 11:30. After work there he goes to his job at Goodwill. He's a very responsible young man, babe. At least let's give the kid a chance."

He was having no luck getting his thoughts together that morning, trying to plot out their next move. Maybe a twenty-minute drive would clear his head. Besides, it was going to be a sunny day. Temperature near fifty. Maybe they could sit on the patio with coffee and a chocolate éclair and watch the old gray duffers in loud sweaters squirting their balls into the sand and high grass. And maybe he could take the dead man's photo along and show it to the golfers and staff. And maybe he should remember that his first priority was to support Jayme and keep her happy and be the man she wanted him to be.

He pushed his chair back. "I'm going to ask Chase about Draco," he said. "Bet you he likes it."

"Bet you it doesn't matter," she said, her smile twice as warm and sweet and devilish as a chocolate éclair.

TWENTY-EIGHT

The only thing that concerns me," Jayme said to Chase Miller, "is not your work ethic or your honesty or anything like that. It's your blog. It seems rather sensationalistic to me, and... sometimes lacking in compassion, I think."

They were seated on the concrete patio at the rear of the Gallery Grille, overlooking the golf course, she and DeMarco in full sun, Chase Miller's face in the shade of the table's closed green umbrella. The restaurant would open for lunch in forty minutes, and the clangs and bangs and clinks already coming from the kitchen jarred DeMarco. He allowed his gaze to wander over the other round wrought iron tables, the simple iron chairs, all empty, and at the closed umbrellas rising like cloth steeples from the tables, the fine stone wall and coach lanterns, and he wished he had a place like this to go to every morning, a place to sit alone in the sun and sip his coffee and steel himself for the day. In the distance down a long green slope, four golfers were converging on a green still twinkling from the morning's soaking from the sprinklers, four silent, unhurried men, each pulling a handcart, each hoping to hit the ball closest to the hole, hoping for the lowest score, maybe hoping they could have their fading lives to live over again.

DeMarco wished Miller had offered them coffee and something sweet, but their tables were empty and a bit dusty and he was having a hard time staying interested in the conversation.

Miller's brow wrinkled in response to Jayme's comment. "Did you read them all?" he asked. "Because if you did, you'd see that I never criticize people who are innocent or deserving of help. I criticize the *system*. Whether it's the system that makes it so easy for criminals to get away with what they do, or the system that makes it easy for lazy, dishonest people to milk the system. Or the system that hides all the nasty stuff it's doing to us. I mean...I have a ton of compassion, I really do. But you have to admit there are some people who don't deserve it."

Here he looked at DeMarco, who had tuned in just in time, and now found himself having to suppress a nod. He knew better than to corroborate Miller's negativity in front of Jayme. He also knew that, in theory, each of them was merely an assemblage of photons and dark matter, and he wished he could kick free of some of his own darkness and shine a little brighter. It was not easy, though, to hold that aspiration paramount in one's mind, not with murderers and ambitious youngsters and a newly emasculated dog to contend with. Usually the aspiration surfaced only in quiet moments when the photons were already beaming. The trick would be to hit the light switch when all he wanted was to be swallowed by the darkness, a desire that was the path of least resistance and unworthy of even a ten-watt photon. He did not know what wattages photons put forth but ten seemed a low enough number to be attainable. He figured Jayme for an assemblage of hundred-watt photons, and knew that if he could illuminate his space even half as brightly as she did hers, he would be well on his way to enlightenment. Time was running out for him faster than ever, though, and more and more often now he wondered what awaited him when the last grain of sand fell out.

So, instead of encouraging the young man's darkness, DeMarco told him, "Forbearance."

Miller's brow wrinkled even more.

"Confucius was asked for a single word that would ensure a good, happy life, and that was his answer: *chu*. It means forbearance. Tolerance and restraint. Patience and self-control."

"It's not like I'm out killing people, am I?" Miller asked. "I'm trying to bring some attention to stuff that's *wrong*. Are we supposed to just let all that stuff slide? Never try to change anything?"

"I still have a hard time with it too," DeMarco confessed. "But it's the anger that will do you in, kid."

Miller wasn't ready to concede. To Jayme, he said, "Do you expect me to love it? All the *crap* in this world?" Here he looked up into the blue firmament, scanned it from side to side. "Okay, you can't see any up there now, but do you know what chem trails are? Tiny particles of aluminum supposed to reflect the sun and stop global warming. But we're *breathing* that stuff. Us, the animals, the plant life—it's killing *everything*. Which makes you wonder if maybe that's not the *real* reason for it, right? Maybe *that's* why they want to keep it so secret."

DeMarco had heard it all before. Was the entire generation obsessed with conspiracies? And why did they have to speak in italics all the time, emphasizing words as if the listener were too stupid to understand? And even if they were right about chem trails…what could anybody do about it? Stop breathing?

"Am I supposed to love all that?" Miller asked.

"No," Jayme told him. "Just don't take it all so personally."

Miller wasn't buying her argument; DeMarco could tell by the look on the kid's face. He wanted to keep arguing but was silently talking himself out of it.

"Okay," Miller finally said. "Okay. I hear what you're saying. But the thing about it is, a lot of it is just my voice. My persona. There are a million bloggers out there. Sometimes you have to get loud to be *heard*, you know what I mean?"

Maybe Jayme was right and the kid wasn't so bad after all. Young and angry, neither condition fatal. And as far as he knew, nobody had ever died from an overuse of italics. DeMarco said, "Tell us something about your history. Where do you come from? What do your parents do?"

"I grew up here, in this dying little town. My dad lives in Columbus. Haven't seen him in six, seven years. My mother has a cleaning business. That's all she's ever done is to mop other people's floors, clean their toilets, do whatever they want done. She started out on her own, has three other ladies working for her now. But she's still doing the same thing every single day. Still mopping floors and cleaning out other people's toilets."

DeMarco heard the young man's resentment, the love for his mother, and he understood it all. Off the job the kid might look like a spoiled preppy, but he wasn't that. He was driven.

"Where did you go to college?" DeMarco asked.

"Allegheny. BA in English."

Private liberal arts, DeMarco thought. *Expensive school.* "What's the tuition there? About forty-five a year?"

"More like fifty after all the fees. Another twelve grand if you live on campus and have a meal plan. Plus the books on top of that. But I commuted. I had a Trustee Scholarship that paid about half the tuition. I did work-study every semester, plus worked here weekends, full-time every summer."

Jayme asked, "How does one get a Trustee Scholarship?"

Miller shrugged. "SAT scores, I guess. Plus class rank in high school. I was a Presidential Scholar there, so that helped."

Jayme smiled, then raised her eyebrows to DeMarco. *You see?* her eyebrows said.

"Okay," DeMarco told him. "My question is, what would you expect to do for us, and what kind of pay are you looking for?"

"You know, ten, twelve dollars an hour would be great. I mean, if I could get an extra hundred a week, I'd work my ass off for you. Day or night, whatever you needed, just so long as I could keep the jobs I already have."

"And what would you do for us?" Jayme asked.

"Like I said, I'm a great researcher. And not just online. I meet all kinds of people here. I mean *all* kinds. This used to be a private country club, and a lot of those people still play or eat here. That's one slice of society I have access to." He leaned against the table edge and lowered his voice. "We have a line cook and servers and at least one busboy who can get you any drug you want. Not that either of you would. I'm just saying I know those people too. The whole drug scene."

He leaned back in his chair again. Held up two fingers on his right hand and enclosed them in his left hand. "So that's two. Three," he said, and enclosed another finger, "are the kind of people who shop at Goodwill. That's half the reason I work there. People on welfare, people collecting unemployment. Dopers, college kids, people doing their best to make ends meet."

He opened both hands and held them out, palms up. "I'm telling you guys, I have it covered. Everybody! If I don't know somebody, I know somebody who does." He turned to DeMarco. "And how effective are you talking to people my age? Nothing personal, but you look and act like a cop. Me, I fit right in. The kids around here know me, they know what I came from. If you want the scoop on what's happening on the street, I'm your man. I can get into places you two never could."

Jayme asked, "And why would you do all that for a hundred dollars a week?"

"It's like I told you in my phone message. I plan to be a writer.

A writer needs stories. A guy nailed to a tree, two women burned to a crisp, that's a hell of a story."

DeMarco studied Miller's face for a few moments. Then he said, "I have the feeling you've been doing some digging already. What have you come up with?"

A small smile creased Miller's mouth. "Am I hired?"

DeMarco turned to Jayme. Her smile was his answer.

To Miller, DeMarco said, "Two weeks probation. One hundred a week. But you do not go off half-cocked. You follow directions. If you even once come within fifty yards of jeopardizing the investigation…"

"My ass is grass," Miller said with a grin. "I got it. And I accept your terms, boss." He stuck out his hand.

DeMarco shook his head and blew out a long breath. Then extended his hand over the table.

"Mrs. Boss," Miller said, and offered his hand to Jayme.

She took his hand and corrected him. "*Ms.* Boss."

"Right," he said. "I just thought…I mean I know you're not married or anything but you're, you know, together…"

She said, "And how do you know that?"

His cheeks flushed a little, but he held her gaze. "I told you I'm a good researcher."

"Who's your source?"

"Unh unh uh. That's on a need-to-know basis only."

"And we need you to give up the blog," DeMarco told him.

"Ah, man, I can't let my readers down like that."

"Are you making any money from it?"

"Not yet, but…"

"Take it or leave it."

"Man, you're hard. Okay. *Dire Wire* is officially on hiatus."

"And you will never, ever, ever mention our names or this investigation online."

"Never ever? Geez, boss. Why don't you just yank out my soul while you're at it?"

"Also," DeMarco told him, "this relationship ends when the case is closed. No guarantees we will be able to employ you afterward. Deal or no deal?"

"Deal," Miller said. When he shoved back his chair to stand, the chair legs made a shrill scraping sound that sent a quick chill up DeMarco's back.

"Hold on," DeMarco told him. "You have some information for us. What is it?"

Miller took a glance to his right and left. Turned to glance at the door to the building. Then said, sotto voce, "The crispy critters? Hundred-dollar hookers. They worked the Hadley and other I-79 rest areas."

DeMarco let his breath slip out between his lips. "Anything else?"

"That's it for now. I'll have more soon."

"We need names," DeMarco said.

"I'll get them. That and more."

To Miller, Jayme said, "Crispy critters is not acceptable language."

Miller flinched. But quickly recovered and said, "Heard, boss," and rapped his knuckles twice on the table's edge. "I'll be in touch."

He turned and walked briskly to the side entrance, went inside, closed and locked the door. DeMarco and Jayme sat there looking at each other. "Am I going to regret this?" she asked.

He gazed up at the sky. A tiny silver needle silently speeding west. Behind it, a long white trail, widening out from the tail of the jet, smearing itself across the blue.

TWENTY-NINE

From the Gallery Grille parking lot DeMarco phoned Trooper Boyd and asked for a meeting with him and Flores in thirty minutes. Boyd suggested they meet for lunch at the Yellow Creek Inn, a small restaurant a couple of miles from the station house.

"Too crowded this time of day," DeMarco said. "And too much butter, batter, or cream sauce on everything. How about if Jayme and I grab some pizza on the way back?"

"That works," Boyd said.

"How many people will be on hand today?"

"Around lunchtime? Six to eight, I'd say."

"We'll bring enough for everybody. Tell the boss he's welcome to join us. If his secondary teeth have come in yet, that is."

Boyd chuckled. "I'll let him know."

Forty minutes later Jayme and DeMarco arrived at the station carrying four large pizzas—one plain, two pepperoni, one supreme. After the other personnel had filled their paper plates and returned to their desks, Captain Boyd closed the conference room door. Took two slices of supreme for himself, then joined DeMarco, Matson, Boyd, and Flores at the table. Their conversation proceeded slowly, between bites.

DeMarco raised a few eyebrows when he informed the others that they had hired the young stringer to help them with research.

"We do our own research," Bowen said.

Jayme jumped in. "Miller has contacts we don't, Captain. Street-level contacts. The kind who freeze up when they see a uniform or even someone older than them. We wouldn't have talked to Miller if we didn't think he would be useful and trustworthy."

Bowen said, after a pause, "You'd better sit on him. Keep him on a short leash."

DeMarco immediately thought of two responses: the first would reference all the years he had been the station commander's babysitter, and the second would point out Bowen's mixing of metaphors. *You want us to sit on him* and *keep him on a short lease?* But with Flores present, he shouldn't tease the station commander. Still, the thought of doing so brought a smile to his face.

"In fact," Jayme continued, "he already gave us something to start with. The two burn victims were prostitutes. According to Miller, they worked out of the Hadley rest area."

"Which means out of a car or truck," Boyd said. "The Santa Fe?"

"We don't know that yet," DeMarco answered. "But it seems logical to assume that the male victim would have been the females' associate in the same line of work."

Flores said, "Do you think they were killed for encroaching on somebody else's turf?"

Bowen said, "We patrol that rest area every night. Anybody hear anything about it being used as a brothel?"

The four others shook their heads. Boyd said, "Flores and I can check the security cameras. See if we can catch anybody moving from one vehicle to another."

DeMarco said, "I think we also need to revisit some of the citizens up in Otter Creek. The ones who got our radar beeping. See what a little extra pressure might shake out."

"Roger that," Boyd said. With a nod toward Flores, he said,

"We've both been digging into those individuals on our lists. All told we have three with drug arrests, two others with non-drug-related offenses."

"Any outstanding warrants?" Jayme asked.

"None," Boyd answered.

DeMarco said, "What about the Reddick family? Joe Loughner all but insisted we focus on Luthor Reddick."

Bowen nodded. "Joe called me after your lunch yesterday. Actually before *and* after. Made the same pitch. Though he, uh… Was he drinking during lunch?"

DeMarco answered with a lift of his eyebrows, knew that Bowen would get the gist of it. "He might have had a beer or two."

Flores said, "I haven't typed anything up yet, sir, but yes, I've been looking into Reddick. Everything Loughner told you about Reddick Jr. and Sr. appears to check out."

"Anything at all new on Reddick Jr.?" DeMarco asked. "Anything we can use to rattle him a little?"

"Not yet, sir. I'm sorry. He does have a business website, but you can't get past the first page without a password. It's restricted to antique dealers. Members of the NWPALRnet Collectors Organization. Of which I can find nothing. It's not listed with the Antiques Dealers' Association of America, or anywhere else, for that matter."

"Northwest Pennsylvania Luthor Reddick network," DeMarco guessed.

"Fake storefront?" Jayme asked.

"Sounds that way, doesn't it?"

Boyd said, "We have Carmichael trying to breach the gate, but no luck so far."

"What about some old-fashioned surveillance?" Flores asked.

"There's only that long gravel driveway up to his place, trees on both sides of it. We could watch that driveway, see who comes and goes."

Captain Bowen's mouth twisted up at the corner. "That's a lot of man-hours dedicated to a hunch."

DeMarco said, "Would you authorize some game cameras?"

"We could do that," Bowen replied. To Boyd and Flores, he said, "Requisition a couple. Take a drive by this afternoon to scout for the best placement. Then contact the property owner for permission, and get the cameras up ASAP."

"Yes, sir," Flores said.

Boyd asked, "What if Reddick owns all that property? The whole way up to the road?"

"What's on the other side?" Bowen asked.

DeMarco answered. "A private home. But it's set way back, a good forty yards off the road. And it's all clear-cut, as I recall. Open yard from the house to the road."

Flores said, "I seem to remember some trees along the edge of that property."

"Okay, check it out," DeMarco told her. "Let me know how it goes."

"Yes, sir. Can do."

To Jayme, he said, "I guess you and I could go ahead and go on up to Otter Creek. Start the follow-up interviews." To Boyd, he said, "Can we get a list of those individuals with a history?"

"No problem, sir."

"And yes, I remember," DeMarco told Bowen. "We need a uniform with us. Who can you spare?"

Flores said, "I can be all squared up here in thirty minutes, Captain. And then scout locations for the game cameras on my way back. If you don't mind me taking a unit out on my own."

Before Bowen could answer, DeMarco said, "Thirty minutes is great. Gives us time to run home and see how much of the house the mutt has chewed up."

"You got a dog?" Bowen asked.

Jayme answered. "Ryan rescued him from his previous owner. And he doesn't chew anything except his dog food. He's remarkably well-trained for a puppy, though we suspect that the training methods were extreme."

DeMarco said, "Jayme had him castrated." And immediately regretted his words. Joking at somebody else's expense—he had to be better than that. Neutering Buddy had been the responsible thing to do, but that didn't lessen the cruelty of lopping off a guy's testicles. He winced every time he thought of it. Though maybe it was a male thing. Maybe only a person with testicles could empathize with a neutered dog.

He added, "Actually we both did it. And now all he does is mope around." He almost said to the station commander, *Is that why you're so mopey all the time?* But only said it inside his head and fought the urge to smile.

Everybody else was frowning, even Boyd, who usually kept his facial expressions to himself. So DeMarco slapped his hands down on the edge of the table and abruptly stood. To Flores he said, "See you back here in thirty."

"Yes, sir," she said.

Outside the building, on their way to DeMarco's car, he apologized to Jayme. "That was stupid of me, saying you had him castrated. One second I thought it was funny, next second I wanted it back."

"Next time pause long enough for the second thought to kick in."

He opened her car door, held it while she crossed behind him.

"I know you told me not to do this for you. But this time I feel like I owe it to you."

She climbed in. "You do," she said, and gave him a soft punch in the belly. "I'll let you know when you can stop."

THIRTY

While Jayme brushed her teeth, DeMarco took Buddy for a walk around the backyard. Then they changed places while DeMarco went inside. After another walk around the yard, Jayme sat on the edge of the porch and held the long snout in her hands and kissed the dog's forehead. "It was for your own sake, I promise," she whispered. "You have no idea how crazy those things would have made you. This way, we only have your daddy's to worry about. And that's my job, not yours. And we can all be happy together."

"What are you two conspiring about now?" DeMarco asked from the threshold, two plastic bottles of cold water in each hand.

"None of your business," she told him, and escorted the dog inside.

≫———————≪

As they neared their first stop in Otter Creek Township, with Flores in a gray state police SUV two car lengths behind, DeMarco put on the turn signal, pulled as close to the drainage ditch as he could, and waved Flores forward.

She came ahead slowly, then stopped her vehicle abreast of his and lowered the passenger window. "You lead the way from here," he told her. "Pull up as close to the house as you can. With your lights on." The flashing lights of a police car in the front yard would add several degrees of gravity to their visit.

At the first and third homes, nobody answered Flores's heavy knocks. At the second, a haggard woman who looked twenty years older than her age told them that her husband was "in a bar somewhere. Probably in Locust Grove." She squinted at the flashing lights and said, "What's he done?"

Flores told her, "We need to talk to him."

"If you arrest him for something," the woman said, "can you get his wallet and let me know if there's anything in it? LaDonna's got this fourth grade party I'm supposed to bake something for, and there's nothing in the house to bake with."

Flores stood there with her mouth grim. Then she looked around. Saw no other vehicles. "Do you have a way to get to the store?" she asked.

"I'll find a way," the woman said. "I can maybe get one of the neighbors to take me. Either that or I'll thumb a ride."

Flores nodded. Then turned away abruptly, returned to her vehicle, and proceeded to their next stop.

At the fourth home, a one-story bungalow whose buckled vinyl siding had once been yellow, with a sullen, hungry-looking rottweiler snugged up to a post in the yard, its chain wrapped tightly around the post, the metal water bowl turned upside down in the circle of dirt surrounding the post, Flores hammered on the screen three times before the owner squeaked open the interior door.

He was a small black man in baggy jeans and a faded blue Southpole T-shirt with the sleeves cut off. His eyes had that sleepy, confused look of somebody who was either deficient in sleep or brain activity. His gaze floated from Flores to DeMarco to Jayme, where they landed. To her, he said, "What are you doing back here?"

Flores held up the photo of the dead black man. "You told Trooper Boyd you don't know this man."

"Yeah? Well?"

"We know you do."

"And how do you know that?"

"Here's what's going to happen," she told him. "You are either going to tell us who he is and how you know him, or we are going to come in and collect what's left of your weed, and then I'm going to throw you in the back of that vehicle and haul you off to jail."

The man squinted and blinked and worked his lips up and down as if they were itchy. "I don't have any weed."

"Your eyes and the smell pouring out through the door tells me otherwise." She reached for her handcuffs.

"Oh, him?" he said, and nodded at the photo. "Yeah, maybe I seen him around somewhere."

"What's his name?" she asked.

"I only know him as Choo Choo."

"Last name?"

He shrugged. "Same as the first one, I guess. Choo."

"*How* do you know him?"

"I think I might've seen him at a party somewhere."

"Where was this party?"

"I don't remember that."

"I suggest that you start remembering, Mr. Palmer. What else do you know about him?"

He scanned the three grim faces staring back at him. The blue and red lights silently flashing atop the gray SUV flickered in his otherwise dull eyes. "I remember he wasn't from around here. The way he talked, he was from down south somewhere."

"Keep going," she said.

"I don't know where from. I didn't ask him. Hardly even talked to him."

"What else?"

"I know his picture was in the paper not long ago. I know he's dead."

"Do you know who killed him?"

"How would I know that?"

"Did he sell you drugs?"

Palmer chewed his upper lip, then his lower.

Flores said, "I am either leaving here with you handcuffed in the back of that vehicle, or I am leaving with information about the man you call Choo Choo. You have three seconds to decide which it will be."

"All I do is buy a little weed now and then. I'm not hurting anybody."

"You were high when you lied to Trooper Boyd yesterday, and you're high now. So it's not just a little weed, is it?"

"I got pain in my back I need it for."

"Do you have a prescription?"

"It costs eighty dollars just to go ask for one."

"Then a bunk in the county jail isn't going to feel very good on your back, is it?"

"He went around with a couple of girls. One of them was a white girl. The other one was from Vietnam or somewhere, I think she said."

"You talked to this girl?"

"Little bit."

"What else did she tell you?"

"Nothing else. We weren't there to conversate with each other."

"And where was *there*? Where did you meet her?"

He kept chewing on his lips. Turned his head, looked at the dog, and kept chewing.

"You know she's dead too now, right?" Flores said. "All three of them are dead. And I am giving you one last chance to tell me what you know about that."

Again, he looked at each of the faces in turn. Not a single smile. Not a single sympathetic eye.

"Damn it all," he said. "There's parties in the summer sometimes. Up in the woods. Out along Fredonia Road. I been there once or twice is all. There's always somebody there with whatever you want. People have to live, you know. Gotta get by some way or the other. Don't mean we go around killing people. I never hurt nobody. Always on the other end of being hurt. And that's it. That's everything I know about them people. And that's all I want to know."

He stood there slumped forward, leaning into the doorframe.

Flores looked over at DeMarco. He gave her a little nod.

To the man, she said, "You untangle that dog and get it some water, Mr. Palmer. And if you hear anything useful, any little thing, you need to call the state police immediately. Do you understand what I'm saying?"

"I understand," he said.

With that she turned, walked briskly back to the SUV, and waited by the door for DeMarco and Jayme to join her. When they did, they all spoke quietly as they watched Palmer come out into the yard and walk his dog around the post, unwrapping the chain.

"You did well," Jayme told her, and DeMarco smiled his concurrence.

"Except that I forgot to ask him about Reddick."

"I don't see Reddick as the kind of guy who goes to parties in the woods," DeMarco said. "A guy so secretive with his website wouldn't be peddling nickel bags at parties."

Jayme asked, "So you think he's not involved?"

"I didn't say that. What we know now is that Mr. Palmer has more or less corroborated what Miller told us. This guy Choo Choo sold drugs, at least weed, and pimped out the two female vics. We know he had a southern accent. What we don't know is their real names or who killed them. Let's go check out Linn Tyro Road for those game cameras."

"You mind if I head back the other way?" Flores asked. "You really don't need me for placing the cameras. I'm thinking I might make a stop in Locust Grove."

THIRTY-ONE

At the bar in Locust Grove, Flores paused just inside the door to let her eyes adjust to the dimness. As the door fell shut behind her, the incoming light was snuffed out, leaving only the beer signs and dirty overhead lighting to illuminate the room. Music was playing off to the side somewhere, probably in the kitchen, Kings of Leon singing "Use Somebody." The air smelled of deep fryer grease, spilled beer, and sweat.

She felt every eye in the place on her, and in an instant she was taken back through time to when she was seven years old and sent inside that very same bar to find her grandfather, who unless he had already passed out would dig a greasy five- or ten-dollar bill out of his pocket and tell her to tell her father that any man who can't feed his own child doesn't deserve to be alive.

She shook off the chill of that memory and surveyed the room, let nothing remain inside but the heat of anger. Four older men seated at the bar, empty stools between them. Two men in a booth; they glanced her way briefly, then continued their whispered conversation. Two men playing pool near the farthest wall, their laughter loud, one of them cackling like static.

That one, she told herself. Blue jeans and T-shirt, unshaven, mussed-up hair, just like a million other guys. But it was his posture that gave him away, that loose-jointed stray-dog slouch, that garbage-stealing smirk on his face.

She strode across the room, looking at no one but him. She loved moments like this and the danger in them, the way the promise of violence sent all five senses into overdrive, her radar on high alert. Later would come the crash, the sadness that had no end. But it *would* have an end, always did anyway, and would lift in the morning after her shower, as she put on a clean uniform, strapped on her resolve once again.

He held her gaze until the last second, as if he had realized himself her target. He turned away and pretended to watch the other man line up a shot. Told him, "Watch it now, boy. You're gonna leave me the nine."

She strode to within a foot and a half, stuck out her hand and said, "Give me your wallet."

He turned, laughed to hide his fear, and said, "Why in the world would I do that?"

"Because you're a deadbeat with a wife and little girl at home. Give me your wallet and do it now."

The other man pulled out of his shot, straightened up and said, "Jesus, Ed. How long you been in here anyway?"

Ed's posture collapsed a little more. As he reached for his wallet, he said, "I was on my way home after this game. I don't know what she's so worried about."

Flores said nothing. Kept her eyes locked on him as he leaned over the table and opened his wallet underneath the hanging light. He fingered a couple of ones, started to lift them free, then cast a glance at Flores, and took out a ten instead. He held it out to her. "I barely got enough left to pay my bar bill."

She snatched it from his hand. "A man who won't take care of his family doesn't deserve to be alive," she said.

She turned away, took one long stride toward the door. Then the man at the other end of the table threw his cue onto the felt, stepped toward her and said, "Hey, Officer." She stopped, tensed, and looked up at him. "Give them this too," he said, slid a hand into his pocket, and brought out several folded bills. He thumbed through the ones and fives, found a twenty at the bottom, peeled it away and handed it to her.

She took it in her left hand. "Thank you," she said, and felt something like a soft blow to her chest, what she always felt from an unexpected kindness. He nodded, turned away and crossed to the bar.

Outside, she climbed into the SUV and started the engine but did not feel ready to drive just yet. Sat there with her hands quivering as the adrenaline drained away, and tried to hang on to the anger that, she knew, was her only fuel.

You did well, Matson had told her. And Sergeant DeMarco had smiled. She *had* comported herself well. She was a Pennsylvania State policewoman, damn it. Not a server in a greasy spoon diner anymore. She was all grown up now, wasn't she? Dynamite Dani, they had called her at the academy. Fuse burning and ready to blow.

Some of the men had used it as a compliment, some only to mock her. She didn't care either way. She had thirty dollars in her hand and now LaDonna would get her cookies, her cupcakes, whatever her mother would bake. Flores would hand the money to LaDonna's mother and say, *And if he so much as lays a finger on you or your girl, you call me. I'll lock his ass up so fast it will make his head spin.*

And she would, too. She would do it and enjoy doing it.

Good, the anger was still there. It would always be there. She looked into the rearview mirror, stared at those brown eyes she hated. Shook the thirty dollars at them. *So what do you think of this, Daddy? You lowlife son of a bitch. What do you think of me now?*

II

I am in blood
Stepp'd in so far that, should I wade no more,
Returning were as tedious as go o'er.
—William Shakespeare, *Macbeth*

THIRTY-TWO

They made one slow pass of Reddick's driveway, with DeMarco looking for a place to turn. Then his cell phone sounded: a text message from Boyd. Jayme lifted the phone from the cup holder and read the text aloud. "'Reddick owns all property forty yards south of driveway, sixty-three yards north.'"

"Great," DeMarco said. "So it will have to be across the road from the driveway." He pulled into the next driveway and made a turn.

The house directly across the road from Reddick's driveway was set upon a knoll at least forty yards back from Linn Tyro Road. The name stenciled on the mailbox was Shaner. DeMarco pulled into the mouth of the driveway but sat with his foot on the brake. "Nobody was home yesterday," he said. "Looks the same today."

"Maybe the car's in the garage," Jayme said.

He drove forward up the sloping drive. This driveway, unlike most others in the area, was blacktopped, the edges neatly trimmed, the yard immaculate and mostly empty, with only two dwarf cherry trees halfway up the yard and spaced widely apart.

Everything about the Craftsman-style house was neat and well maintained. No clutter in the yard and only a metal-frame glider on the porch. Halfway up the driveway DeMarco lost sight of the porch, with the front yard rising higher on his right, so that he parked directly facing the basement door in an area cut out from the hill. Through the glass panel in the basement door, a yellow light burned.

They climbed out. DeMarco pressed the doorbell. The man who opened the door to them was of medium height and slight build, his thin gray hair parted at the side and combed back over his head. He was dressed in moccasins, olive-green khakis and a white short-sleeved shirt.

DeMarco introduced himself and Jayme.

"Fred Shaner," the man said, and took the card Jayme held out to him.

She said, "You might have heard that we were visiting the neighborhood yesterday."

"I've been visiting my grandkids in Arizona," he answered. "Got back just this morning. What's going on?"

DeMarco had brought along a headshot of the dead black man. "This individual and two other bodies were found in the woods a couple of miles away."

The man scowled and shook his head. "Drugs, I take it."

Jayme said, "Why do you say that, sir?"

He motioned them inside. "This neighborhood used to be a nice place to live. I'd move if my wife's grave wasn't up the road a piece. But where can you go to get away from it? For three nights out in Flagstaff I laid awake listening to police sirens. I finally couldn't take it anymore."

"Have you seen this individual around?" DeMarco asked.

"I pretty much keep to myself. Keep the curtains drawn up front. I don't want any part of any of it."

"Here's the thing, sir," Jayme said. "We need to do surveillance of the road in this area. And we need an inconspicuous place to hang a camera or two."

"Stick them up wherever you want," he said.

They went upstairs so that DeMarco could check the view from the front of the house. He parted the living room curtains far enough to look out. A straight shot down across the yard to Reddick's driveway. "How far is it from here to the road?" he asked.

"A hundred and thirty feet, give or take a few inches."

Game camera detection range topped off at under fifty feet. DeMarco said, "Excuse me while I make a call."

Trooper Boyd answered on the second ring.

"Problem," DeMarco told him. "We have a prime vantage point for a camera, but it's a hundred and thirty feet from the top of the target area."

Boyd thought for a moment. "Our IR cameras can pick out a license plate number from three hundred feet, day or night."

By the end of the conversation, Boyd had agreed to meet with the homeowner at a restaurant in town within the hour. Boyd would come dressed in civvies, driving his own car. In the parking lot he would place the camera in Fred Shaner's car with instructions on how to mount it on the front porch.

"Don't worry about that," Shaner told DeMarco. "I'm an electrical engineer. Retired." He walked them back downstairs to the basement door. "I take it you want the camera on that fella who lives down that gravel driveway," he said.

"A view of that part of Linn Tyro will be fine," Jayme said.

"Young lady," the man said with a smile. "I'm not an idiot. You want to see who's coming and going from that place. How long is that camera good for?"

DeMarco said, "We'll review the footage every forty-eight hours, if that's okay with you."

"You can sit in my living room and review it minute by minute, as far as I'm concerned."

Jayme asked, "Are you familiar with the gentleman who lives down that driveway?"

"I've never spoken a word to him. But I will tell you this. There are some things you notice without even wanting to. Like when I'm out working in the yard, which I do a lot of these days. And what I notice is a lot of cars coming and going. They're either the friendliest people in the world living down that road, or something funny's going on."

"They?" Jayme said. "How many people live there?"

"That I do not know."

"Is there a particular vehicle you see most frequently?" DeMarco asked.

"Black Ford Explorer. Tinted windows all around. It comes out to the end of the driveway every afternoon to pick up the mail. There's either a big bald fella driving it, or a woman."

"Can you describe the woman?"

"Better than I can describe him. She gets out of the car to get the mail. Her arm's not long enough to reach the box, I guess. It's hard to say exactly how tall she is, but a mailbox is supposed to be no more than forty-five inches off the ground, and that one comes to about her throat."

"So," Jayme said, "five four to five six?"

"Sounds about right. Fairly stocky. Forties, I'd say. Blond hair. Bleached."

"How do you know it's bleached?" she asked.

"You know how a woman's hair gets after it's been bleached too many times? So thin you can almost see through it. Especially when the sun shines down on it. Looks like yellow cotton candy then."

Jayme smiled. "We really appreciate your help with this, Mr. Shaner. We'll let you get to your dinner now."

He glanced at his wristwatch. "I should say so. Early-bird prices only last till five. Are you going to write me a ticket if I pass you on the way back to town?"

"We have no authority to issue tickets, sir."

"That's all I needed to hear."

THIRTY-THREE

Ĥ ow you build it is up to you," DeMarco told her, and handed Jayme a deep enameled bowl.

She considered the ingredients they had prepared, some still on the stove, others in bowls and saucers and bottles on the table. Yellow rice, grilled and chopped chicken breasts red with creole seasoning, chopped spinach, chopped sweet onions, steamed corn, chopped romaine lettuce, chopped sweet peppers, chopped jalapeños, salsa verde, pico de gallo, soy sauce, sriracha sauce, kalamata olives, and pickled banana pepper rings.

She followed DeMarco, adding layer after layer to her bowl. "What do you call this mess?" she asked.

"Rice bowl," he said.

"How about United Nations rice bowl?"

"Whatever floats your boat, my love."

Buddy watched from beneath the table, his chin on the floor. In the living room, Van Morrison was singing about being caught up on Cypress Avenue. The back door was open, the last warmth of the day streaming in with the rose-tinted light.

She wondered why food they cooked together always tasted better than restaurant food or anything she cooked alone. Maybe there was something real to the notion of cooking with love. Maybe love was an additive as real as salt and pepper and the other spices.

"It was a productive day," she said, and topped off her bowl with some pico de gallo.

"If you like this dish, we can make it with pulled pork sometime. Or grilled salmon. Or seared tuna."

She asked. "Coffee table or dining room?"

"Dining room okay?"

"I'm right behind you."

In the dining room they sat across from each other at the oval table, each with an empty seat beside them, and ate in silence for a few minutes. Then Jayme said, "I hear he's kind of a jerk." When DeMarco looked up, she nodded toward the living room, where Van Morrison was now singing "Ballerina."

"We geniuses often are," he said.

"It must be tough living among the rest of us."

"You have no idea."

No one else could look at her the way he did. Hit her with a sarcastic insult yet a devilish smile that warmed her entire body, made her almost want to cry.

She said, "We should fill in our assistant. Get him busy on Choo Choo and Reddick. He's working at Goodwill right now."

DeMarco nodded. "Make him earn his kingly wages."

"I'll call him after dinner."

Again the conversation faded. She studied his face for a while. Could tell by his smile that he knew she was watching him eat.

"Why do you do this work?" she asked. "State police. Private detective."

"Why do you?"

"I wanted the challenge, I guess. Physical as well as mental. Plus I wanted to help people. Now you. You told me about how you saw Tommy Lee Jones in *The Fugitive* and all, but I want to know the real reason. In your heart of hearts."

He shrugged. "I wanted to be a better person."

"And did joining the state police do that for you?"

"Some, I guess. But being a father did more. And you... I think you've done the most."

She knew he meant it, could read the truth in his eyes. And yet...what she had felt in those few weeks when she had been alone with her secret, the life in her womb, guarding it, even hoarding it...how to describe that love? When you know you are not alone, you are two. Two in one. It was a different, deeper connection than anything she had ever felt. Missing it made her entire body ache.

She rubbed her foot over Buddy's hip, concentrated on the softness there, the warmth. When she felt it was safe to talk again, she softly cleared her throat, then asked, "Which is your favorite song?"

"Favorite Van Morrison song? Tough question. Probably either 'Philosopher's Stone' or 'When the Leaves Come Falling Down.' Which is yours?"

"Gotta be 'Tupelo Honey.'"

"That's a good one too. Do you know what it's about?"

"About a girl who's as sweet as Tupelo honey, right? Though I have always wondered why it has to be honey from Tupelo, Mississippi. Unless that's where the girl is from too."

He smiled. Returned to his rice bowl.

She said, "I'm wrong, aren't I?"

"It's a natural mistake." He took another bite.

"Tell me!"

"Tupelo honey comes from the nectar of the tupelo tree blossoms. It's a very light honey that doesn't granulate. Mainly from the wetlands of Georgia and Florida."

"God, you disgust me sometimes. But okay," she said, "so I got the state wrong."

Again he smiled into his rice bowl.

"I hate you," she said. "Tell me what else I got wrong."

"The song is about freedom. The first verse alludes to the American Revolution, the second verse to the Irish battle for independence. And the chorus is about his wife, Janet, who gives him the sweet freedom to be the best artist he can be."

"Ah, that's beautiful, babe. Do I give you that freedom?"

"You make me better than I am. Which makes you a whole lot sweeter than tupelo honey."

She blinked back the dampness pooling in her eye. Nothing was sweeter than one of his compliments. Though she wished she could control her emotions better. Why must every kind word sting?

Dog at my feet, she thought, and felt the warmth against her naked toes. *My man across from me.* What more could she want? It was almost perfect.

But for two empty seats at the table.

THIRTY-FOUR

A *lone again*, Flores told herself. *Naturally*.

It was her first thought upon awakening in the dark room. Every time she had that thought, and it happened frequently, she heard the first two words in a resigned deadpan, and the third word sung to the tune of Gilbert O'Sullivan's suicide song. She knew all the words to that song by heart, had memorized them when she was only thirteen.

The romance novel she had been reading had fallen shut; she would have to search through the pages tomorrow night to find her place again. At some point she had turned off the table lamp and curled up on the little sofa, though she could remember doing neither. Now she lay there with her head on the armrest and listened to the sounds through the large windows overlooking the street. She had chosen this apartment because of those windows. And because the rent was so cheap. And because the hardware store on the first floor closed at five every weekday, at two every Saturday afternoon, promising silence beneath her.

She had imagined that the windows would provide a perfect vantage point for viewing the night sky, since the nearest streetlight was two blocks away. She had not counted on how far its glow would spread at night, or on the lights from the Sheetz station three buildings away, or on the cigarette smoke that somehow seeped in from the kids who liked to hang out below. She had acted impetuously, three days before her first day with Troop D. Had believed, naively, that now everything would change.

The routine of her days changed but little else did. And now she would have to drag herself up off the sofa and into the bathroom. Have to undress and brush her teeth and shake out the twisted sheets on the bed so that she could climb between them again. And then lie awake for another hour or two probably, her mind playing back every moment of the day. It had been a good day but her churlish mind would not remember it that way. Would say *you should have done this, you should have said this*. And if an older moment happened to pop into consciousness, one of those festering grievances, she would rehash it again and again until her eyeballs felt swollen from the escalating blood pressure.

Sometimes she would repeat the Lord's Prayer, as her mother had taught her to do when she was still tiny and afraid, only four or five years old: *Our father who art in heaven, hollowed be thy name…* She had been eight when her mother caught the mistake and corrected it.

Hallowed, baby. Not hollowed.

Like in Halloween, you mean?

No no no. I don't think so, anyway.

What does it mean then?

Hallowed? Made holy, I think.

And now every time she thought *hallowed be thy name*, a quick *not hollowed* followed, destroying any soothing, mantric possibilities. But it was the only prayer she'd ever learned. Not that she expected anything from it now other than a soporific numbing, the white noise of her own voice. Her mother had filled their apartment with candles and crucifixes and plaster figurines and what good had it done either of them?

Sometimes the only way she could find sleep was to masturbate.

She kept a small pink vibrator in the drawer of her bed table but seldom used it. Too mechanical. Its whir under the sheet made it too hard to imagine a man's finger or mouth in its place. Her own hand worked better. Had more speeds. Different pressure settings. Didn't whir.

She usually started out with Michael Peña because he was gentle and sweet and his soft voice reassured her. Toward the end, though, by the time she tossed the sheet aside, there was no telling who might take over. Ryan Gosling. Ryan Reynolds. Vin Diesel. The Matt Dillon from *Crash*.

Tonight she was afraid to get started. She kept seeing herself in the car with DeMarco, sitting along the side of the road, watching the sun sink below the hill and the "great shaggy beasts" as he'd called them. She did not think he would be the one to climb into bed with her but neither did she want him watching her with whomever did. It was a crazy thought but she knew what could happen in the heat of the moment. She had been intimidated by him but now she wasn't, and that could be a problem too. Every time she felt a bond with an older man had been a problem.

No, the problem was her own freaking mind. She needed a way to shut it off. *Silencio!* she wanted to scream.

There was a little shop behind Citizen's Bank with a sign that said *Reiki & Healing Oils*. Just last week it had been a candles and crystals shop. Maybe she could try it out before it became a pole dancing or vape shop.

She had to do something. Damn her chattering monkey mind. It was almost two thirty and she had to get up at six.

Okay, there he was again popping into her thoughts. She hadn't been able to look out his window at the sleeping bison without seeing the side of his face. No, she did *not* want him, not in that way. She was sure she didn't. But it was all mixed up, wasn't it? She was all mixed up.

It's okay, he told her, and slipped an arm around her shoulders, pulled her close. She laid her head against his chest, felt his heart beating against her ear. *It's okay to cry*, he told her, and so she did. She cried long and hard and he held her close to soften the way her body shook against him. And after a while the tears subsided and she felt herself drifting into sleep finally, safe in his arms, his heartbeat strong and steady, synchronized with her own, a small distant drum beating softly inside her head.

THIRTY-FIVE

S aturday mornings always felt different to DeMarco. As a boy
he would wake up wary, immediately tensed and alert, as if
his body knew the day before his mind did. Usually there was no
sign of his father throughout the week but he might stumble in
late on a Friday or Saturday night, as dangerous the next morning
as a hungover grizzly. So it was wise for a boy to wake up with
his senses wide open for a smoky, sour scent or the sound of his
father's snoring, which always reminded Ryan of tires spinning
in heavy gravel. If either of these indicators was present, the boy
would dress quickly and quietly, creep into the kitchen to fill a
plastic grocery sack with whatever he could find in the refrigerator,
then slip outside in the chill of morning and head for the woods.

The first sound he heard this morning was the whimper of the
dog standing with its snout close to his. He looked at the light in
the windows. Leaf-smoke gray.

"Okay," he whispered, and scratched Buddy between his ears.
"Give me a minute." Leaf-smoke gray meant the sun was about to
rise. Coal-smoke gray and wet-wood-smoke gray meant fumbling
in the dark for his boxers.

Boxers located, he followed Buddy downstairs and to the back
door. The dog surprised him by bounding forward off the porch.
"Hey!" DeMarco said, and stepped down into the damp, chilly
grass.

Buddy gave him a look, then went through his usual sniff and squirt routine, watering three or four spots before turning back toward the porch. But this time, instead of stepping daintily up the three wooden steps, the animal paused and stiffened where the brick path met the small concrete pad at the bottom of the steps. He sniffed at the bricks, then went down low on his front legs and growled. A moment later he backed up and started barking at the brick path.

"Hush," DeMarco told him, but the barking continued, loud and jarring. DeMarco squinted at the spot. Had another dog or a skunk or possum urinated there? It was impossible to tell. What he did notice, though, was that one brick appeared to be set unevenly, with the corner slightly higher than the other bricks. Was there something under the brick that the dog was smelling? A rodent maybe?

With his left hand DeMarco clutched the collar and held Buddy at his side. Then he squatted, leaned over and delicately lifted the brick up, keeping the near end low to the ground in case a brown recluse or late-season snake lay there ready to strike. Both were ectothermic and probably too numbed by the chill to do any damage, but why take a chance?

What he saw beneath the brick was dizzying. It made no sense. What was it doing there? He heard his breath popping out in startled little gasps.

A shotgun shell, its red crimped top visible inside a small metal cylinder. Positioned to aim at the underside of the brick.

He pulled the dog back, more sharply than he intended, stood, and went up onto the porch. He was still holding the brick in his right hand as, with his little finger, he opened the screen door and went inside. Then shoved the wooden door closed and locked it and laid the brick on the counter and released the dog and walked briskly upstairs.

He picked his phone off the bed table and sat on the edge of the bed, turned so that he could lay his hand on Jayme's hip and nudge her awake. "Hmm?" she said.

"Honey, get up. You need to get up and get dressed."

His mind was racing. *Nearest bomb squad in Allegheny County. Sheriff's office closest. Secure the area.* He tapped 9-1-1.

Jayme sat up. Asked, "What's going on?"

He held up a finger, then spoke into the phone. Gave his name and address, said, "Possible explosive device" and heard Jayme suck in her breath. He kept talking to the dispatcher, kept his voice even and steady, though his throat felt strangled by a Saturday morning fear he hadn't experienced in almost forty years.

THIRTY-SIX

An hour and fifty minutes later, the bomb tech came in through the back door. "Hello?" he said.

"Back here," DeMarco told him from the dining room. Jayme, Flores, Boyd, and Captain Bowen were seated at the table, drinking coffee, with DeMarco, the Mercer County sheriff, and the Jefferson Township chief of police standing nearby, coffee mugs in hand.

The bomb tech, still wearing thick yellow neoprene gloves, held out a three-inch-long piece of dirty pipe, now empty. "It obviously wasn't meant to kill," he told them. "But it might have taken off a couple of toes."

Jayme leaned closer. "How does it work?"

"The pipe functions basically as a short gun barrel," he explained. "There's a firing pin attached to the bottom cap. Then the shotgun shell was set atop the firing pin. We took a flat rock from beneath the pipe. So the whole thing sat atop that rock like a loaded barrel. Then the brick was on top. Theoretically, if somebody stepped down hard enough on the brick, the shell would have been depressed and the firing pin and primer would have collided."

"Would it have worked?" Bowen asked.

"I see no reason why not," the tech said.

Outside, dogs were sniffing the front and back yards, crawling under the back porch, walking over every inch of DeMarco's property. "We're just about done outside," the tech said. "Everything's clear."

"You swept the garage and the vehicles?" DeMarco asked.

"Yes, sir. Inside and out. All we have left is inside here."

"Come in whenever you're ready."

"You folks might like to go out and have breakfast somewhere," the tech suggested. "Best to err on the side of caution."

The group inside had already dissected all possibilities. A call to Chief Brinker in Youngstown, who was in touch with the FBI in Erie, informed them that there had been no reported sightings of Daksh Khatri since the one in Ottawa, which was almost a week old. Khatri or one of his disciples could easily have traveled to Mercer County by now. Could have easily removed a brick last night, dug a little hole and buried the device. Any moron with a soldering iron could have built it.

"My question," said Bowen, "is why? Why you two?"

"We're the ones who uncovered his secret," Jayme said. "So now he's taunting us. He could have killed us last month when he slipped that first letter inside. I think he just wants us to know that he has the power to get to us anytime he wants."

"Sick son of a bitch," the sheriff said.

The chief said, "We can put your place on our regular patrol every night, but the township doesn't have the manpower to—"

DeMarco waved him off. "We'll have a full security system installed by the end of the day. Video, motion sensors, lights, alarms…" He laid a hand atop Jayme's and told her, "Nobody will get near this house again without our knowledge."

Everybody in the room nodded. Flores leaned to the side in her chair and looked at the dog curled around Jayme's feet. "Smart dog," she said. "What's his name?"

"It was Buddy," DeMarco said, "but I think he just earned a new one. Scout maybe. Or Sentinel."

"Hero," Jayme said, and rubbed the warm belly with her foot.

"Oh yeah," Boyd replied, and nodded solemnly at DeMarco. "Hero. That's the one."

THIRTY-SEVEN

M aybe we need to step back from this thing," DeMarco told her. The Denny's was crowded and noisy that morning, so instead of sitting across from him in the booth, Jayme had chosen to sit beside him, their heads lowered together so as to keep the conversation private. "We could take another road trip," he said. "At least until the feds can draw a bead on Khatri again."

"You don't want to do that and neither do I," she told him. "We've barely gotten started."

"The beginning is the best time to walk away. Boyd is more than capable."

She shook her head. "I know what you're doing, babe. But I don't need you to hide me away somewhere. Okay? Let's just finish this. Then we can drive some place warm for the winter and not have to feel like we got chased away by a scrawny little lunatic."

DeMarco pursed his lips. Scowled down at his Grand Slam breakfast. "Do you think it's because he has a crush on you? I always felt like he did. I mean, the way he looked at you those times at the Humane Society…"

"He stuck a *knife* in me," Jayme said. "And I have the scar to prove it."

"Well. Yeah. There's that, I guess."

The home security people had promised to show up at 11:30, the same time the bomb squad would be wrapping up, so there was still time to finish their breakfast without rushing. But of course he was restless. Wanted nothing more than to go home, pack up the RV, and drive Jayme and Hero down to Key Largo or Baja or maybe all the way up to Prudhoe Bay. Let the rest of the world go to hell in a hand basket; he and Jayme had already paid their share of dues.

But she was ten years behind him and still wanted to make a difference. Probably needed another victory to wash away some of the sting from the recent defeat.

He smiled at her and thought, *All right. One more. Once more unto the breach.*

Her phone vibrated on the tabletop and startled both of them.

"It's Chase," she said. Then read the text aloud. "'Lots of info. Meet up today?'"

"Tell him we'll be heading home soon. He can meet us there if he wants."

She sent the text. Held the phone while she waited for the reply. DeMarco considered his pancakes. He had eaten only one of the three. Wanted the other ones too but knew if he ate them he would spend the next few hours feeling fat and lazy.

Again the phone vibrated. She read the text, then held the screen up for him to read: C u there. With a grinning smiley face.

"He seems happy about something," DeMarco said. "You know who he reminds me of? Lennie from Steinbeck's *Of Mice and Men*. Always hopping up and down with optimism. 'Gonna live off the fatta the land! And have rabbits!'"

"You know who you remind me of?" she said. "The old you, when you're angry. But you're angry at Khatri, babe, not at Chase. Try to remember that. He only wants to impress you. The same as all those people who showed up this morning. They all just want to do right by you."

He nodded, properly reproached. Then said, "I just want to do right by you."

"Have another pancake," she told him.

And he had to laugh. He couldn't get away with anything.

THIRTY-EIGHT

W ho do you want to hear about first?" Chase Miller asked. "This Reddick guy, or Choo Choo and the ladies?"

DeMarco had set up three chairs on the back porch while the new security system was being installed inside. A tiny video camera and motion-activated light were already in place above the back door, with others mounted on the garage and out front. If anything bigger than a raccoon strolled onto his property, the image and an annoying ringtone called Tuning Fork would burst from his and Jayme's cell phones.

The air was clear but cool enough to require the sweatshirts he and Jayme had pulled on. Miller wore a pale yellow Columbia fleece. As usual, he was cleanly shaved, the khakis with a sharp pleat, his hair gelled and neat. He sat leaning forward on the edge of his chair, facing the others, a mug of coffee in his hands, heels raised as his legs bounced up and down. His eyes were red but Jayme could detect no quivering of the pupils, no discernible dilation.

She said, "How much coffee have you had today?"

"Too much," he said. He took another sip, then set the mug on the floor. "I usually only have one with my mushroom powder first thing in the morning, but this morning I—"

DeMarco interrupted. "Mushroom powder?"

"Yeah, but not the kind you're thinking. It's a blend I buy online. Lion's Mane, which is a nootropic, for enhanced cognitive function. Chaga, which is just loaded with antioxidants, triterpene, and melanin. And cordyceps, which enhances energy levels. That's my morning blend. Usually I have a cup of reishi tea at night to help me sleep, but there was just too much to do last night and I was too wired to sleep."

"All this is legal?" Jayme asked.

"Absolutely legal. You guys should try it. I'll give you the website."

Jayme pointed to his jittery legs. "And that?"

"This? This is caffeine. Like I said, I skipped my reishi tea last night and went straight for the french roast. Don't worry; I'll crash for a couple of hours before I go to work today. I have the dinner shift at the Grille."

He seemed completely open to her, and she wanted to trust him. "I won't have you ruining your health over this, Chase."

"I'm fine. Seriously. One night without sleep is no problem. And the mushrooms are good medicine. You really ought to give them a shot. I'll bring you guys a couple of tea bags next time we get together."

Just then Hero rose from his spot at Jayme's feet, walked over to Chase and sniffed his knee, then lay beside him. "Dogs like me," Chase said.

She thought, *They liked Khatri too.*

DeMarco asked, "What did you find out about Reddick?"

"Yeah, that guy," Miller said. "There's something funny going on with him. He has a good-looking website but you can't buy anything from it. Every button I clicked came up the same: *Verified Collectors Only*. So I kept digging and came up with a phone number. It was about ten last night, but I figured what the heck, give it a shot."

"And?" Jayme said.

"Some woman answered. Deep voice for a woman. Harsh, you know? Like a lifetime of cigarettes and whiskey. So I tell her I'm interested in an item on the start page, and she's like, 'We're not accepting any new clients right now.' So I'm all, 'You're going to turn away a guaranteed sale? How can you stay in business that way?' We go back and forth a couple more times and then she tells me to eff off and hangs up."

Jayme leaned back, her eyes going wide.

"I know," Miller said. "What legitimate business would act that way?"

"Anything else?" DeMarco asked.

"About Reddick? Not much. But if you can get me a headshot, I'll show it around. Somebody will know him."

"What do you have on Choo Choo?" DeMarco asked.

"Ah, the Choo man," Miller said. "Now this is one colorful guy. He and the two girls—I'm sorry, women. Or should I say ladies?" he asked Jayme. "It's hard to know these days."

"Females will be fine," she said.

"Cool. So he and the two females seemed to have popped up in the area last summer. Some of the people I talked to knew him from the rest stop, some from other places. Have Hyundai, will travel."

"The Santa Fe was his?" DeMarco said.

"He was the guy behind the wheel anyway. You want fifteen minutes with a girl? A hundred dollars. A gram of good weed, one Andrew Jackson. Mollies, coke, smack, meth, chocolate suckers, these were all hit or miss. Sometimes he was carrying, sometimes he wasn't. And oh yeah. One guy I talked to said he remembered once when there was another guy in the car with Choo Choo. Sat in the passenger seat and didn't say anything. He was the guy holding the drugs that time."

"Any description of this guy?" DeMarco asked.

"White. Scrawny. Little moustache, big ears. My contact said he looked like a real burnout."

"Anything else?"

"That's all I could get out of him."

"Tell us about the females," Jayme said.

"Usually it was Suzi and Lady D. Vietnamese and Southern belle respectively."

"Why Southern belle?" DeMarco asked.

"Accent, I guess. Plus her attitude, kind of sad and aloof, my guy said. There were also a couple of other females Choo Choo would shop around too. Not as frequently as Suzi and Lady D but now and then anyway. Both Caucasian. The younger one called herself Sylvia, and the older one, who my contact described as—and these are his words, not mine—a fat-assed slob not worth fifty cents. Though one other guy said she gave good head. So, you know, one man's poison and all that."

"What about Sylvia?"

"This is interesting," Miller told them. "One guy said he recognized her from high school. Commodore Perry. He couldn't remember her name, only that she was a couple years younger than him. Very pretty back in the day, he said. Thin, long brown hair, the quiet type, you know? He said she hung out with a couple of other artsy types. Until she started dating an older guy her senior year. He's the one who turned her on to coke. And it was all downhill from there, I guess. When my contact saw her with Choo Choo, he said she had that full-blown junkie look on her face. Heroin chic, he called it. He wasn't even going to do her at first, but he couldn't see any tracks on her, so, you know…"

"How old is this contact of yours?" DeMarco asked.

"Hmm… Maybe thirty, give or take a year. He said he tried

to strike up a conversation with Sylvia but she just acted like he wasn't there. Just lay there and closed her eyes, if you know what I mean."

DeMarco said, "So if he is thirty, that would put Sylvia between twenty-seven and twenty-nine."

Jayme asked, "He couldn't remember anything else about her?"

"He was fairly sure her real first name was Alice or Alyssa or Amy, something with an A. I plan to visit the school on Monday, see if they will let me look through the old yearbooks."

"They aren't online?" Jayme asked.

"Not the more recent ones. A half dozen older ones that alumni have posted, but nothing later than 1992. Don't worry; I'll track her down. I know a couple of other people who went to Commodore Perry around the same time as her. I'll touch base with them from work tonight if I get the chance."

DeMarco let a few moments pass, then asked, "What do you tell people when they want to know why you need this information?"

Miller looked hurt by the question. "I'm not stupid, you know."

"I didn't suggest that you are. I just need to know your cover story."

"Do you think I'd just come right out and say, *hey, I'm working with the police? Tell me what you know?*"

"That isn't what he meant," Jayme said.

But he kept looking at DeMarco. "I was pretending to be a collector when I called Reddick, okay? I already told you that. As for Choo Choo and the females, I'm a journalist and a blogger. The people I talk to know that about me. And as long as I don't say something bad about them or mention their names to anybody, they don't care what I write."

"We know you're being careful," Jayme told him. "We're all being careful."

He said, his tone less aggressive now, "I forgot to tell you that I know where Choo Choo, Suzi, and Lady D came from. Last known address before coming here, I mean. They lived in Lost City for a while."

DeMarco and Jayme looked at each other with furrowed brows.

Jayme asked Miller, "Where is Lost City?"

"Yeah, I guess maybe it is sort of an underground place. It's down in Washington County, a couple of miles off I-79. It's this village, I guess you could call it, of old shipping containers and flatbed trailers. Some old campers, single-wides…stuff that people just dump there because it's too expensive to get rid of them legally. The only way to get there is to walk a half mile or so through a pine forest."

"And you're saying that Choo Choo and the females lived there?" Jayme asked.

"From what I hear, and I've never been there myself, but yeah, as many as a hundred people might be living there during the summer. Most of them head south for the winter, but in the summer there's gardens and whiskey stills, patches of marijuana growing, everything a person would need except for electricity and flush toilets. It's rumored to be the reason Washington County has so many heroin overdoses. And why nearly a whole fraternity at W&J ended up with gonorrhea a while back."

Jayme shared another look with DeMarco. She said, "We need to get out of Mercer County more often, babe."

"Do the local police know about this Lost City?" DeMarco asked.

"That I can't answer," Miller said. "If they do know, they don't bother with it. Probably happy to have the riffraff out in the woods instead of sleeping on their streets."

"I need to see this place," DeMarco said.

Miller grinned. "We could take a trip down tomorrow. Might be a treasure trove of information."

Out front, a van door slammed shut. DeMarco said, "I think the guys are finished inside. I better get in there." He stood. "You too," he told Jayme. "They'll need to show us a few things."

Miller stood and faced him. "So how did I do?"

"Good work," DeMarco muttered.

Jayme stood and put her hand on Miller's shoulder. "Very good work. We'll be in touch. Go home and get some sleep."

He said, "So a road trip tomorrow?"

DeMarco raised his hand, and for a moment she thought he was about to tousle the boy's hair, but before she could cringe he stopped himself, bent down and picked up Miller's coffee mug, and went inside.

"He's pleased," she whispered to the young man. "He just doesn't want you to know it."

"Copy that," Miller said, but she could not read the look on his face, that squint of eyes and the crooked twist of his mouth. It was either embarrassment or rage.

THIRTY-NINE

The oddness of the rest of the day would not dissipate, even after everyone else had cleared out and she and DeMarco had swept away all visible evidence that a dozen others had been tramping through their house all morning. She couldn't help taking furtive glances at the security cameras and at the windows with their motion sensors.

It made her wonder about her ancestors in their walled estates and castles. Had *they* seen themselves as prisoners locked inside by fear? Had they stood at their windows gazing out and filled with longing? And when they rode out through the gates, did they tremble? Feel exposed and vulnerable? Long to be safe behind their thick walls again from the rampaging brutes outside?

What troubled her most was the knowledge that this suburban fortress had been made for her alone. Ryan, if living on his own, would never have installed a security system. He would have bought a couple of extra boxes of ammunition and slept in his chair with the Glock between his legs. He would have *defied* someone to breach his will. If not for her, he would probably be miles from here right now, scouring the landscape for Khatri. In fact, if left to her own devices, she would be doing the same thing.

She had to wonder what their love had made of them.

≫———≪

After the initial hellos, DeMarco put the call on speaker so that Jayme could listen in. There was no mistaking the slurred voice, though Loughner sounded so intoxicated, at not yet four in the afternoon, that much of what he said was incomprehensible, though the gist of his tirade was clear: "son of a bitch needs in the fucking ground...the gene for evil...stop pissing around and get this done...I will if you can't...when he does it again who's to blame?"

The conversation lasted most of five minutes, with DeMarco making an occasional reply, his voice soft and low and hoarse: "Okay, Joe...I hear you...I understand...I know what you're saying."

When Loughner abruptly stopped talking and the call ended, DeMarco slipped the phone into his pocket and said nothing, only looked at her and shook his head. He had been on his knees on the back porch when the call came, brushing out Hero's coat, and now he picked up the brush again and returned to that task. Jayme wondered what to say to him, knew how deflated he felt, the sense of loss he must be experiencing, especially after a day such as this one.

But what was there to say?

She slid off her chair, knelt beside him, bent down to kiss Hero's snout. DeMarco leaned over her and kissed the back of her head. "Our wounded soldier," she said to mask what she felt and to shift the sorrow to another place. But then she went a step too far. "We should do something nice for him."

He said, "What do you do for a guy who's been neutered?"

"I really wish you would quit mentioning that. Am I asking too much for you just to be quiet about it?"

He kissed her head once more, lighter this time, then rose and went into the kitchen.

≫------------≪

In the late afternoon he wandered from room to room, his movements so aimless that she finally said, "Let's go out for dinner. That
barbecue place in Grove City has a patio, don't they? Maybe we
can take Hero along."

His face gladdened a little. "If they won't let him on the patio,
we can get the food to go, walk over to the park."

"I like the way you think, DeMarco."

"I need a shower."

"So what are you waiting for?"

He was rinsing the shampoo out of his hair when the shower
door slid open and she stepped inside. Ten minutes later they were
on the bed, their skin and hair still damp. Afterward, catching their
breath, with him on his back and Jayme rolled against him, the
slow seeping away of oxytocin and dopamine, he chuckled out
loud.

She said, "That's not the reaction I would expect at a time like
this."

"I made up a joke," he told her.

"So let's hear it."

"What's the best thing about sex for a pirate?"

"Hmm. Taking off his wooden leg?"

"Nope. The arrrrrghasm."

She groaned, laughing, and told herself, *Okay. Okay. We're
going to be all right.*

FORTY

On Sunday morning DeMarco woke early, a full hour before sunrise. For a few moments he lay there and listened to Jayme and Hero breathing, both still sound asleep, Hero on the floor at his side. The dog had a habit of going from one side of the bed to the other throughout the night but he usually found his way to DeMarco's side by first light, making it impossible for DeMarco to climb out of bed without Hero coming suddenly alert too.

Mornings were the best part of the day for DeMarco and always had been, especially Sunday mornings. He loved the stillness and quiet of not just the house but the entire neighborhood, and therefore of the world. As a boy it would take him only a couple of minutes to leave the house and sneak away in the damp dark of morning, delaying even his morning urination until he was on the edge of the nearest woods.

This morning he delayed only until he reached the downstairs bathroom, yesterday's clothes in a bundle in his left hand, Hero following him into the bathroom to watch how humans got the job done. Sometimes when Hero stood there watching, looking up at DeMarco and then down into the bowl and up at DeMarco again, it was easy to think of the dog as a substitute for a little boy, and as himself as the kind, indulging father he'd always wished he had. And when he had such thoughts, a sweet ache of longing filled his chest.

But he was well past the normal age for fathering a child, so a dog would have to do. He finished up, looked down at Hero, and asked, "You getting the drift of it?" Hero wagged his tail in response.

It was too early for starting breakfast, and besides, Hero had yet to practice his newly learned skill of an upright tinkle. DeMarco dressed quickly, shut off the alarm, opened the back door, and followed Hero outside. Once there, however, after a couple of deep breaths of moist, clean air scented with fallen leaves and Mrs. Craig's marigolds, DeMarco had no desire to wait inside for the sunrise. He stepped back into the kitchen long enough to scrawl a note for Jayme and check the cash in his pocket. Then he attached Hero's leash and, pulling the door closed and locked behind them, headed out toward the street.

The local Sheetz was over a mile away but as a boy he would regularly venture five times that far on a morning as peaceful as this one. Most houses were still dark, the streets empty, and gratitude came easily. When you and your dog and a couple of birds are the only living things on the planet, it is possible to forget about the evil afoot in the world. Possible to experience an appreciation and even a sympathy for whomever had created this morning. Any being who could sculpt such serenity in such muted colors was truly an artist.

DeMarco wondered what a god like that would be doing right now. Probably the same thing DeMarco was doing—savoring those few minutes before the world came awake, not really wanting it to come awake but knowing that it would. DeMarco had only two messes to deal with when the rest of the world climbed out of bed, the triple homicide and Daksh Khatri, whereas God must have tens of billions of messes on his plate.

He remembered reading somewhere about a Buddhist belief

that after God created the world, he was too busy with other work to pay any attention to a bothersome humanity, and it certainly did appear as if that were true. And DeMarco could muster no resentment over God's neglect. Not far ahead he would collect two large mocha cappuccinos, three sausage and egg breakfast sandwiches, and two apple fritters, and he would carry them home in white paper sacks and enjoy them with his family. It was a small family and not likely to get any bigger, but on a morning like this, just to have Jayme and Hero in his life seemed a kind of miracle. So he could not rule out the possibility of another miracle. Even an otherwise neglectful God must get the urge to tweak his creation now and then.

FORTY-ONE

M iller said, "Does it seem to you guys like Big Pharma is trying extra hard these days to get people addicted? In ninety minutes last night, I saw ads on TV for drugs to treat sweaty armpits, bent penises, inappropriate laughter, falling asleep during the day, and bad breath. It's like they want us to believe that everything about being human is a disease, and they have the cure."

He was seated in the center of the rear seat, from which point he could see DeMarco's eyes in the rearview mirror and the side of Jayme's face. She had only to turn a few degrees to smile at him. Whatever emotions he had left with when he departed their home the previous afternoon, all now seemed forgiven.

"Seriously," he said to Jayme when she turned. "What kind of medications do you guys take? Everybody I know is popping at least a couple kinds of pills."

"Neither of us takes anything," she told him. Only an hour earlier she and DeMarco had visited their children's graves, now a regular Sunday morning routine for both of them, and both remained subdued.

"Neither do I! A cup or two of coffee, some mushroom tea, maybe a candy bar once a week or so. Are we freaks or what?"

DeMarco took another glance in the mirror. The kid's energy was amusing. But he was also correct. R. D. Laing's observation that life is a sexually transmitted disease, mortality rate 100 percent, seemed truer every day. The sadness of that reality lingered in stark contrast to the brightness of the Sunday morning sunshine, which came streaming in through DeMarco's window to warm the car and tighten the skin on the side of his face.

Because he wanted to see how Miller would react, he quoted Dostoyevsky. "'To be too conscious is an illness.'"

Miller thought for a moment, then nodded. "That's cool," he said. "But does that mean that the *awareness* is the disease, or that *life* is the disease, and therefore…" He could not find the end of that sentence.

"Maybe both," DeMarco offered. "Life is a disease, but obsessing about it only makes it worse. The Roman philosopher Seneca said that if you want to be less angry, be less aware."

Miller slid forward, leaned closer to DeMarco. "Yeah, I don't know about that, though. When is it ever a bad thing to be too conscious of something negative and destructive?"

"When it makes you too miserable to appreciate your blessings," DeMarco answered, and slid his hand over the console to squeeze Jayme's hand.

Sometimes he liked this kid a lot. Sometimes he was as annoying as a swarm of gnats. But today DeMarco was determined to extend equanimity to all. Not only to Miller but also to Boyd and Flores following in Boyd's anvil-gray Jeep Renegade. And also to any residents of the Lost City they encountered.

He had little idea of what to expect of the place. Boyd had notified the Troop B station commander that their party would be traipsing around in the woods nearby, but the commander had little intel to share. The Lost City property was owned by the Floridian heirs of a now defunct mining company, who probably did not know or care that their land had been taken over by squatters. The station commander's primary concern was that the few residents who wintered over in their storage containers and derelict trailers would not freeze or starve to death or catch a stray bullet from the hunters who would fill the woods in November. He told Boyd that unconfirmed reports had suggested that a few bodies were buried in those woods but that the police did not go around digging for corpses without a missing person report or reliable tip. The residents of Lost City were those forgotten by society, and they would not have hiked into the woods unless they wanted to remain that way.

DeMarco tried to envision the scene. Acre after acre of old flatbed trailers and shipping containers? It seemed apocalyptic somehow, a devolution from his own experience growing up in a trailer park. Those furnished trailers, no matter how run-down, had plumbing and electricity, running water and toilets. What must the hygiene be like in Lost City? What of the daily accumulation of trash and human waste? He imagined the place as one huge crack house, and could only hope that he would be proven wrong.

"Exit 30, you said?" he asked.

"Correct," said Miller. "Then toward Lone Pine."

"Four more miles."

As far as DeMarco was concerned, even if they learned nothing new at Lost City, the day had already been productive. Before the two-vehicle caravan had pulled away from his house an hour earlier, Miller, Flores, and Boyd had added more brushstrokes to the criminal portraits they were assembling.

One of the servers at the Gallery Grille had a friend who had purchased every Commodore Perry yearbook from her seventh through twelfth grades. But when the server called her friend with the information Miller supplied, the friend knew exactly who "Sylvia" was. Amber Sullivan. Smart, beautiful, daydreamy and shy.

Ran cross-country until her senior year. A member of the English Club. Wrote poetry. Especially adored the work of Sylvia Plath. And now had a Facebook page under the name Sivvy en Ruine, where she posted her poetry about drug addiction and struggling to get clean and praying for the strength to commit suicide.

Miller told them, "Sivvy was Sylvia Plath's nickname. I already checked out Sullivan's website; her poetry is bleak as hell. No photo, though. But my friend's friend is going to copy Amber's page from the yearbook. I'll get it from her tomorrow."

Unfortunately, there was no known current address for Amber Sullivan. "We can start with her parents," Jayme had said.

Boyd and Flores had reviewed the footage from the IR camera placed on Mr. Shaner's front porch on Linn Tyro Road in Otter Creek Township. Over the course of the previous forty-four hours, only one vehicle had entered or left Reddick's driveway. Flores explained that the vehicle, a red Corolla, contained two passengers, one male and one female. It entered the driveway at 4:29 the previous afternoon, and, as of 8:12 that Sunday morning, had not yet exited.

"The video gives a short but clear look at the side of the driver's face," Boyd had added. "And it matches the license photo of the registered owner. One Timothy Jakiella, a.k.a. Sonny. Forty-six years old, five eight, 143 pounds. Previously arrested on two separate charges of breaking and entering, once of a dentist's office, once a Rite Aid drug store. Served a combined twenty-eight months, plus three stints in rehab, all voluntary admissions for heroin addiction. Currently employed part-time as an electrician with a general contractor by the name of Mark Heeter. Works out of Conneaut Lake. Which is also Jakiella's home address. He lives alone, divorced, two daughters living with their mother in Linesville. Ages eleven and eight."

"Conneaut Lake is less than thirty minutes due north of Luthor Reddick's address," DeMarco had said.

Now, alone in the car with DeMarco and Miller, a short drive and long walk from their destination, Jayme said, "So putting it all together, everything new from Chase and Boyd and Flores, Chase's contact saw Amber Sullivan, a.k.a. Sylvia, a.k.a. Sivvy, in a vehicle with Choo Choo. The same or another contact saw a scrawny burnout of a guy with Choo Choo."

"Same contact," Miller corrected her. "He saw both the scrawny guy and Sylvia on the same night."

"And according to Flores," Jayme said, "Sonny Jakiella could easily be described as a scrawny burnout of a guy."

"Which means," Miller said, "that both Amber Sullivan and Sonny Jakiella are known associates of the male vic."

Jayme finished his sentence. "And of Thomas Reddick Jr., a.k.a. Luthor Reddick. Which means," she said, and looked straight at DeMarco, "that Joe Loughner might have hit the nail on the head."

But for the usual packed lanes from the Cranberry exit to the turnoff toward Pittsburgh, the Sunday morning traffic on I-79 had been conducive to reflection. DeMarco was eager to get north again to act upon the new information, and, were it not for his curiosity about the place called Lost City, he would have preferred to spend the day in Mercer County, where he and the team could maybe have things wrapped up by nightfall. It would be intense work—a lot more intense than driving. And he would welcome the distraction.

But now he was slowing for the exit ramp. Coasting to a stop. Where he sat there staring at the stop sign.

"Left," Miller reminded him.

"Yep," DeMarco said quickly, snapping out of it. "Toward Lone Pine." He made the turn, glanced in the rearview mirror, saw Boyd's Jeep not far behind.

The sun was coming straight through the windshield now, hard in his eyes, nearly blinding. DeMarco flipped down the visor but still he had to squint. Jayme popped open the console, took out his sunglasses and handed them to him. "Doing okay?" she asked.

He heard the concern in her voice. Smiled. "Let's not waste the day on this," he told her and Miller. "Thorough but quick."

She said, "You think this is inconsequential now?"

He shrugged. Tossed another smile her way. "I hear there's a great pizza place back in Washington. We can hit it on the way home."

But he knew by her look that she wasn't fooled. He had something else on his mind, and it certainly was not pizza.

FORTY-TWO

Y ou look familiar," DeMarco had said. "Do we know each other?" He nearly groaned aloud to hear the lamest pickup line of all time coming out of his mouth. But it was the only one he could think of. Besides, she did look familiar; she looked like a dream he had had a hundred times.

And to see her here, tonight, at the first high school basketball game he had attended in years. He had come on a whim because the routine was wearing him down, the long days of manning a radar gun or breaking up domestic arguments, long nights of studying for his corporal exam. She was working the concession stand where he purchased a bottle of water. The long bob of brown hair, large eyes and long chin and full, luscious mouth.

"I think I would remember you," she said. "I teach here."

"Name's Ryan," he said, and switched the perspiring bottle to his left hand, quickly dried his right hand on his slacks, then extended it over the counter. "I know I've seen you somewhere. Your face looks so familiar to me."

"Do you read poetry?" she asked, with a challenging tone that said she knew what was going on here, she had dealt with jerks like him her entire life.

"Does Willie Nelson count?"

She straightened, lifted her chin. Then laughed. Such music

in her voice! "Some people say I look like Sylvia Plath, the poet. Have you ever heard of her?"

"Isn't she with the Dixie Chicks?" he said, and made her laugh again, and knew suddenly that he was going to marry her, if for no other reason than the music of that laugh.

And over the next couple of years, Laraine taught him all about Plath and Dickinson, all the great poets and fiction writers and playwrights. She took him to readings and lectures, read to him in bed nearly every night, taught him to appreciate the alchemical power of story and the even more mysterious power of love. She made him a better man, and in turn he drove her to a humiliating promiscuity that culminated in a failed suicide attempt.

He thought he had gotten over that guilt, but it all came back to him that morning when Chase Miller first mentioned Amber Sullivan and her love for the poetry of Sylvia Plath. He hadn't talked to Laraine since August, hadn't called to ask how she was doing, or to ask her to file for divorce, as he had promised Jayme he would. And Amber's story broke his heart. In his mind's eye he pictured her as a young Laraine who had been knocked off course by drugs.

All the way to Washington County, the guilt and sadness had been scratching at a corner of his mind. In a strange, uneasy way, all the players seemed connected, like the pieces on a three-dimensional chessboard. If he were alone with Jayme now, he might tell her about it. She would say what she always said. *Just stop it, Ryan. You can't take care of the entire world, so just stop feeling guilty about it.*

She was so sensible, so right. Such wonderful medicine. He wished he could tell her that now. But Miller was seated two feet behind him, breathing down his neck, hanging on every word. And he resented Miller for being there, then immediately felt guilty for that resentment. The realization made him chuckle. *You are so messed up, DeMarco.*

"Got a tickle?" Jayme asked.

"Remind me to tell you later."

Miller leaned forward and stuck his head between them. "Up there on your right," he said. "You'll need to park in that pullout."

DeMarco flipped on the turn signal. "I thought you said you've never been here."

"Got excellent directions," Miller answered.

He was too glib sometimes. Too quick with a partial answer. DeMarco glanced in the mirror again. But Miller was grinning, peering out the windshield; he was loving this role he had cast himself in. Expedition leader.

Jayme must have noticed DeMarco's jaw tightening, because she reached across the console and patted his thigh. "Nice and easy today, okay, boss?" she said.

He eased the car off the side of the road, slipped the gearshift into Park, and shut off the engine. Then turned to look at her. Smiled. Said, "Weapon, please."

"Just curious," Miller said as Jayme removed both handguns and clips from the glove box, "but if I had a gun and a concealed carry permit, would you let me strap on too?"

For the first time in over an hour, DeMarco turned to look at him directly. "Dream on," he said.

FORTY-THREE

From the trunk of his car, DeMarco took two backpacks he had filled with bottled water and energy bars. He handed one to Boyd, then swung the other one onto his back. "Distribute as needed," he said.

Boyd slipped an arm through the shoulder strap. "Distribute to us or the people we talk to?"

"Yes," DeMarco said.

They were all dressed in civvies, doing their best to look like day hikers. Miller hurried five yards ahead, acting as if he knew the way. Then DeMarco and Jayme, with Boyd and Flores close behind, all four wearing paddle holsters concealed beneath untucked shirts. They had all dealt with homeless people before, knew that most were docile, a few full of rage, all of them unpredictable. Jayme carried a manila file folder containing several copies of Choo Choo's photo.

They followed a wide, deeply rutted trail through the pines, the ruts sparsely covered with browning grass, only the hump down the center showing signs of recent foot traffic. Somebody had carved out the road many years earlier, made it wide enough for heavy equipment to pass. It reminded DeMarco of old grassy lanes up in Mercer and nearby counties that frequently led to old farmsteads where nothing remained but a foundation gradually filling in with weeds.

The red pines on both sides of the road stood forty feet high, the ground beneath their branches matted with brown needles. Dry, broken branches and limbs lay everywhere. High in the canopy, a blue jay squawked its warning. Seed husks from a pine cone ticked down through the brittle limbs.

The topography of southwestern Pennsylvania seemed much hillier than it was an hour north, where the Allegheny Plateau leveled out just east of Mercer County. Here, West Virginia lay twenty miles west and forty south, with not much in between but hills and hollers, softly rounded ridges and deep, ancient valleys. DeMarco's heart soared in places like this. The sweet pine-scented air. The wide, unfettered spaces.

After twenty minutes of silent walking, they had their first glimpse of Lost City. It lay spread out on the side of a hill long ago cleared of all timber. From the edge of the pine forest, it looked like a box of twenty or so shipping containers dumped out by a giant, petulant child. Some lay on their sides, canted dangerously toward a creek at the bottom of the rocky valley. A couple were upside down. But most of them sat upright, often with one end resting atop boulders or logs to approximate a level setting. Two Porta-Johns were stationed at the far side of the encampment, their blue plastic hulls faded and dirty. Gray smoke could be seen rising from four or five different spots, all blending into a thin cloud high above the encampment, where it drifted northeast in a languorous breeze.

DeMarco recognized the scent of that smoke, full of sap and resin. After Iraq he had gone on several solo big two-hearted camping trips of his own, and had always looked for pine deadfalls for his fires; found the pop and snap of the burning wood comforting in the dark.

The site laid out below, however, was anything but comforting. "It looks half-abandoned," he said.

"As I mentioned yesterday," said Miller in a professorial tone, "most of the residents have headed south by now. Rumor has it that people have frozen to death here in the winter."

Jayme looked down upon the dented, rusted shipping containers. "I can't imagine having to live like this."

And Flores said, more softly, "I can."

The others turned to look at her, but she stared straight ahead.

DeMarco looked at her pretty face and the set of her jaw and the sudden hardness in her eyes. They reminded him of his own eyes when he was younger and of the eyes of fellow soldiers in Panama and Iraq. They had all been boys when they enlisted but their boyhoods hadn't lasted long enough.

Often back then he had heard the phrase *war makes men of boys*, which was said mostly by those who saw a little killing at a distance but not enough action up close to fully decimate the boy. A man grown from a decimated boy had small hope of ever outgrowing the damage. That was what war did but it was sometimes what life did too, not only to boys but also and maybe more frequently to girls. Flores's eyes were evidence of that. The only difference between the effects of war and the effects of life were that war did it faster. There was no subtlety in war or in life and nobody apologized for the casualties afterward.

Boyd stepped up beside DeMarco then and asked, "How do you want to do this?"

DeMarco blinked and brought himself back to the woods. "Same as Otter Creek," he said. "One badge per team. Miller, you can pick your team."

"How about I be my own team? I work better alone."

"Not safe," Jayme said, and DeMarco added, with a more somber look in Miller's direction, "Pick a team and stay with it. Flores and I will head over to the Porta-Johns and work our way back from there. You guys work toward us from the other end. Everybody grab a pic of Choo Choo from Jayme. We need to learn everything we can about him and anybody who came here with him. If nobody mentions Reddick, ask about him."

Flores gathered a photo from Jayme. With that, DeMarco gave Flores a nod, and they headed off. Half a minute later he looked over his shoulder; a resentful Miller was trudging along behind Jayme and Boyd.

FORTY-FOUR

On their half of the encampment, Flores and DeMarco spoke briefly with five individuals who considered themselves permanent residents. One skinny, scraggly man in his early thirties; one woman in her seventies, who bewitched DeMarco with her rosy cheeks and air of serenity; and one burly man in his fifties living with two women, one who looked old enough to be his mother, the other his daughter, though he claimed that both were his wives. Like the two solitary residents, this trio had made the shipping container their permanent home with pieces of scavenged or donated furniture and a combination furnace/stove fashioned from a metal drum and ductwork chimney.

Jayme and Trooper Boyd encountered a man who claimed to be a retired millionaire stockbroker from Pittsburgh who had come to Lost City to "get straight with God." A male and female couple who looked barely out of their teens—"We're the Warblers"— and who sat side by side on a ratty love seat, each with a cheap guitar resting on their laps. And a gnarled but robust man in his sixties who claimed to be the president of Lost City. His shipping container served both as his home and workshop. Hanging neatly from the walls was an array of antique wood chisels, files, rasps, handsaws, planers, and scrapers. Lined up along the walls were twenty or so crude sculptures of dogs, cats, ducks, geese, hawks, whales and other animals, some tiny, some as much as two feet tall, which he would sell from April through September at the craft fairs throughout Western Pennsylvania and Ohio.

"I have a buddy who swings by and picks me up every year," the man said. "He's a painter, works in oils. You'd be surprised how well we do. And the damn government don't get a penny of it."

When Jayme asked the man if he wouldn't rather be somewhere warm for the winter, he smiled as if at a child. "Do I look like a man who plays shuffleboard, sweetheart?"

Ninety minutes later, everyone but Miller met up at a doorless metal shed near the center of Lost City. Deep inside the interior was a haphazard pile of windfall branches and limbs gathered from the outlying woods, plus a few pieces of two-by-fours and other framing ripped from inside the unoccupied containers. A sawhorse and stump sat close to the open end, with an ax blade embedded in the stump. A skinny yellow dog came out from behind the wood to watch from a corner of the container, but the dog remained as soundless as the rest of the place. All that could be heard were a couple of jays squabbling in the woods.

DeMarco nodded, eyebrows pinched, at the dull brown object Jayme held in her left hand. "It's a duck," she explained, and showed him the little sculpture. "A mallard, he said. I thought you might like it." The unpainted wood showed every chisel mark and cut, with only the head and beak sanded smooth.

He set it in the palm of his hand. Crude, but somehow beautiful. Somehow delicate. As if the rough-cut facets and the tiny drill-hole eyes gave it life.

"Thank you," he said, and slipped it into a pocket. Then he looked around. "Where's Miller?"

Boyd said, "We turned around and he was gone. We haven't seen him since the top of the hill."

DeMarco told himself not to be angry. Not to be worried. He said, "Get anything we can use?"

Boyd said, "We emptied out half of the backpack on four people, two in the same container, but it didn't buy us much. Jayme took some notes."

She opened the manila folder and read what she had written. "Choo Choo liked his coke. Wished he could go back to Louisville but it was still too dangerous for him there. He wouldn't say why. Only that he hated all the effing hillbillies around here. All the effing dirt. Hated the Porta-Johns and had knocked one over when he was drunk on grain alcohol. Everybody was glad to see him go and hoped he never came back. And that's all anybody knows about him."

Flores said, "We got the same story. He was mean, short-tempered, and would steal anything that wasn't nailed down. And he did not like to share. Not a very neighborly attitude in a place where sharing is a means of survival."

"We got a little more about Suzi and Lady D," DeMarco told them. "Suzi was the Vietnamese girl. Thought to be under twenty-one, because she made some comment about not being able to get a drink in town. Lady D was closer to thirty. Had stretch marks from having at least one baby. And, allegedly, she would do anything and anybody for crack or heroin. They came here with Choo Choo and they left with Choo Choo. In the Santa Fe he stole in Kentucky. They weren't here for more than a couple of weeks. No idea why they left."

Boyd said, "That should be enough for us to ID them all. At least one of the three had to have left some kind of record behind. I'll call Carmichael and have him contact Louisville."

"At least it's something," DeMarco said. He looked around. "Where is that kid?"

Jayme took out her phone and called Miller's number. The call went to voicemail. She said, "Chase, we're pulling out. If you don't want to walk back home, meet us at the cars. We're heading back now."

They retraced their path through the pine forest, more somber now, Boyd and Flores in the lead and speaking softly to one another, DeMarco and Jayme a few yards behind. He touched the lump the duck carving made in his pocket. "Thanks again for the duck," he told her.

"He wanted to give it to me. Free. I gave him ten dollars anyway. You should have seen all the pieces he'd made."

DeMarco slipped his hand into hers. "It's strange, isn't it? We go in there feeling sorry for them, but they don't want our help. They just want to be left alone."

"They do seem happy. But they don't care much for the kind who come and go."

"Like Choo Choo, Suzi, and Lady D."

"Those three were running from something or somebody in Kentucky, I bet. Laid low here for a while. But what made them pick up and head for Otter Creek?"

DeMarco shook his head; he had no idea.

They were close enough to the cars to see them through the trees when running footsteps pounded up from behind. They turned. Miller and a girl. She looked tiny in a man's quilted coat, dirty orange, the sleeves nearly covering her fingers, the hem hanging mid-hip over baggy, rolled-up jeans.

Miller was grinning and out of breath, panting as he came to a halt in front of them and said, "We need to take her with us. She knows Reddick."

FORTY-FIVE

She looked young, too young, and DeMarco was reluctant to acquiesce on Miller's word alone, especially because Miller's story was so rushed and pixilated. "She needs to get out of here. The guy could come back anytime. She knows Reddick, Choo Choo, the females, but she doesn't want to be here anymore, needs to get her head straight. I told her she could come with us."

Jayme was looking back and forth from the girl's face to DeMarco's eyes, so when Miller stopped talking, DeMarco gave Jayme a little nod, then said to the girl, "Why don't you come sit in the car with Jayme and me for a minute while we figure this out?"

Jayme took the girl's hand and said, "We're not cops, sweetie. You're safe with us."

And when Jayme started walking toward the car, the girl, with a last frantic glance at Miller, followed along.

Miller started after her, until DeMarco touched his shoulder and said, "You wait here."

"Hey, I'm the one who found her. You wouldn't even have known—"

"Wait here," DeMarco said.

Jayme sat in the back with the girl, DeMarco in the front passenger seat, his body turned to face the girl as directly as possible. He smiled, but said nothing.

Jayme said, "What's your name, sweetie?"

"Cookie," the girl said. She looked no more than fifteen, frightened, her face with a few pale freckles, long hair too black for her skin, her fingernails short but painted black, ears poking through the stringy hair showing three piercings each but naked of any jewelry.

"What's your real name?" Jayme asked.

"Georgina," she said after a moment's hesitation. "My mother calls me Georgie."

"How old are you, Georgie?"

"I'm nineteen."

"You don't look it. Are you really?"

"I'll be twenty in February."

Every question Jayme asked was voiced as a compliment, lacking any suggestion of accusation. *She's so good at this*, DeMarco thought, and strove for the same tone when he said, "That's my birth month too. The twelfth. Aquarius. What are you?"

"I'm Aquarius too, but on the cusp. The eighteenth."

"Uh-oh," Jayme said. "I'm surrounded by Aquarians."

The girl smiled. Looked down at Jayme's hand still holding hers. Made no effort to withdraw it.

Jayme asked, "So did somebody bring you here against your will?"

Georgina shook her head. "I wanted to come. But I don't want to stay here anymore."

"Okay, we can help you with that. Right, Ryan?"

"Of course," he said.

"Who did you come here with?"

"Some guy."

"Oh, I know him," Jayme said, which made the girl's smile broaden.

Georgina said, "He picked me up in Wheeling. Told me he knew a place where life was easy. Where I could have anything I wanted."

"Did he hurt you in any way?" Jayme asked.

Another shake of her head, more adamant than the last. "I just… I don't want to do this stuff anymore. I want my life back."

"We can get you home if that's what you want. Where do you live?"

"It's not good there," the girl said. "That's why I left."

"Okay," Jayme said. "Do you have other relatives somewhere?"

"Yeah but I don't want to see any of them yet. Not the way I am now." The girl touched her hair, flicked a strand over her ear.

"What's your natural color?" Jayme asked. "Judging by your skin tone and those beautiful blue eyes, I'm going to guess brunette."

Georgina nodded. "It needs cut too. I don't like it this long."

Jayme squeezed her hand. "Sweetie, we'll take you anywhere you want to go. You're an adult, so it's your choice to make."

The girl thought for a few moments before she spoke, then did so with her eyes cast down. "I think I need to be around other people for a while. People who can help me stay on track."

Jayme nodded. Patted Georgina's hand. Then turned to DeMarco. "Ryan?" she said. "What do you think?"

"I think," he said, "we need to get us some lunch and figure out the best options. Anybody here like pizza?"

Georgina lifted her eyes to his and smiled.

"I knew it," he said. "Aquarians *love* pizza."

He turned in his seat, popped open the door, climbed out and called to the others, who were waiting beside Boyd's Jeep, "Pizza on me! Chase, you can ride with Boyd and Flores."

Miller's sullen glower bloomed red. "Why can't I—?"

But then DeMarco was inside his car, and slammed shut the door.

FORTY-SIX

Not only did DeMarco not want Chase Miller participating in the rest of the conversation, he did not want Boyd and Flores eavesdropping and making Georgina nervous. As he drove toward the interstate, he told his phone, "Pizza shops Washington PA," then handed the phone to Jayme.

"Whoa," she said as she scrolled through the list. "Over twenty places. This town loves pizza."

"Any with New York style?" DeMarco asked.

"Hmm…yep. Ricci's? Plus it's the only one with five stars."

"Gets my vote," he said.

She punched it in and passed the phone back to DeMarco. He took a quick glance at the screen before setting the phone in the cup holder. Eighteen minutes. He set the cruise control at 55.

"I'm curious." He glanced in the rearview mirror. "How did you and Chase find each other?"

"What do you mean?" Georgina said.

"I guess what I meant is, where were you today when he found you?"

"Where I told him I would be."

I knew it! he thought. This time he looked in the rearview mirror toward Jayme, and found her questioning eyes meeting his.

"So I guess you must have heard us knocking," Jayme said to

the girl. "Between the four of us, we hit every door or looked inside every single container."

"Yeah, we were in one of them," Georgina told her. "Chase said just to ignore it, we'd catch up with you soon. Which we did."

"Gotcha," Jayme said.

DeMarco asked, "So how long have you and Chase known each other?"

"I don't really know him. I just met him today. My friend Lori said I could trust him."

"And Lori lives up our way?" he asked as nonchalantly as he could.

"She lives near Jamestown. Where the dam is? I've never been there. She says there's a place where there are so many fish that—"

DeMarco chimed in to finish the sentence. "—the ducks walk on their backs. Yeah, I know that place. It's a big attraction up there."

"That's what Lori said."

"So I guess Lori and Chase must be friends?" DeMarco asked.

"She said she sees him at the Goodwill store sometimes. He works there. He was asking her about some other people whose names I must've mentioned to her, those ones who got murdered, and she called to tell me about that. And then I guess she must've told him that I was looking for a ride out."

"Well, that makes sense," DeMarco said. "I just wish Chase had told us we were coming to pick you up."

"I'm sorry," Georgina said. "I thought you knew."

"Don't worry," Jayme told her. "All that matters is you're here, right? We got to meet each other."

Georgina said, "I don't know why he didn't tell you."

"Hey, that's Chase," DeMarco said. "That name is perfect for him, isn't it? We have to chase him down to get any information out of him." He hoped she couldn't see the flush of anger in his neck. He said, "Georgina, how long has it been since you've had a good piece of New York–style pizza?"

"Long time," she said.

"It's my favorite. And if you say it's your favorite too…I just might start believing in astrology."

Four seconds later, she said, coquettishly, while sharing a secret grin with Jayme, "It's my favorite too."

FORTY-SEVEN

Pepperoni pizza, salads, iced tea and coffee. Jayme was quick to seat Georgina between herself and DeMarco, with Flores, Boyd, and Miller across the table from them. The troopers followed Jayme's lead and kept the tone of their questions light, allowing Jayme to do most of the questioning, with Boyd silent as usual, Flores offering only an infrequent comment. On occasion, when DeMarco sensed a heaviness descend on the young woman, he leaned close to tease her or crack a joke. Miller made a single attempt to join the conversation, but, when his comment was ignored, he seemed content to slouch in his chair and glower.

Jayme: "So where did you say you're from originally? Was it Wheeling?"

Georgina: "We lived outside the city."

DeMarco: "It's freezing cold in here, isn't it?"

Georgina: "Not really."

DeMarco: "What's that coat rated for? Minus forty?"

Georgina grinned, eyes averted. "I wouldn't know."

DeMarco: "It's none of my business, but you might find it easier to eat if your sleeves weren't dangling in your food."

Georgina unzipped her coat and shrugged it off so that it hung over the back of her chair. "Does that make you happy?"

DeMarco: "If it makes you happy."

Her body seemed diminished by half without the coat, arms and shoulders thin in a red Oglebay Festival of Lights T-shirt.

Flores, with a nod at the T-shirt: "I've always wanted to go there. Is it as pretty as people say?"

Georgina, with a shrug: "I guess."

DeMarco to himself: *She comes from money.* The way she held her knife and fork. Her enunciation.

Except for the passive-aggressive attitude, her mannerisms were more like Jayme's than anyone else's at the table, all four of the others with blue-collar backgrounds. The difference between her and Jayme, he guessed, was that Jayme had grown up loved, handled gently, supported in all she did. Georgina's pitch-black hair, the chewed black fingernails, the thrift store coat, the drug use and other behavior he didn't want to think about…it all pointed to a life of polite disdain and belittlement that grew into a desire to hurt those who had hurt her.

But now she had grown to despise herself, who she had made herself into. How quickly she had responded to his and Jayme's kindness! Just as Hero had.

Jayme: "Would you mind if we talk a little about Luthor Reddick now? It would be helpful if Troopers Boyd and Flores hear this too."

Georgina: "Do you think he killed those people?"

Jayme: "We just don't know that yet."

Miller: "He went to Lost City to buy drugs. This whole thing is about drugs. Drugs and prostitution. Tell them, Georgie."

She lowered her head, dropped her hands away from the table.

Miller: "He had a connection with her boyfriend and—"

DeMarco raised a finger and cut Miller off with a look. Then, to Georgina: "As far as you know, what was Reddick up to when you met him?"

Georgina: "He was talking to the guy I came there with."

Jayme: "About what in particular?"

Georgina: "Buying drugs. Crack."

DeMarco: "Who was doing the buying?"

Georgina: "Reddick wanted to. But Slick didn't have it on him. He said he could get his hands on four or five cookies to start."

DeMarco thought, *Crack cookies. And her nickname is Cookie.*

Jayme: "So they made a deal?"

Georgina nodded. "They shook hands. But it wasn't long after that we heard about what happened to Choo Choo. I woke up two mornings ago and Slick was gone."

Jayme: "You think he was afraid the same thing would happen to him?"

Georgina: "He was scared, I know that. We both were. I still am."

DeMarco: "You're with us now. Nobody is going to let you come to harm. Okay?"

Georgina: "Okay."

Flores: "I'm a little confused about the whole timeline here. When did you meet Choo Choo, Lady D, Suzi, and Reddick? Was it all at the same time?"

Georgina nodded again. "They came back with Reddick about…a month ago? It was right after Slick and I got here. Slick sold them some weed and coke. That was the first time I saw any of them. Lady D told me they used to live there. And Reddick, he was…"

DeMarco: "Take your time."

Georgina: "He told Slick he ought to put me to work. Said he had a clientele that would make us all a lot of money. And I told him to go screw himself."

DeMarco: "Good girl."

Jayme: "And it was how long before you heard about the murders that Reddick came to talk about the crack cookies?"

Georgina: "A couple weeks maybe? But almost right away the deal for the cookies fell through. Slick told Reddick by phone, said he'd keep trying, and then he told me afterward that Reddick was seriously pissed. So when we heard about what happened to Choo Choo and the girls…"

DeMarco: "Gentleman Slick up and disappeared on you."

Georgina nodded; sat with her hands in her lap. "That's everything I know about them," she said.

Jayme: "You did great, sweetheart."

"I mean," the girl began. Then she shook her head and looked down at the table.

Softly, because of the glimmer of moisture in her eyes, DeMarco asked, "You mean what?"

After a few moments, she raised her eyes to him. "I keep thinking about D and what happened to her. Her and Suzi both. But D and I were friends."

He nodded, said nothing, held her gaze with the softness of his own.

"She wanted out of all of that craziness too. She just wanted to go home."

He said, "Lady D told you this?"

She answered with a nod. "It was just that one time that we talked. But I don't know. I liked her. We both knew we'd screwed up our lives. We just didn't know how to make things right again."

He asked, "Was Choo Choo holding them against their will?"

"He wasn't tying them up or anything like that but," and again she shook her head. "You can't understand until you've been there."

DeMarco did not intend to refute her, though he believed that he did understand. Threats, drugs, maybe a nasty slap now and then. Rape, probably. All these would have been Choo Choo's tools. Break down an already splintered spirit, take away her last shred of dignity and self-worth. No wonder D had seemed sad and aloof to Miller's contact. And no wonder Georgina and she had become friends so quickly. Two gullible girls from nice homes. And the one who called herself Sylvia made a third.

DeMarco leaned close to Georgina and whispered. "You're going to be okay. You're out of it now."

When she leaned up against him, burying her face in DeMarco's shoulder, Miller shoved his chair away from the table, startling everybody with the shriek of the metal feet. Face red, he stood. "I'm going to the bathroom." Turned and strode away.

Georgina stared after him, then asked, "What did I do?"

"Not a thing," DeMarco told her. He smiled across the table at Flores and Boyd. "Too much iced tea for me too. Excuse me, please."

Quietly he pushed back his chair, stood, and crossed to the restroom.

FORTY-EIGHT

Miller was standing with his hands on the edge of a sink, leaning close to the mirror, cursing at the glass. The door swung open, and there was DeMarco. He stepped inside and let the door fall shut behind him. "This isn't your show," he said.

Were it not for the flicker of fear in Miller's eyes, he would have rained fire down upon the young man. Miller stood motionless for a few seconds, then straightened, and released a breath. He placed a hand under the soap dispenser, then both hands under the faucet, which sprayed water into his palms.

It was the first time DeMarco had been alone with the boy, and the banality of their situation, the boy intently soaping and washing his hands so as not to look DeMarco in the eye, brought DeMarco a sudden understanding. He knew of people who had had wonderful childhoods filled with large families that loved and protected them and took them on vacations to places that now existed in their memories as magical wonderlands peopled by humorous characters and creatures. Everything in those memories was warm and bright and healthy and wise. Jayme had memories like that and she loved to talk about them and they always made DeMarco nostalgic for what he had never experienced. He had no memories of his own that did not make him sad or angry or ashamed of himself. Except for his memories of being alone in the woods. In his own best memories he was always alone, and now as a man beginning the autumn of his life he had come to realize that this was not a healthy way to be.

He had learned to recognize this kind of childhood in others as well. He might not know the particulars of their unhappiness but he could see the damage it had done and the way it made them now as adults. When you have no warm and comforting memories into which to retreat, you are always pushing forward toward an imagined happiness that can never be achieved. You are always trying to prove yourself worthy of love and respect and worthy of existence. If you are lucky you will grow to have moments when you know that you are as worthy as anybody else, but those moments will be fleeting and you will find no comfort in them in the dark of the night. The night itself will be your comfort because it hides you from the eyes of others, just as the woods always hid DeMarco as a boy. He could feel comfort and confidence in the woods because trees and birds and squirrels did not look at you with disdain and contempt. Well, sometimes the squirrels did but only because you had invaded their territory. They had a territorial right to their contempt. But when you grow up judging yourself in the damning eyes of another, no amount of logic will ever fully erase the damage. For you the past will never be a wonderland and your ability to find a satisfying future will always be in doubt.

That was why he knew he had to go easy on the boy. He could start by not thinking of him as a boy. Miller was a young man in earnest pursuit of his destiny and he deserved to be treated like one, even if he made lots of mistakes along the way. How many mistakes had DeMarco made, and well before he'd reached Miller's age? Too many, and most of them far more severe than any Miller had made or was likely to make.

"You did good work," DeMarco told him, no longer angry, his voice firm but soft. "But you withheld information from us. You manipulated us. Because you wanted to look like the big shot. Like you were in charge of it all."

"You never would have found her without me."

"You need to shut up and listen," DeMarco told him. "Don't talk."

Miller drew away from the faucet. Stood there with his hands dripping water.

"No," DeMarco told him. "We would not have found her without you. That's what I was referring to when I said you did good work. But you let your ego run wild. You used me, Jayme, and Georgina to make yourself feel important. And that's not why we do this work, Chase. If you want to keep doing it with us, you need to understand that. Otherwise, you're done. I will not allow your ego to jeopardize this investigation."

He paused for a moment to let it sink in. "However. I am willing to cut you some slack this time. This one time. You need to learn what I had to learn. What everybody out there at that table had to learn. Our job is to serve and protect. To do what's right not because it makes us look good but because it's the right thing to do, no matter how tired or lonely or sad it makes us. No matter how little thanks or recognition we get from it. Because it's not about us. We do it because helping people is the right thing to do. It's as simple as that."

He paused; wasn't used to making such speeches. He could only hope that he had made his point. "Is that something you are capable of learning?"

Miller looked like he wanted to melt into the sink and slide away down the drain. Finally, he nodded. "I'm sorry."

DeMarco held his gaze for a moment before speaking. "Boyd will drive you back to your car. We'll be in touch."

He turned, exhausted, pulled open the door, and returned to the dining room.

FORTY-NINE

After Boyd's Jeep pulled out of the parking lot and drove away, DeMarco and Georgina sat in the front seat of his idling car while Jayme, in the back, scrolled through web pages on her laptop. "There's one women's shelter in Washington," she said. "It appears to have a good training and education component. There are also several to choose from in Pittsburgh. It's your choice to make, Georgina."

The young woman turned in her seat. To Jayme, she said, "What's it like where you live?"

"Small towns mostly. Lots of cornfields. Not much in the way of nightlife or other excitement."

"That sounds good to me," Georgina said.

Jayme shot a look at DeMarco via the rearview mirror.

He said, "I'm not sure it's a good idea to have you so close to Reddick."

"How will he know where I am?"

Jayme said, "He won't. But let me ask you this, sweetie. You said you want to get straight. Should we be searching for a rehab facility instead of a women's shelter?"

"I'm not addicted," Georgina told her. "I just need a reason to not use. People who will help me."

DeMarco said, "And you don't want your family to do that?"

She shook her head no. "They're the reason I'm like this."

He said, softly, "Your reaction to them is the reason you're like this."

She nodded. "I know. I just want to be…" She looked down, blew out a breath, moved her head back and forth.

Jayme said, with her eyes on the mirror again, "There's a good place in New Castle. That's only twenty minutes from where we live. We can stay in touch by phone, help you find a job when you're ready…"

"I think I'd like to go back to school."

"That would be great," DeMarco told her. "Though even the state schools aren't cheap."

"Money's not a problem," she said.

"Well then. Shall we make a stop in New Castle? Have a look at the place?"

She lifted her eyes to his. "Thank you for everything." Then to Jayme. "Thank you so much."

"Hey, no tears," DeMarco told her, blinking. "We'll flood this car. Buckle up, buttercup."

She grinned at him and pulled the harness across her chest.

Out on the road, he said, "One last thing. Are you attached to that orange monstrosity you call a coat?"

"I hate it," she told him.

"Ms. Matson?" he said. "Suggestions?"

"Exit 59A to 376. The Galleria at Pittsburgh Mills."

FIFTY

B y the time they had bought a new coat and a few other articles of clothing for Georgina, then drove to New Castle and got her checked in at the women's shelter, then drove the last eighteen miles home, Miller's car was long gone from the curb out front and the light had faded to a crepuscular gray, the air noticeably cooler.

DeMarco drove around the corner and parked next to Jayme's vehicle and the RV in the backyard. Immediately the new motion sensors filled the yard with a startling brilliance. "Wow," Jayme said softly. "I didn't know it would be so bright." A moment later, both her phone and his beeped an alarm.

"The system works," he said.

"You don't sound very happy about it."

"I don't think we'll ever look at this place the same way we used to."

"Which is strange, seeing as how it's now maybe the only place we can count on being safe."

He frowned. "Khatri got what he wanted, didn't he?"

"You think this is what he wanted?"

"I do."

He shut off the engine but made no move to open the car door. Kept looking through the windshield at the yard, the brick path leading up to his porch, the neat little house where he had been happy for a while, the happiest he had ever been, then the most sorrowful he had ever been, then happy again thanks to Jayme. And now…

"What I wonder," Jayme said, "is just how far Khatri will go. He could have killed us with a bigger explosive but didn't. Will the next one be bigger?"

"It would be unwise not to expect an exponential growth in his attacks."

"So you *do* think he will try to kill us?"

He turned to look at her. Felt a warm flush of shame and guilt. Took her hand and said, with a smile that could not hide his sadness, "You're the one with a master's degree in psychology. You tell me."

She nodded. "He'll need more and more titillation. Until finally only one thing will satisfy him. The change could take a long time, or it might be immediate."

They sat in silence for a few minutes. When the motion sensor lights blinked off, the effect was palpable—a heaviness to the twilight; a chill.

"In the meantime," he told her, "we need to keep our heads in *this* game. It's just getting so freaking crowded, though."

"It's been a long day, hasn't it, babe? I'm sorry if dealing with all those people has worn you out."

"I'll live."

"What did you say to Chase in the restroom? He came out looking properly chastised."

"I went easy on him, I think. Tried to anyway. Remembered all the mistakes I made when I was his age, and how his mistakes don't even compare."

"He's so hungry for your approval," she told him. "We all are. Why do you have that effect on us, DeMarco?"

"Search me," he said. Because he truly did not understand. He counted himself among the least impressive of men. As far as he could tell, the only virtue he held in abundance was that of defiance. He had spent his life defying the forces of the universe trying to destroy him. Pain, loneliness, betrayal, death—he had stood up to all of them, and was doing so even now. But he did not count that as courage or strength or intelligence; just the opposite. An ox-like stubbornness. Obstinacy was the best response he could muster, and it certainly was not a virtue to admire.

"Will we be going in the house tonight?" Jayme teased. "Or should I make myself comfortable in the back seat?"

He returned her smile. "I have always found that sitting in a car is a good way to gather one's thoughts."

"Okay," she said. "Let's gather them."

"Sonny Jakiella. That scrawny burnout Boyd identified from the video."

"And who is probably the same burnout Chase's contact saw handling the drugs for Choo Choo. With Amber Sullivan, a.k.a. Sylvia, also in the car."

"Jakiella was last seen driving into Reddick's place yesterday afternoon. A red Corolla."

"Correct," she said. "And as of this morning, his vehicle had not been seen leaving the property."

"Burnouts rattle easily. Especially if we suggest holding him in a cell for seventy-two hours. But I don't want to approach him at Reddick's place. Don't want to show Reddick our hand yet."

"According to Boyd's intel, Jakiella lives and works in Conneaut Lake. He has to leave Reddick's place sooner or later."

"So, first thing tomorrow, we go have a look at the IR camera in Otter Creek. And, with luck…"

She nodded. "So can we go inside now? I miss my Hero."

"I do too."

She popped open her door. "Are we bad parents for leaving him home alone all day?"

"Let's go ask him."

The moment they stepped out of the car, the motion sensor lights flared back on. Then their phones beeped. She said, "This could get annoying really fast."

"It already has," he said.

FIFTY-ONE

After returning to the station house in midafternoon, Flores and Boyd went to their desks, Flores to write up a report of their day's activities, Boyd to coax more information out of his computer regarding their growing list of persons of interest.

Not even halfway through her report, Flores was sent out on a call. A single vehicle incident, Route 58, two miles northwest of Grove City. No injuries reported.

She checked out a unit and drove 7.2 miles to find a blue Ford F150 axle-deep in the mud and high weeds, facing south fifteen feet off the northbound lane. The only visible damage to the vehicle was the driver's side mirror, sheared off when the vehicle slid past a telephone pole. The driver was seated in the vehicle with his hands on the top of the steering wheel, his head laid back against the headrest.

She spoke first with two bikers standing in a yard off the southbound lane; one of the bikers had called in the accident. Both bikers had been following the truck for several miles, had watched it swerving erratically and had dropped back to a safe distance only to see the vehicle cut across the highway for no visible reason and sail into the weeds. They had spoken with the driver, who claimed to have fallen asleep.

Flores walked across the road and checked in with the driver. Fell asleep, he sheepishly repeated. Just finished a double shift. Had already called a tow truck. Thank God he hadn't hit an oncoming vehicle.

She walked back across the road and thanked the bikers for reporting the accident. No sign of intoxication, she told them. She believed his story. Feel free to continue your ride. Be safe.

She cited the driver for careless driving, the least severe penalty, but assured him that if it happened again he would be cited for reckless driving or even criminal manslaughter in the worst-case scenario. She then waited in her vehicle for the tow truck to arrive. Watched the bikers still standing in the yard, in no hurry to leave, laughing and telling each other stories, no doubt. She wished she could climb out and join then and listen to their stories. *Where do you go on your rides?* she would ask. *What's the most interesting place you have been?*

Both bikers were in their fifties at least, their faces tanned and lined but in a way she found attractive. The taller one especially. He was slender and graying and spoke only occasionally, happy to let the other man do most of the talking. There was a stillness to him that she found very appealing. A quiet kind of contentment sparkling in his eyes.

But it would be too awkward to approach them now. She would look foolish. Needy. She refused to give that appearance to anyone. Never again.

She waited until the tow truck driver pulled into position to winch the pickup onto the flatbed. Then she returned to the station house to finish both incident reports.

It was her seventh day on duty in a row and she was scheduled now for five days off. She felt the slide into depression beginning as she parked at the curb in front of her apartment above the hardware store. She hadn't eaten anything all day but for two slices of pizza and a small salad, and knew that when the depression fully bloomed she would not have the energy to make anything or go out to a restaurant. So she walked to the Sheetz and bought three sandwiches to go—one six-inch steak sub, one pulled pork, and one Italian. She carried these back home and put all but the steak sub in the refrigerator. She sat at the kitchen table and unwrapped the sub and took a bite, but though the meat and cheese were still warm, her taste buds were already shutting down, going offline until further notice. Still, she finished the sandwich, if for no other reason than not wanting to have to contend with hunger later, then balled up the wrapper and put it in the trash, then drank from the bottle of orange juice in the refrigerator, the juice soured by too much oxygen, which made her tell herself, sourly, *Just like me.*

In the bedroom she changed her clothes, put on a pair of sweats and a T-shirt and looked at the bed and thought about lying down. But lying down was always a dangerous thing to do. Lying down meant staring at the ceiling and hearing the town lapse into quietude and darkness. She would fall asleep too early, then awaken at one in the morning, unable to go to sleep again.

She could maybe slide her little keyboard from beneath the bed and get her journal and write another song about loneliness and heartbreak, but that was the epitome of futility too. She would only make herself even more depressed. She had no talent and no training and who did she think she was, anyway? She was no Taylor Swift, no Katy Perry, no anybody.

She returned to the living room and plopped into the corner of the sofa with her feet tucked beneath her and turned on the TV. Early that morning she had watched *Fox & Friends* while she dressed for work, as she did every morning, and now Martha MacCallum was discussing the world's news. Flores thought about switching to Epix on Demand and selecting her favorite mature audience offering. But that was dangerous too because afterward she would start crying and there was no telling how long that would last. So she watched Martha MacCallum and then Tucker Carlson, and the voices droning and scolding and arguing were a good antidote for a while. But eventually her attention and resistance ebbed and she told herself *oh grow up, there's not a damn thing wrong with it*, and switched the channel to Epix on Demand.

Later, when she was curled up and sobbing, with a full darkness filling the window and a long empty week stretching ahead of her, and with the scent of cigarette smoke drifting up from the kids who liked to hang out in the hardware store entryway after dark, and with nothing and nobody in her life full of nothings and nobodies, she lay there staring at the glass and told herself *you can call Boyd if you have to, you can call DeMarco, you can call Jayme*, but soon told herself *no you can't, you can't, you can't*. She would have to wait this out as she always did. She wasn't her mother, she was a Pennsylvania state trooper now. She was living her dream, wasn't she? She had nothing left to prove to anybody. She was exactly where she had always hoped to be. As always, she would have to endure the misery of her downtime alone.

FIFTY-TWO

"Y ou feel like meeting us up in Conneaut Lake this morning?" Jayme asked. "I know you're off today, but Boyd said you might be available."

It was barely 8:30 in the morning, the air still gauzy with the last lingering wisps of fog. After reviewing the video from the camera mounted on Mr. Shaner's porch along Linn Tyro Road in Otter Creek Township and seeing the red Corolla departing Luthor Reddick's driveway at 1:48 that very morning, DeMarco had first telephoned Boyd, who reported that his plate was full until later that afternoon. DeMarco did not want to wait, and so, when told that Flores was off duty, he handed his phone to Jayme and told her, "See what you can do."

Flores, who was lying in bed staring at the ceiling when the phone rang, feeling too ponderous to move, all but shouted "No problem!" in response to Jayme's query. And suddenly the weight that had been sitting on her chest dissolved. She sat up, swung her feet over the edge of the bed, stood and headed for the bathroom. "Where and when do you want to meet?"

"We're a little over twenty miles away, but it's local roads so, even if we left now, we couldn't be at Jakiella's place until a quarter after nine."

"I'll shoot up 79 and then swing over on 285 West. Give me ten minutes to get on the road?" She put her phone on speaker and laid it on the corner of the sink while she loaded her toothbrush with paste.

"Whatever you need. So you'll be coming in on Water Street?"

"Correct."

"Then let's meet at the Sheetz there. Say...9:30ish?"

"Excellent!" Flores said. "See you soon!" A second later she had the toothbrush in her mouth and was simultaneously soaking a washcloth with warm water. She tried washing her face with her left hand and brushing with her right but it did not work, too much mutually occupied territory, and no hand free for the liquid soap. So she draped the washcloth over the edge of the basin, and, while brushing and gargling, shimmied out of her sweatpants and T-shirt before grabbing the cloth again and doing a quick once-over of her body.

She really wanted a coffee but figured she could run on adrenaline for another thirty minutes. Or she could grab a coffee at the station house. She needed to check in with Captain Bowen anyway to get his okay. Earlier she had been a useless slug of nothingness but now she could do anything she put her mind to.

It felt good to be so unexpectedly alive again. She loved being with Jayme and DeMarco, even though she wondered if there might be something sick about that. Headed north, however, with the light pouring in through the passenger window, she had no doubts that hers was a healthy kind of attraction. They made her feel good about herself, about who she was and where she was headed. She saw her own potential in them. She was only messed up in the darkness or alone. In uniform she was purposeful and resolute. In uniform she was living the dream.

FIFTY-THREE

S onny Jakiella's home near the corner of South Fourth and Richmond Streets, with the blue Conneaut Lake Area Ambulance Service building across the street, was as far as a resident could get, both in miles and merriment, from the lake to which locals and tourists swarmed every summer and that had given both the historic amusement park and the town their names.

Back in the summer before DeMarco's senior year in high school, when the amusement park and hotel were fully operational, he had brought a girl to the park one afternoon and spent the day with her riding the Blue Streak and the Tilt-A-Whirl and the bumper cars, playing arcade games and eating boardwalk fries and making out on the little beach beside the Beach Club. He could remember her face now and the way she had lifted her mouth to his for their first kiss, but her name was gone from his memory.

He thought it strange how he could feel that experience as if it still lingered several blocks behind him as he knocked on Sonny Jakiella's door, as if the boy and girl were still kissing their first kiss, the girl's lips salty from the fries, the couple patiently hanging out in the haunted hotel lobby waiting for his return.

He knocked a second time, waited, then turned to Jayme and Flores. To Jayme he said, "You have the address for the contractor's office?"

She held up her phone.

He gazed east over her shoulders. Could almost smell the corn dogs and hear the laughter of the long-gone children splashing in the lake. Their laughter when he was young and kissing a girl he did not love had only made him lonelier. He had wondered then if he would ever love or be able to love somebody.

He smiled at Jayme and Flores and felt better and said, "Let's roll."

⇒⸻⸻⸻⸻⸻⸻⇐

"I knew that man would be trouble sooner or later," the office manager had told them.

She was a stern-looking woman in her late fifties, broad and full-bodied, with enough makeup on her face to make three corpses presentable. She had provided the address of the new home build the contractor was supervising, and had confirmed that Jakiella was on-site. With that information in hand, DeMarco said, "We need to ask you to not notify your boss or Mr. Jakiella that we are on our way."

That was when the office manager, scowling, shook her head. "I knew that man would be trouble sooner or later."

"Why do you say that?" Jayme asked.

"You can tell just by looking at him. He's a loser. The only reason Mark puts up with him is because electricians are hard to find these days. Especially ones who will work piecemeal. So I suppose I should start beating the bushes for a new one?"

DeMarco smiled. "You might want to hold off on that for a bit."

"I'd just as soon be rid of him," she said. "If it wasn't for his ex and their kids…"

"Are the names Choo Choo or Luthor Reddick familiar to you?" he asked.

"Never heard of either one of them. And I have a strong feeling I don't want to."

"Thank you for your time," he said.

FIFTY-FOUR

While the contractor and three of his other employees watched, Sonny Jakiella walked the trio of investigators across the hardened mud surrounding the large two-story, three-stall garage build. The home had been roofed and wrapped with Tyvek but the interior was unfinished. They had found Jakiella installing electrical boxes and switches to the naked two-by-fours framing the interior walls. Now he walked slowly toward the rear of the property, taking his time as, with trembling fingers, he drew a cigarette from the pack and lit it and released a stream of smoke.

The thinness of Jakiella's face accentuated the size of his nose and ears and the sharpness of his chin. His fingers too seemed unnaturally long, the fingernails yellowed by nicotine, his arms as thin as a child's. He hadn't shaved in a couple of days, probably hadn't changed his clothes either: a sweat-stained camo ball cap, a gray long-sleeved Henley shirt with all four buttons undone at the neck, dirty blue jeans worn white at the knees and with cuffs that bunched up atop dirty black sneakers.

He turned near the edge of the property, stood crookedly with one knee locked, the other cocked to the right, his shoulders hunched. He kept his head down for another long drag. Then lifted his eyes to DeMarco. "So what's this about?" he said.

"What were you doing at the home of Luthor Reddick this past weekend?"

"Who says I was there?"

"Our surveillance camera. You arrived in your Corolla on Saturday afternoon, left early this morning. Would you like the exact times?"

Jakiella's smile was weak; it lifted only one corner of his mouth. "Since when is it a crime to spend time with a buddy?"

"What kind of business is your buddy in?"

"Antiques and such. You looking to buy something?"

"I'm looking for information about him. And about a man named Choo Choo, a woman named Suzi, and another woman called Lady D."

Jakiella was doing his best to appear nonchalant, working hard to keep his body still, but tiny twitches kept erupting everywhere. His mouth, his nose, his eyebrows, his fingers, his right leg. One every fifteen seconds or so. "Sorry to say you made the trip for nothing. I don't know nothing about nobody."

With her next breath, Flores discovered that she was downwind of Jakiella and quickly suppressed the ensuing wince; he reeked of the burned hay scent of weed and the distinctive vinegary stench of old sweat infused with black tar heroin. She said, "We have a witness who claims otherwise."

"What witness?" he asked.

Flores said, "How about pushing your sleeves up for us."

"How about showing me your breasts."

Flores smiled. He was afraid; otherwise he would have said *tits*.

"Look," DeMarco told him. "We know you were in charge of the drugs when Choo Choo was out dealing. He was driving the stolen Santa Fe from Kentucky, and you were in the passenger seat. We know that Amber 'Sylvia' Sullivan was in that vehicle at the same time."

Something like a snarl pulled at Jakiella's mouth. He said, "She don't go by either one of them names."

"Which names?" Jayme asked.

"Amber or Sylvia. We call her Sully."

DeMarco said, "Who do you mean by 'we'?"

"I mean me, okay? To me and her, she's always been Sully."

Flores read the shadow in his eyes. She said, "Because Sylvia is her working name, right? And Amber is who she used to be."

His lips parted as if he were about to speak. But then only a small breath escaped. Followed softly by, "You don't need to be asking about her."

DeMarco said, "When did you and Sully first meet?"

Another incipient snarl. "I don't remember."

DeMarco reached toward his back pocket. "Let's see if you remember this." And produced from his pocket a square of folded paper. He unfolded it twice, then held the photo of Choo Choo in front of Jakiella's face, the photo showing a shaft of rebar protruding from Choo Choo's throat.

Jakiella's face went white, then alarmingly red as he looked away. His hand shook as he raised the cigarette to his lips again. "That's a helluva thing to be flashing around in front of people."

Jayme said, "It must have been even worse to see it in person."

"I have no idea what you're talking about, lady."

DeMarco gave the paper a shake. "You have no idea who did this?"

"How would I know something like that?"

DeMarco looked down at Jakiella's shoes. Then at Flores. "Trooper, did you happen to bring the photos of those impressions we took at the scene?" Before she could answer, DeMarco asked Jakiella, "What size are those?"

Flores said, "They look like the right size to me. Same tread pattern too, I bet."

Jayme said, "You have two daughters, right, Mr. Jakiella? Eleven and eight years old?"

He was visibly trembling now. Shivering. "What's that have to do with anything?"

"Think of what's going to happen to them," Jayme said, "when you can't pay child support. Because you're sitting on death row."

Jakiella jabbed a finger at the photo. "I had nothing to do with that. I wasn't there or anywhere near it."

"Who was?" DeMarco asked.

Jakiella swallowed. Blinked. Worked up a gob of yellowish phlegm and hawked it off to the side. His head moved jerkily, bobbed back and forth like a pigeon's.

Jayme said, "You doing okay, Mr. Jakiella? Not going to pass out on us, are you?"

He said, "If I'm going to be arrested, I'm not telling you nothing."

Flores said, "Did anybody here say anything about arresting you?"

"You're sure acting like you're going to."

DeMarco said, "At this point, we are more interested in Luthor Reddick than in you."

"So does that mean you're going to arrest me or not?"

"What I am going to do," DeMarco told him, "is to ask three questions. If you answer honestly, we might just let you walk away from here and go back to work. If you don't, Trooper Flores will take you in for questioning while we get a warrant to search your house and car. Afterward, whether we find anything in your home and vehicle or not, you will be arrested for obstructing justice and interfering with a criminal investigation. We are fully prepared to do that. Am I right, Trooper Flores?"

She laid a hand on the restraints attached to her belt.

"What are the questions?" Jakiella asked.

"One: Is anyone else living in or a regular visitor to Reddick's house, and, if so, who are they? Two: What kind of business does Reddick really operate out of that house? And three: What was the association between Choo Choo and Reddick?"

"Huh," Jakiella said. "That sounds like more than three questions to me."

Jayme said, "The clock is ticking, Mr. Jakiella."

"Am I getting immunity for this? Cause if there's nothing in it for me, I got nothing to say."

DeMarco asked, "Why would you need immunity unless you were directly involved?"

"*Were* you directly involved?" Jayme asked.

"I already told you I wasn't." His body was sagging, going limp.

"We need your full cooperation," Flores told him, her voice empty of all harshness, almost plaintive. "Think about your daughters, Sonny. Think about how your actions are going to screw up their *entire* lives."

He gazed into the distance. Spit a piece of tobacco off his tongue. Considered the ground. He was breathing loudly through his nose, his breath quick and shallow. "There's a couple of women sometimes live there too. With Reddick. Sully's one of them, though she mostly comes and goes. She ain't been there for a while. Anyway she never done anything to nobody, so you can just keep your distance from her."

"Who is the other woman?" Jayme asked.

"Micki, we call her. Cheryl McNulty. She's been with Luthor since long before I ever knew either one of them."

"They're married?"

"Hell, I don't know. She wears a bunch of jewelry. Maybe one of them's a ring. I never looked at her close enough to tell."

DeMarco said, "You've looked closely at Sully, though, haven't you?"

Jakiella jerked his head up, glared at DeMarco.

Flores smiled. And Jayme asked, "What else can you tell us about Micki?"

"I don't like her, I can tell you that."

"Why not?" DeMarco asked.

"Because of the way she treats everybody. Especially Sully."

"And how is that?" DeMarco said.

"Like she's Queen Shit and Sully is her toilet paper. Sully and me both."

DeMarco and Jayme said nothing, waited for him to fill the silence.

"She's epileptic," he continued. "Thinks that gives her the right to boss everybody else around."

"Even Reddick?" Jayme asked.

"Naw, not him. He'd grab her by that beehive hair and knock her head against the wall."

DeMarco said, "Have you seen him do that?"

"I've heard him threaten to. That and worse."

Flores asked, "So if he's such a monster, why did you spend last Saturday night at his place?"

Jakiella blew out a long, heavy breath. "You figure it out."

Jayme said, "What about Suzi and Lady D?"

"What about them?"

"Who are they? Where are they from? What were they doing messing around with Reddick?"

"They come up from Kentucky with Choo Choo. Wanted to get into business with Reddick."

"Exactly what kind of business would that be?" DeMarco said. "And if you say antiques, you're going straight to jail."

"Drugs and women—what do you think it is?"

"Were all four women involved?" Flores asked. "Sully too?"

"She didn't want to be, but… People need money to live."

DeMarco said, "So why did Reddick kill Choo Choo and the females?"

"When did I say he did?"

"If it wasn't him, then who?"

Jakiella had switched to breathing through his mouth now, taking large gulps of air. "I knew it wouldn't be just three fucking questions. I knew it. I'm done talking now. If you want to search my place, go ahead and fucking search it. I'd rather go to jail for a couple ounces of weed than end up nailed to a tree." With that he sidestepped DeMarco, turned and squeezed past Jayme and Flores to head back to the job site.

DeMarco said, "Keep your head down, Sonny. And keep this conversation to yourself. If you make a phone call, we will know. Do you understand?"

"Yeah yeah."

"We'll be in touch soon."

Jakiella walked faster and muttered, "Tell me something I don't fucking know."

FIFTY-FIVE

L isten to this," Jayme said. She was seated beside Flores in a booth in the Water's Edge restaurant, overlooking the marina on the southwestern shore of Conneaut Lake. DeMarco sat across from them, finishing his omelet. Jayme had ordered a croissant and fresh fruit, and Flores, who had really wanted a couple of bagel egg sliders, had followed Jayme's lead and now picked at the last chunks of pineapple on her plate and wondered if it would be gauche to soak up the fruit juice with the rest of her croissant.

Only a few boats remained docked at the marina, mostly pontoon party boats and a couple of sport fishing boats. These too would soon be hauled out and stored in one of the local storage yards or, for those who could pay more, inside a huge steel building. The water was too cold now for swimming and jet skiing but tourists and retirees and those who owned a weekend home along the shores of the lake still wandered around on sunny days, drawn to the glittering water and the memory of more festive times.

"She posted this one last Saturday night," Jayme continued. "It's called 'Mirror Image.'" And she read from Sivvy en Ruine's Facebook page:

> These fingers could be my grandmother's
> the ones I stole from her grave to wear
> and wrap around the bowl of a pipe

the ones I will leave behind for no one.
This mouth I stole from my father
so that he could never curse at me again
his dirty little whore lips plump with poison
nobody wants to kiss.
These eyes I stole from ages past
blinded to beauty by the film of smoke
that wreathes my head which is
also not my own, though whose
I do not know.
All this stolen self I take with me
through the valley of the shadow of death
where I fear all evil, where
I walk hand in hand with this ugly stranger
lost in the evil we both have become.

Neither Flores nor DeMarco spoke. They shared a look.

"We need to get this girl some help," Jayme said.

≫————≪

A phone call to Boyd and a ten-minute wait got them the address for Amber Sullivan's parents. Another thirty-five minutes passed before the State Police SUV and DeMarco's black sedan pulled to the curb in front of the Fredonia residence. Only Mrs. Sullivan, a thin, pretty woman with dark half-moons under her eyes, was at home. She stood in the doorway behind the locked screen door and considered the smiling Hispanic woman in the state trooper uniform on her front porch, plus the older man and woman waiting below the steps.

"What do you want to talk to her for?" Mrs. Sullivan asked. "Did she do something wrong?"

"We have no reason to believe that," Flores said. "We just have a couple of questions we would like to ask."

"About what?"

"I can't discuss that, Ms. Sullivan. I'm sorry. Is Amber at home or not?"

"She's not. She got a phone call about an, I don't know, an hour ago? We were down in the basement doing the laundry together. Next thing I know she's going up the stairs. Five minutes after that she yelled down that she was going out awhile. Last thing I heard was the front door slamming shut."

"Do you have an idea where she might have gone?"

"No, I don't."

"No idea at all? Any friends nearby? Did she leave on foot or did somebody pick her up?"

Four seconds ticked past before the woman spoke. "Is she in trouble of some kind?"

Flores knew the meaning of those four seconds. "She might be. We need to find her and find her now. So if you have any idea where she is, it is in her own best interests that you tell us."

Three more seconds. Then Mrs. Sullivan pulled a cell phone from her hip pocket. "I texted to ask where she was going."

"And did she respond?"

Amber's mother held the phone out to her.

Flores read the text: Going up to the lake awhile ttyl. "Conneaut Lake?" she asked.

The older woman nodded. "She has a friend up there she visits sometimes. I don't know anything about him. Not even his name."

Flores returned the phone. "Thank you," she said, and turned away.

"Can you let me know when you find her? Let me know she's okay?"

"Absolutely," Flores said.

The three investigators walked quickly to their cars, then paused between them. DeMarco said, "Jakiella called her after we left him. Maybe even drove down and picked her up."

"They could be back at his house by now," Jayme said.

Flores had her own phone out. "I'll call Conneaut Lake PD and have them watch the house. Make sure Amber and Jakiella don't go anywhere."

Jayme said, "Better have them go inside. From the sound of that poem, she's already suicidal. And now, with the cops closing in…"

To Flores, DeMarco said, "Use your flashers. We'll be riding your tail."

FIFTY-SIX

B y the time they arrived back at Sonny Jakiella's house, Amber Sullivan had been taken away in an ambulance. Sonny was handcuffed in the back seat of a police car, sleeping with his head laid back, mouth open.

Acting on Flores's phone call, a pair of local officers had knocked on Jakiella's door but received no response. His vehicle was in the driveway, the hood still warm. All doors on the residence locked, all curtains drawn. The senior officer then kicked open the back door. They found Jakiella on the living room sofa, Amber nonresponsive and curled up on the floor between the coffee table and the sofa, heart rate 26 bpm, respiration negligible. On the coffee table were a half-empty pint of Jack Daniel's whiskey, a still-burning candle, a plastic straw, and a square of aluminum foil black with burned residue. In a small ziplock bag in Amber Sullivan's jeans pocket were three tabs of Ativan.

"We're monitoring his vitals," the local officer told them. He and a female EMT stood outside the open end of the remaining ambulance. Inside, a male EMT sat beside Jakiella, who lay strapped onto a gurney, an oxygen mask over his face. "As soon as we get the green light, we'll take him to Saegertown for booking on the drug charges. You guys are looking at him for that triple homicide in Mercer County?"

"Both he and Amber Sullivan are persons of interest," DeMarco said.

"Well, you know where to find them. If the girl makes it, she'll go to Saegertown too."

Flores said, "Would you mind if we take a look inside the house?"

"Have at it," the officer said. "We bagged everything we need."

"His vehicle too?"

"Sure, it's unlocked. We took a dime bag out of the glove box. Not much else in there but a lot of fast-food wrappers and empty beer cans. Plus about a hundred pictures of his kids. You've got to give him points for that."

The thirty-minute search of the house produced nothing of relevance but for a computer folder loaded with photos of Amber. In none was she looking into the camera. Jayme said, "My guess is she wasn't even aware that he was taking them."

Flores said, "What do you bet his phone's loaded up with them too? Pictures of Amber and his kids. Judging from what's in the house, those are the only kind of pictures he took."

"Maybe the only people who mattered to him," Jayme said.

"Some of the backgrounds might be inside Reddick's house," DeMarco added. "We need to get copies of those."

When they finished, only the patrol car remained parked at the curb. One of the local officers had departed in the ambulance with Jakiella for the Crawford County Correctional Facility in Saegertown, but the other remained to secure the residence. DeMarco asked him, "Any chance your guys could seize that laptop inside for us? It has photos and maybe emails relevant to our investigation."

To Flores the officer said, "Shouldn't be a problem. Have your station commander contact the chief."

"Thanks," Flores said. "We'll need Amber's and Jakiella's cell phones too."

Jayme said, "How did the girl look to you when she left here?"

"Honestly?" the officer said. "Like a ninety-pound corpse."

FIFTY-SEVEN

S orry to have used up one of your days off," DeMarco said. He handed a cardboard cup of coffee to Flores and another to Jayme, then picked the remaining one off the counter.

"Hey, I'm glad to be here," Flores answered. "I'd work every day if they'd let me."

They crossed to a table at the window. Jayme and Flores again sat side by side; DeMarco set his cup on the table but did not sit. "Anybody want an apple fritter or a muffin? I have a lot of free points on my Sheetz card."

"Not for me, thanks," Jayme said, and Flores added, "Yeah, my stomach's kind of jittery from all that. I probably shouldn't even be drinking another coffee."

DeMarco nodded, slid a chair away from the table, and sat. Amber Sullivan was in the cardiac/coronary care unit and still too unstable to be questioned; they would try again later before heading home.

"Good work today," he said to both Jayme and Flores. "Everything is falling into place finally."

"Boyd's going to be green," Flores said.

Jayme smiled. "We'll let him go through the photos and emails. Make him feel useful. Men need to feel useful sometimes," she added with a wink to DeMarco.

He was already ticking off other things to get done after they spoke to Sullivan and Jakiella, if they were permitted to do so. Had all of the tasks been related, he would have been able to file them chronologically in his mind, but several were only tangentially relevant to the investigation, others not at all, so he told himself to simply recognize each one for now so that tonight or better yet in the morning he could make a list and prioritize his obligations: two voicemails from Ben Brinker, probably a status report concerning any news on Khatri's movements and maybe a reminder about the upcoming sentencing hearing for Connor McBride; a text from Chase Miller, probably an apology or plea to be brought back into the fold; a message from Joe Loughner, most likely a drunken wtf's going on down there.

DeMarco also needed to get Hero scheduled for his post-op checkup; needed to contact Laraine and get her to file for divorce; wanted to check in with Rosemary O'Patchen for any word from the editor about Tom's book of reflections and observations, see how the editor felt about DeMarco's and Jayme's selections; get both his and Jayme's cars scheduled for overdue oil changes or else buy the filters and oil and do it himself; and ask Jayme to call Georgina to find out how she was handling life in the women's shelter...

God, there were so many people in his life suddenly. A population explosion. How had this happened?

"Ground control to Sergeant DeMarco," Jayme said for a second time.

He looked up from his coffee cup. Both Jayme and Flores burst out laughing.

He smiled sheepishly. "Still waters run dry," he said.

Jayme said, "Daniella would like to know how we do it."

"How we do what?" he asked.

"This," Flores said. "What we did today. I mean...I do enjoy my work, I really do. But there's another part of me that has to wonder. Does it ever get to you? The kind of people we have to deal with? It never changes, does it?"

"You mean like Sonny Jakiella?" DeMarco asked.

"Him and everybody like him. I mean, we get one body in this life, right? Yet everybody we deal with seems hell-bent on screwing it up with one kind of poison or another."

DeMarco shrugged. "When you're right, you're right."

Jayme said, "It's hard, I admit. But every once in a while, you know, there's somebody like Georgina."

"You've been thinking about her too?" DeMarco asked.

"I feel like we're sort of responsible for her now. Like we sent her away to camp and I need to call her and see how she's doing."

He had to smile. A couple of mother hens, that's what they were turning into.

"Can I ask you guys something else?" Flores said. "I'm not even sure how to ask it, but…how did you two find each other? And how do you keep being so good to each other? How do you, I don't know… How did you get what you have together?"

DeMarco said, "She chased me until I ran out of breath and passed out. And when I woke up, she had me in handcuffs."

Jayme chuckled. "There's some truth to that."

"I wish I had what you have," Flores said. "I must be doing something wrong."

He felt that he had to say something, but what? She was looking for words of advice, an older man's wisdom. But hell, everything good that had ever come his way had come not because of who he was or what he had done but in spite of it.

Time to steal from somebody smarter. "There was this ancient Roman philosopher," he told her. "Also an emperor for almost twenty years. Marcus Aurelius. And he said this: 'A rock thrown in the air, it loses nothing by coming down, gained nothing by going up.'"

"Okay," Flores said. "And what does that mean?"

"That a rock is always a rock, whether it's lying on the ground or sailing through the air. And you are always you, whether you're all jazzed up or feeling low. So just keep being what you are—which in your case is a good, kind person and a damn fine trooper—and everything will work out."

She smiled, but weakly. "Do you really believe that?" Then looked at Jayme. "I mean I know what you guys have been through lately. I know it's been... There have been some painful times recently."

Jayme nodded. "And still painful." She reached across the table, laid her hand atop DeMarco's. "But we're still here, right, babe? Up or down, we're still here."

DeMarco smiled. Then shared the smile with Flores. Said, "There's your answer, I guess. Keep on keeping on. That's all anybody can do."

FIFTY-EIGHT

In the lobby outside the cardiac/coronary care unit, they waited for permission to enter Sully's room. Flores sat in a dark-green Briar chair across from Jayme and DeMarco on the sofa, but soon wished she hadn't chosen that seat. Not only were the squarish arms of the chair uncomfortable, but there was no reading material available and she had nowhere to look but at DeMarco and Jayme, their hips touching, or the elderly man who stood in the corner, head down, his lips moving as if he were praying over the cardboard cup of coffee held close to his chest.

She wondered whom the old man had come to visit. Probably a wife, maybe a dying parent. His clothes looked slept in, wrinkled and baggy on his thin frame. DeMarco had his eyes on the tile floor as Jayme leaned close and spoke too softly for Flores to hear. He answered with a little nod, then touched Jayme's hand with his fingertips.

Everybody has somebody, she told herself, and wondered who would visit her if she were dying. Her mother, of course, but who else? Boyd and DeMarco and Jayme, sure, and some of the other guys too, certainly Captain Bowen, but so what? They wouldn't come out of love for her, not the kind of love she wanted. No, she was more like Sully herself than any of them. More or less on her own. If she were ever shot or in a car accident or dying from some disease, she would be dying more or less alone.

And then she thought about Georgina too, another lonely girl. Dropped off in a shelter and left to fend for herself. And what about Suzi and Lady D? If they had been loved by someone, really and truly loved, they would never have ended up as they did. Would not have given in to such evil.

What was that Bible verse she had learned so long ago? *From the book of John*, she remembered. *We know that we are of God, and the whole world lies under the sway of the evil one.* Under the sway. Why would she think of something like that now? At eight or nine years old, however old she was at the time, she had said, after first hearing the quote, "So that means the evil one is stronger than God." No, she was told. God is stronger than anything. He gives you free will. The right to choose.

But that didn't seem right either, not back then and not now. It meant that God didn't really care. He didn't care about Sully, didn't care about Georgina, didn't care about Lady D or Suzi, didn't care about her.

She stood and turned quickly toward the door, said, "Got a bad case of dry mouth. You guys want anything?"

Jayme and DeMarco answered no, thank you, but she was already moving, blinking hard, telling that first sting of tears *don't you dare, don't you dare.*

|||

WISELY AND SLOW; THEY STUMBLE THAT RUN FAST.
—WILLIAM SHAKESPEARE, *ROMEO AND JULIET*

FIFTY-NINE

It was nearly 8:00 p.m. before DeMarco, Jayme, and Flores were granted a few minutes in Amber Sullivan's room in the cardiac/coronary care unit. Amber had been connected to a biventricular pacemaker, a heart monitor, a glucose drip, and an oxygen tube, yet her chances of survival were deemed low owing to the damage done to her heart by ten years of drug use. Amber's mother had been seated at her daughter's bedside since early evening, softly weeping, and the attending nurse was reluctant to evict her. DeMarco convinced the nurse that a few minutes with Amber might lead not only to the arrest of the individual or individuals who had supplied her with the drugs but also to those responsible for the brutal murders in Otter Creek Township. The nurse spoke to Amber's mother, who came briskly out of the room to seize DeMarco by his shirtfront and say, "You get him! You put him in jail and don't you ever let him out!"

He promised he would do his very best. And hoped he could keep that promise.

Jayme and Flores were forced to stand on the threshold while DeMarco leaned close to the young woman, his cell phone in hand to record the interview. He spoke in a voice as soft and gentle and clear as he could muster.

"Amber, I need to ask you about Luthor Reddick. I know that he's responsible for everything that happened to Choo Choo and

Suzi and Lady D. I just need to hear you say it. Tell me why he killed them."

Her eyes were glassy and damp, but she held his gaze. She blinked but did not look away. The oxygen tube hissed each time it released another puff of air.

"I did it," she said. Her lips barely moved when she spoke.

"No," he told her. "You didn't. I've read your poetry, and it's beautiful. Poets don't kill people."

She blinked. Nodded. "I did it. Just me."

"You drove Choo Choo's car into the woods?"

"Made D drive."

"And how did you accomplish that?"

"Threatened her."

"With what?"

"A gun."

"Whose gun?"

"Mine."

"Where is that gun now?"

"Threw it away."

"Where?"

"Don't remember."

"What kind of gun was it, Amber? What caliber?"

"Don't remember."

"Okay," he said. "And how did you get Choo Choo into that car? We know that he was drugged first. So how did you get him into the car?"

Another blink. "Carried him," she said.

"You did?"

"With Suzi and D."

"I don't think so," he told her. "Because they were drugged too, weren't they?"

She blinked. Said nothing.

"Okay," he said. "Who drove the rebar into Choo Choo?"

This time she held her blink closed for five full seconds. Then opened her eyes sleepily and said, "I did."

"Who held Choo Choo up while you nailed him to the tree?"

Pause. "Nobody."

"Amber, we know that Choo Choo was drugged. He was unconscious. He weighed close to two hundred pounds. Somebody had to hold him up while somebody else nailed him to the tree. Was it Sonny? Is that why you don't want to tell me the truth?"

Weakly, she shook her head. "I did it all."

He wasn't going to push her. Her eyes told him that she knew she was going to die, and he had no desire to hasten her death with more questioning. He had never felt love for an absolute stranger before that moment but he felt it now and it was anything but pleasant.

Outside the room he bent close to Amber's mother and told her, "She's a beautiful girl. I am so sorry this happened."

With Flores and Jayme following, he went down the hall to the elevator and punched the Down button. When the door opened he stepped into the corner and stared at the floor. Jayme entered next, pressed the Lobby button and stood facing DeMarco. Flores came in and said to him, "Did you get anything?"

He shook his head no; looked down at the cell phone in his hand, still recording. He tapped the Stop icon, then Delete. "We'll get it from Sonny," he said.

SIXTY

The town of Saegertown, Pennsylvania, with a population of approximately one thousand, sits in the northwestern corner of the state, one county shy of Lake Erie. It is known for two things: the birthplace of actress Sharon Stone and the Crawford County Correctional Facility, a medium security jail located, ironically, on Independence Drive, housing inmates awaiting trial or sentencing. According to IMDb, Stone, named one of *Men's Health*'s "Hottest Women of All Time" and one of *People*'s "50 Most Beautiful People," has an IQ of 154. It is unlikely that any of the 280 or so residents of the correctional facility could match her beauty or intelligence, but, if any could, it would not be Timothy "Sonny" Jakiella.

When DeMarco caught up with Jakiella in a small windowless room at the facility, Sonny, dressed in an orange jumpsuit, looked small and weak and twenty years older than his forty-six years. DeMarco set a cardboard cup of coffee in front of Jakiella and took a seat across from him. Flores stood near the door while Jayme and one of the facility's three sergeants watched behind a one-way mirror.

Jakiella wrapped both hands around the cup, bent close to it and took a birdlike sip. Then asked, "How's she doin'?"

"She's probably going to die, Sonny."

"No, man, no. Don't even say that."

"Her heart is ruined."

"Can't they get her a new one? I'll give her mine. Tell them I don't even care, they can cut it out of me right now and give it to her."

"Yours? You've been a junkie even longer than she has."

"They gotta do something for her. They can't just let her die."

"They're doing their best to keep her alive. Probably won't be enough, though."

He waited and watched. Saw Jakiella's body shrink even more, saw him caving into himself. Then said, "I know you cared about her, Sonny. You too were close, right?"

"Yeah. But not the way you're probably thinking."

"How then?"

"I love her. I do. But she didn't want to ruin our friendship with that. With, you know…"

"With sex?"

"She only did it when she needed the money. She tried quitting dope but just couldn't. She was always trying to quit."

"You didn't help her much with that, did you?"

"I couldn't stand to see her sick!"

"And now you've killed her."

"Don't you say that to me, you son of a bitch."

"Face the facts, Sonny. You picked her up, you took her to your place, you supplied her with the alcohol and heroin. And now her life is hanging by a thread."

"The cop told me she had pills on her too. I didn't know anything about the pills. That's what did it to her, not me."

"Ah, Sonny, you're living in a delusion. You know that, right? She called you for help and you killed her. Period."

"She's not dead, man. You said so yourself."

"She knows she's going to die."

"You don't know that."

"She told me." *With her eyes*, DeMarco thought. "She told me everything."

"Like what?"

"Like the truth about what happened to Choo Choo and Suzi and Lady D. All the truth you are too cowardly to tell."

"I don't believe that. She wouldn't tell you nothing."

"She told me all about Reddick. All about how it went down in those woods. About you holding up Choo Choo while the rebar went into his throat."

Sonny shook his head no, breathed loudly through his nose as his head jerked back and forth in short, quick movements. His eyes looked crazy, pupils wide with panic. He was squeezing the cardboard cup so hard, thin arms shaking, that coffee squirted out of the hole in the plastic lid. "If she told you that, she was just making it up to get rid of you. Reddick wasn't even there. He didn't know a thing about it till it was all over with."

"That doesn't make any sense to me," DeMarco said. "A scrawny guy like you?"

"It's the truth, goddammit! I hated that black bastard."

"Hey hey hey, pardner. Let's not get racial here, shall we? You have the God-given right to hate anybody you want to, but keep it on an individual basis, all right? Not an accident of birth. Would it be fair for me to hate you just because you were born stupid?"

Sonny drew himself up a bit straighter. "I wasn't born stupid."

"You got there honestly, is that what you're saying? Because you have to admit, Sonny, you're looking fairly stupid now, aren't you?"

He sagged again. "You don't know what it's like."

"Here we go. You're going to whine like a little baby and play the victim, blame the big bad drugs for forcing themselves inside you. And yet you're willing to take the fall for a guy like Reddick? What's that all about?"

"I had plenty of reasons to hate Choo Choo."

"Such as?"

"He was a bully. Always shoving me around, telling me to do this, do that. And putting his hands on Sully where he shouldn't have."

"Is that why you killed him? If you really did."

"I caught him and those girls stealing from the cache, that's why. Reddick would've blamed me for it. So I did it, okay? Just me. Sully didn't have any part in it."

"Sonny," DeMarco told him, "you're a junkie and a liar. You're sitting there twitching like a dying bug and you expect me to believe that you stood a big man like Choo Choo up against a tree and drove three pieces of rebar into him? And watched Lady D and Suzi burn? I don't believe you."

"Then fuck you, okay? Fuck you. I want a lawyer." He turned and shouted at the mirror. "Get me outta here and get me a lawyer!"

SIXTY-ONE

The night was dark and had turned cold and the air smelled like winter. The lights blazing in the correctional facility's parking lot wiped out every star and rendered the sky a uniform black. A thick stand of trees far behind the facility and partially lit by the sodium vapor lights formed an uneven colonnade that made the low white building seem set in the middle of a vast wilderness.

Flores leaned against the door of her red Subaru, with DeMarco and Jayme facing her. He said, "You logged a lot of miles for a day off."

"Better than logging them on my butt watching television," she said. "So how do you figure their stories? Sully says she did it, Sonny says he did it. Both say Reddick wasn't involved."

"Maybe he isn't," Jayme said. "Maybe we're guessing wrong. Maybe because of Joe, and how adamant he's been."

DeMarco said, "Forget about Joe for a minute. Just stand here and ask yourself, what makes the most sense? Knowing what we know for certain—that Reddick met Choo Choo and the female vics down in Washington County. That they wanted in on Reddick's business. That Sonny and maybe Sully spent last Saturday night at Reddick's place. That Choo Choo was drugged, carried, and stood up against a tree, and that Sonny and Sully combined probably couldn't lift a heavy bag of groceries. Knowing all that, who's the most logical suspect?"

"Reddick," Jayme said.

"Reddick," said Flores.

"And now ask yourself," DeMarco continued, "why would Sonny and Sully both be so adamant that Reddick wasn't involved?"

"Fear," Jayme said.

Flores nodded. "They saw what Reddick did to the victims, and he promised them some of the same if they didn't keep quiet about it. No doubt he threatened their families too."

"Sonny and Sully aren't killers," Jayme added. "Sonny holds down a job and pays child support like a good father despite being a junkie. Sully is sensitive, artistic, probably loves her mother, at least enough that she wouldn't want to see her hurt. And I think Sully and Sonny really care about each other."

"Reddick, on the other hand, was discharged from the military for what?" DeMarco asked.

Jayme nodded. "Homicidal tendencies."

DeMarco addressed Flores. "There's this thing called an evolution of skills that I learned from a friend of mine. A writer. The more you practice something, even if you only practice it inside your head, the better you get. Reddick got booted from the army in his early twenties. What would you say is the natural evolution of violent tendencies?"

"Depends," said Flores. "For somebody intelligent, who doesn't want to get punished again, I'd say it would be to become more circumspect about where and when the violence happens."

"You and I talked to him," DeMarco continued. "Did he strike you as intelligent? Do you remember what you wrote in your notes about him?"

She nodded. "He was smooth. Too smooth. Too confident. Like a bald Ted Bundy."

"You said he seemed skeevy. Tell Jayme what you meant by that."

"I understand skeevy," Jayme said.

Flores told her, "He literally left me with a bad taste in my mouth. Not from anything he said, just...like I'd taken a mouthful of something disgusting."

"So Joe Loughner is probably right after all," Jayme said. "We come back to that. Question is, how do we prove it? How do we nail Reddick?" Hearing her own words, she winced. "Sorry. No pun intended."

DeMarco gave her a smile. Turned to Flores. "We might need you again tomorrow. Is that okay?"

"Sweetest thing anybody has ever said to me," she answered.

"Watch out for deer on your way home."

"Hey, I grew up on these roads, remember? The deer need to watch out for me."

SIXTY-TWO

It had been a long, full day and DeMarco was surprised when he slid into bed beside Jayme and found her naked. She snapped the waistband of his boxers and said, "Skin to skin, babe. I need to feel you against me."

He peeled off his boxers and T-shirt and they rolled against one another and made love that was gentle and slow until the last two minutes, which were desperate and dizzying. She kept her body pressed hard to him afterward and said nothing for so long that he thought she was falling asleep. But then she asked, "Do you ever look at another woman and wish you could be with her?"

"What? No, I never do," he said. "Why would you think that?"

"Not even for just an hour together?"

"Not even for just a minute."

"A minute would do neither of you much good."

"Nor would an hour," he told her. "Only with you."

"I know that women look at you that way, though. I've seen it."

"I think maybe you imagine you see it."

"Don't say that you've never noticed it."

"Only when it's obvious," he said. "But that hasn't happened in a long time now. And only then with the old grannies. One of those eighty-year-old grannies in yoga pants."

"I don't care how old she is," Jayme said. "If she tries to steal you from me, I'll cut her."

"When did you start carrying a knife?"

"There's always a knife nearby somewhere. I will cut her and I won't care how many grandchildren she has."

"What about in the woods?" he asked. "You would have to carry your own knife to have one in the woods."

"I'll break off a twig and sharpen it with my teeth and then I'll cut her. I'll slice her like a block of soft cheese."

"Hard cheese is easier to slice than soft cheese," he said.

"Then I'll slice her in all the hard places."

"What about in a clothing store?"

"I'll break off a mannequin's arm and slice her up with that."

"What about in a library?"

"Have you forgotten how much a paper cut hurts? Imagine getting a thousand of them. That's what I will do to her in a library."

"It's comforting to know that you are so protective of me," he said.

"I'm not protecting you, I'm protecting me from losing you."

"Either way I feel safer."

"What would you do to protect yourself from losing me to another man?" she asked. "Would you cut him?"

"No," he said. "I would drive his head through the wall. Then I would shove the rest of his body in through the hole his head made. Then I would patch up the wall and paint it and hang a picture of a dead man over the patch. As a warning to every other man."

"That's so romantic of you," she teased. "You make me feel safer too. But I think a picture of flowers would be even more romantic, don't you? Not to mention ironic. A picture of a bouquet of roses."

"Van Gogh did one with a vase of pink roses. Would that be okay?"

"Yes but get a reproduction. I don't need the original painting."

"That's good. I would have to rob several banks in order to afford it."

"A good reproduction in a nice frame will be more than sufficient."

He said, "I love it that you're so frugal."

She kissed his chest and closed her eyes. "Thank you for the way you touch me and the way you love me. You really do make me feel safe. I'm going to dream about pink roses now, okay?"

He kissed the top of her head. "Sweet dreams, my love."

Twenty minutes later he was asleep too, but he did not dream of pink roses or of any kind of flowers. It was not a nightmare nor even a bad dream really but it made him sad when he was dreaming it and again when he awakened and remembered the dream. In this dream he had died in his sleep, not in any spectacular or important way, not even in old age but as the man he was then. He had simply awakened, in his dream, to a place of total darkness that felt soft and temperate and nonthreatening and knew that he was dead. He was inside this place that he suddenly understood to be the womb of God and then a voice that was also soft and warm and nonthreatening inside his head and all around him asked if he wanted to go back or not. His first thought was *no way am I going back to that place*, but then immediately he thought that maybe he would. *If I can go back without losing what I've learned*, he thought, and the voice inside and around him said without hesitation, *you know that's not how the game is played*. He thought, *I want to have Jayme if I go back, and my son and daughter too and everything I lost this last time*, and the voice replied, *don't play games with me*. So then he thought, *in that case this place isn't so bad, I'll just stay here*, but the voice chuckled and answered, *nothing ever works out the way you expect it to. Let's get that straight*. Then suddenly the voice retreated from him in a kind of silent whoosh and he awoke and was left with a ringing in one ear and a bottomless sadness that was all the worse because he could not distinguish it as sadness for something he had lost or for something he would never have.

SIXTY-THREE

DeMarco lay awake a long time after his dream. A cold front had swept in and made the house shudder and creak. Only when the wind subsided was he able to drift into sleep again. When Hero's damp nose woke him to the rosy tint of dawn, he slid out of bed and realized how cold the room was. He pulled on his boxers and T-shirt and eased a sweatshirt out of the dresser drawer and pulled it over his head while tiptoeing down the stairs. At the back door he slipped into his sneakers for the chilly trip outside.

He hadn't expected to be startled by the morning, but he was: the world had changed overnight. Frost sparkling on every blade of grass, most of the leaves that had been brightly colored little flags filling the trees now lay scattered on the ground, many with their paler bellies exposed as if some mad giant had raced throughout the neighborhood taking angry swipes at the trees. Even Hero was flummoxed. He walked gingerly about the yard, not quickly as he usually did but lifting his paws high and slowing frequently to look at and sniff the ground. Tentatively he tasted the frost, and then, apparently finding it to his liking, he went about more confidently, pausing only to lick or tinkle or sniff.

DeMarco thought how oddly lovely the morning was and how interesting that the change could fill him with such ambivalence. *So much beauty, so much pain.* Hero must have felt the same way because he stopped for a few moments to consider the red horizon, then to turn and regard DeMarco with a grin that seemed to ask, *Are you seeing all this?*

DeMarco chuckled. "I know." The coming winter would be Hero's first, whereas DeMarco had experienced half a hundred of them and enjoyed not one. To his mind the beauty of winter was the beauty of death, sterile and imprisoning.

As Hero occupied himself with an old bird nest that had been blown to the ground, DeMarco, shivering, turned his thoughts to the day ahead. The bad guys were still at large, and not just his bad guys but tens of thousands more of every ilk, in tattoos and leather jackets and cleric robes and tailored suits, in the alleys and barrios and classrooms, in the halls of Congress and every secret government agency in every government in every country, in the mosques and churches and synagogues, in the homes in all of the Otter Creeks and all of the Georgetowns and all of the Nuevo Laredos everywhere, and in every neighborhood and town and city. Despite the burst of color scattered over his yard and the bracing chill and the glittering frost, evil still populated every corner of the world, every shadow, and there would be no abatement of misery on this day or any other.

"It would be a beautiful world, wouldn't it, Hero," he said, "if only there weren't any people in it?"

Hero stopped in place, cocked his head and gave DeMarco a long look, as if considering the possibilities of that proposition.

"Hunh," DeMarco said in the silence, and felt a last shiver rattle his spine. "We done here? My toes are cold and I need coffee."

SIXTY-FOUR

B y the time Jayme came downstairs, mumbling and groping for a coffee mug, he had cleared all the recent texts and voice messages from his cell phone, had a skillet filled with scrambled eggs and fried ham warming in the oven, and had devised a plan of action for the day. She was wearing a pair of flannel pajamas pants, checkered black and red. He watched her fill a coffee mug from the decanter, and when she turned to the table he was sitting sideways on the seat, a soft smile on his lips.

"What?" she said.

"Every morning, another work of art."

"Shut up," she said, and kissed the top of his head. As she took the seat to his right, Hero stood and moved from beneath DeMarco's chair to hers. She rubbed him with her heel and asked, "What kind of trouble has your daddy cooked up for the day?"

"We need to get him back to Dr. Lisa for a checkup soon."

"Today?"

"We can wait a day or two. Did you realize we missed group Thursday night?"

"I did remember that once or twice."

"Mac sent me a text yesterday, asking if everything was okay."

"I love Mac," she said. "Did you return the text?"

Mac Vanko, group leader, the burly Gulf War vet with what he called a pogo stick for a right leg. "Told him we'd be back as soon as we wrapped up the case. He wished us luck."

"Are we going to need it?" she asked, and tapped the yellow legal pad that lay in front of him. Half of the page was covered with his messy handwriting. He sometimes wrote so quickly that only the first letter or two of a word was legible, the remainder a squiggle. Several greasy fingerprints also marked the paper, indicating that he had gone back and forth from the stove to the paper, thinking and cooking and writing and thinking.

"I also had two texts from Chase Miller. I haven't answered them yet."

"I've gotten three. He's chomping at the bit for something else to do for us."

"I also had a text from Ben Brinker."

"He said with an ominous tone."

"The FBI traced the explosives to a plant in Canada. Which suggests that either Khatri or one of his lackeys is already here."

She shook her head. "I just don't get it. Why would he risk capture to come back here and taunt us?"

"Because we're the mice that got out of his trap and sicced the feds on him. His entire MO is manipulation. He needs to show us that he can do whatever he wants. He needs to keep playing with us."

"Cats usually end up eating the mouse," she said.

"We need to keep our heads on a swivel. Every single moment of the day."

"Such a lovely, gut-twisting thought to start the morning," she said, and sipped her coffee.

"Ben offered to send us a couple of vests. It might not be a bad idea."

"He wants us to wear body armor?"

"The new ones are down to about seventeen pounds. That includes the metal inserts."

She pursed her lips but offered no immediate response.

The look on her face broke his heart. He said, "I thought one of us might check in on Georgina today too. See how she's adjusting."

"We're collecting quite a little brood, aren't we, Papa?"

"It's exhausting," he said with a smile.

"I'll call her later. What else?"

"Carmichael still hasn't cracked Reddick's website. If we want to nail him for anything, we need somebody to talk. And the only person left is Cheryl McNulty. Micki. According to Jakiella, she's been with Reddick the longest."

"Then let's go get her. Do we have enough for a warrant to search the house?"

He shook his head. "There's no sheet on her. All we have is what Jakiella told us."

"If she has epilepsy, like he said, what do you bet she's collecting SS disability?"

"Good thinking. You want to track down her vitals? It would be good to know if her mailing address is the same as Reddick's."

"Can do," she said. "Are you going to feed me first?"

"*Immediatamente*," he said, and pushed back his chair, startling Hero.

As the conversation continued, DeMarco took plates from the cupboard and filled them with cheesy scrambled eggs and ham. "And that leaves us with Mr. Miller."

"Be nice," she told him.

"I have been. Haven't I?"

"You know there's this strong father-son vibe going on between you two, right? You're aware of that?"

He nodded. "Flores, Georgina, Chase…"

"Don't forget Sully."

"My football coach in high school had eight kids. Eight. Can you imagine that?"

"It hurts to even try," she said. He set a plate in front of her. "This smells so good." She took the fork he handed to her. "So back to Chase. Are you cutting him loose or what?"

"I'm thinking we send him to Reddick's house. Posing as an antique collector." He returned to the table with his own plate and fork.

"I don't know about that, babe. In light of Reddick's homicidal tendencies and all."

"I'm betting that if a young, handsome college kid shows up with a handful of cash, Reddick might be downright friendly. As I see it, the worst that could happen is Reddick slams the door in his face. The best is that Chase comes away with a bag of coke or a good description of this McNulty character."

"Whoa, babe. A sting operation? You could get crucified for that. We both could."

"Not if it gets Bowen's stamp of approval."

"He's never going to approve that. Chase would go for it, I'm sure, because he's young and stupid and desperate for your approval. But Captain Bowen? I don't see it happening."

"You can be very charming sometimes," he told her. "Eat up. I'll text Chase to meet us at the station house."

She laid down her fork. "Seriously? You would seriously put Chase in that kind of situation?"

"We'll coach him first. About staying outside the house, getting either Reddick or McNulty in the doorway. Boyd has a brand-new toy he's itching to put to use."

"A drone?"

"Correct. Plus, you, me, Boyd, and Flores will be stationed a few seconds away. We'll wire Chase, and the moment Reddick incriminates himself or McNulty shows her face, we get him out of there."

She was shaking her head. "I still don't like it. Not in the least."

"We have to get Reddick or McNulty on *something*. Just a few words. Enough for a warrant. Then we can search the house and maybe actually nail him. With him in jail, Sully or Sonny or Micki is going to have second thoughts about covering for him."

She said nothing. Looked at him with her jaw set.

He said, "Can we at least leave it up to Chase and the captain? They both have to agree."

"We haven't even talked to Micki yet. Why don't we try that first?"

"Because it will put both her and Reddick on high alert. As it is, he's probably already expecting to see us at his door again. What he will not be expecting is a street-savvy kid looking to get wasted."

"Oh, Ryan," she said.

"You say you want me to respect the boy. The young man. You want me to trust him. Well, I'm doing that. I'm trusting and respecting his ability to help us out with this. To be part of the team. Which is exactly what he wants to be."

She seemed unable to stop shaking her head. "I do not feel good about this."

"Baby, I have spent the entire morning trying to come up with another way. How about if you finish your breakfast, get dressed, and I'll clean up here. And if you can think of any other option, we'll go with that instead. Okay?"

She said nothing.

"Okay?" he repeated.

"Damn you, DeMarco."

"I know," he said. "Believe me, I know."

SIXTY-FIVE

By 10:00 a.m., Flores, Boyd, Miller, DeMarco, Matson, and Captain Kyle Bowen were seated around the conference table in a room in the Troop D station. Most had cardboard cups of coffee in front of them, Miller's a thirty-two-ounce cup from the Sheetz in Greenville, DeMarco's and Jayme's sixteen-ounce cups from the Country Fair on the way to the station house, and Bowen's and Boyd's ceramic mugs from the Troop D break room. Flores held a bottle of apple juice. Only Miller was grinning.

"This is what I *do*," he told them. "It's what I'm good at. I can be very convincing. Besides, Reddick has no idea who I am. None whatsoever. My photo's not on my website, not in the papers I write for, nowhere. He doesn't know me from Adam. He's a *businessman*. What's he going to do?"

"A possibly homicidal businessman," Captain Bowen said. "Whose businesses are, in all likelihood, illegal."

"So I knock on his door," Miller said. "What's the worst that can happen?"

Flores told him, "You haven't seen this man."

"There's a picture of him on his website," Miller said. "He doesn't scare me."

"He's a head taller than you and twice as wide."

Miller grinned. "I'll wear my running shoes. He'll never lay a hand on me."

Even DeMarco had grown uneasy with the plan. But what were their options? To Boyd, he said, "How noisy is that drone of yours?"

"Reddick won't be able to hear it inside the house. And I'll keep it high enough that he won't hear it even if he steps outside."

"And if he sees it?" Jayme asked.

"He won't unless he's outside or has a big skylight. And if he sees it, I see him seeing it."

"And then what?" Jayme asked.

"Then I zoom away. Leave him wondering."

DeMarco looked to Chase Miller then, was about to speak but saw movement at the door, a face in the pane of glass. Trooper Carmichael. Bowen saw it too and waved him inside.

Carmichael entered and held up a small sheaf of papers. "Louisville finally confirmed IDs of the three vics." He reached between Jayme and DeMarco and laid one sheet of paper in the middle of the table: a mug shot of a thin, pretty white woman with jet-black straight hair, purple lipstick and eye shadow, flecks of glitter on her cheeks.

"Diana Constance Moore," Carmichael said. "A.k.a. Lady D, Princess D, Vixen Queen of the Night."

"Queen of the Night?" Bowen asked.

"I don't make this stuff up, sir. She was an exotic dancer. That was her stage name. This photo is from her one and only arrest. Two years ago. Which would have made her twenty-six at the time of her death. Solicitation and misdemeanor possession. Two years probation."

He gave everybody a few moments to look at the photo, then laid another sheet of paper beside it. "Phan Thi Vinh, a.k.a. Suzi Phan. She was eighteen when this photo was taken." Large dark eyes in pools of black eye shadow, a broad, flat nose, sensual lips closed atop an overbite. "Picked up at the same time as Lady D, but Suzi got belligerent with the judge and pulled thirty days along with the probation."

Seeing the young women's faces, DeMarco felt a heavier gravity fill the room. Suddenly the vics had become actual people, flesh and blood, daughters and sisters. He remembered the scent of the smoldering vehicle in which they had lain, the acrid stink of burned rubber. Nobody should have to die like that. He felt a particular sympathy for Lady D, who had been, if only briefly, Georgina's friend. And in both of them, he saw Sully. Three young women derailed by drugs but hungry to redeem themselves and reclaim their lives. The same sad history three times told.

"And this," Carmichael said as he laid down the final sheet of paper, "is Mr. Clarence Barclay Knox, a.k.a. CB, Choo Choo Charlie, Choo Choo, and K-man. Charged four times for assault, and all four times the charges were dropped."

Jayme said, "Can you say *witness intimidation?*"

DeMarco asked, with the hint of a grin forming on his lips, "His first name is Clarence?"

"Yes, sir. Clarence Barclay Knox."

DeMarco offered Jayme a smirk, which caused her to scrunch up her mouth and thumb her nose at him.

Bowen said, "You two want the rest of us to leave the room?"

"Sorry," DeMarco said. "Inside joke."

"You will appreciate this, Sergeant," Carmichael told him. "Do you know how he got the name Choo Choo?"

"I bet it wasn't from eating Good & Plenty."

"Star running back in high school. KFCA Class 4-A Player of the Year. He had this jerky way of running, like a train picking up speed. Was offered full rides from Georgia, UK, and South Carolina. He went with the Wildcats but was cut halfway through the first season for peddling PEDs to his teammates. Second offense."

DeMarco studied the photos a few moments longer. "So now we know them," he said. "Now they're real."

Captain Bowen added, "And whatever their crimes were, it doesn't justify what happened to them. They didn't start out life wanting to be what they became. They were somebody's children, and they probably had the same dreams that all of us had. We need to keep that in mind moving forward."

Everybody in the room nodded their agreement.

To Miller, DeMarco said, "Reddick has to buy your pitch. How are you going to convince him that *you're* for real? In thirty seconds or less."

Miller thought for a moment. "I have a couple names I can drop. Names he'll recognize."

"Customers?" Jayme asked.

Miller nodded. "But you all have to promise to never repeat those names or hassle the people. If word gets out that I can't be trusted, nobody will ever talk to me again. And some of these people, you know…it's hard to tell what they might do to me."

Jayme said, "That is exactly why this is a bad idea."

Everyone sat silent for a few moments. Then Flores said, "We don't even know if Reddick is at home, do we? He might have spooked after our door-to-door."

Boyd said, "We need to review the most recent footage at Mr. Shaner's place." To DeMarco, he said, "I had planned to head up there until you called."

"Then let's do that first," DeMarco said. "Let's get Chase rigged up, then he can ride to Otter Creek with Jayme and me." He turned to Jayme. "We haven't used your car at all since we started this, have we?"

"I haven't driven it in at least a week."

"Or mine," Flores said. "Except yesterday, I mean. But nobody involved would have seen it."

"Okay," Bowen told them. "So you check to see if Shaner is home. If he is, you ask if it's okay to park two vehicles behind his house. You enter his house through the back door, review the footage so that we know what we're sending this kid into. Or if we even do."

DeMarco smiled at Bowen's use of the word *kid*, and Bowen caught the smile. To DeMarco, he said, "Don't even think about it."

DeMarco pinched his smile closed but could feel the muscles twitching. "Never crossed my mind, Captain, sir."

Bowen turned to Boyd. "Keep someone inside Shaner's house on the camera. That way you know if anybody else comes or goes from Reddick's place. You launch the drone from behind Shaner's house and let the team inside know if there's any kind of activity at Reddick's, or if there are additional vehicles parked there. We know what Reddick drives, right?"

"Black Ford Explorer," Boyd told him. "That's the only vehicle registered to him."

"Okay, then," Bowen said. "If things look good, you send Miller across the road."

"Walking?" Miller asked. "Or would it be better if I drive my own car there?"

"Too many vehicles," DeMarco said. "It's an isolated place, but still… If anybody sees three vehicles pulling into Shaner's place and driving around back…"

"You can take my car," Jayme said to Miller.

"Nothing personal," Flores said, "but mine looks more like something a college kid would drive. If that's your cover."

"What do you drive?" Miller asked.

"Subaru Crosstrek. Red."

"Perfect," he said.

DeMarco thought he caught a glimmer of something between them, something in the way they smiled at one another. It troubled him, but he wasn't sure why.

Captain Bowen interrupted his thoughts. "If anything you see on the camera or with the drone seems amiss, strange, out of place, worrisome, whatever—and I mean *anything*—you abort." He looked around the table from face to face. "Is that understood?"

He was answered by a mumbled chorus of affirmations.

To DeMarco, he said, "Why is it that every time I approve one of your plans, I feel like I need to get my head examined?"

DeMarco shrugged. "I don't know, boss. Maybe you should get your head examined and find out why that is."

SIXTY-SIX

The footage on the IR camera showed Reddick's Ford Explorer leaving the driveway at 10:47 Sunday night. As of 12:19 Tuesday morning, it had not yet returned. Sunday night had been clear and cool, with a third quarter moon hanging white in the sky. The Explorer could be seen exiting the driveway and turning left without stopping at the top. There Flores paused the tape for a closer look. No one but Luthor Reddick could be seen inside the vehicle.

"So what that means," DeMarco said to Flores and Miller, and inadvertently to Fred Shaner, who was listening from the threshold, "depends on what the drone sees. According to Sonny, Micki is Reddick's live-in. And apparently she didn't leave with him on Sunday night."

"Unless she left horizontal," Flores said.

DeMarco nodded. "Always a possibility."

They all leaned back from the screen and waited. Fred Shaner said, "I have some coffee and orange juice if anybody is interested."

"Not right now, thank you," DeMarco said.

Minutes later, a shrill sound like a spinning drill bit could be heard, muted by the building's walls. The sound rose in volume for a moment, then began to fade. They waited.

DeMarco's phone vibrated. He tapped the phone icon. "Yeah," he said.

Jayme, in the backyard with Trooper Boyd, told him, "Nothing. No vehicles in sight. No activity outside the house. There's a light on downstairs but we don't know what room it is. My guess is the kitchen, judging from the window size and placement."

"Copy that," DeMarco said. He put the phone on speaker so that Flores and Miller could hear too. "So it looks like Micki is the only one home. Or else Reddick left a light on."

"That's our guess," Jayme told him. "You want Boyd to get lower? He said he can peek in the window if you—"

"No," DeMarco said. "Tell him to back off and assume a position above the house. I'm sending Miller over. Keep your phone on."

"Ten-four," Jayme said.

"Okay," DeMarco told Miller. "You will probably be dealing with Cheryl McNulty. Late forties, platinum-blond hair. Supposed to be bossy and not very pleasant. You still want to do this?"

"Absolutely," Miller said.

DeMarco heard the answer from Miller's mouth and simultaneously in the wireless earbud in his other ear. "You have the money?"

Miller patted the bulge in his side pocket.

DeMarco nodded at Flores, who handed her car keys to Miller. "Bring it back in one piece," she told him.

He grinned. "Do you care which piece?"

DeMarco told him, "You had better be taking this seriously."

"Chillax, man," Miller said. "I got this." He turned and headed for the back door.

"He's on his way out," DeMarco said into the phone.

"Copy that," Jayme said.

SIXTY-SEVEN

M iller barely had time to get used to the feel of Flores's car or to the cinnamony scent emanating from the fragrance sticks in her air vents before he was parked in front of Luthor Reddick's door. He wished he could sit there for a few minutes longer and talk his heart into not tapping against his chest at such a pace that he felt short of breath even while sitting motionless behind the wheel. He had been brash and confident in front of DeMarco and the others but now all certainty was gone. He was always doing things like this, going all the way up to the very edge of danger before asking himself *what have you gotten yourself into this time*, yet he always moved forward even further because the thing he feared most was being a failure and a coward. So now there was nothing to do but to climb out of the car and knock on the door. "Getting out," he said, as much to urge himself forward as for the microphone under his shirt.

He climbed out and looked up and saw Trooper Boyd's drone thirty or so feet above the house. There was a slight hum in the air, so as he turned to close the door he tilted his chin down and mumbled, "I can hear the drone." The drone rose higher.

Fourteen strides to the porch. Four long inhalations and exhalations. Two more deep breaths while standing at the door.

He pressed the doorbell. Heard no echoing chime from within.

Raised a hand and knocked, rapped his knuckles three times on the heavy wooden door.

Nothing. No sound.

He knocked again.

Out of the corner of his eye he glimpsed a movement at a window. Forced himself to keep his head still. Smiled a little. *Not too much*, he told himself. And knocked again.

A part of him hoped that the knock would not be answered, that he would knock one more time, louder so that everybody back at Fred Shaner's house would hear, and then could return to Flores's car and drive away. But a larger part of him did not want that to happen. If it did he would later castigate himself for being a coward. All talk, no action. It would be worse than—

A lock clicked open and his heart jumped, his breath caught. He stood a little straighter, moved back half a step.

The door opened by eight inches. A woman's face, pale and fleshy, only slightly darker than the brittle nest of hair. Her eyes were more gray than blue, as soft and friendly as bullets. "What do you want?" she said.

"Oh, hi," Miller answered. "Is, uh…is Luthor at home?"

"Who are you?" she said.

"My name's Kenny, ma'am. Kenny Martz? I live down in Clark? I mean, that's where I grew up, I actually live on campus now. I go to Thiel. I'm a senior there. I graduate in May."

"What do you want with Luthor?" she asked.

Suddenly his mind went blank. What was he supposed to say? "Oh, well, I, uh…I was told that he might be able to help me out with a couple of things I need."

"What things?"

"Well, uh, you know…I'd rather talk to him about that?"

"You'll talk to me or you'll get your ass off my porch."

"Okay. Uh...it's stuff for a party tonight. On campus? I was told Luthor was the man to see. Something to, you know, make the party a party?"

She stared at him for a full five seconds. He tried to keep his smile from quivering. Then she said, "How do you know Luthor?"

"Yeah, well, I don't know him personally. But a friend of mine told me this was the place to, you know, take care of my needs? He said Luthor was the man."

"What's your friend's name?"

"Mundy?" he said. "People call him Redball?"

"How do you know Redball?"

"We hang out together from time to time."

"You don't look like somebody who'd know Redball."

"Oh, he gets around. Anywhere there's a party, he'll find it. You know what he's like."

She looked at him awhile longer. Then lifted her gaze and considered the Subaru. Then beyond it, up the empty gravel lane. Then she yanked open the door, grabbed him by the wrist and said, "Get inside here."

SIXTY-EIGHT

D amn," Jayme said, and DeMarco, inside Shaner's house, barked in Miller's ear, "Get out of there, Chase. Now!"

In the foyer, McNulty swung the door shut behind Miller, then stood to the side to give him a long, unblinking once-over, which made him feel small and vulnerable. With her beehive hair she stood nearly as tall as him, but wider. In her pink velour jogging suit, baggy in some places and tight in others, she looked to go at least two hundred pounds and probably considerably more; her bare feet, nails painted red, appeared tiny for a woman her size. And her fingers, seven of them adorned with gaudy rings, were, he noticed, as slender as Flores's though not as tanned, the fingernails long and squared at the tip, painted red with white polka dots. One fingernail on each hand had a tiny white plastic bow glued to it.

She said, "You have money?"

He patted the bulge in his side pocket.

"Let me see."

He reached into his pocket and brought out a small roll of hundred-dollar bills, then closed his fist around them.

She said, "How much of that are you here to spend?"

He smiled. "As much as necessary."

Behind Shaner's house, Jayme said, "Are we going in?"

"Hold on a minute," DeMarco answered.

McNulty said, "You said you have some needs. What are they specifically?"

"I was thinking maybe some mollies to start? Maybe a bag of good weed?"

She nodded. Moved a step closer to him. "Anything else?"

"Uh...no. That ought to do it."

She touched a fingertip to his cheek. "Boys like you are always looking for something else."

He looked around. "Is Luthor home?"

"Wouldn't matter if he was," she said. "What else did Redball tell you about me?"

"About you? Gee, I, uh..."

"I know he told you. He tells everybody. It's okay. I want to hear you say it."

"I'm not sure I, uh..."

"You want me to trust you or not? There's only one reason Redball comes to me. What is it?"

"Well, uh..."

"I'm waiting."

"He said you give one hell of a blow job."

"Ha," she said, and ran a hand down over his arm. "I knew the moment I saw you what you were really here for."

"Actually, I'm just sort of the party supply man, if you know what I mean."

"Unh uh," she said. Her hand trailed over his fingers and onto his crotch, then cupped his genitals. "You don't get any party supplies until you pass the test."

"I, uh..." he said, and had no idea what to do next. How far was he expected to go?

As far as necessary, he told himself. And said to her, "How much would that cost?"

"How much did Redball tell you?"

"He said a hundred."

"Redball's full of shit. It's three hundred and always has been."

"Well, I, uh…I'm not sure I have enough money for that *and* the mollies."

"Feels to me like you do," she said, her hand moving. "Feels to me like you have plenty."

"Uh…whew," he said.

"Take it out," she told him.

"Excuse me?"

"Take it out and show me you're not a cop."

"Seriously?" he said. "Me a cop?"

She pulled down his zipper. Reached inside. Worked her hand inside his boxers. She chuckled. "A little nervous, are you?"

"Yes, ma'am," he said. "I am."

"You'll get over it fast. Just let Mama do what she does best."

She fondled him until he grew hard. It took a while. But she knew what she was doing. And then she released him and held out an open palm. "Three hundred," she told him.

He opened up the roll, peeled off three bills, and handed them to her. "There you go," he told her, "three smiling Ben Franklins," and prayed that the microphone was still working.

With her free hand she took the bills and shoved them into a pocket. With her other hand she pulled Miller toward the adjacent room. "Come into my parlor, said the spider to the fly."

"Go, go, go!" DeMarco said into the phone.

By the time he and Flores were outside, Boyd had landed the drone behind the house and Jayme was waiting at the wheel of DeMarco's car, the engine running. Then the other three jumped inside, and Fred Shaner, standing at his front window, watched the sedan disappear down Reddick's driveway behind a cloud of gravel dust.

SIXTY-NINE

M icki pulled away from Miller at the sound of a vehicle sliding to a halt outside. As she hurried toward the front door,
Miller zippered up.

The front door sprang open as she was reaching for the lock, so
that her hand was rammed by the metal and wood, bending back
her fingers and breaking two nails. A tiny plastic bow clicked as it
skittered across the floor.

On the other side of the door, Trooper Boyd felt the contact
and shoved harder; she stumbled backward and managed to scream
"Who the fuck do you—" before a uniformed state policeman
came inside with his weapon drawn, followed closely by Flores,
DeMarco, and Jayme.

Within seconds Boyd had her braced against the wall, both arms
behind her back as he secured the restraints. "You are under arrest
for solicitation of prostitution," Flores told her, even as McNulty's
right ankle was kicking harmlessly against the trooper's leg.

"Are you fucking kidding me?" McNulty screamed. "You
fucking broke into my house!"

"I will let your face out of the wall when you calm down,"
Boyd told her. She kept cursing, writhing and kicking, but
Trooper Boyd held her in place with his shoulder as he patted
her down. She had a face like Ronald Reagan's death mask,
fleshy and soft but contorted now as she struggled against him,

her body with more undulating folds of flesh than a walrus. The image flitted through his mind of her and Reddick having sex. He envisioned her lying there utterly still and quiescent, feeling nothing through all that flesh, her eyes on the wall. Meantime Reddick sweated and grunted atop her, loving her the way a guy on death row loves his mattress—bitterly and hard. They did not talk as they went at it, her as silent as swamp gas, Reddick as quiet as a night crawler defecating by the light of the moon. It gave Boyd the shivers.

DeMarco and Jayme walked past them and into the living room, where Miller stood waiting. He seemed unsure of whether or not to smile, whether or not to hold his hands in front of his crotch. "Nice work," DeMarco told him, then looked around the room. Other than the worn leather sofa, the room was filled with small tables and a hundred or more vases, lamps, and figurines, none of any apparent value. He said, "It looks like a bunch of yard sale stuff."

Jayme glanced at Miller's red cheeks and asked, "You doing okay?"

"Doing great," he said.

"Good. You'd better wait outside now, okay?"

"No problem," he said. Turned and headed for the door.

DeMarco was moving slowly about the room, peering into every vase, down into every lamp shade. Flores walked up beside him and spoke very softly. "Sir. We have no warrant. No drugs were purchased."

"Just looking," he said. "I haven't touched a thing."

"Sir," she said. "Please. We need to leave now."

"If there's something out in the open…"

"Please, sir," she said. "Please stop. We have her on solicitation. Please exit the house with me, sir. Please."

The soft plaintiveness of her voice pulled him up short. He looked at her. Smiled. "You're right. I'm sorry. Let's go."

Micki McNulty's voice echoed throughout the house as she carpet-bombed Trooper Boyd with f-bombs.

SEVENTY

C heryl McNulty, when questioned by troopers Boyd and Flores, remained obdurate and rancorous, refusing to account for Reddick's current whereabouts or for his and hers during the time of the triple murders. A Mercer County sheriff's department vehicle was dispatched to the home for McNulty's transport to the county jail. The three one-hundred-dollar bills taken from her jogging suit pocket were bagged as evidence, along with the recording of her conversation with Chase Miller.

Because of McNulty's condition as an epileptic, as reported by Sonny Jakiella, Trooper Flores, prior to securing the home on Linn Tyro Road, inquired of McNulty, as she sat cuffed in the rear of the sheriff deputy's SUV, where to find her medication. This, too, McNulty refused to reveal, leaving the troopers no choice but to search the master bedroom and bath. Recovered from the master bathroom were a prescription bottle containing Tegretol XR antiseizure capsules, and another plastic phial containing eighteen four-milligram tabs of Suboxone, both labeled with an active prescription for Cheryl McNulty.

Just prior to his partner's discovery of the medication in the bathroom, Trooper Boyd opened a drawer in the bedside table and there observed an open Altoids box containing a white powdery substance, a ziplock bag containing approximately one-half ounce of what appeared to be cannabis, and $2,743 in cash. After conferring with his station commander by cell phone, Trooper Boyd photographed those items but did not remove them from the drawer.

Throughout the booking process at the county jail, while being fingerprinted and photographed and divested of her pink velour jogging suit, McNulty refused to answer all questions and instead loudly berated every individual with whom she came into contact. She also refused her right to a telephone call, because "you motherfuckers will be listening in on every word I say!" She refused the offer of a public defender to represent her in court.

In her cell, awaiting arraignment, McNulty turned her face to the wall and continued talking, though at a lower decibel level. A passerby might have assumed that she was praying, but anyone within range would hear few words included in any prayer book. At that point, the only charge against her was for solicitation of prostitution. In hopes that she might soften her attitude and give up some information, she was informed that she would likely remain in that cell for up to seventy-two hours before the DA scheduled an arraignment.

Because McNulty would answer no questions regarding her Suboxone dosage reduction schedule, or for which drug or drugs she was being treated with Suboxone, she was placed on a two-hour watch schedule for possible withdrawal symptoms and was allocated one Tegretol capsule with breakfast and dinner.

Before vacating the Reddick home at the request of the troopers, the civilian consultants Matson and DeMarco were able to observe that one large room in the house was set up for the fulfillment of orders from Reddick's website: rolls of mailing labels and shipping tape, stacks of Priority mailing boxes of various sizes, rolls of Bubble Wrap, and bags full of foam peanuts all neatly lined against the walls. A digital scale, presumably for weighing packages about to be shipped, sat atop a small folding table.

≫————————≪

After McNulty's arrest, Miller, Matson, and DeMarco returned to the Troop D station house, where Miller had left his car. During the twenty-five-minute drive, DeMarco speculated on the fact that neither of the three, during their brief time inside the Reddick home, had seen a desktop or laptop computer.

"Wherever Reddick is," he said, "he either has it with him or he got rid of it entirely. It's impossible to guess what lake or river it might be in. He cleaned up everything before he left."

Jayme said, "I wonder why he didn't take McNulty with him?"

DeMarco pursed his lips and shook his head. "Let's hope he lives to regret that decision."

Jayme said, "Maybe she was his listening post. Keeping him apprised of any developments."

"Makes sense," DeMarco said. "I'm fairly certain this was a closed system. Reddick, McNulty, Jakiella, and Sullivan. With Sonny and Amber in jail, McNulty would be his only source of information."

"Which means there must have been some phone contact between them. Something to track down."

"Not necessarily. If they were smart—and it's clear that Reddick is no dummy—she would have a burner hidden somewhere but would use it only once."

"Either to give him the all clear or to tell him to keep running."

"Exactly."

"Do you think McNulty will crack?" Miller asked.

"I'm betting no."

Jayme said, "If she doesn't, we'll have to break one of the softer ones."

"You never know," DeMarco said. "Another night in jail might soften Sonny up. Especially when we tell him that we have Cheryl too. Boyd might have some qualms about lying to him about what she has or hasn't told us, but we're all just stupid civilians. Who knows what we might say?"

Minutes later, DeMarco pulled into the parking lot and eased into a space near Miller's car. He turned then to address Miller, who had been silent throughout most of the drive. "We won't be needing you tomorrow, Chase. But what you did today...it got us where we are. You delivered, and we're all grateful for that."

"Thanks," the young man said, but without lifting his gaze to the rearview mirror. He popped open the door to climb out.

DeMarco said, "Hold up. I'll walk you to your car."

Miller walked briskly and DeMarco had to hurry to catch up to him just as the young man thumbed down the remote button to unlock his door. "Hey," DeMarco said. "You understand that you can't write about any of this yet, yes?"

"Of course," Miller said.

"Not a word. Not anywhere. I need your promise on that."

"You have it," Miller said. "I promise."

The young man was too subdued and DeMarco thought he knew why. He softened his voice even more. "Listen," he said. "If you're feeling like things went a little too far with McNulty—and nobody needs to know how far they went—just forget about it. She solicited you, you handed her the money, end of story."

Miller stared at the gravel. Then looked up. "What about when it goes to court? Is she going to talk about it then? Will I have to?"

"Nah," DeMarco said. "It will never get that far. She'll plead guilty in exchange for a reduced sentence. There won't even be a trial."

"Are you sure?"

"Ninety-nine percent," DeMarco said. "She didn't video anything, did she?"

"No, thank God."

"Then we're good. Go home, take it easy, get some rest. You don't work tonight, do you?"

"I took the whole day off. Wasn't sure how long you would need me."

"Then enjoy your free time. Do you have a girlfriend somewhere?"

"No. Not really."

"Take it from me," DeMarco told him, and placed his hand on the young man's shoulder, "the right girlfriend changes everything. You just need to find her."

"I'll keep looking," Miller told him. "Thanks."

DeMarco nodded and turned away. Took a few steps from the car, then turned again. "Have you ever considered a career in law enforcement?"

"Me?" Miller asked, surprised. "No, sir, I haven't. I'm probably not very trainable."

DeMarco laughed, turned and headed for his own vehicle. "Singing my tune, son. You're singing my tune."

SEVENTY-ONE

The bad news came early in the morning in the form of a 3:14 phone call from Trooper Boyd. "Amber Sullivan passed away, Sergeant. Heart failure. They brought her back a couple of times but she wouldn't stabilize. I just now left her mother."

"Oh lord," DeMarco said.

Jayme was lying beside him, awake, eyebrows raised. Hero, when the phone first vibrated, had already risen from the floor on Jayme's side to come around the foot of the bed and stand there looking up at DeMarco.

"Thank you, Mace," DeMarco said into the phone. "Let's get together this morning, okay? How's nine for you and Flores?"

"Nine's good. See you then."

DeMarco ended the call and told Jayme, "It's Amber. Heart failure."

"She's gone?" Jayme asked, her eyes already shining with tears.

He nodded.

"That poor girl."

He nodded again. Put his hand out and rubbed Hero's snout. "Lie down, boy. It's okay, lie down."

Hero licked his hand once, then walked in a tight circle before lying down next to the bed.

Jayme said, "I'm going to pray for her."

DeMarco placed the phone back on the bedside table, then

turned to lie facing her, their hands touching. "I will too," he said.

"Tell your boy she's coming."

"I hope she's already there."

"I don't even like to think about the life she must have led. All that pain every day."

He nodded. "Georgina and Diana too. And Suzi. Let's hope they're all out of it now. No more pain."

"We should go to her funeral."

"We could, if you really want to. Though that's all just for show, you know."

A tear slid across the bridge of her nose. "Do you think we had anything to do with her death?"

"I think everybody who ever hurt her or used her had something to do with it. Us included."

"Oh, baby. That makes me feel so bad."

"It makes me angry."

"That too. But right now I just want to cry awhile."

He tightened his arm around her. "You go ahead. We'll be angry together tomorrow."

They held each other, shuddered and wept for the girl they hardly knew, Jayme's tears falling onto his chest, his into her hair.

SEVENTY-TWO

D eMarco said, "We need one team to drive up to Saegertown and push Sonny hard. Three counts of murder one, manslaughter for Amber, possession and distribution, whatever else you can think of. Lay it on thick. Promise him we'll press for the death penalty. Don't play nice. Bring up his daughters. What it's going to do to them. He's been without drugs for a while now, so find every weak spot you can and rip it open."

"You're looking at me," Trooper Boyd said with a small smile, "so...you want Jayme and me to go?"

"Actually, no," DeMarco said. "I guess I was just thinking out loud. Flores and I are a better fit for this one. You guys take McNulty. Everybody okay with that?"

They were spread out around the conference table this time, at least one empty seat between each of them, as if each had come into the room already isolated by their own thoughts, their own emotions, and were in a state of mind to preserve that isolation. Boyd had started the meeting by informing them that Reddick's website had disappeared, that a BOLO for Reddick had been issued, the Washington County State Police alerted to the possibility that he might be hiding out in Lost City, the Elk County State Police surveilling his mother's home in Benezette and checking on all rental cabins in the area, Canadian Border Services Agency alerted, all precautions being taken.

"Cell phone data?" DeMarco asked.

"No pings," said Boyd.

"So he's on high alert," Jayme said. "He's running."

DeMarco nodded. "Or hiding."

Boyd said, "McNulty will probably make bail today."

Flores asked, "What if the DA argues that she's a suspect in a murder case?"

DeMarco shrugged. "You can run it past Captain Bowen, but I doubt it will fly. There's zero evidence to support it. In fact, Jakiella's confession contradicts McNulty's involvement."

"She's still a person of interest," Jayme said.

Boyd told her, "To us she is. Her lawyer's going to claim entrapment. We have the recording to rebut that. But right now we don't have a thing to suggest that either she or Reddick was involved in the murders."

DeMarco frowned, acknowledging the truth. "Do we know where Reddick banks?"

Boyd said, "Both Citizens and Farmers have been notified. They're watching the accounts."

"Okay, then," DeMarco said. He looked from face to face. "We do what we can do. Any questions?"

Flores started to raise her hand, then pulled it back down. She asked, "So our job is to get Sonny to *un*confess? And their job," with a nod toward Boyd, "is to get McNulty to…to what? Turn on Reddick?"

"He abandoned her," DeMarco said. "That's the only pitch that's going to make her flip. They've been together awhile; she's more of a partner than the others were. She has to be convinced that Reddick doesn't share her loyalty. That he sold her out. Left her behind as the sacrificial lamb. If she can be convinced that he isn't coming back for her, she'll be ours."

"You don't sound very optimistic about Sonny being of any help."

"I'm not. I expect that his cowardice will overrule what's left of his neocortex. But we're going to give it our best shot, aren't we, partner?"

Flores nodded. "I'm looking forward to it."

SEVENTY-THREE

DeMarco: "You screwed the pooch this time, Sonny. Killed that pretty young woman."

Jakiella (weeping): "You can't put that on me. She *called* me to come get her. I didn't even know about those damn pills."

Flores: "Wa wa wa. Dead is dead, Sonny. How long have you been her supplier?"

Jakiella: "We were trying to get her clean! That's what both of us wanted."

DeMarco: "And you do that how? By getting her drunk and snorting heroin?"

Jakiella: "She was freaking out, man. It was her idea. She needed to calm down, that's what it was all about. I would've done anything for her."

Flores: "Well, you sure did, didn't you? All the way to the grave."

Jakiella fell forward against the table's edge, lay atop his hands secured at the wrist, pressed his forehead to the metal tabletop. His body shook convulsively with every sob. They allowed it to continue, waited for him to wear himself out with misery. After a couple of minutes, the interrogation began again.

DeMarco: "You owe her the truth, Sonny. We know you didn't kill those people. We know you don't have it in you."

Flores: "You need to start thinking about the living now. Think about your children. You love your daughters, don't you? Do you realize how screwed up they're going to be if they go through life believing you killed three people? Every time they close their eyes they will see two women burning up in a car, a man screaming because you're driving rebar into his chest. *My father did that,* they'll think. *I'm the daughter of a monster.*"

DeMarco: "Is that what you want, Sonny? You want to ruin your daughters' lives?"

Flores: "Sit up, Sonny. Sit up and look at us, you coward!"

Jakiella lifted his head off the table. He sat hunched over, his head barely high enough that he could look at Flores's chin, his arms hanging limp as if he were holding on to something heavy, something like two buckets of lead that were pulling his shoulders down and making his head lag forward, made his knees ache all the time for no apparent reason, made the base of his spine feel on the verge of being crushed. Something weighty and awkward he could not release, an integral part of him as indelible as a massive keloid scar. Something like guilt.

DeMarco: "We have McNulty too. She's in the Mercer County Jail right now. And you know what? She agrees with you. She's blaming everything on you. Her words, if I recall correctly, are that Sonny Jakiella is the worst kind of scum. A weasel, I think she called you. A worm."

Flores: "How do you feel about that, Sonny? You said you aren't responsible for Amber's death but you are responsible for the others. How does that work? Why don't you just take all the blame for everything and let Reddick and McNulty skate? Let them go off and do it all over again to somebody else."

DeMarco: "What do you say we do a polygraph, Sonny? How about we get one in here and get you hooked up?"

Jakiella: "Those things aren't admissible and you know it."

DeMarco: "They carry some weight with the jury though. Juries love polygraph tests."

Flores: "And how is that going to look when you fail the test? The whole world will think you're the biggest fool in the universe. You will go down in history as a bad joke. Your children, your grandchildren, that's how they're going to remember you."

DeMarco: "The only way you change any of that, Sonny, is to tell the truth."

Flores: "Did Reddick hold a gun on you to make you help? Or was it Micki? I can see her with the gun. Reddick gives the orders and Micki holds the gun. Tell me if I'm wrong."

Again they waited. Jakiella's sobbing had abated but his body still quivered. Whether from the drug and alcohol withdrawal or the chill of the room was unimportant. His eyes had gone blank— cold wet marbles gone blind to everything but misery.

Jakiella: "I need to think about this. You need to let me alone awhile so I can think straight."

DeMarco: "We've laid out your options fairly clearly, Sonny. There are only two of them."

Flores: "Hold to your lie and be despised by your children, or man up and tell the truth. Which are you going to do?"

Jakiella: "Just leave me alone awhile. Please just give me some time to think."

DeMarco looked at Flores; nodded.

Flores: "All right, take a little time, then. Talk to Amber about it. Ask her what she would want you to do."

At the mention of Amber's name, he collapsed into sobs again, chin tucked into his chest, eyes squeezed shut. DeMarco and Flores stood.

DeMarco: "We'll see you again soon."

Flores: "Think about Amber. Think very, very hard."

Jakiella, hoarsely: "Sully. Call her Sully."

DeMarco: "She was Amber Marie Sullivan. Intelligent, beautiful, sensitive…a poet. A good, decent person with a lifetime of bad breaks. And she was your only friend. The only person in the world who trusted you. That's who she was, Sonny. And don't you ever forget it. That is precisely who she was."

SEVENTY-FOUR

I can tell you how they did it and everything," McNulty said. She wore a carefree, foggy-eyed look and spoke in a lilting, almost musical voice wholly unlike the belligerent Micki whom Jayme and Boyd had first encountered. McNulty's face was relaxed, her body loose, eyes unfocused as her gaze drifted from one pale-green wall to another in the interview room at the women's section of the Mercer County Jail.

The change was so curious to Jayme that while Boyd informed McNulty of her right to have a lawyer present, Jayme went to the door and asked the female guard if McNulty had gotten hold of some drugs somehow. "She got her epilepsy medicine with breakfast," the guard said.

"That's all?" Jayme asked.

"No way she got anything else," the guard said.

Jayme returned to her seat beside Boyd. McNulty smiled at her and said, "I wish I had hair like yours. It's so thick and pretty. You should wear more makeup, though."

Jayme said, "Thank you for the advice. And now let me give you some. We already took a statement from Mr. Jakiella, and one from Amber before she passed away. And they both told us the entire story, start to finish. And it's a different story from the one you're telling. So, right now you are looking at charges for prostitution. And let's see, what else? Obstruction of justice, defrauding the government, conspiracy to commit murder, accomplice to murder…we can stack up the charges as high as we want."

"Okay, sweetheart," McNulty said.

Boyd said, "Do you still want to blame it on Jakiella?"

"Do you want to know how he did it? Skinny little man that he is?"

"Go right ahead."

"Okay," McNulty said. "So Sully and Suzi, they did not like each other, not one bit. Especially after Sully caught her and Sonny going at it."

"Why would Sully care?" Jayme asked. "She and Sonny weren't lovers."

"He wanted it worse than anything, though. All she wanted was a big brother. And she didn't like seeing her big brother banging a little Vietnamese whore." McNulty opened her mouth and laughed, a deep *hunh hunh hunh* rising up from her chest.

"So then what?" Boyd asked.

"Sully made him promise to get rid of her. Which meant getting rid of all three of them, of course. They were all of a piece. So Sully knocked them out at dinner one night. I watched them falling over in their chairs, one two three, just like that." She tried to snap her fingers at the word *that*, but made no sound.

"How did she pull that off?" Boyd asked.

"Sully?"

"How did she knock them out?"

"She had some syrup she used. Soaked some of those little orange slices in it and fed it to them as an appetizer."

Chloral hydrate, Jayme thought. And asked, "And where did she get her hands on that?"

"Oh I don't know. She had it around somewhere. She put some more in a pitcher of margaritas she made."

"All right," Boyd said. "And then what?"

"Then she wanted me to help carry them outside to the car, but I said unh uh, don't involve me in any of this."

"Did Luthor help?" Jayme asked.

"Luthor? He wasn't even there."

"Where was he?"

McNulty wrinkled her brow, scratched behind an ear. "I don't remember where he was that time."

"You're sure about this?" Jayme asked. "He wasn't even in the house when it happened?"

"We had chicken fajitas that night," McNulty said. "I made a big platter of them. Choo Choo bought the groceries and I cooked them up."

"You remember that," Jayme said, "but you can't remember where Luthor was?"

"He's always coming and going. Got a business to run, you know. Collectibles. Household stuff mostly. Now and then a religious statue or two." And again she laughed, that same deep-chested grunt.

Boyd said, "Tell us how they got Choo Choo and the women out to the woods. And what happened out there."

"I wasn't a part of any of it," McNulty said.

"But you know what happened," Jayme said.

"She bragged about it afterward, Sully did. She could be a mean little bitch when she wanted to."

Again Boyd asked, "How did they get them into the woods?"

"In a car, of course. Kept them taped up till dark, then made the girls help drag Choo Choo out and cram him into the back end. Same thing once they got where they were going. Stood him up against that tree and tortured the poor man. For what? For bringing those two girls into our lives. Personally, I liked them. I liked them all."

Boyd rolled his eyes at Jayme. To McNulty, he said, "Okay. And then what?"

"Then they drove home. Sully and Sonny."

"Drove home in what?" Jayme asked.

Again McNulty's brow wrinkled. "Oh, okay. Yeah. They walked out, didn't they? That's what they done."

Jayme leaned back in her chair. Shot a glance at Boyd, a tiny shake of her head. To McNulty, she said, "Is this the way the Tegretol always affects you, Micki?"

"What way, honey?"

"You seem a little too happy to me."

"Why wouldn't I be happy?"

"You're in jail," Boyd told her.

"Oh, you know. Everybody has to be somewhere, don't they?"

Before leaving the facility, Jayme stopped at the infirmary to speak with the RN, a tall, sturdy, fiftyish woman in a navy-blue pantsuit with white piping around the pockets and the tunic's short sleeves and mandarin collar. Her dark hair was pulled back in a bun.

"I'm curious about the Tegretol," Jayme said. "The epilepsy medicine? What exactly are its effects?"

"Are you asking about the side effects?" the nurse asked.

"No, just the overall effects on the patient. How do they manifest themselves?"

"Well, the active ingredient is carbamazepine. It comes with a long list of possible but generally rare side effects, but the desired effect for epileptics is to manage seizures. It is also prescribed for bipolar disorder to manage mood swings. Why do you ask?"

"Is it ever used recreationally?"

The nurse cocked her head and looked puzzled. She turned away and stepped up to a table on which lay several open folders.

Skimmed the names on the tabs and picked up one folder and glanced at the patient's sheet inside. "You were here to see Cheryl McNulty, correct?"

"We just now finished talking with her."

"She gets a 200 milligram chewable at breakfast and dinner. Prescribed by Dr. Sanjay Narang. Was she having a negative reaction of some kind?"

"Negative?" Jayme said. "I don't think so. In fact, just the opposite, considering where she is. She seemed a little dopey to me. In a euphoric kind of way. Have you seen that reaction before?"

"I haven't, no."

"Was she administered Suboxone today? Could that have done it?"

The RN looked at the file, then said, "No, none. She gets that only as needed. And no withdrawal symptoms have been reported."

"Hmm," Jayme said. "Okay. I was just wondering."

"It's not uncommon for Suboxone to be abused," the nurse told her. "Some people crush it up and snort it. It isn't terribly effective except in those who don't use opioids."

"But there's no way she could have gotten hold of some this morning?" Jayme said.

"No. I'll go have a look at her, though. Just in case."

"Give me a call if you notice anything usual."

Trooper Boyd was waiting for her on the other side of the metal detector in the lobby. They walked together to the State Police SUV in the parking lot. Boyd agreed that McNulty's behavior did not fit his expectations, given their first meeting, but attributed it to her guile. "She had her story down pat," he said. "Knew we'd be coming sooner or later. I think she was just having fun with us. Her kind of fun."

"You didn't think she seemed a little spaced-out and dopey?"

"They all seem dopey to me," he said. "Or else they wouldn't be in there."

SEVENTY-FIVE

Leaving Boyd and Flores to write their reports, DeMarco unlocked the front door to find Hero on the threshold, tail wagging. "There's my boy," Jayme said, and knelt to kiss his skull and rub his fur. "We owe you a walk, don't we? You want to take a walk?"

"I'll get the leash," DeMarco said.

"You don't have to come if you don't want to. You seem tired."

"Frustrated is all. Be right back."

Jayme sat on the edge of the porch, her hand gripping Hero's collar, until DeMarco returned. As he fastened the leash, he said, "No phone messages. Do you think we need to change real estate agents?"

"It's a slow market, babe."

"We've had two showings since the sign went up. At this rate you'll be a…"

"I'll be a what?"

"We'll both be old before this place sells."

"That isn't what you were going to say."

"Never mind, baby."

"No secrets, remember? I'll be a what?"

"I was going to say that you'll be a widow before this place sells."

She looked at him with sad eyes. "Don't you ever die on me, DeMarco."

"It was a stupid thing to say. That's why I didn't say it. Until you made me."

She stood there for a moment looking at him. Then Hero shoved his head between her legs. "Okay, boy, we're going." To DeMarco, she said, "Let's go somewhere he can run free. He deserves that after being left alone all week. And not the dog park. Somewhere there's just the three of us."

DeMarco nodded. One stupid word and now both of them were sad. Now both of them were heavy with presentiment and fear. He said, "Let him pee first while I give it some thought."

SEVENTY-SIX

A s he drove he was thinking about how difficult it was to keep his promise to have no secrets from her. It was an impossible promise to keep, even excluding the secrets he had burned, those dirty secrets about the war and his father and the things he had done when he was drinking too much. And there were always new secrets to take their place, memories that returned to him unbidden and made him wince.

His father had possessed all of the usual weaknesses of a man and none of the virtues and that was why DeMarco would always despise him. Nor would he ever be able to rub out the memory of him. At least once each week as a state trooper he had come across a man identical to his father in his behavior, a man who was mean, petty, and weak, a man either too stupid to recognize his own flaws or merely devoid of any concern for the damage he did to others. His father would always stand as DeMarco's best model of what a man should never be.

Thomas Huston, on the other hand, had been the perfect counterpoint to his father's example. Huston had made his family a priority, even after they had been slaughtered. Went half-mad with grief yet managed to track down the killer. Huston was as fine a man as any DeMarco had ever known, a man deeply troubled and flawed, as every man is, yet a man who did his best to face each day with courage and kindness and love and resolution and an understanding that he alone was responsible for everything he said and did. DeMarco had loved Huston in a way he had always wanted to love his father but never could. It was strange that a younger man coming so late into DeMarco's life should finally show him the full measure of what a man should be. DeMarco's father had died a coward and a liar and a parasite on society, a drunk and abuser, but Huston had died bravely, in a self-orchestrated way that only he and DeMarco would ever know and understand. And that was only one of the secrets he could never reveal, not even to Jayme.

The Pymatuning Reservoir straddled the Pennsylvania-Ohio border, with their nearest point of access just outside the village of Jamestown, Pennsylvania. DeMarco turned into the gravel lot above the dam and was glad to see only one other vehicle parked there, a black pickup truck. He parked in the rear corner of the lot, away from the road. Two young people, one male and one female, stood fishing side by side in the pool below the dam. He said, "I think we can turn him loose in the woods here. There's nobody else around."

He glanced at his cell phone: no service. Placed the phone in the glove box, took out his weapon and Jayme's.

"You really think we need those?" she asked.

"No. But let's take them anyway."

Released from the back seat, Hero immediately bolted for the spillway, ran full-out for twenty yards, wheeled around and returned to where they stood watching, wheeled around them and completed the same route another four times before Jayme called for him to stop. "He's so happy," she said. "I guess he's recovered from the surgery."

"A dog has to run. If we head into the woods here we can pick up a trail down the slope a little."

Should he tell her that after his mother died and he had beaten up the neighbor Paul—who was almost an old man then but still detestable—he had not been able to stay in the trailer where she died, but had packed a duffel with canned fruit and crackers and a bottle of Jack Daniel's and had hiked into those woods with nothing else but a tarp and blanket? If he kept that information to himself, did it become a secret and yet another violation of his promise? Should he tell her that he had remained in those woods until he ran out of whiskey, and that he fully intended to go AWOL, but outside the liquor store had a change of heart and telephoned his squad leader and apologized because he would be returning half a day late and then broke into helpless sobs? Or that his squad leader cleaned the mess up for him because DeMarco had always been such a good soldier and followed orders and killed when he was told to kill and sometimes when he was not? He had burned those killing secrets but not the part about almost going AWOL and he did not ever want her to know that about him, that he now saw his entire time in the service as a time of mindless weakness, and that everything he had done since then was an attempt to cauterize that wound just as joining the army and being a dutiful soldier had been a failed attempt to cauterize his youth.

She took his hand as they entered the woods, with Hero running ahead to sniff every tree and fern and to chase every chipmunk. When she paused to gaze into the stream, DeMarco stopped beside her and looked at the water too and said nothing. When she gazed up through the canopy at the browning leaves and the bright broken sunlight and the uneven patches of blue, he paused and looked too. And when she slowed and then looked up at him with tears in her eyes, he slowed too. And when she turned and leaned into him and began to cry, he wrapped his arms around her and kissed her hair and said nothing because she had been remembering too, had wandered upon painful memories more recent than his, memories not yet scarred over but so fresh that every time her mind quieted, those memories washed into her as chilling as ever. And, knowing this, he was ashamed of his own misery over long-past youthful behavior, those memories he should have jettisoned long ago. It was time to hold the good and throw the rest away. She was all and everything that mattered or should matter to him.

So he held her and said nothing and smelled the sunlight on her hair, and when her body trembled against him he held her even closer, and with his eyes closed and his mind quiet he could hear their Hero racing through the leaves. He could smell the forest and the stream, the shadows and the light. He could hear the ugliness back home scratching like dry leaves, like brittle twigs twitching against the sky. But that was there and now was here, and, for a while longer, her love and grief and his love for her were all and everything that mattered.

SEVENTY-SEVEN

The sun was low when they came out of the woods. They emerged a couple of hundred yards from the parking lot, and as they walked back up along Dam Road the sun was to their right, throwing a glassy sheen of gold across the quiet water and shining red through the trees along the horizon. "The magic hour," Jayme said. She was holding the leash but had wrapped it around her hand several times so that only the last foot or so hung limp as Hero trotted along beside her, his snout high and ears perked as if he was taking it all in, absorbing all this new territory through his eyes and ears and nose and tongue. DeMarco took it in too but with an appreciation that did not want to possess, only experience. He was aware of a kind of contentment he had known only rarely in life, that absence of desiring anything more, which he had not experienced since holding Baby Ryan asleep on his chest.

The pickup truck was gone from the parking lot and the young couple who had been fishing in the pool below the dam were gone too. Everything was still except for two people and a dog moving through the stillness like the world's last survivors, the reservoir flat and long and peaceful to their right, the woods hushed and dim to their left. He wished he could freeze it all in that moment and never have to go home again. And with that thought, the contentment faded away.

At the car, while Jayme opened a bottle of water and held it dribbling onto Hero's lapping tongue, he pulled the holster and Glock from his pocket and stowed them in the glove box. Then he sat on the edge of the seat with his feet outside the car and used a large chunk of the limestone gravel to scrape mud off his shoes.

"Anybody hungry?" he asked.

"We're starved, aren't we, boy? We need sustenance."

"There's an Italian place back in town. Plus the ice cream and burger place. And a few other choices back in Greenville."

"But it's not exactly Charlotte, North Carolina, here, is it?" she said. "I don't want to have to leave him in the car while we eat."

They returned to the little brightly colored ice-cream shop on Main Street, where they ordered chili dogs and cheeseburgers and a basket of fries. A retired couple was enjoying their sundaes at the round table on the porch but the grassy patio area was empty, traffic sparse, the town settling into a Mayberry somnolence. DeMarco picked up their order on an orange plastic tray and followed Jayme to a shaded picnic table along the side of the building. He was halfway through his first chili dog when he remembered that he had left his cell phone in the car. He retrieved it, came back to the table, and sat, placing the phone between himself and Jayme. "Voice message from Joe," he said, and tapped the speaker icon.

"What the hell are you people doing down there?" Loughner said. "I thought you were supposed to be some kind of hot-shit investigator. I'm sitting here outside the lab wondering if you even know what you're doing." His voice was scratchy and low and created a picture in DeMarco's mind of Joe sitting hunched over in his car, leaning down to speak into the microphone, the doors and windows closed, the car like a greenhouse, and Joe with a thermos cup of coffee and scotch in his other hand.

"So you raided Reddick's house and what did you come up with? Diddly squat, that's what. If you people had been on the ball you would've gotten there before Reddick bolted. You give a man time to do his spring cleaning, that's what you're going to get. So what's your brilliant plan now? If it was me, I'd be turning the place upside down to find that dirtbag. Go on up to Elk County and shake every fucking tree until he falls out of one of them. Have you even questioned his mother yet? Jesus, DeMarco, are you just sitting on your hands down there or what? Go pull my incident logs, why don't you? I know there's stuff in there could help you find him. Check out that cabin he hid out in after he got discharged. I don't remember the dates but you can get them easy enough. Look at the week his old man died; Junior was back for the funeral. What was he doing that week, who was he hanging out with? Man, this thing is not going to solve itself. You keep dillydallying like this, he's going to be sunning himself in Cancun if he isn't already. Jesus fucking Christ, man. Do your fucking job."

Both Jayme and DeMarco had winced with each f-bomb, had looked at each other with sorrowful eyes. When the call ended, Jayme said, "Apparently he doesn't know that Boyd's been in touch with Elk County."

"Boyd would have told him that." DeMarco shook his head and laid the hot dog back into its paper boat. He did not want to be too hard on Loughner. He looked at Jayme and smiled. *He's me if I hadn't found you*, he thought. And told her, "You think I should change my number?"

She smiled. "I feel kind of sorry for him."

"I do too, though we shouldn't. He's a grown man."

She nodded. Fed a french fry to Hero.

"Since when are we allowed to feed him at the table?" he asked.

"It's a picnic, right? And he's hungry too."

DeMarco looked down at Hero seated behind them, his chin

on the wooden seat. "Do you like mustard on your chili dogs?" he asked.

Hero lifted his chin. And Jayme said, "That's dog sign language for yes."

DeMarco held out the remainder of his chili dog; it disappeared in one gulp. He rubbed Hero's head, then faced the table again.

Jayme said, "Now what, Brainiac?"

A grin twitched at the corner of his mouth. "Do you even know who Brainiac is?"

"Somebody smart, I take it."

He kept smiling. Tapped a fingertip against the table. Eight times he tapped it, then held his fingertip poised in the air. Then a final tap. And said, "What do you think Boyd is doing right now?"

"Probably writing his daily report."

DeMarco reached for his phone and told it, "Call Boyd."

When Trooper Boyd answered, DeMarco said, "When were you going to let me know about the lab results?"

"I was thinking that the morning might be a good time."

DeMarco blew out a breath. He understood Boyd's reaction. The old DeMarco would have gone ballistic.

Boyd said, "I'm guessing you heard from Joe Loughner?"

"You could say that."

"He gave me an earful too."

"Yeah, well," DeMarco said. "Next time, whatever information comes in, I would appreciate knowing it right away. Like three seconds after you know it. Even if the information is no information."

"Yes, sir," Boyd said.

"Please don't call me sir anymore," DeMarco told him, then tamped down the frustration. "Mason, listen. Technically, I'm working for *you*. I'm not your boss. I would like to think that we're partners, though. And partners keep each other apprised."

"Copy that, sir—Sergeant. Can I still call you Sergeant?"

"Of course. You might even throw in a Ryan every now and then. If you think you can pull it off."

"Ha," Boyd said. "That might take some practice."

"You'll get the hang of it. Meantime, you've been in contact with Troop C, right? And they're keeping an eye out for Reddick?"

"They spoke with his mother and she claimed to have no idea where he is. Hadn't heard from him in months, she said. Plus no reported sightings of his vehicle in the area."

"I figured," DeMarco said. "So fill us in on what has Joe so ticked off. Jayme's here too, by the way. Got you on speaker."

"Sure. So…nothing more from the crime scene in Otter Creek. We'll be taking down the tape today. And now that Reddick's website is down…"

"No way to backtrack and find a path to his sales and customers?"

"Not without a fistful of warrants. And even then…"

"Does the DA know all this?"

"The lab faxed him, yeah. He has my and Flores's reports on McNulty's arrest too."

"And let me guess. No search warrant to get back inside the house?"

"He said McNulty will claim the weed was for her epilepsy. And even if it wasn't prescribed, no jury will fault her for finding some relief wherever she can. But we got her cold on the prostitution charge."

"And now what?"

"Now we wait, I guess."

"I'm still not very good at that," DeMarco told him, and

received a knowing smile from Jayme. "Maybe I need to have a conversation with the DA. See where we stand."

"Yeah. I don't think he's gotten back to the captain yet."

"In other words you're telling me to sit tight."

"I just…don't think he's gotten back to the captain yet."

DeMarco laughed. "You know, Mason, I never really appreciated your sense of humor before. But you can be a very funny man sometimes."

SEVENTY-EIGHT

T he DA was a sharp dresser. That was the one thing DeMarco liked about him. He did not like the excessive amount of hair gel. Or the manicured fingernails. Or the pointy-toed leather shoes. He did not like the man's win-at-all-costs attitude. Or the way an hour in the younger man's company made him feel as if he had spent that hour standing over a bubbling deep fryer full of old grease. And that was why DeMarco decided to make contact by phone from the comfort of his car. Besides, the view of the quiet street through his windshield, the Mark Twain Manor and, beyond it, the Randall Funeral Home, was somehow soothing. Jayme at his side, Hero standing on the back seat, panting in his ear. He noticed a chili stain on his pant leg.

To the DA's secretary, he said, "Tell you what, Jeannie. Please inform Mr. Cooper that if he doesn't have three minutes for me now, I will be happy to come to his home tonight. In fact I'm headed in that direction right now. Tell him no hurry, I can wait in his driveway."

DeMarco was put on hold for twenty seconds. Then the line clicked open again. "Sergeant DeMarco," the DA said with a discernible lack of enthusiasm, "what can I do for you?"

"I need to know where we stand on Luthor Reddick."

"Well, sir, by all appearances, we don't stand anywhere on Mr. Reddick."

"Meaning what?"

"Has your team gathered some evidence I don't know about? Something a little more concrete than mere suspicion? Because what I have before me to implicate Mr. Reddick in any way is… let me see here…oh yes, there it is. Absolutely nothing."

DeMarco's left hand clasped shut, stretched open again, fingers rigid. Jayme laid her hand atop it. Into the phone, he said, "I don't like what I'm hearing."

"What's not to like?" the DA said. "We have in custody two witnesses. One has confessed to the murders, and the other has corroborated that confession. As soon as I get McNulty's testimony under oath, we are prepared to move forward."

"She's going to want something for that testimony."

"That's the game we play—is it not?"

"We need to go back out to Reddick's property. He's too smart to hide anything in the house but he has lots of land to hide it on. Where's the rebar he used? Where's the hammer? Where did he burn his bloody clothes, and how about Choo Choo's clothes, and all the drugs he ships out of that office of his? Every so-called collectible in that house is hollow. What do you think he fills them with, bubble bath?"

"Mr. Reddick's property is no longer a crime scene, Sergeant. If you want it searched again, you know what I need."

I know exactly what you need, DeMarco thought. But said, "Have you scheduled your press conference yet?"

"The public has the right to know that the guilty parties are in custody. You wouldn't deny them that right, would you, Sergeant?"

Jayme squeezed his hand. He looked at her. She squeezed again. Into the phone he said, "Have a good night," and ended the call.

SEVENTY-NINE

I t was best to say nothing for a while. Let him drive with his hands strangling the steering wheel, his eyes locked like laser sights on the center line. The evening was cooling, streaming in through the vents, but Jayme knew his opinion of the DA and imagined that DeMarco's body was flush with heat now, so she left the air conditioner vents open and shivered a little and tried to think warming thoughts.

After a while she retrieved her earbuds from inside the console and plugged them into the car's stereo. He said, surprising her, "You don't have to use those."

"I didn't want to disturb your thoughts," she said.

He said, "Channel 49 on Sirius is Motown."

"You sure you wouldn't rather have Ozzy's Boneyard or some nice Liquid Metal?"

He smiled. "Whatever you want, snarky."

She turned on the radio, moved the dial. The Trammps were sixteen bars into "Hold Back the Night." Twelve bars later, she saw his fingers relax. "One of Ozzy's greatest hits," she said.

He smiled as he drove. They listened to another song in silence. Then he said, "Have you ever seen the elk?"

"By *the* elk, you mean…?"

"The elk in Elk County. October is a great time to see them. The stags are full of vinegar and the hinds are strutting their stuff."

"Lots of head bashing and lovemaking, that kind of thing?"

"Precisely."

"Who wouldn't want to see that?"

He smiled again. She rocked her shoulders back and forth to the Elgins' "Heaven Must Have Sent You."

Some twenty minutes later he pulled alongside the RV in the backyard, slipped the gearshift in Park but did not shut off the engine. Behind them, the garage light flared on and threw a long shadow of the car toward the house. Everywhere else lay in twilight. "Dusk," he said aloud, barely a whisper.

"The gloaming," she said.

"I like that word. It's Scottish, like the love of my life."

She felt no need to correct him, say *it's Old English, from the Germanic.* A new song had started. She glanced at the digital readout. Jimmy Ruffin. "What Becomes of the Brokenhearted." "Are you ever going to dance with me again?" she asked. "Like we did on my grandma's porch?"

He looked at her for a moment, then shut off the engine but turned the key back to engage the alternator and keep the music playing. Then he popped open his door and climbed out and left the door open as he walked around to her side. Sensors in the yard tripped lights mounted on the porch roof and along the side of the house. Moments later, both of their phones beeped. He silenced his and opened her door and held out his hand. "It's mating season," he said.

She silenced her phone and climbed out and they danced in the grass to the next three songs. The Spinners. Love Unlimited. Martha and the Vandellas. Hero stood on the rear seat and watched out the window, his tail batting rhythmically back and forth like a conductor's furred baton.

EIGHTY

They headed due east a few minutes before eight in the morning, aiming to reach their destinations in Elk County by ten.
The air was clear but the sky Confederate gray, and though no
glare of rising sun blazed on the windshield, DeMarco wore his
sunglasses to soothe eyes that felt full of sand, despite the eye drops
he had applied twice that morning. Thanks to Loughner's phone
message or the one and a half chili dogs or the conversation with
the DA the previous evening, his few hours of sleep had failed to
refresh him.

After returning home that night, he had telephoned the Troop
C station in Ridgway to let them know that he and Jayme would
be visiting Benezette to question Luthor Reddick's mother, and
asked if he, DeMarco, could also have a look at Joe Loughner's
incident logs for the weeks before and after Thomas Reddick Sr.'s
death, as per Loughner's suggestion. The trooper who had taken
the call said, "Let me speak to the station commander and I'll get
back to you ASAP." DeMarco knew that a call was being placed
to Joe Loughner and expected to have to wait quite a while for an
answer, but was surprised when his phone rang no more than two
minutes later. "No problem, Sergeant. We'll have everything you
need when you get here."

The plan was to drop DeMarco off in Ridgway at the Troop
C station, from which point Jayme would proceed southeast to

Benezette and, with luck, surprise Mrs. Reddick with a visit. They expected the interview to take no longer than thirty minutes. Then Jayme would drive back to Ridgway, pick up DeMarco, and both would travel to one of the elk-viewing areas north of Benezette. "Unless Luthor's mother sets your radar beeping," DeMarco said, "and you get the feeling she knows where he is. In that case we'd better check out some of the cabins and other possibilities before seeing the elk."

"When is the best time to watch all that testosterone in action?" she asked.

"A couple of hours after sunrise and a couple of hours before sunset."

"Just like you," she teased.

"I don't bugle like an elk, though."

"Sometimes you do," she said.

He appreciated that she was trying to keep the mood light. He did not like the heaviness that sometimes came over him during an investigation and made him feel like he was slogging through deep mud or, this time, was knee-deep in quicksand. It helped to be mobile and to have a solid plan for the day but he worried that his mood might be even darker by afternoon if neither destination provided some momentum to the case.

He hated his moods. And wondered what his life might be like if he gave up the profession completely. What would he do to keep from going stir-crazy? They both had some retirement money coming in and a moderate savings account, but a life as world travelers was beyond their reach. If the house sold, half of the money would go to Laraine and a big chunk of it to the real estate agent; not enough would be left over to pay off the RV. He would be fifty in a few months. And, if Jayme got her wish, a father. She was no longer taking birth control pills, a fact he reminded himself of every time they made love. A couple of times he had been unable to ejaculate. The erection never failed him but he wondered if the recalcitrant ejaculation was a subconscious form of birth control on his part.

At her age, prenatal checkups would be frequent and costly; the insurance they paid for as retired troopers would cover only part of the costs. Then there would be a few tons of disposable diapers to buy, then solid food and designer sneakers and electronics and college tuition. Maybe retiring was a big mistake. But did he want to go back to that routine, to having his daily schedule determined by somebody else? A self-directed life had always been his secret dream, but this dream like most came riddled with hidden pitfalls and perils. What had he gotten them into?

"Looks just like ours," Jayme said, which shook him out of his reverie. The Troop C station house was fifty yards ahead and nearly identical to the redbrick building in which they had worked. "The setting and everything," Jayme said. "You should feel right at home."

He smiled and flicked down the turn signal. When had he ever felt at home?

EIGHTY-ONE

N early every business in the town of Benezette seemed to have the word *elk*, *buck*, *stag*, or *antlers* in its name. The air was thick with wood smoke, and despite the last of the colorful leaves in the surrounding woods, every surface appeared weathered and drab. She knew from the research she had done during the drive from home that the population of the entire township was under three hundred people, which meant fewer than two people per square mile. Still, until she read that 7 percent of the population lived under the poverty line, and that the median family income was only $36,000, she had been expecting a small version of Breckenridge or Killington, with expensive chalets and lodges studding the hillsides, and trendy boutiques and bistros lining the streets.

None of that was visible here. Judging by the number of muddy pickup trucks, Jeeps and SUVs in front of every motel, restaurant, and B&B, either every local citizen was in town that morning or she wasn't the only tourist come to watch the elk spar and hump and graze.

The Reddick home was a rambling two-story clapboard on a large weedy lot two streets north of Main, the exterior's blue paint gone chalky and algae-stained. At least three exterior stairways led to second-floor decks, their weathered boards long ago stained the color of redwood. The roof shingles were buckled and all of the windows but one were black in front of heavy, closed curtains.

Only the bay window on the first floor showed any sign of habitation inside: the flickering light of a television screen.

Jayme knocked twice before Mrs. Reddick appeared in the corner of the bay window. No matter how she twisted she could not get a look at Jayme, and so she knocked on the glass. Jayme stepped back from the door, showing herself, and waved. A minute later the door squeaked open partway, letting the loudness of the television burst out.

"Mrs. Reddick?" Jayme asked.

The woman looked well past eighty, was stout but feeble and wary. Her thick lenses on black rims were filmy with dust. She had thin gray hair, parted in the middle and hanging in limp strands over her ears, and she was wearing at least two bulky sweaters, the top one olive green, over a long wool skirt, black, atop gray sweatpants and heavy woolen socks. The scent coming off her body or clothes or wafting from inside the house was strong: old smoke, old sweat, old food, old woman.

"Who wants to know?" she said.

"My name is Jayme Matson, Mrs. Reddick. I'm working with the Pennsylvania State Police on a—"

At the words *state police*, the old woman's eyes narrowed. "I got no time for the police. They never done a damn thing for me. Besides, I already talked to them. What do you want with me now?"

"We're trying to locate your son Thomas—"

"He goes by Luthor now. Has for a long time."

"Yes. Okay. We would like to ask him some questions—"

"I already told them I don't know where he is. If I did I would've said so."

"Okay. That's good," Jayme said. "Would you mind if I come in for a couple of minutes? It's been a long drive up here."

"Where you coming from? Back there where he lives?"

"Yes, ma'am. Back in Mercer County."

"Well, you drove all the way up here for nothing, I hope you know that."

"It's a beautiful drive, though. All those hills and forests and valleys. It's much flatter back home."

"So what do you want to ask him?" she said. "Those other police wouldn't tell me what's going on."

"Well, his housemate, Cheryl McNulty—"

"I know Cheryl. She used to come up here with him. Invited me to come visit them sometime. Though how she expects me to get there without a car, I have no idea."

Jayme smiled. Nodded. Said, "Anyway, Cheryl hasn't seen Luthor for several days, and she's worried about him. I promised her I would try to track him down."

"If she's so worried, why wouldn't she just call me then? It makes no sense sending you up here instead."

"We were coming up anyway. To look at the elk. So we just figured we'd stop in here on the way."

"Well, you're wasting your time and mine too. If Luthor don't want found, nobody's going to find him."

"I was hoping you could help me with that."

The old woman snorted and looked like she might spit. But then she swallowed and turned away. "Come on in then if you have to. And close that door tight behind you. You're letting all the heat out."

EIGHTY-TWO

Twenty minutes passed from the time DeMarco walked into the station house until he was able to sequester himself in a small room with a cup of coffee and Joe Loughner's daily reports. He first had to shake eight hands and answer numerous questions, not only about the current investigation but also about the Huston, Aberdeen, and Youngstown cases too. One trooper joked, "We figured you must be at least nine feet tall," which made DeMarco so uncomfortable that he lied about having another appointment in an hour. He was shown to the windowless room and told, "This is the quietest room in the building. Joe said to give you any and everything you need. He sure thinks highly of you."

And again he felt guilty and confused. And sat down to smother those emotions with work.

Two rectangular wooden tables, each approximately two feet by three feet, their surfaces scarred and scratched and stained, had been pushed together to make one table, with a single wooden chair placed against the edge. Atop the table and centered beneath a hanging light in a rectangular metal shade was an accordion file containing a short stack of individual sheets, a single white legal pad, a blue gel pen, and an ashtray. DeMarco pulled out the chair and sat, set the ashtray on the floor and gave it a shove with his foot.

The daily reports were dated consecutively for two weeks in

the summer of 1989, loose unless a day's log ran to two pages, in which case those pages were stapled in the upper left-hand corner. Seeing those dates, DeMarco realized for the first time that Reddick Jr. and he had been in the army at the same time. He didn't know why that realization should startle and upset him, but it did.

Joe's typing was uniform from page to page and showed no signs of misspellings or typos. And it had been typed on a typewriter, not printed from a computer screen, which meant that Joe had been a very careful and possibly slow typist. He cared about the appearance of his work. Took pride in it, no doubt. Even his cursive initials at the end of each report were clear and precise.

He would have been close to forty back then. Probably clean and sober and ambitious. Fully invested in his vow to serve and protect. What was different now? Maybe only the clean and sober part. When and why had things changed?

DeMarco pulled the legal pad in front of his right hand and picked up the pen. Slid the incident logs directly in front of his chest, the oldest one on top. And read.

Then the next. The next. The next. Taking each by the bottom corner and turning it upside down onto the table, gradually stacking them up again. They read much as he remembered his own former reports. Domestic disturbances, vehicular accidents, driving violations, drunk and disorderlies, providing assistance to citizens with car troubles, reprimanding noisy, disruptive, or truant children and teens, investigating thefts, assaults, shoplifting, and other generally stupid behavior. A few drug busts or arrests for possession, most of them involving cannabis. A typical day in the life of a trooper. The nearest municipalities of St. Marys and Emporium had their own police departments but tiny Benezette did not, so many 9-1-1 calls from local citizens were dispatched to the nearest state police vehicle.

DeMarco read seven daily reports without making a notation on the legal pad. Then came the eighth report. 4:29 p.m. A Thursday afternoon. Troopers Loughner and Stottlemeyer had responded to a 9-1-1 call placed by a distraught woman who returned home from work to find her husband bloodied and dead in the living room, wearing only a white T-shirt and white crew socks. Victim, Thomas Reddick Sr. Wife, Elsie Campbell Reddick, employed as cashier at Shaffer's Market on Main Street. Manager confirmed that Mrs. Reddick was in the store from a few minutes before 8:00 a.m. until 4:10 p.m. Mr. Reddick's body was found in a state of advanced rigor when the troopers arrived. Multiple traumas to the face and head. Couple has one son, Thomas Reddick Jr., active army, currently stationed at Fort Leonard Wood in the Ozarks.

The remaining reports all included information pertinent to the ongoing investigation into Reddick Sr.'s death. Coroner confirmed death by multiple blunt trauma to the head and face. Evidence suggested a motive of robbery; traces of white powder later identified as cocaine were found on the coffee table and between floorboards. All known associates were questioned. No arrests made.

According to the logs, Luthor Reddick had returned home to Benezette the evening before his father's funeral. When questioned by Loughner and Stottlemeyer, the younger Reddick stated that he "didn't know anybody who *wouldn't* want to kill the old man. He was a piece of shit to everybody he met. Good riddance to bad rubbish."

And that was it. One single piece of information about Reddick Jr., and it was of absolutely no value in helping DeMarco locate Reddick. Why had Joe insisted he come here and read reports that would be of no value? Bad memory? Or was DeMarco missing something?

EIGHTY-THREE

Jayme stepped inside the house and immediately understood why the old woman was dressed in several layers of clothing. The air was stale and odorous and chilly, several degrees cooler than the outside air. She said, "I bet these old houses are hard to heat, aren't they?"

"I wish somebody would burn it to the ground. With me in it." Mrs. Reddick settled herself in the center of an old sofa facing the blaring TV, a fifty-inch flat-screen on a black plastic stand. She lifted up the quilt hanging to the floor and pulled it over her legs and up to her chest.

Jayme nodded at the remote control on the arm of the sofa. "Any chance we could turn the volume down a bit? I have an inner ear thing, makes it hard for me to hear a conversation sometimes."

"You seen a doctor about it?" The old lady picked up the remote and held it out to Jayme, who lowered the volume by half.

"A couple of times," Jayme said. "Might as well have flushed my money down the toilet."

"Tell me about it," Mrs. Reddick said. "You can set down if you want."

Jayme's choice was sit in the corner of the sofa, close to the old woman's feet, or in the darkly stained wing chair with its back to the drafty window. She chose the chair.

"I'm going to need that remote back when *Wheel of Fortune* comes on."

"Oh, I love that show!" Jayme said. "What time does it come on here?"

"Eleven. I never miss it."

Jayme glanced at her phone. 10:32. "So about Luthor," she said. "When was the last time you heard from him?"

"Heard from him or seen him?"

"Both."

"He calls me every week on Sunday morning. Usually around this time."

"And did he call you this past Sunday?"

"You didn't let me finish. It's been a while since I heard from him. At least a month, I'd say."

"And how long since you have seen him?"

"For a while there he was coming by every month or so and taking me into St. Marys for dinner. They got a Bob Evans there I like. Sometimes he'd stay the night and make breakfast for us the next day."

Jayme held on to the remote, smiled and nodded. With each deep breath, she wanted to wince. The air smelled as stale as old crackers, as sad as…as an old woman alone in a cold, empty house.

"They make this pot roast hash, I think it's called. At the Bob Evans there. With an egg on top of it however you want it done. Luthor always got his scrambled but I like my yolk runny. Over easy, I'd tell them, or else I'm sending it back."

"Luthor sounds like a very considerate son."

"He's always been good to me. He's a good boy. Always has been."

"But you haven't seen him for a while? Is that correct?"

"Anything I want, he gets it for me. Has my groceries delivered every week, has those Meals on Wheels coming every Tuesday and Thursday. My Visiting Angel comes on Saturday to do the laundry and help me in and out of the tub. That last one, though, she was no angel, I'll tell you that. Boozer, I think. She'd get here and the next minute be snoring in the chair. Luthor got her fired is what he did. They shouldn't have a person working if they hate their job so much they have to get drunk to do it."

"I couldn't agree with you more," Jayme said. "Luthor's business must be doing well."

The old woman shrugged. "It's not like I ask for a helluva lot. I wasn't brought up that way."

"Is it true that Luthor had a little problem with the army when he was younger?"

"He was just a boy! Damn government has no right taking boys away from their home like that."

The old woman looked as if she were about to say more, so Jayme remained silent.

"They have this pot roast hash, I think it's called. That's what I always get. Last time it was a little dry, though. Not enough gravy. And I told them so. I don't believe in paying for bad food."

"Nor should you," Jayme said. "So how *were* things at home when Luthor was a boy? Between you and Mr. Reddick, I mean."

"Huh," she said, and yanked at a thread of yarn on the quilt.

"Not good?"

"You ever made a mistake with a man? A bad mistake?"

Jayme smiled. "Isn't every man a bad mistake?"

The old woman laughed, showed her yellowed teeth. "You got that right, don't you?" She looked around the room. "You seen my cigarettes anywhere?"

Jayme scanned the room. "I'm sorry, I don't see them."

"Maybe I'm setting on them." She leaned to the side, slipped a hand under her body, down between the cushions. Then leaned to the other side, felt around with her other hand. "I'm always losing the damn things."

"I can get up and look around for them," Jayme said.

"Look out in the kitchen on the table. That's where I usually leave them."

Jayme was happy to stand and move. Her hands were cold, her nose was cold. The chilly air coming off the window had made the hair at the back of her neck stiff.

On the kitchen table, a pack of Marlboro Lights lay beside a butane lighter and a saucer already half-full of butts and ashes. Dirty dishes in both sides of the double-basin sink. Foil pans with baked, dried-on food sticking out the top of the trash container. A Campbell's soup can on the stove, a layer of white, congealed bacon fat two inches from the top.

"They out there?" Mrs. Reddick called.

On the door of the refrigerator, along with a three-by-five-inch magnetic sign listing the county's emergency numbers, plus five restaurant flyers with the phone numbers circled in blue ink, were two photographs of Luthor Reddick. The image in the first photo had yellowed from age and showed a young Luthor in his army camo fatigues, pointing a rifle and snarling at the camera. In the second photo, a middle-aged Luthor and a woman were standing in front of a waterfall, both in shorts and T-shirts, Luthor grinning while the woman smiled sleepily, her head against Luthor's shoulder.

"Still looking!" Jayme said, and lifted the second photo by its untaped bottom edge; nothing was written on the back. That woman posing with Luthor—who was she? Jayme took out her phone and captured three shots, the last one zeroing in on the woman's face.

"What the hell you doing out there?"

"Sorry!" Jayme called. "I got distracted admiring the view from your kitchen window."

"I don't know what you think is worth looking at out there."

"I found your cigarettes!"

"Get 'em in here, then. I always have a smoke when *Wheel of Fortune* comes on."

Jayme pocketed her phone and returned to the living room, where she handed the pack of cigarettes and lighter to Mrs. Reddick, then set the saucer ashtray on the sofa's armrest and took her seat again.

The old lady asked, "Where did you find them? On the table?"

"Actually they were on top of the refrigerator."

Mrs. Reddick wrinkled up her face as she lit the cigarette and sucked in a lungful of smoke. She blew it out again. "That's odd. I never leave them there. I don't even know why I would."

"I do things like that all the time. Sometimes I'll walk into a room and then forget why I even went there in the first place."

"Ha," the old lady said. "Happens to me a dozen times a day."

"Those are nice photos of Luthor on your refrigerator," Jayme said. "That waterfall in the second one is beautiful. Do you know where it was taken?"

"Umm, it was down in West Virginia somewhere. Down past Morgantown, as I recall. Black Falls or something like that."

"Blackwater Falls?"

"That's it. Him and Cheryl brought me back a jar of maple syrup and a ball cap from an Indian trading post there. I asked them what's a ball cap have to do with Indians? Insulted her, I think, though I didn't mean to. She's not been back to see me since."

"That's Cheryl in the photo?"

"Who else would it be?"

"How long ago was the photo taken?"

"Years ago. Luthor always says it's because of her epilepsy getting worse, why she never comes with him here no more. I think he just don't want me to feel bad is all. Me and her always got along good before that. I didn't mean nothing by it. Just couldn't see no connection between a ball cap and them Indians. People are too sensitive sometimes."

Jayme smiled. Said nothing. Pretended to watch the TV for a minute. Then slapped a hand over her pocket. "Whoops, there goes my phone." She pulled the phone out, looked at it, and said, "It's my partner calling. I'll just step out into the kitchen for a second so I don't bother you. Be right back."

In the kitchen, facing the refrigerator, she whispered into her phone, "Call Ryan."

Eleven seconds later, he said "Hey," and she said, "Hey, babe. I'm going to head your way in a few minutes. Any chance you could call Boyd and get him to send you a photo of McNulty?" Her voice was hushed, a hand cupped around her mouth.

"What's going on?" he asked.

"We have a kind of development here. It would be great if Boyd could get that photo to you before I arrive. A close-up of her face."

"Are you whispering because Reddick is nearby?"

"No, nothing like that. You know what? I should've just waited a couple of minutes. I'll call you from the car." She ended the call, took a couple of quick breaths. Suddenly her heart was racing. She took one measured breath after another, a little deeper each time, and gradually felt the thumping of her heart lessen.

She stared at the photo. *No, no way. Nobody changes that much over the course of a few years. Wrong nose. Wrong mouth. Wrong hair. Wrong eyes.*

She went from the kitchen to the edge of the foyer. "I'm so sorry, Mrs. Reddick," she said, "but I need to get back to my partner now. I enjoyed our conversation."

The old woman drew the blanket from her chest and struggled to slide her legs off the sofa. "You can't stay and watch *Wheel* with me?"

"I'm sorry, I can't. Please don't get up. Thanks again." She strode to the door, didn't wait to see if the woman managed to lift herself from the sofa or not.

EIGHTY-FOUR

Two troopers were huddled together looking at a computer screen, one man seated, the other standing, when DeMarco approached from the side. The area outside the little room where he had spent the past hour seemed inordinately bright, almost dizzyingly so. He said, "I need Trooper Boyd back home to shoot me a photo of Cheryl McNulty. If he emails or faxes it here, could you maybe print it out for me?"

The trooper sitting at the desk pulled a notepad his way, scribbled a number on it, tore the sheet off, and handed it to DeMarco. "There you go.".

The other trooper asked, "What's it for?"

"Jayme thinks the woman we arrested isn't Cheryl McNulty."

"Seriously? But that's the name she gave you?"

"Yes, sir."

"What makes Jayme think that?"

"Be right back," DeMarco said. He went back into the little room, picked up his phone from the table beside Loughner's incident reports, called Boyd and asked him to call the county jail and request a current photo of McNulty to be sent to his phone and also to the Troop C fax machine. "Here's the number for the fax," he said.

"Whoa," Boyd said. "She's out."

"She's what?"

"As of 9:30 this morning. She proffered to the prostitution charge, gave her statement under oath, and made bail."

"Please tell me you're kidding."

"No, sir, I am not."

"What did she swear to?"

"Same thing she told us. Sonny and the girl did it."

DeMarco's head was spinning. "You and Flores need to get out there right now, out to Reddick's place. Get a few photos of her and send them to Jayme's and my phones ASAP. And whatever you do, do not let her go anywhere."

"If she's not the real Cheryl, she's been defrauding the U.S. government. Collecting the real Cheryl's disability checks."

"At the very least," DeMarco said.

"How sure are you that she's an impersonator?"

"Jayme's 90 percent. She saw a photo of the real one at Reddick's mother's house."

"Holy mackerel," Boyd said. "So where *is* the real one?"

"That's our second problem. Let's take care of the first one first."

"Roger that, Sergeant. I'll let you know when we have her."

DeMarco pocketed his phone. Stood there looking at Loughner's papers. Took his phone out and checked the time. Twenty minutes until Jayme arrived. Laid his phone on the table and sat, pulled Loughner's papers close, peeled off the top one and started to reread it. The letters swam across the page. Formed into words and broke apart again.

He pushed away from them and leaned back and stared into the overhead light, even though the neon glare stung his eyes. "What the hell?" he asked the light. "What the bloody hell?"

EIGHTY-FIVE

Pulling in, said Jayme's text.

He texted back, Out in three.

Get the photo?

Sit tight.

He gathered up Loughner's reports and slid them back into the accordion folder. Stood and left the room. To the trooper still at his desk, he held up the folder and asked, "Can I take these copies with me? I need to read through them again."

"They're yours," the trooper said. "Joe said to give you whatever you needed. We haven't received any faxes yet."

"Yeah, cancel that. I'm having it sent to my phone. Thanks for everything, by the way. Thank everybody for me, okay?"

"Just let us know what you come up with."

DeMarco nodded and turned away, took two steps toward the front door, then stopped. Turned and walked back. "You're Lowry, right?"

"Yes, sir, I am."

"Did you know Joe Loughner?"

"He retired before I came aboard. But he's stopped by a few times to say hello, so I've been introduced to him."

"How about his partner Stottlemeyer?"

"I've never met him, sir. He retired before Joe did. His picture's on the Wall of Fame back in the lounge, though. They both are."

"Hunh," DeMarco said. "Joe was insistent that I have a look at his reports, but I can't see why. Maybe I should read Stottlemeyer's reports too. Do you know if he's still around so I can ask his permission? Or just talking with him would be great too."

"Pretty sure he's in a personal care home," Lowry said. "In St. Marys, I think. The captain might know which one, but he's in town at a meeting now. HR could tell you, though."

"I'll try that, thanks." From where DeMarco stood he could see out a large window in the far wall, saw nothing out there but a long sunlit field of high brown grass leading to a low blue wall of distant trees. "I thought I lived in the boonies," he said, "but you guys are really far out, aren't you?"

"Yes, sir," Lowry said. "It's too much for some guys. Me, I like to hunt, fish, got a bike I like to ride, so I don't mind it at all."

"Mountain bike?"

"Yamaha Road Star. 1600 ccs of rolling steel and sex appeal."

"Cruiser," DeMarco said, nodding.

"One of the best. I've been as far east as Maine on it, as far west as Montana."

"Not to Sturgis yet?"

"One of these years. My wife's afraid of it."

"Afraid of the bike?"

"She loves the bike. She's afraid of Sturgis. Thinks she'll be expected to run around topless like you see on TV."

DeMarco smiled. It would be nice to have a motorcycle, Jayme seated close behind with her hands on his waist, all that hair streaming out behind her helmet like a sunlit flame. Except that she wouldn't want to be a passenger. Would insist on a bike of her own. That would be nice too, very nice. They could go anywhere they wanted to go. Stay, leave, wake up and go again, as free and easy as they wanted to be. Yeah but what about Hero? *I'd get him a sidecar*, DeMarco thought. *Get him a helmet and goggles.* The thought made him chuckle out loud.

Trooper Lowry glanced his way. "Something funny?" he asked.

"Thinking about me and my partner and our dog on motorcycles."

"My dog rides a crotch rocket," Lowry said.

"Oh yeah?"

"He's hell on wheels. Costs me a fortune in speeding tickets."

EIGHTY-SIX

D o you still want to see the elk?" DeMarco asked after he had slid the passenger seat back a couple of inches and buckled up.

"It's up to you," she said.

"I promised you we'd do it."

"But you don't want to now. I can tell."

He shrugged, wagged his head back and forth.

"So where to?" she asked. "Home?"

"I'm not sure yet. Maybe just drive for a few minutes. I think better when we're moving."

She decided to head southeast, just in case they needed to visit Mrs. Reddick again. But she drove slowly, several miles under the fifty-five-mile-per-hour limit.

The sun was high and bright, the faded blue sky smeared with gray. DeMarco jumped a little when the phone rang in his pocket. Took it out. Boyd. Pressed Answer and then Speaker.

"You're not going to believe this," Boyd said.

"Don't you dare tell me she's not there."

"Sorry, Sergeant. But guess who *is* back?"

DeMarco looked at Jayme. She gave him a quick glance, eyes open wide, then faced the road again and started looking for a place to pull over.

DeMarco said, "She's gone and Reddick's back?"

"And he's acting like there's nothing in the world wrong. Cool as a cucumber. Said he was off shopping for inventory, moving from swap meet to swap meet. He even showed me a bunch of junk he hadn't unloaded yet from his vehicle."

"And McNulty?"

"Said he tried to call her a few times when he got home and saw she wasn't there. Showed me the calls he made, as if that proves anything."

"And let me guess. He has no idea where she might be."

"Correct."

"Do we know who picked her up from the county jail?"

"She was seen walking out the door and heading down the hill toward 208. That's all."

"Somebody picked her up. Did you ask Reddick if her clothes are gone? Any sign that she had been there and left?"

"He said he couldn't really tell. Of course."

Jayme put on the turn signal and pulled onto an asphalt lane. Drove forward ten yards, pulled onto the shoulder and slipped the gearshift into Park.

"The IR camera!" DeMarco said.

"Already checked, sir. The only vehicle into the property was his, at 11:47 this morning. No other passengers visible. Doesn't mean she wasn't huddled up in the back somewhere."

DeMarco tried to figure it out. "So if she was released at 9:30 a.m., and caught a ride with somebody..."

"If she went straight back to the house, she would have arrived around ten. But there's no evidence that she did. I asked Mr. Shaner to check the camera from time to time to let me know if Reddick leaves the house or not. So far he hasn't."

"Which suggests either that she's still at the house hiding out somewhere, or he never picked her up in the first place." He felt like banging his head against the padded dashboard. Had Jayme not been present, he would have done so. "Just like that," he said. "She's gone."

"I'm sorry, sir. We're checking into bus schedules, cell phone data, everything we can. But right now we have nothing."

"Nada y nada."

"Sir?"

Jayme motioned for DeMarco to hold the phone closer. He did so, and she said into it, "Did you or Flores say anything to Reddick about Cheryl not being Cheryl?"

"We did not," Boyd answered.

"Good," DeMarco said. "Good. So he doesn't know we're onto that."

"We're working to ascertain if the suspicion is correct," Boyd told them.

Jayme said, "I have three shots of the photo from Mrs. Reddick's place. The one we know is the real Cheryl."

"She certainly looks like a different person," DeMarco added. "But you're right, Mason. How do we prove it?"

"We do have the photo from when she was booked."

"Thank God for that," DeMarco said.

Jayme said, "According to what Mrs. Reddick told me, the last time she saw the real Cheryl was a few years ago. So that's probably when the switch happened."

"Could she give us a more specific date?" Boyd asked.

"I doubt it. She's foggy on just about everything except *Wheel of Fortune*."

"Okay," Boyd said with a chuckle. "We have the info from the prescription bottles, so we can interview the doctor and the pharmacist and maybe get something there. But if neither woman's fingerprints are in the system, and Jakiella is the only known associate…"

"And he's only ever met the second one," DeMarco said. "So he wouldn't know that she isn't really McNulty."

"Exactly," Boyd answered.

"We're thoroughly screwed," DeMarco told him.

"I wouldn't say thoroughly, sir, not yet anyway. I sent a car up to watch the driveway, plus two officers from Greenville are watching the woods behind the house. We can't legitimately stop him from going anywhere, not until we confirm McNulty's identity. But we can slow him down and keep an eye on him."

DeMarco gazed out the window. Up on a hill some two hundred yards away was a huge stone house with a five-car garage. In the front yard was what appeared to be a ten-acre lake with a stone wall around one end, fountains spraying high from the middle of the lake, the sun painting a little rainbow across the spray, the pin and red flag of an impossibly green pitching green off to the right. He thought, *I wonder what the rich people are doing right now.* Then answered himself, *Not chasing their tails, that's what.*

Into the phone, he said, "Give our DA a call, Mace. Tell him he's free to use McNulty's statement for toilet paper."

"Will do, Sergeant. Though not in those words."

"At least tell him what a dumbass he is."

"He'll probably figure that out for himself."

"Don't count on it," DeMarco said. He pressed End Call and looked at Jayme.

She said, "I forgot to ask. Anything helpful in Joe's incident logs?"

"That was the second nada in nada y nada."

"Joe seemed so sure you would find something there."

"Yeah," he said. He sat with his chin stuck out, lower lip pushing up the other one. Then asked, "Was there a park back in Benezette?"

"I don't remember seeing one."

"Okay. Well... No, wait! Swing east at the next left. Head for St. Marys."

"What's in St. Marys?"

"Maybe Stottlemeyer, Joe's old partner. I'll call HR and see if they know which personal care home. But first let's find a quiet place to read through Joe's logs again. Even an empty parking lot, I don't care where. Maybe you'll notice something I missed."

"Sure, put all the pressure on me," she teased.

EIGHTY-SEVEN

B y the time Jayme parked the car in the corner of an Exxon station lot and shut off the engine, he was two pages ahead of her. He handed her those pages and kept reading. Every time he finished a page he laid it in her lap. When she finished a page, she picked up another one and laid it atop the previous page.

The only sounds inside the car were of pages sliding back and forth and the muted rumbling of traffic coming through the windows. With barely eleven miles between Ridgway and St. Marys, the traffic in both directions was heavy with pickup trucks, empty and loaded logging trucks, delivery trucks, and cars. DeMarco sat hunkered over, legs spread, holding each sheet of paper between his knees, concentrating hard.

He finished the final page and held on to it though he was no longer reading, just staring at the gray surface of the glove box, a blank wall for his thoughts. Then Jayme said, "You done with that, babe?"

He held it to her without speaking or looking. Stared at the gray.

A few minutes later, she said, "Okay. I'm done."

He leaned back in his seat. Looked at her.

She said, "What do you think?"

"I would prefer to hear your thoughts first."

"There's only one report here, out of what, all fourteen days, that is of any interest whatsoever."

"How so?"

"It doesn't have anything at all to do with Luthor or Cheryl or any of that."

"Then why is it of interest?"

"Well," she said, "that's the day of Reddick's murder. When his wife found his body late that afternoon."

"Yes?"

"Everything happens that day," she said. "Starting with the dentist's appointment."

"And how is the dentist's appointment relevant?"

"I don't know why it bothers me, but it does."

"Keep going," he said.

"So on the morning of"—and she thumbed through the pages—"the twenty-first. Early that morning, Joe called in to say he was going to be late. Said he'd lost a filling. So he needed the morning off to see the dentist."

"Nothing unusual about that, is there?"

"Not until this entry for...11:14 a.m."

"What entry would that be?"

"'Observed adolescent female walking along South Second Street,'" she read. "'Appeared to be under the influence. Stopped and questioned her. Took her home to her mother. Then returned to station house and reported for duty.'"

"We would have done the same, right?"

"Of course," Jayme said. "And after that, for...the next five hours or so, it's all routine. Nothing special."

"Until?"

"Until Mrs. Reddick's 9-1-1 call."

"Responded to by?"

"Troopers Loughner and Stottlemeyer."

"Okay," DeMarco said. "Dentist's appointment. Girl under the influence. Reddick's murder. So how do they tie together?"

"Let me just check something," she said, and gathered her phone from the cup holder. To the phone she said, "Dentists in Benezette, PA."

"Okay, here you go," her phone responded in a pleasant female voice, and provided a list.

"Three currently in town," Jayme told him. "All with addresses on Front Street."

"Some of them probably weren't around back when this happened," he said.

"Maybe none of them. But I'm betting that at least one of those offices has had a dentist occupying it all these years."

"Okay," DeMarco said. "And?"

"Reddick's house is on Second Street. And that's also where Loughner picked up the adolescent girl."

"Probably just a coincidence," he said.

"It's a tiny little town, Ryan. Second Street isn't very long. And the way I accessed it from Front Street was by traveling east on Pine."

"Okay," DeMarco said.

"But on the way up here, where did you tell me Joe used to live?"

"In a little town a few miles west of Benezette."

"You already figured this out, didn't you?" she asked.

"I haven't figured anything out. Just tell me what you're thinking."

"What I'm thinking is," she told him, "Joe leaves his home west of town, travels east to a dentist on Front Street. He gets his filling replaced. If he even had a dentist's appointment. But if he did, why would he then continue east on Pine to Second Street, where he encountered the girl, when the Ridgway station house is northwest of the dentist's office?"

"Good question, isn't it?" DeMarco said.

EIGHTY-EIGHT

The Silver Cloud assisted living facility sat on a ridge overlooking the city, with tall, stately pines to its rear, a flagstone
courtyard with south-facing wooden benches out front, and a
white split-rail fence surrounding the grounds. Lou Stottlemeyer
showed them to the library down the hall from the front lobby.
"Only place to get some peace and quiet," he told them. "Who
reads at my age? It's all screens and audiobooks nowadays."

He was a good ten years older than Loughner, and every one of
those eighty years showed in his face, from the frown lines to the
deep creases across his cheeks and forehead. His hands were swollen, fingers bent, his walk steady but slow, a stiff yet determined
shuffle. "You said Joe sent you?" he asked before stepping into the
room.

"More or less," DeMarco answered.

Stottlemeyer slid his hand along the wall, found the dimmer
switch and added a soft glow of illumination to the room. "You're
going to have to explain that," he said, and crossed to a set of
three red velvet wing chairs beneath a stained-glass window, with
floor-to-ceiling shelves filled with books and DVDs at his back.
He settled into the chair facing the other two and waited for Jayme
and DeMarco to sit before asking, "So what's that supposed to
mean, he more or less sent you here?"

DeMarco smiled. "He strongly suggested that we read his

incident logs for the week before and the week after Thomas Reddick Sr.'s murder."

The creases around Stottlemeyer's eyes pinched together for a moment. "And why would he do that?"

DeMarco explained the case they were working on, and Joe's certainty that Luthor Reddick was involved in the triple homicide. "Luthor went missing right after Jayme and Trooper Boyd first questioned him."

Jayme added, "Joe thought his incident reports might give us an idea or two about where to look for Luthor."

"And did they?"

"No," DeMarco said. "And we learned just an hour ago that Luthor has returned back home."

The old man cocked his head. "So why are you here then? Joe have you checking up on me? How the hell is he doing, by the way?"

"Doing okay," DeMarco said. "Still working with the Evidence Recovery Team out of Erie."

"He's drinking a lot," Jayme said. "Excessively."

DeMarco flinched at that. Too brusque. He waited for Stottlemeyer to tell her to mind her own business.

Instead, Stottlemeyer looked at her evenly for a few moments, then lowered his gaze and nodded. "He wasn't like that when we worked together. As sober as a corpse, I used to tell him."

"What changed?" Jayme asked.

"You said you both were with the state police till recently? Then you oughta know the answer to that. Occupational hazard."

Jayme nodded. "He was also wounded in the line of duty. I imagine that must have had a big effect on him."

"He was a good, good cop," Stottlemeyer said.

DeMarco asked, "Did he have something personal against the Reddicks?"

It took a while for the old man to answer. "You have any characters back in your jurisdiction you'd just love to put away but can't? Somebody you know is evil to the core but you just can't get enough on him to do any good? That's how it was with old man Reddick. We knew he was garbage. Knew he was selling drugs to kids. Bad drugs. Not just weed and watered-down coke. And yeah, Joe took it personal."

Jayme said, "We've never talked to him about family, and, as far as I recall, he's never mentioned having one. Does he?"

Again, another pause from Stottlemeyer. Then, "You probably hit the nail on the head there, young lady."

"He has a family?"

"Past tense. Wife and little girl came here with him. She hated the place. Nothing to do but hunt and fish and stare at the trees, she said. And she hated his job, and not just him being away at all hours, having to get up and go every time his phone rang. Deep down I think she hated cops in general. So one day he comes home from a long shift and they're gone. She'd scribbled him a note and left it on the table. *This isn't working and it never will. Kimmy isn't yours anyway.* Kimberly being the little girl's name."

"Good lord," DeMarco said.

"He tracked them down later, but by then the girl was in her teens and her mind so poisoned that she refused to even talk to him."

"And of course it affected his work," Jayme said.

"You had to really know him to see it, though. But we were close, the two of us, so I knew. He was seething inside. The only thing that gave him a moment's happiness was dragging some piece of crap up before a judge. That's why he took it so hard that Reddick was too slippery for us. Believe me, there wasn't a decent person in the county who wasn't happy when Reddick got what he had coming to him."

He blew out a long breath then, his eyes on the floor. When he looked up to DeMarco again, he said, "That's all I have for you. Sorry. I know it has nothing to do with the case you're working on."

Jayme looked at DeMarco, one eyebrow cocked. He caught the question and gave her a little nod that said, *Yeah. Go ahead.*

"Sir?" she asked. "On the day of Reddick's murder, about six hours before you and Joe responded to the 9-1-1 call, Joe was driving along Second Street and spotted a teenage girl under the influence."

"I know about that," the old man said. "He put her in the car and took her home. He wasn't about to arrest some girl barely in her teens."

The phrase *barely in her teens* jumped like a rabbit in DeMarco's mind. Loughner's report hadn't been that precise.

"The thing is," Jayme said, "that happened only a few blocks from Reddick's house."

The old man waited for a few moments, then responded. "And?"

"And we can't come up with a good reason why Joe would have even been on Second Street. According to his report, he returned to work after visiting the dentist. But the station house was in the opposite direction."

The old man slowly pushed himself erect and straightened his shoulders. Then leaned back in the wing chair. Said, "You're asking me to read another man's mind, and I can't do that. Joe's the only one can tell you where he was and what he was doing that day."

"Yeah, that's what's bothering us," DeMarco answered. "We think he *was* telling us what he was doing. By sending us up here to read his incident logs."

"I'm not following," the old man said, but with a tone that suggested the opposite.

DeMarco said, "We think maybe he was coming from Reddick's house when he spotted the girl. And that maybe the two things are related."

For a full fifteen seconds, the old man sat silent. Then he said, "I wasn't there. I have no idea what did or did not happen to anybody but me."

"Do you have any idea of the girl's address?" Jayme asked. "Where she used to live, or where she lives now?"

"Didn't know then," he said, "don't know now. And I have no need to ever find out." He smiled at Jayme. "It's nice to have met you folks. Thanks for coming by. Tell Joe for me that I remember him well and still think of him highly. And good luck with your case. Do me a favor and turn the lights off on your way out."

With that he clasped his hands atop his belly and closed his eyes.

EIGHTY-NINE

J ayme paused at the visitors' book in the lobby, checked her phone, and signed them out. DeMarco waited with his hand on the lever across the front door.

When they walked outside together, he reached into a pocket for his sunglasses but they weren't there. *Left them in the car*, he thought and squinted across the parking lot.

Jayme took his hand. Squeezed it. "I'm sorry," she said.

He nodded. Walked stride for stride with her to the car.

Seated inside, DeMarco at the wheel this time, still squinting, his movements slow. He slipped the key into the ignition but did not turn the key, only sat there with the key between his fingers.

"We don't have to do anything, babe," she said. "Just keep working the case."

He turned her way. "He wanted us to know. So that we *will* do something."

"You think he's been living with it too long, and this is his way—"

DeMarco was nodding. "He wants it over with. And he picked us—me—to do the dirty work."

"So you give what we have to IAD, and then what? It's all speculation. And even if it weren't, even if we knew exactly what happened in Reddick's house that day, every case Joe ever worked on will be impeached. Every single arrest challenged.

You're talking about probably hundreds of arrests. A man's entire career."

"He knows that. He just wants somebody to put him out of his misery. Can you blame him? I don't. I was there once. Exactly where he is now."

She shook her head. "It's not the same, babe. He could go to jail. He will still have to keep living with it. Whatever exactly *it* is."

"You know what it is," he said.

"I know what I'm thinking and that you're probably thinking the same thing."

"Okay, what? There's only one expert on human psychology in this vehicle, and it's not me."

"Hardly an expert and you know it. I could have six master's degrees and I would still be hypothesizing."

"So hypothesize for me, okay? It helps to hear it out loud."

She breathed in through her nose, let the air slip out between her lips "Maybe he didn't even have a dentist appointment that morning. Maybe he was watching Reddick's house. Maybe that had become part of his day, every morning before he went to work. But on that morning, something happened. The girl, who should have been in school, went to Reddick's house instead. His wife was at work. And maybe he sold the girl some drugs."

"You're forgetting how Reddick's body was found."

"I'm not forgetting. T-shirt and socks."

"She was probably trading sex for drugs. Joe watched her go in, then he got inside somehow, picked the lock on the back door probably, if it even was locked. He caught them going at it, and he lost it."

"He was a father too," she said. "Even though his little girl wasn't with him anymore."

DeMarco nodded. "Multiple blunt trauma to the head. Then

he put the girl in his car, gave her a lecture she'd never forget, and dropped her off in front of her house. Drove back home as fast as he could, cleaned up and changed clothes, and was back at work thirty minutes later."

"I hear you," she told him. "It's a credible scenario. But it's still just speculation. Do you really want to try to track down that girl and force her to give Joe up? We could check with the dentists but records that old have probably been destroyed by now. And Boyd would need a subpoena to even get them, and no judge is going to issue a subpoena based on what we have."

DeMarco held out his hands, palms up. *What am I supposed to do?*

Jayme said, "What if he just wanted somebody to know?"

"And he picked me?"

"Of course he picked you. The moment he heard the name *Reddick* associated with Choo Choo and the others, he picked you. I saw the way you two were drawn to each other. You *recognized* each other. And you know exactly what I mean."

He nodded. "Nathaniel Hawthorne called it the shock of recognition. The first time he met Herman Melville."

"And the first time I saw you, babe. The first time you met Thomas Huston. You see somebody and you just *know*."

He let a few heavy seconds tick past. "So now what?"

"Let's go home," she said. "Let's get some rest and then go back to work on putting Reddick away."

He nodded again. Started the car. Asked, "How would you feel about getting a couple of motorcycles when all this is over? We could tour the country. The continent. The hemisphere."

"What about Hero?"

He smiled. Took his sunglasses out of the cup holder and put them on. "That's one thing I *do* have figured out."

NINETY

The doctor's office was in an old house in Greenville, a Craftsman-style building, square but with a punch-out upstairs and a covered front porch that ran the length of the place. The front door opened onto the sitting area, where there were four old folks scattered around the room as if they had all agreed to sit as far from each other as possible, three leafing through old magazines while the fourth, a female, squinted and scowled at her cell phone.

In a little room in the back corner partitioned off from the rest of the room, with an open area above a shelf, stood the secretary/receptionist/office manager, a middle-aged woman with too much makeup and sagging jowls and startled eyes, who looked like she had stepped from behind the counter at the nearest greasy spoon and now found herself facing two Pennsylvania state troopers.

Directly across from the woman's tiny office was a hallway leading to two examination rooms and a half bathroom. Boyd stepped up to the shelf with Flores just off his left shoulder, handed the woman two photos taken of Cheryl McNulty's prescription bottle labels before she had bonded out, and said, "We need to see this patient's records."

Before the woman could answer, Flores stepped up and held out a sheet of paper. "Here's the warrant," she said.

Rather than reaching immediately for the warrant, the woman

turned to look at the waiting patients, all of whom were looking at the troopers now. One very old male patient in a wrinkled brown suit grinned as if thinking, *What an interesting twist to another dull morning!*

Then the woman behind the shelf, holding the photos in her right hand, took the warrant in her left hand, looked at it, and laid it on the shelf. She said, "Give me a minute." Then turned away and crossed to a bank of filing cabinets along the near wall of her little room.

It took her a while, working down from the top row of cabinets to the next-to-bottom row, to find what she was looking for. By then she was on her knees, which allowed both Flores and Boyd to see that she was wearing men's green cloth bedroom slippers and that her ankles were fat and swollen. Then she found the appropriate folder and pulled it out and laid it open atop the others still inside the drawer. "Hmm," she said. And sat motionless for a moment before closing the folder and picking it up in her left hand. With her other hand to the cabinets, she pulled and pushed herself back up.

To Boyd she said, "Let me see if the doctor can speak with you," and opened a blank door on the far side of her room and disappeared inside.

Boyd and Flores kept watching that door, and both were mildly startled when a door opened behind them instead, along the hallway to the examination rooms. They turned to see the white-smocked Dr. Sanjay Narang leaning out of one of those rooms.

He was well past retirement age, with only a thin band of white hair in an eroded horseshoe shape around his ears. His head seemed too small for his body, which started out thin at the neck and shoulders but expanded quickly from the chest to the stomach to the buttocks, then decreased gradually past the hips to the calves and feet. His skin was dark, his face round, eyes looking too large behind tight brown frames holding round no-line bifocal lenses. He jerked his head to motion them back, then disappeared inside the room again.

He was seated at a small desk when they entered, the low chair swiveled their way. He tapped the folder open on the desk. It lay adjacent to a clear plastic container holding a spoon buried in a brown mound of tabbouleh—bulgur, chopped tomatoes, and parsley and mint—the source of the pleasant minty aroma in the room. "I haven't written a prescription for this patient in quite a while," he said. "Three years and seven months, to be specific. She stopped coming here. Marylou sent her a few reminders, but received no response. We assumed she had moved or switched doctors or passed away. Why is she of interest to you?"

"Thank you for the information," Boyd said. "We're going to need those photos back."

Outside, as they crossed the street to their vehicle, Flores noticed that Boyd was smiling. "What are you so happy about?" she asked.

"Social security disability fraud," he said. "Identity theft. And now forging a prescription."

"How could she get away with it for so long? Aren't there safeguards to keep something like that from happening?"

"Of course," he said. "But it happens anyway. A lot. That's why I love it so much when the bad guys trip over their own messes."

She smiled too. Almost told him, *You're really handsome when you smile.* But didn't. Took the warmth of the thought and kept it to herself.

NINETY-ONE

The pharmacist came through!" Flores said.

DeMarco was sitting on the edge of his bed, wearing a clean white T-shirt, a damp towel wrapped around his waist. Hero lay across his feet, soft furry belly against DeMarco's ankles; he could feel the animal's heat on his skin. The light through the window was lemony and soft, the magic hour, one of his favorite times of day, second only to sunrise. When the phone rang, he had been waiting for Jayme to emerge from her shower wearing nothing, her skin soft and cool and soap-scented, her face washed clean of everything but the freckles.

"He named Reddick?" he said.

"Didn't name him but recognized him from the photo. Said he was usually with McNulty when she filled the prescriptions, and that she didn't look like the woman in the photos Jayme took."

"Excellent," DeMarco said. "So you have Reddick in custody?"

"Headed up there right now. We thought you and Trooper Matson might like to join the party."

"You know," he said, "we're sort of tied up here at the moment. Besides, you guys don't need us there. It's your party. Give us a call if you get anything out of him, though I suspect he'll stay true to form."

"I agree," she said. "We have a BOLO out on the fake McNulty.

I have a feeling she'll be the talkative one once we catch up with her."

He heard the faucet running in the bathroom, which meant that Jayme was brushing her teeth. Then she would gargle and then be his.

"Listen," he said. "How about we meet up in the woods in Otter Creek tomorrow? The full team and a couple of dogs?"

"You think Cheryl's body is up there?"

"He trusted that place enough to take Choo Choo and the female vics there. I'm betting he's trusted it before that too."

"The ERT should've scraped the place clean already, though, right?"

"It's easy to miss something when you're not looking for it," he told her. "If there's a grave up there, it won't be on top of the crime scene. But not far away either."

"I'll talk to the captain," she said.

He heard the water stop running. "Gotta go," he told Flores. "Excellent work, Trooper. We'll see you in the morning."

He laid the phone on the bedside table just as the bathroom door came open. Turned and looked her way.

"Did I hear you talking to somebody?" she asked.

Something fluttered in his chest at the sight of her. There was a soft radiance to her body that always took his breath away. So this was no time for a prolonged conversation. "Singing to myself," he told her, and held out his arms. "The 'Hallelujah Chorus.'"

IV

THESE VIOLENT DELIGHTS HAVE VIOLENT ENDS
AND IN THEIR TRIUMPH DIE, LIKE FIRE AND POWDER
WHICH AS THEY KISS CONSUME.
—WILLIAM SHAKESPEARE, *ROMEO AND JULIET*

NINETY-TWO

Reddick's cockiness had morphed into a simmering rage by the time he was cuffed, booked, and shackled to a metal table in the interview room of the county jail. The room was otherwise empty—one table, two chairs on one side, one chair on the other—and several degrees below comfortable. Reddick's lawyer, seated beside him in a slim-fit, skinny-legged suit only someone forty pounds lighter and thirty years younger should wear, with enough gel in his hair to grease a small elephant, kept grinning at Flores and flipping his black eyebrows up and down in a way that made her want to stomp on them. She stood against the wall beside the closed door, hands clasped loosely below her belt, her face expressionless, a portrait of disdain, while Boyd sat facing Reddick and the lawyer. Captain Bowen, with a sheriff's deputy at his side, watched from the observation room and nervously sipped coffee from a cardboard cup without tasting a drop of it.

Reddick denied that the missing Cheryl McNulty was not the real Cheryl McNulty. Denied any knowledge of either McNulty's whereabouts. Denied that he or anyone he knew had forged prescriptions. Denied that he sold drugs out of his house. Denied any acquaintance with anyone named Choo Choo, Suzi, or Lady D. To all other questions he answered with some variation of "I have no knowledge of that" or "I have no recollection of that."

Boyd, who sat tilted back in his chair, finally said, "Look at me. I'm not the FBI, and you're not Hillary Clinton. So how about an honest answer for a change? I'm going to give you one last chance to do yourself some good. Who is, and where is, the woman pretending to be Cheryl McNulty?"

Reddick stared at Boyd's forehead. "I have no idea what you are talking about."

Flores laughed a single-syllable, "Hunh." She shook her head and chuckled. "You know," she told Reddick, "for a while there you were giving a fairly decent impression of being moderately intelligent. But now that I see you up close, you look as dumb as a fart."

"Hey," the lawyer said, which she ignored.

"Trooper Boyd," she said, "may I have the pleasure of informing this scum-sucking knuckle dragger of what's going to happen to him if he fails to cooperate?"

"Be my guest," Boyd said.

"So," Flores told him, and smiled at the ceiling before looking down at Reddick again, "we *are* going to find your fake Cheryl. And she *is* going to give you up in exchange for reduced charges. And then Jakiella *is* going to corroborate her story. And where will that leave you? Sharing a prison cell for a very long time with a tattooed man with a look of love in his eyes."

Reddick smirked.

His lawyer flipped his eyebrows up, then down. He said, "You are attempting to intimidate my client."

She stepped closer. Put both hands on the edge of the table. Leaned toward Reddick. And said, "Do you feel intimidated, Mr. Reddick? Would three or four first-degree murder charges intimidate you?"

"Hey hey hey," the lawyer said. "Who said anything about murder? Nobody's talking murder here."

She smiled at Reddick. And said in a near whisper, "We're just getting started with you, *gilipollas*."

"Hey," the lawyer said, "what did you just call him?"

She stepped back to lean against the wall. "Ask his tattooed lover when you meet him. Maybe you and your twitchy eyebrows can get in on the action too."

Reddick's face was slowly going pale. The lawyer looked confused. Boyd was trying not to laugh out loud. Behind the glass, Bowen raised his cup for another sip, sucked only air, then stared into the empty cup, saw no coffee, looked to see if he had spilled the coffee on the floor, saw none, and asked the trooper, "Where did all of my coffee go?"

NINETY-THREE

The woods were damp in the early morning chill, the branches dripping. A lingering scent of wet ash hung in the gray air. Two troopers with their dogs on leashes worked outward from the burned car and the tree to which Choo Choo had been nailed. Jayme, DeMarco, Flores, and Boyd followed behind, spread well apart, eyes on the ground. They were looking for a depression in the earth, a disturbance in the matted leaves, a mound of freshly turned dirt, a shred of clothing. Staring so intently at the monochromatic ground made their eyes hurt. Nobody talked.

Chase Miller stayed several yards back from the others so that he could keep everyone in sight. He had dressed too lightly, in a hurry after Jayme's call, and now shivered every fifteen seconds or so. But he would not let the chill ruin this opportunity. He had promised DeMarco that he would be inconspicuous, a fly on the wall, and that his subsequent narrative of the search, if the search proved successful, would not be released until DeMarco gave the green light. But even if no body was found, he could use this experience again and again, the scent of wet branches, the wet, decomposing leaves, the numbing chill in his feet and hands and on his face, the eerie hush of the searchers' movements. Even the stiffening shivers, each one an icy hand pressed to the small of his back, and the way the chill raced up his spine to explode soundlessly across the scapulas—yeah, that was good stuff; he could build a library out of experiences like this.

He held his cell phone close to his mouth, whispered so that even he could barely hear the words, "the mood is somber, even reverent...the dogs appear to enjoy their work and hurry from place to place, then stop suddenly, consider a scent, then move forward again...you can almost feel something dark hovering in the air...some shadow...death...violence...evil. There's been only one chipmunk so far, not a single squirrel...all the animals seem to be in hiding... Now and then a crow's caw, it surprises me every time, makes me look but I can never see it... I wonder what the birds are doing now, where do they go when they hide? All of those little eyes watching us, maybe laughing at man's folly..."

Ever since the trip to Lost City he had been more than a little ashamed of himself. Had thought he could run the show, be the big hero. But he saw now, following the others, that it would never be like that. Not with this kind of business. The dogs were running this show, the six humans, seven including him, at the dogs' mercy. And willingly so. Even his blog seemed foolish to him now. What gave him the right to be a pontificator? Social critic, huh. If he was going to be a writer of any value he needed to disappear behind the material. The way Stephen Crane had. Jack London, Nellie Bly, Ambrose Bierce, all of those pioneering journalists he had read about in school and after. Let the story do the talking. Let the bones and the heart and the ghost of the story say it all.

But there was a thrill in that too. He hadn't noticed it until this morning, the thrill of being the invisible eyes and ears and mouth for the story. The funnel through which the story ran. He was actually *doing* something here. Preserving the moment, the experience. All that new journalism bullshit, all that me me me, it devalues the story. He saw that now. Felt it. It was what DeMarco knew too, all of them up ahead. The case was bigger than them and they didn't try to become the story. Just as the story was bigger than the person writing it. Every good writer knew it was so. The rest was nothing but ego.

DeMarco was a hard man to please, but he wasn't unfair. He could learn a lot from DeMarco. From Jayme too. And Boyd.

As for Daniella…yeah. It would be nice to talk to her alone sometime. Maybe coffee? *Could I interest you in a cup of coffee some afternoon?* She probably had a boyfriend. But no engagement ring, in fact no jewelry at all. *May I ask, is there a man in your life?* Naw, too formal. Old-fashioned. *You wanna grab a drink tonight? I mean, I'm not a drinker myself, but you shouldn't let that stop you.* God, what a joke. She would probably laugh at him. Look at her. Armed and dangerous. Probably knew six different ways to subdue a man. Not that that was a turnoff. *Ever use those cuffs for recreational purposes?* Dude, you're such an ass. Pay attention to what—

"Over here!" a trooper called.

Everybody changing direction, making a beeline. Gathering around a spot he could not yet see.

"Chase!" DeMarco called. "Can you run back to the car and grab the shovel?"

"I'm on it!" he called, turned and jogged back though the leaves, talking into the cell phone louder now, "Okay they found something, I'm running for the shovel now, it might be a body or something else I don't know but what else would they be digging up out here? I'm betting it's a body. I hope they let me do the digging…"

NINETY-FOUR

Before they climbed into their own vehicles and headed back to town, DeMarco approached Trooper Boyd, stood close to him, half smiling, and asked in a conspiratorial tone, "You know anybody at the jail who could maybe whisper to Sonny that we found the real Micki?"

Boyd cocked his head. They had no idea whose body had been found.

"Just a hint," DeMarco told him. "Just a tease. Let's see if Sonny is smart enough to put two and two together."

"You're going to talk to him again?"

"I'm going to run home and get a shower and then, yeah, I might pay him another visit. I miss his smiling face."

Boyd nodded. Allowed himself his own small smile. "I'll see what I can do."

NINETY-FIVE

W hat are you doing back here?" Jakiella asked.

DeMarco had come to the jail alone this time. All of the sheriff's deputies and guards knew him, knew that he was still attached to the state police, though in a vague way, and therefore did not question his right to interview the prisoner. He took a seat facing Jakiella across a plastic-surfaced table in the mess hall. The room was beginning to fill with the scent of that day's lunch, meat patties and dark-brown gravy. From the kitchen came the clangs and thumps of meal preparation and the muffled conversations of the kitchen staff, all of it coming hollow and empty into the dining room.

"Just thought we might have another chat before they send you off to detox."

"How soon's that going to happen?"

"You getting a little antsy, are you?"

"I shoulda been there already."

"I was thinking I might suggest they keep you here awhile longer. See how you handle cold turkey. Depending on how our conversation goes, of course."

"Why would you do something like that?"

Sonny Jakiella looked even smaller than the last time DeMarco had seen him. Shrunken. Defeated. He was sitting sideways on the wooden bench, both legs on the outside, knees together and arms crossed over his stomach, hunched over, his body turned away from DeMarco, only his head inclined DeMarco's way. With DeMarco's last statement, Sonny's face pinched even tighter.

"Sonny, are you about to start crying on me?"

"I never done nothing to you. You're a real son of a bitch if you keep me out of detox."

"You lied to me. You know that and so do I."

Sonny's eyes swiveled back to the floor, his head rocking back and forth.

"Oh, hey, guess what?" DeMarco said. "Guess who we found this morning. The real Micki. What was left of her anyway, in a gully up in Otter Creek. She was covered with a couple feet of dirt and leaves. And not more than forty yards from where you nailed Choo Choo to a tree."

Instead of appearing startled by that news, Jakiella remained motionless. "I don't even know what that means. The real Micki."

"It means that the one you knew was a fake."

And now Jakiella's head shifted again, his eyes coming back to meet DeMarco's. "Are you shitting me? This is for real?" His voice was shallow and hoarse. Grief and fear will do that to a man. Not to mention heroin withdrawal and living inside a cage with a bunch of animals. Jakiella was a weak man but he had a conscience, a memory, a heart, all of which DeMarco planned to use against him.

More than once DeMarco had looked at an incarcerated individual and thought how inhumane such treatment was, how primitive. But what were the alternatives? Those who did harm to others needed to be removed from society. Rehabilitation worked less than a third of the time, with around 70 percent of all criminals, regardless of the offense, returning to crime. Jakiella did not view himself as a criminal but the law did, and DeMarco did too.

A young woman struggling to avoid drugs had been given drugs; whether the intent was her death or not, the supplier of those drugs remained culpable. DeMarco could gaze at Jakiella with pity yet find his behavior reprehensible.

"Of course, that was just another lie, wasn't it?" DeMarco asked.

"What was?"

"That you didn't know the second Micki is a fake. You're Reddick's business partner, are you not? You've already copped to killing Choo Choo, Suzi, and Lady D because they stole from Reddick's cache, so it only makes sense that you were in on killing the real Micki too."

"That's bullshit."

"What did she do to tick you guys off? Was she not generous enough with the goodies?"

Jakiella's head rocked back and forth. "I don't have to sit here and take this from you." He put a hand on the edge of the table but seemed too weak to do more. His hand twitched like an electric shock was running through it.

"Yep," DeMarco said. "The DA is going to love this. Four counts of murder one, Sonny. Choo Choo, Suzi, Lady D, and now Cheryl McNulty. No, wait. For you it will be five. I forgot about Sully."

This time his whole body twisted toward DeMarco. "I did *not* kill her! Don't you say something like that. I never done anything to hurt her!"

"Okay, so maybe manslaughter for Sully. But you helped with the others. Four is still a nice round number. Plus obstruction of justice, conspiracy, three counts of abuse of a corpse, the drug charges, misprision of felony…"

"What's that last one mean?"

"Failure to report a crime. Man, the charges keep piling up, don't they? All in all, Sonny, if I were you I'd be hoping for the death penalty. Just take the needle and get it over with. Of course, you will have to wait your turn. Pennsylvania has almost two hundred people like you on death row. I can't imagine what that must be like, can you? Day after day after day, waiting for your number to be called? Just sitting there in your cell, counting the minutes, remembering all the people you hurt. And doing all of that stone-cold sober. That's got to be excruciating. Especially for a jittery guy like you."

"What are you even doing here, man? I told you everything I know."

"Tell me how the real Cheryl died."

"I didn't even know there was a real Cheryl! I thought the one I knew was the real one! She's the only one I ever knew."

"So you're saying it was all Reddick's doing? His and Fake Cheryl's?"

"How would I know that?"

"They must have mentioned it once or twice. You all being so close."

"I wasn't close to anybody but Sully. Reddick treated us all like garbage."

"And yet you're willing to go to prison for him? And be somebody's punch for the next decade or so before you even get sent to death row? What's wrong with this picture, Sonny?"

Jakiella shook his head, squeezed his arms against his stomach. "I need to think about this awhile. I can't even think straight anymore."

"You'd better think hard. Think about what Sully would want you to do. What your daughters would want you to do. Do you teach your kids to lie, Sonny?"

"Of course not."

"And yet that's exactly what you're doing. Your little girls are going to grow up, graduate from school, get married, have children, all while you rot away like a bag of potatoes. Give that some thought, Sonny. Think long and hard. Because if you stick with your story, you will never hug your children again."

"I never will anyway."

"Why is that? If things went down the way I think they did, and you cooperate with the prosecution, you could do your time right here, never even go to prison. One to two years and you're out."

At that, Jakiella looked up at him again. "That's never going to happen."

Such a pitiful look on Jakiella's face. DeMarco almost felt guilty. "Let's say that Reddick threatened you. That he forced you to help him with Choo Choo and the others. Let's say you feared for your life. Maybe he even threatened your kids. That sounds just like him, doesn't it?"

Jakiella had no response. Yet he did not look away.

"You haven't talked to a public defender yet?" DeMarco asked.

"Just a couple minutes or so. He couldn't even pronounce my name right."

"He'll be back around. They're busy people. And he'll tell you the same thing I'm telling you. You have one way out and one way only. Cooperate. Tell the truth. Don't let yourself be Reddick's sacrificial pig."

Even Jakiella's blink was pitiful. Slow and heavy. Resigned. "He's in here now, right?"

"Luthor? That he is. You two can get reacquainted at your next meal. Maybe even get some private time together in the showers."

Jakiella aligned his head with his body again. Stared at the space between his bony knees.

"Do you know what a scapegoat is, Sonny? Do you know where that word comes from?"

Jakiella offered no response.

"It's used in the Bible. Do you ever read the Bible?"

"When I was a kid I had to."

"Then maybe you know. The ancient Jews would have a ritual. Send all their sins into a goat, then drive the goat out into the wilderness to die. To get torn apart and eaten by wolves. That's sort of what Reddick has done to you, isn't it? He's made you his scapegoat."

Jakiella rubbed a hand over his face. Said, "So you guys have Reddick on the other Micki? The real one? I mean you know for sure it's her and that he put her there?"

"We have enough," DeMarco told him. "With lots more to come."

"So he's going down no matter what? For doing the real Micki?"

"Unless he claims to have knowledge that you did it all on your own. And seeing how you've already confessed to the other three…"

As of that morning, the decomposed remains discovered in the woods had not been identified, nor had the cause of death been established. In dry earth the body might have been better preserved, but in the dampness of the Otter Creek woods, with fewer than three feet of earth and rocks and wet leaves atop it, the individual's own bacteria had gotten the party started immediately and were soon joined by maggots, insects, worms, rodents, and other subterranean beasties. It was a wonder that the bones hadn't been dug up and gnawed into pieces. So no, there was of yet no evidence that Reddick had murdered anybody. It was even possible that, if the body was that of the real Cheryl McNulty, she had died during an epileptic seizure or of some other ailment, and Reddick and the other woman had merely disposed of the body so as to continue collecting her disability checks. It was possible. But DeMarco would not have laid money on it.

"And just so you know, Sonny. Prison is nothing like the county jail. A year here is a cakewalk compared to that circle of hell."

"You think I don't know that?"

"That's right, I think you don't. Not really. You may have done some time here but all you know about prison are the stories you've heard. And stories can't compare to the real truth."

"I know what I'm looking at."

"I have to disagree. You ever read Dante, Sonny?"

"I don't know who that is."

"The nine circles of hell. Guess which circle is life in prison?"

Jakiella said nothing. His body seemed to have reached its critical mass in weakness. All voluntary movement had ceased. Two low-level currents, one of fear and the other of withdrawal, were coursing through his wasted body, making him quiver like a wet kitten, or like a dying bird in the snow, or like a man facing life without parole in a prison filled with monsters and beasts.

"Prison is the ninth circle of hell, Sonny boy. The absolute worst. It's where the devil himself lives. He walks the corridors every night. Slips in through the bars. Tortures you so that you beg, *beg* for death. But you're already dead, aren't you? That's what prison is, a living death that you can never escape. 'Abandon all hope, ye who enter here.'"

When Jakiella spoke, he sounded drugged, out of breath, his words a sour exhalation. "Like I said. I need to think about things awhile."

He lacked the strength to even lift his head. And DeMarco wondered if he should keep pressing. Keep pushing pushing pushing until Jakiella fell apart?

Even as a boy DeMarco had heard people say that words are only words and can do no lasting damage, but he knew that claim to be false. You could cut a man with a knife and if the cut is not too deep it will heal and leave a scar that the man can be proud of. He can show the scar to people and tell a story about the time he was cut and survived and he can embellish that story so that the person who cut him ends up being a miserable cur who got what was coming to him. The wounds made by words, however, are less visible and harder to treat, and sometimes those wounds never heal but only fester and fill the victim with poison and offer little opportunity for storytelling. Nobody goes around proudly recounting a story about the time they were cut deeply by an individual who said *you are a worthless human being* or *you make me sick* or *you deserve to rot in your own filth*. You have to be very careful when inflicting wounds such as those. You have to want to cause permanent damage to the victim. DeMarco had known some despicable men who deserved not an ounce of sympathy or consideration yet it was always difficult for him to hurt anyone in a permanent way. Maybe that was a flaw in his character. He did not know for sure one way or the other.

In the end, he decided that he had done enough damage to Jakiella for the day. "Good talk," he said. Then stood and walked to the door and left Jakiella alone with his misery and his shakes and his brutalizing imagination.

NINETY-SIX

The team decided not to interrogate Reddick again until they had something close to proof that he was responsible for Cheryl McNulty's death. The pharmacist's identification of Reddick threw a bright light of suspicion onto him, but little more than that. The fact that Cheryl's social security disability checks had continued to arrive in Reddick's mailbox every month, uninterrupted by her death, added another beam of light. But what they needed to keep him where he was, without bond and no hope of being granted it, was evidence that showed his hand in Cheryl's demise. They had no choice but to wait and let the forensics lab do its stuff.

To keep from drilling holes in their desks with their tapping fingers, Flores and Boyd turned their minds to other work. They had schedules and routines to fall back on. DeMarco and Jayme searched online for a distraction, a way to fill their evening, and found a motorcycle show at Erie's Bayfront Convention Center, forty thousand square feet filled with chrome and leather and freedom-thrumming engines.

They held hands and strolled through the displays, sipped weak coffee from foam cups, dined on soft pretzels and undercooked hot dogs, traded TV commercial dreams of cruising up Highway 1, New England in the fall, lobster rolls and chowder for every meal, then into Canada and west across the Trans-Canada Highway all the way to the Rockies, into the Yukon for a while, the Takhini Hot Springs, the midnight sun in Yellowknife. Eventually they would turn south to follow the Pacific Coast Highway, Monterey, Big Sur, Carmel-by-the-Sea.

"This trip will cost us a fortune," Jayme said. "How are we paying for it?"

"We could take the RV instead," he said. "Trade in the one we have on a toy hauler. Or just hitch up a bike trailer."

"I love that idea! It would be so much better than camping out or paying for a motel every night. And it would be better for Hero too, wouldn't it?"

"I don't know," DeMarco said. "He looks like a biker to me. I bet he has a dozen tattoos under that fur."

"And what would be our favorite place?" she asked. "The place where we would all want to stay forever?"

"That's a hard one. You like beaches, I like mountains."

She stuck out her lower lip in a fake pout. "Why aren't there any mountains with beaches at the top?"

"God tried that. The water all ran downhill."

"Stupid water," she said.

He smiled; her remark reminded him of Flores when he had showed her the hay-bale bison: *Stupid white man.*

"I wonder what the team is up to," he said.

"You're missing them, aren't you?"

"Not a whit."

"Liar. You miss them all, I know you do. Even Chase."

"Chase who?" he said.

They had paused beside a Victory Vision touring bike, azure blue, Jayme on one side, DeMarco on the other, both of them pretending to consider the curve of the tank, the height and width of the handlebars, the probable comfort of the deep leather seat.

"It feels kind of anticlimactic, doesn't it?" he said.

As always, she understood his shorthand language, knew where his mind had gone. "You can't end every case with a shootout, babe."

"I guess not. Besides, we still have a lot of loose ends to wrap up." He was thinking not only of Chase and Flores and Boyd now, but also of Laraine, and especially Joe Loughner. How was he going to deal with what they knew about Loughner? He said, "If this were a novel, the reviewers would be saying 'too many characters, too many plots.'"

"Ignore the reviewers. Life is messy."

"Ours has certainly become that way. How did we let this happen? All these people in our lives."

"Don't ask me. I'm not the one writing this novel."

"I wonder who is. God or Max Planck?"

"Max who?"

"The father of quantum physics. He had something to do with the discovery that photons and electrons sometimes behave like particles and sometimes like a wave."

"Stop it. You're getting me all aroused."

"Ha ha," he said, and came around the bike to take her hand again and lead her away to another aisle. "The experiment suggests that the observer influences, or, in Planck's mind, creates reality."

"So which one of us is creating *this* reality?"

"Not me, that's for sure. My reality wouldn't have all these noisy people in it. And the coffee would be better."

It was full dark when they left the convention center, with a cool breeze rich with the scent of water. Both had fallen into an easy silence, pleasantly worn out by three hours of slow walking and dreaming through row after row of beautiful machines. Beneath the lights of the parking lot, while Jayme walked with sleepy eyes on the softer lights along Lake Erie, DeMarco spotted something stuck to his windshield, and felt a chilling certainty that it was not a welcome or thank-you note or even a coupon for 20 percent off their next purchase.

He guided Jayme to the passenger side, unlocked and opened the door, then strode quickly to his side and snatched up the slip of paper under the wiper. He read the three typed sentences, every letter in caps, while standing beside his door, then quickly crumpled the paper and stuffed it into a pocket.

Then he climbed in and smiled at her, buckled up and started the long drive home. Every mile of the way, he was aware of the small ball of paper in his pocket, felt it like something alive and dangerous against his leg, resting now like a coiled snake but poised to strike, and he could hear the words on it as if Daksh Khatri were whispering in his ear: DID YOU AND YOUR LADY ENJOY THE NIGHT, GOOD SIR? HAVE A PLEASANT DRIVE HOME. WE WILL MEET AGAIN SOON.

NINETY-SEVEN

I t's her, Boyd's text message read. Lab says 94% certain based on match with known medical stats on record, height weight age race etc, including childhood fracture of right ulna. Evidence of subdural hematoma AND strangulation.

They had parked the car and were walking toward the house, the security lights all ablaze, when Jayme paused to turn her eyes to the sky. DeMarco paused beside her. She said, "I wish we could see the sky better."

He read the text silently, then showed it to her.

"Do you need to call him back?" she asked.

"It's nearly midnight. If he had anything urgent to say, he would have called. Let's enjoy the stars for a minute."

Using his phone, he extinguished the security lights. The yard and house went black, but the sky, second by second, filled with more and more stars. "There you go," he told her. "They are all yours, my love."

Instead of feeling vulnerable in the darkness, he felt safer. Invisible. Besides, Khatri would not ambush them tonight. Probably he never would. He thought of himself as some kind of social or spiritual warrior but he was just another demented punk. If he came he would show himself first, would want to be seen. Probably he had no intention of physically harming DeMarco or Jayme, had never intended to. Why kill your audience? In St.

Margaret's he had probably intended only for Connor McBride to die, ideally after wounding DeMarco. But McBride had bungled the job and Jayme had come up the wrong set of stairs and Khatri had been unable to slip away after watching the show. He considered himself smarter than everybody else but his plan in St. Margaret's hadn't worked out, so to save face he would continue to taunt DeMarco and Jayme from afar.

But they could not live their lives in fear of Khatri's letters, of that he was certain. He already regretted and resented the security lights and alarms.

He and Jayme had had a few hours of distraction at the convention center that night but the exposition had been noisy and crowded and now the night sky was a good antidote for that, a slow, still soak in the infinity of the stars and their invisible planets and moons. The night was cool but neither he nor Jayme was in a hurry to go inside. For him the dark was not only concealing but also protective and healing; he looked at her with her head tilted back and eyes wide and imagined what she must be thinking: *Are we really all alone down here, God? Is my baby with you? Can my baby see me looking up?*

For DeMarco the night concealed wounds and injuries, broken homes and hearts and all the misery of the world. The stars promised something better but were vague enough in their promise that any dreamer's dream could be accommodated. The night sky offered beauty but no explanations. Showed the past but teased the future.

So they remained there with their eyes turned to the stars. DeMarco squeezed Jayme's hand and quoted Rumi. "'When someone mentions the gracefulness of the night sky, climb up on the roof and dance and say, Like this?'"

She squeezed his hand in return. "I love when you say something I have never heard before."

"I wish they were my words and not somebody else's."

"I'm yours and nobody else's."

"And because of that, I know there is a God."

"Me too," she said. "What do you think he, she, or it is like?"

"Not like us, I hope."

"Meaning what, babe?"

"Meaning…" What did he mean? He meant not like humans. Not driven by greed and lust and power. Not infused with anger and desperation and jealousy and hate. But he would not say those things now and diminish her enjoyment of the moment, not introduce more sadness into the mix. And so he said, "Meaning more like the best part of us than we are. More love and kindness and selflessness. I hope that's what God is."

"And more patient," she said.

"Patient for what?"

"We do terrible things, but God still loves us. Because we're still just babies. And a good mother and father love their babies no matter what. No matter how many tantrums they throw."

"I like that," he said.

"So God must be patient, I think. Like the stars. Waiting forever for us to grow up."

"Hmm," he said. Then, half a minute later, "'For my part I know nothing with any certainty, but the sight of the stars makes me dream.'"

"Are whose words are those?"

"Vincent van Gogh's."

"Before or after he cut off his ear?"

"Before, probably. But it was after the ear that he painted *The Starry Night*."

She moved her head slowly from left to right, took in the sky from one corner to the other. "Thank you, Vincent," she whispered.

In his mind's eye the image of Van Gogh materialized, the self-portrait of the artist bundled in a heavy coat and cap, his mutilated ear beneath a dirty strip of cloth wrapped around his head, those melancholy eyes, that sad, pinched mouth, Mount Fuji in a picture behind his head, a place of mystery and wonder he would never reach.

DeMarco lowered his gaze to the darkened house. It was time to return. Reddick and Loughner were waiting for him in there. Laraine was waiting too, and Daksh Khatri, Boyd, Captain Bowen, Flores, and Miller all awaiting their due.

"Let's get some sleep," he said, though he knew that he would not.

've been waiting for you," Reddick said. For a man with his wrists chained to a heavy table, he seemed inordinately comfortable.

He ran his smile from face to face, from Jayme to DeMarco to Flores to Boyd to Captain Bowen to the county sheriff, and finally allowed it to settle on DeMarco. And said, "I have some good news for you, sport."

DeMarco told him, "Troopers Flores and Boyd are in charge. Talk to them."

Reddick held his eyes on DeMarco. "Have a seat. I like your face."

DeMarco considered pushing back, reminding Reddick where he was and that he was no longer giving the orders. But that was pride talking. Information was more valuable. So he pulled out the chair and sat opposite Reddick. The others stood in an uneven line behind him.

"Where's your lawyer?" DeMarco asked.

"I'm a hands-on kind of guy. Besides, he knows what I'm going to say. He's writing it up for the plea bargain."

"Writing up what?"

"My confession."

Those two words hit DeMarco and the rest of the team like a wave of hot air. Trying to hide her movements behind DeMarco, Flores fumbled in her pocket, pulled out the cell phone, tapped her thumb to the voice memo icon, then tapped the record button.

"Hey, chica," Reddick said. "Set it down here in front of me. I wouldn't want you to miss anything. But I retain the rights to the recording." He looked up at the sheriff, a tall, sinewy man with an Abe Lincoln chin. "I want that in the agreement," Reddick said.

The sheriff did not nod or speak. Kept his face hard, his expression mute.

Flores laid the phone in front of DeMarco. He slid it closer to Reddick.

Forty minutes earlier, DeMarco and Jayme had been cleaning up their breakfast dishes when he received a call from Captain Bowen. "Reddick wants to talk to you," Bowen had said.

"Say again?"

"According to the sheriff, Reddick said he has a news flash and he wants it to go through you."

"Through me? Why me?"

"Sheriff thinks Reddick believes he'll get more publicity that way. Because of your history. He wants The Rock to play him in the Netflix series."

"Is this a joke?" DeMarco had asked. He was in no mood for jokes. Had been planning to call the FBI as soon as Jayme went upstairs for her shower. The crumpled ball of paper was still in his pocket, the khakis on the bedroom floor, and his stomach had been sour ever since he had so heedlessly handled the paper. And now another psychopath had singled him out for some cat-and-mouse playtime?

"Tell him I'm not interested," he told Bowen.

"Yes, you are interested," Bowen said. "Boyd and Flores will meet you there. Fifteen minutes."

DeMarco had looked across the table at Jayme in her shortie pajamas. "We're not even dressed yet."

"Twenty minutes, no more. The sheriff and I will be joining you."

And now Reddick had his audience. His shaved head had been polished for the occasion, his smile bright. DeMarco suspected that the man had probably requested cameras too, a news crew, but the sheriff would have shot that down. *This better be good*, DeMarco thought.

He asked, "So what are you confessing to, Luthor?"

"Let's start with Cheryl. I slammed her head into the wall and then I choked her to death. You already know that, right? Or will soon enough. As to why? She had become useless to me. It's as simple as that."

"So you know we found her."

"Found and identified, yessirree. I also know that you won't find any trace of me on or near the body, but, juries being what they are, I'm going down for it."

DeMarco nodded. Considered his words. "And what about the fake Cheryl? She had a hand in it too. What's her name and where is she?"

"Unh uh. That's one thing you don't get."

"Hey, you're talking to the wrong guy here. I have nothing to do with your negotiations."

Again Reddick looked up at the county sheriff.

"Go ahead," the sheriff told him.

"You will all back off and leave her alone," Reddick said. "Call off the dogs. She walks."

DeMarco remained motionless, his eyes locked on Reddick's.

Flores said, "You hoping for connubial visits, or what?"

He grinned at her and said, "I like my women the same way I like my bananas—firm and slightly green."

"You're a real shitwad, aren't you?" she asked.

Reddick held his grin a few moments longer, then turned to DeMarco again. "So do we have a deal or not? Either she walks or we're done talking. And you go back to looking for the monster who killed my friend Choo Choo and his lovely girls. Oh, how I miss them all."

Seven more ticks of the clock. DeMarco leaned forward and started to rise. Then felt Captain Bowen's hand on his shoulder.

The sheriff said, "Let's just move forward here, Luthor. You know the DA is going to give you what you want. As long as you give us what *we* want."

"I want my good man here to say it."

"He has no authority in this matter."

"He has my authority, Sheriff."

Bowen said, "Go ahead and tell him, Sergeant."

Instead, DeMarco leaned back in the chair. "What's this game you think you're playing?"

Reddick grinned. "Let's call it the game of life. *My* life."

"Your life is a short dead-end street, my friend."

"There's more than one road to immortality," Luthor told him. "In fact, I can think of seven, just off the top of my head."

DeMarco turned to Captain Bowen. "This is a farce and a waste of time."

"Humor him," Bowen said.

DeMarco felt his hackles bristle. "In case you've forgotten, Captain, Jayme and I are volunteers here. Not employees."

The sheriff said, "The county would greatly appreciate your cooperation, sir."

He was being used, this much DeMarco knew. Reddick hoped to tie his star to DeMarco's alleged celebrity. The sheriff and Captain Bowen hoped to hasten and ensure what DeMarco saw as an inevitability—Reddick's conviction. It galled him that they would allow a homicidal maniac to call the shots. But it wasn't the first time such had happened, and it would not be the last. Plea agreements were built on giving the guilty a final titillating victory.

Reddick kept grinning. To DeMarco he said, "I don't sign the statement until you say, 'Yes, Luthor. We have a deal.'"

"A deal with me is worthless," DeMarco told him. "So why should I mind giving you something of no value? Yes, Luthor, we have a deal. Why did you kill Choo Choo, Suzi, and Lady D?"

"Because I caught them breaking into my cache. My inventory. They were brain-dead, every one of them. I couldn't work with people who would rather fry their brains than make a profit. I should have left them to freeze to death in that filthy storage container."

DeMarco asked, "Who all helped you do it?"

"To what *it* are you referring?"

"Torching the females. Crucifying Choo Choo with rebar."

"Oh, that *it*. Well, who do you think helped me? Sonny and Sully, of course. But they were under what you might call duress. It takes a firm hand to get anything useful out of a couple of junkies."

"Not the fake Cheryl?"

"You have a short memory, don't you? They make drugs for that, you know. Better living through chemicals. I can hook you up if you're interested."

When DeMarco offered no reply, Reddick added, "The woman you call the fake Cheryl is a nonentity. As far as all of you are concerned, she no longer exists."

And then came the epiphany. DeMarco said, "Here's what I think. I think you realize that we already have you on defrauding the government, and that we'll nail you for Cheryl's death, no matter if the evidence is circumstantial or otherwise. And that sooner or later we'll get through the maze you set up online and see for a fact that you were engaged in interstate racketeering by shipping drugs through the mail. You know that you're never going to see the light of day again. So why not go inside with a rep as a homicidal maniac, and buy the fake Cheryl's loyalty at the same time."

"I don't have to buy anybody's anything. I take what I want."

"Then why protect the fake Cheryl? You know she would give you up in a second flat."

"You're the genius here; you tell me why."

"Because you want her to watch after your mother, the only person for whom you have ever felt anything remotely like love. You're a momma's boy."

Reddick's eyes narrowed, but his grin remained.

DeMarco straightened his back. "Since you're in a talkative mood, Luthor, I have another question for you. Why go to the trouble of destroying the car and the females, yet leave Choo Choo standing there for all to see?"

"Ha. That was limp dick's doing. He was supposed to take the shovel out of the car *before* striking the match." Reddick shrugged. "Hey, you get what you pay for."

"You are referring to Sonny Jakiella?" Bowen asked.

"My Sonny boy. With all the brains of a sock puppet."

DeMarco wanted to punch his face. Wanted to knock him down and stomp his head flat. He said, "I hear you think your story will be made into a movie."

"A movie, no. I'm thinking twelve episodes minimum. Either Netflix or HBO."

Unfortunately, it wasn't impossible. The more gruesome the crime and the more twisted the perpetrators, the more likely to be turned into entertainment. DeMarco cringed on the inside but kept his expression unchanged. "You know you can't profit from anything like that. Not a single dollar will come your way."

"I can watch it, though. Over and over and over again. It's a different kind of profit but just as satisfying."

"Sick," DeMarco told him, "yet so like you, Luthor."

"I'm going to insist on creative control. I'll get that little red-headed weenie from *The Italian Job* to play you. What's his name— Seth somebody?"

"You think you'll have time for Netflix in prison? What with all the gangs wanting to beat the crap out of you?"

Reddick laughed. "I'm not afraid of prison. Word gets around about how I handled Choo Choo, I'll be a rock star. A month from now I'll own the place. There's nobody in there but a bunch of two-bit hillbilly crackheads."

"What makes you think you'll go to the Mercer facility? Sheriff," DeMarco said, but kept his eyes fixed on Reddick, "we should look into getting our friend here a room at Polunsky, down in Texas. Lots of dangerous gangs in there, Luthor. From what I hear, shanks and razors are issued with the jumpsuits."

Reddick flinched. Looked up at the sheriff. "That goes in the agreement. I stay in Mercer. Or else I withdraw everything I said. I was coerced."

Again the sheriff stood stone-faced.

Reddick glowered at DeMarco. "You think I'm afraid of gang-bangers? You know my history. I scared *the U.S. Army*, bro. You think I can't handle a bunch of mindless, tatted-up minions?"

DeMarco smiled. "Well, wherever you're sent, you will have a good long time to get yourself elected president of the student body before they ship you out to death row."

"Oh, I'll be seeing you again long before that."

"On the outside? How do you plan to pull that off?"

"You'll see. If you live long enough."

"And what is that supposed to mean?"

"Word is, soldier, you're a wanted man."

"And where did you hear that?"

"The spirits talk to me."

"Is that right?"

"Oh yeah. They whisper in the wind."

"Well, enjoy your hallucinations, Luthor. We're done here. I think I'll go have a nice long walk in the fresh air and get this stink out of my nose." He stood, turned, winked at Jayme, walked away, and choked down the bile rising in his throat.

NINETY-NINE

He had to tell her about the note on the windshield. She would come out of the jail feeling victorious, another bad guy nabbed and stowed away, no injuries to the team, and he did not relish having to rain on that parade, but she had to be forewarned, just in case. He waited beside his car, leaned against the front fender, facing the jail. The hood had cooled already. Gunshots popped somewhere behind him, down on the firing range between the jail and the state correctional institute. The third blue sky day in a row. *The chem trail guys must be on vacation,* he thought.

A chill in the air. The trees were looking barer and browner than they had the day before, more leaves on the ground. And not yet November. An early winter on the way? Most falls he would be alert to the movement of the birds, know when they started massing for the long flight south, but this year he had forgotten to look for them. Too many distractions. Too many people.

All he wanted was to be alone somewhere with Jayme and Hero. He did not want to be responsible for all the others. Wished he and Jayme could pack up the RV and leave today. But he had never been a runner.

Then told himself *Ha, what a lie.* His entire childhood had been an attempt to escape his life, all those solitary days in the woods and along the railroad tracks, losing himself in the city parks, where he could never get deep enough. The army had been another escape.

Ditto the state police. Laraine. The bottle. Maybe even Jayme. No, not her, she could never be reduced to that. Jayme was a blessing. Undeserved. He had to keep her safe.

She came striding out of the door with a wide smile on her face, that beautiful open face that always broke his heart. He smiled in return but also took a quick glance to her left and right. Maybe Khatri *was* stupid enough to attack them there. He would probably find the challenge and the irony of it invigorating. Sick, sick bastard. The world was full of them.

He opened the passenger door as she approached but she did not slide inside as quickly as he would have liked. She paused for a moment beside him, a hand on his arm. "Can you believe that?" she said. "Just to make sure his mother is looked after?"

Yes, it was easy for him to believe. How many times had *he* cursed himself for not being there when his mother took out the razor to slit her wrists? But he answered Jayme's question with a smile, waited until she had lifted both legs inside, then softly closed the door.

Behind the wheel again, a little less nervous ensconced in the illusion of safety, he said, "Coming out of the convention center last night? I don't think you saw it, but there was a note under the windshield wiper."

"What kind of note?" she asked.

"I have it at home. I'll show it to you. I need to get it to the FBI."

"Oh God," she said. "Was it from him again?"

He nodded.

"What is he *doing*? Following us everywhere we go?"

"Him or one of his loony disciples. If he even has any. He wants us to think he does, but I don't know. I doubt it's true."

"What did it say?"

"Just that he hoped we enjoyed our evening, and that he would see us soon. See me soon, I mean."

"Why is he doing this?"

DeMarco shrugged and shook his head. "From now on we need to carry our pieces. Everywhere. Even taking Hero out in the yard for a pee."

"We can't let him control us like that."

"Sweetheart," he said. "Promise me you will carry your piece."

"You don't think he's bluffing? That he would really do something if he gets the chance?"

"He's had lots of chances already," DeMarco said. "That's what puzzles me. On the other hand, there was that little explosive device under the sidewalk. So I think we have to expect that he *will* do something."

"Damn it, Ryan," she said. "I hate the way I let him suck me in. I feel so foolish about that."

"You lead with your heart. I wouldn't want that to ever change."

With her eyes on his, she took one long breath and then another through her nose. Then faced the jail. Three more breaths, this time exhaling through a slit between her lips.

He turned the key and started the engine but did not reach for the gearshift. He watched the jail door a few moments longer. "Where is everybody?" he asked. "Aren't they coming back out?"

"Oh geez, I forgot. They're going to talk to Sonny now. To see if he'll flip and corroborate Reddick's version. I was supposed to ask if you wanted to join them."

He considered their options. Go home, stare at the walls, sit and wait for another good reason to leave the house? Go for a drive, listen to Van Morrison and Jackson Brown and Eva Cassidy, get hungry, have some lunch, then keep driving? Jump in the RV and run forever, eyes always on the rearview mirror? Or finish this job, deal with Loughner, deal with Laraine and the divorce, deal with life and every other three of spades Fate dealt him?

He shut off the engine, extracted the key. Reached for his cell phone. "I need to call the FBI first. I'll catch up with you inside."

She laid a hand on his thigh. "We'll go in together, babe."

ONE HUNDRED

J akiella sat in a slump, not merely broken but dissolving, as if his bones had softened and begun to melt. Flores and Boyd sat facing him; Jayme and DeMarco joined the others standing or leaning against the wall. An odor emanated from Jakiella that DeMarco was surprised to recognize as his father's odor, both sour and musty, almost sulfurous, like a newly opened bottle of cheap red wine but devoid of any floral or fruity scent.

"So what good are you doing by lying now?" Boyd was saying. "Reddick copped to everything we've known from the start. It was his plan, he orchestrated it, you and Sully helped carry it out. That's how it's going to go down in the books. What are you gaining now by not admitting to the truth?"

Fifteen seconds passed in silence. Then Jakiella looked up at DeMarco. "Is this on the level?"

"One hundred percent."

Jakiella dropped his head again. Said, "Okay," a hoarse, guttural croak. He was bent so low, forearms on his thighs, that his words dropped straight down, barely audible. Flores pushed her phone closer to his head.

"Okay what?" she asked.

"Okay, that's what happened."

"You and Sully did what he told you to do," Boyd said. "Yes or no?"

"Yes."

"Who poured the gasoline and torched the vehicle?"

"I did."

"Who told you to do it?"

"Reddick."

"Who held Choo Choo up against the tree?"

"Me and Sully and Micki. Except that Sully didn't want to. She was crying the whole time." His words ran together in a monotonic slur.

"Then why did she do it?" Flores asked.

"Afraid of him. Both of us were."

"Afraid of Reddick?" Boyd asked.

"Yeah."

"Did he threaten you?"

"All the time."

"Then why did the two of you hang around? Why didn't you just go your own way?"

Jakiella lifted his head, regarded Boyd with the most sorrowful eyes DeMarco had ever seen. "He would have cut us off."

"From what?" Boyd asked.

"Black eagle."

"I thought Sully wanted to quit using."

"She tried. Was always trying."

Flores asked, "Did *you* ever try to stop, Sonny?"

He dropped his eyes. Shook his head.

DeMarco thought, *Who administered the chloral hydrate?*

And Flores asked, "Who knocked Choo Choo and the others out to begin with? So that you could get them into the car and out to the woods?"

DeMarco smiled and thought, *Good girl.*

"Micki," Jakiella said. "She put it in their dessert."

"Why?" Boyd asked. "Why did Reddick have them killed?"

"Said they tried to steal his stuff. Money and drugs."

"You sound as if you don't believe that, Sonny."

"Choo Choo wasn't afraid of him. None of them were. He didn't like that."

"So he decided to get rid of them?"

"Him or Micki did. She didn't like extra girls taking business from her."

Boyd asked, "What else was Micki involved in?"

"Everything. Start to finish. Everything he did."

"And you and Sully never knew she wasn't the real Micki?"

Again Jakiella shook his head. "Only one we ever met. I told you that before."

"You told us a lot before," Boyd said. "But most of it was lies. Are you lying to us now?"

"No."

"Everything you have told us is the truth?"

"Yeah," Jakiella said.

Flores said, "Swear it on your daughters' souls."

"Unh," Jakiella moaned, and drew himself tight in a shiver. "I swear."

Boyd turned, looked to Captain Bowen. Bowen nodded.

To Jakiella, Flores said, "A life well-spent, Sonny. Are you proud of yourself?"

"Don't," he whimpered. "Please don't."

"It's a little too late for your pathetic little don'ts, isn't it?"

He made no answer. Collapsed with his forehead on the hard edge of the table, sobbing, body shuddering. And DeMarco thought, *Welcome to the ninth circle of hell, my friend.*

ONE HUNDRED ONE

In the afternoon DeMarco spent a couple of hours in the basement, sweeping the concrete floor, using a broom to chase cob-
webs down off the rafters and walls, sorting through moldy boxes
he hadn't opened in a dozen years—Christmas ornaments not used
since Laraine moved out, tax papers, old books with their pages
stuck together now, a pasta maker he had forgotten he owned—all
the ballast of a shipwrecked marriage. He tinkered with a couple
of lamps that had quit working and had been relegated to the darkness, but even after trying three different bulbs they refused to
produce a glimmer. The dehumidifier had stopped working too,
though he didn't know when, and nothing he touched seemed
worth salvaging. He dragged or carried everything close to the
bottom of the stairs and told himself that he would spend the next
day hauling them out to the curb for Monday's garbage pickup.

The Realtor had told them that clutter was their enemy; clutter
would blind prospective buyers to the "good bones" of the house
and send them scurrying for the door. So while he cleaned up the
basement, Jayme organized the first floor, clearing off the coffee
table and other surfaces, vacuuming, dusting, making mental notes
about what colors would work best for the new sofa pillows and
area rugs the Realtor had suggested she buy.

For the first fifteen minutes Hero followed her as she moved
about the room, but then went to his usual spot at the end of the

coffee table, walked in a circle and then flopped down on the floor. Every time she moved to the other end of the coffee table, he lifted his head, checked to see that she was still there, and rested his chin on the rug again.

DeMarco emerged from the musty dimness near five, his face and hands smudged black with dust, his T-shirt streaked from holding the moldy boxes to his chest. He came into the living room and said, holding his hands at his sides as if they were diseased, "I told the FBI I would bring them the letter."

She had her back to him when he spoke; had been considering the curtains and whether or not they should be replaced. She turned. "You have to drive all the way to Erie again? They couldn't even meet you halfway?"

"I figured I might as well get everything over with at the same time. I'm going to meet with Joe afterward too. I don't think you should be there."

"Oh, baby," she said. "You're going to do that tonight?"

"It has to be done."

"And then what, after you tell him? Are you going to the IAD?"

"I don't know. I guess I'll just play it by ear."

"I can at least ride up and back with you," she said. "I don't have to sit in on the meeting."

"I'd rather you stay home. Just please be careful, okay? We both have to start being a lot more careful now."

"What time do you think you'll be back?"

He glanced at the clock on the cable box. "An hour up, a few minutes to hand off the letter and answer a couple of questions, an hour with Joe, an hour home. So before nine, I hope."

"You're going to take a shower first, right?"

He held out his hands palms up, smudged black with the years. "Want some company?" she asked.

"I wish I had the time. Hold that thought, though, okay?"

"Call me when you leave Joe. Where are you meeting him?"

"Brannigan's on State."

"Does he know why you're coming?"

"We didn't discuss it. But I'm sure he has an idea."

"You should eat something before you see him."

He nodded. "I'll grab something along the way."

"Fast food?" she said. "All that grease and fat? You know what it will do to your stomach."

"My stomach is already a mess, just thinking about going up there."

"I'll make you a fruit smoothie to drink on the way. With ginger to settle your stomach."

"Thank you, baby. That would be perfect."

"If he gets angry, just walk away."

"He won't get angry. He *wanted* me to find out."

She crossed to him and, despite the filth, slipped her hands around his waist. Laid her head against his dirty cheek. "Come home to us as soon as you can."

Her warmth and scent went into him, filled him up and hollowed him out. "You're the only place I want to be."

ONE HUNDRED TWO

Loughner was already two sheets to the wind, red-faced and laughing out loud at the flat-screen on the wall when DeMarco arrived. *The Big Bang Theory*. Four dysfunctional geeks and a gorgeous, ditzy female. Loughner was seated at the near corner of the bar, his back to the door.

DeMarco paused for a moment to scan the room: the heavy, dark-brown nineteenth century furnishings, the thick bar and stools, the plank floor and paneling on the walls—all the same shade of liquid cocoa except for the area covered with checkerboard floor tiles, dirty yellow and cinnamon. The few tables on the little platform on the other side of the room were occupied, all with customers younger than the solitary men at the bar. From the dim larger dining room farther back came a soft rumble of conversation.

The place hadn't changed an inch since the last time DeMarco had set foot in it, the week before he ended things with Laraine. He had used to stop there for a quick one after leaving the street in front of her home, after sitting in his car and listening to music while she entertained a new friend.

It seemed so long ago. Everything seemed so long ago.

He stepped over to the bar. Leaned in between Joe and the burly man next to him, the man's round face close to a shepherd's pie he was busy shoveling into his mouth, chasing every other spoonful with a gulp of stout. DeMarco could smell the rich beefy scent of the shepherd's pie in its white enameled bowl, felt the pulse of the din like a bass drum in his ears. He leaned close to Joe and said, "Want me to see if there's a table open in the back?"

Loughner turned his way; the older man's eyes seemed unfocused. "I like sitting at the bar."

"It's a bit noisy, don't you think?"

"Suit yourself," Loughner said, and raised his glass to his mouth. Scotch on the rocks; DeMarco recognized that scent too.

He crossed to the hostess station and spoke briefly with a pretty brunette in a plaid skirt and white blouse. She looked at her table chart, then placed an X over one of the icons and told him to follow her. He said, "Let me tell my friend," went back and spoke to Loughner, then returned to follow the hostess to a booth against the wall midway into the larger room. Not three feet to the left of the booth was a row of tables, all of them full. It would be impossible to speak there without being overheard. He thanked the hostess for her trouble and said they would stay at the bar.

This time he crossed to the opposite side of Loughner and wedged himself in between Joe and the wall. He did not like the feeling of being boxed in and having to lean down whenever he wished to speak. Things needed to be said that should not have to compete with the laughter and chatter of a hundred people having a good time. His conversation with Joe deserved a closed room with soft lighting, with maybe one of them on his death bed, the other one dressed like Max von Sydow in the original *Exorcist* movie.

Joe finished his scotch and signaled the barman for another one. "And whatever he wants," he said with a nod at DeMarco.

"Water is fine," DeMarco said.

Loughner had to lean a little to his right to look up at him. "You're not even going to have a drink with me?"

"I've pretty much given it up, Joe."

"That's a stupid thing to do."

DeMarco waited until the drinks arrived and the barman moved away before he spoke again. "So Jayme and I made that trip up to Elk County you suggested. Read the logs and talked to Reddick's mother too."

Loughner swished the liquor in his glass, raised it to his lips and took a sip. Held the glass in front of him as if he were checking it for bugs. "I hear you finally got the prick locked up. Took you long enough."

The change in Loughner's tone was obvious. Almost confrontational. But DeMarco recognized it not as anger but preparation. As a boy he had stood before his father a hundred times and had heard that same tone in his own voice, that almost-angry moment of acceptance of what was to come, the slap across his face, the damning curse.

But DeMarco wasn't his father. Would never let himself be such a man. "I wish you hadn't put me in this spot, Joe. Jayme's in it now too."

"What spot would that be?" Loughner asked.

"Why did you carry it around with you all these years? Why didn't you take it to your station commander? Or maybe you did."

"You're talking gibberish, Sergeant. If you have something to say, spit it out."

"You were watching him every chance you got. Reddick Sr. You became obsessed with putting him away."

"Obsessed?" Loughner said. "I don't like the implication of that word."

"I didn't mean it that way, Joe. I'm sorry for my word choice."

"He was the sick one. You would know that if you really knew what you're talking about." His words were coming slower now, thick and low and sticking to one another.

"What all was he into?" DeMarco asked.

"You tell me."

"He was peddling drugs, of course. I'm not sure what else."

"He was selling it to kids. To children. Getting them hooked and then using them for his own sick pleasure."

DeMarco leaned a little closer. "You caught him with that girl, right? The one in your report you described as 'under the influence.'"

"Did I?"

"You didn't say she was only thirteen, though."

"Don't know that I even asked her age."

"You must have. Your partner knew it."

Loughner smiled, gazed down into his glass. "Lou's still kicking, huh? Son of a bitch beat three kinds of cancer. Tough, tough bird."

"I'm thinking you used your baton on Reddick. At first I figured he was pistol-whipped, but I don't think you meant to kill him. That was never your intention."

Loughner continued to smile. "You have a good imagination, I'll give you that. Might want to rein it in a little, though."

"Multiple blunt force traumas to the head and face. Bruises to his stomach, chest, and legs consistent with being kicked."

Loughner's smile twitched at the corner, then he broadened it. "Somebody did a number on him, that's for sure."

"And then you took the girl home. Cleaned up and went back to work. And you've had the truth eating at you every day since."

Loughner sipped his drink, set the glass down on its napkin. Picked up his beer glass and drained it. Signaled to the barman for another one.

Both men watched the barman draw the beer, tilting the glass from slanted to straight up under the tap so as to form a perfect head of brown foam. Only after the beer had been served and the barman moved away did Loughner speak.

"It's a good story," he said. "Too bad it's bullshit."

"Why did you want me to know this, Joe? To do what with it? Take it to IAD?"

"It's your fiction, Sergeant. You can sell it to the movies for all I care."

"If you wanted to get clean of it, why didn't you report it yourself?"

Loughner sipped from his beer glass, wiped the foam from his lips, then leaned to the man on his right, who was sitting back with his eyes on the shelves behind the bar, the white ceramic bowl in front him now empty but for the smears of gravy. "How was that pie?" Loughner asked. "You recommend it?"

"It's always good," the man said. "Very satisfying."

Loughner turned to DeMarco. "You want to try one? It's on me. Gentleman here says it's highly satisfying."

"I'm not very hungry, Joe, but thanks. Why don't you have one?"

He picked up his scotch glass. "Liquid diet. Doctor's orders."

DeMarco leaned in close, his hands on the edge of the bar. "What do you want me to do, Joe? You want me to turn you in? It doesn't make any sense but I can't figure it any other way."

Loughner lifted his chin slightly, raised his eyes to the crowded shelves. The mirror behind the bottles made the shelves appear overloaded, in danger of crashing down. He said, "You ever hear of a guy named Sophocles?"

"I have, yes."

"I used to read those inspirational quotes in *Reader's Digest*.

When I was a younger man. Trying to improve myself, you know? For some reason, one of them stuck with me. I've never been able to get it out of my head."

"I would love to hear it, Joe."

"Who was that guy anyway? That Sophocles? I never bothered to look him up."

"He was a playwright in ancient Greece."

"A playwright, huh? I always figured he was something more important than that. Like an emperor or something."

"What's the quote that stuck with you?"

"Eh. It's all bullshit anyway, isn't it?"

"What is?"

"Inspirational quotes. Philosophy. Religion. What good are they when the shit hits the fan?"

"I don't know, Joe. I think they might be of some benefit. I sort of collect quotes myself."

"Is that right? Let me hear a couple."

"I had this friend, a writer. Thomas Huston."

"I know that name."

"From the murders last year in Mercer County. That case I worked on."

"That's where I heard it," Loughner said.

"Tom wrote fiction but he also left behind a lot of notes. His thoughts on just about every subject in the world."

"So are you going to tell me one or not?"

"He said that we are all aliens somewhere."

"Aliens?" Loughner said. "Like illegal aliens?"

"I guess. Plus the outer space kind. All kinds."

"You sure know how to pick them," Loughner said.

DeMarco answered with a smile. "What he meant is that we all feel out of place sometimes. Like we don't belong here. Strangers in a strange land. It's just another way of saying that we're all the same. We all get lonely, we're all afraid, we all feel lost sometimes."

Loughner shrugged and lifted his glass. "That's why single malt scotch was invented."

"What's that quote from Sophocles you remember?"

"Forget it," Loughner said.

"Come on, Joe. I gave you one of my favorites. Let me hear yours."

"'I would prefer even to fail with honor than win by cheating.'"

DeMarco felt a sudden stab high in his chest. "That's a good one," he said.

"Seemed like it to me, anyway. When I was young and stupid."

DeMarco stood with his hands on the edge of the bar and gazed down the counter. Every stool full, all men his age or older. He could have been one of them. Another solitary man at the bar, trying to fill his emptiness the only way he knew how. The heaviness of that thought, that image, nearly knocked him off balance, made the room cant for a moment. Then he thought of Jayme and the room righted itself.

He pulled away from the bar and crossed behind Loughner and went down to the opposite end and signaled to the barman. He took out a twenty and handed it to him and said, "Get my friend up there a shepherd's pie, will you? You might want to switch him over to coffee too. He's had more than enough for one night."

"I can do that," the barman said.

DeMarco returned to Loughner, then laid a hand on his shoulder. "It's been good talking with you, Joe. Be careful on your way home."

"Yeah, yeah," Loughner said. "You too."

DeMarco went outside and onto the street with the traffic noise and lights and turned north toward the lake and started to walk.

The air was cool and the sky black, every star blacked out by the lights from the city. He pulled out his phone and pressed the Call icon. When Jayme answered, she said, "I've been waiting to hear from you. How did it go?"

"I'll be on my way home soon, baby. Going to go stand on the dock for a while."

"You don't want to talk about it yet?"

"I'm just going to listen to the water for a while, okay? I won't be long. How has your night been?"

"Quiet," she said. "Hero and I have been taking turns reading to each other. *The Hundred and One Dalmatians*."

"Ha," he laughed, and felt the pain and heaviness subsiding from his chest. "You are such a lovely little liar."

ONE HUNDRED THREE

S he was soundly asleep when he returned home, so he undressed and eased into bed beside her. His movements woke Hero, who stood and came around the bed to lie on the floor on that side for a while. DeMarco reached out and scratched between the dog's ears and then lay on his back with his hands crossed atop his chest and began to wonder about all the drama in his life and whether or not any of it really mattered. It all felt very real and often troubling but what if life *was* nothing but a simulation or a hologram as many people said? Before the quantum scientists came along, Poe had written, "All that we see or seem is but a dream within a dream." And before that, Shakespeare had said, "All the world's a stage." Plato had said that everything we see is a mere shadow of the real thing. And Descartes had said, "I think, therefore I am," but had he stopped to consider that maybe he was thinking that thought because somebody else was thinking him thinking it?

Less than 5 percent of the universe is composed of light, he told himself, and nearly six times that amount is composed of dark matter. So it made sense to calculate a human being as composed of a comparable ratio. As above, so below. The odds, then, were six to one that dark matter would eventually win the race. The big question concerned the nature of the remaining 68 percent of the universe and a human being. Some scientists called it dark energy and others called it empty space and it was called quintessence by others, including the ancient Greeks. Whatever it was called, it was the part making the universe expand at a faster and faster rate against all the rules of physics that predicted it should collapse into itself instead. And no one understood why.

DeMarco had a hard enough time keeping track of his own shrinkages and expansions, let alone those of the known and unknown universe. He thought that maybe Jayme was the quintessence breaking all the rules of his personal physics, and he was not bothered in the least by that insubordination. He enjoyed every second of it and hoped it would never cease.

And maybe, now that he thought about it, dark energy was the true nature of the being called God—that 68 percent of the universe that keeps growing and creating more of itself. He hoped it knew what it was doing. But it was too big an issue for a puny human being to ponder, especially when he was trying to fall asleep. So he turned his concentration to his quintessence instead, to the sweet sibilance of her breath as she slept and the warmth and scent and love that, if anything could, would be the only thing that might prevent him from collapsing into himself.

Easy peasy, he thought. *Like picking grape seeds off a wet tile floor.*

ONE HUNDRED FOUR

As a very small boy he had learned the value of being quiet on the outside, keeping his hands and feet and downcast eyes perfectly still even though on the inside his emotions were raging, but on this night nearly half a century later he became aware of an expanding quietude on the inside as well. He had never learned that particular discipline and had always believed it could not be taught without years of practice, and so was surprised to lie there in his bed beside the woman he loved and recognize while she slept his own inner stillness. This was not the same as the stillness after sex or the quiet contentment and gratitude he sometimes felt in her presence. This was a kind of sleepy emptiness he had previously experienced only as a soldier, usually prior to an especially dangerous patrol or when bunking down with the knowledge that an explosive device could land nearby and send him into a permanent sleep. He had never felt this kind of quiet as a civilian. He had counted on it as a form of resignation borne of knowledge that what might or might not happen was wholly out of his control—a necessary resignation during times of war or else one's fear would get the better of him and possibly infect others as well. But it was odd to be swaddled in such quietude now. *Thank you*, he thought to no one in particular, and was surprised and amused when he heard *You're welcome* softly but clearly in a voice not his own inside his head.

That too had never before happened to him, so he explained it away by telling himself that the answer was also his own thought, though not consciously generated. But then he heard, *Your thoughts are my thoughts*.

That, too, was puzzling, but not enough to make him want to fight the sleep that was settling in. He allowed all bemusement to slide away and his body to grow heavy and his mind to fill with a soft and comforting darkness. He was well out of the war and no mortars or rocket fire or IEDs would be slung his way tonight or tomorrow or the next day. There wasn't much in life a man could count on or predict but waking in one piece in the morning finally seemed to be a fairly safe bet to make.

V

Full fathom five thy father lies;
Of his bones are coral made;
Those are pearls that were his eyes.
Nothing of him that doth fade
But doth suffer a sea-change
Into something rich and strange.

—William Shakespeare, *The Tempest*

ONE HUNDRED FIVE

Sometimes even after a good night's sleep he would wake heavy with a nameless sorrow, as bereft and hopeless as if he had lost a fortune the previous day or had lost everyone he loved or had been humiliated beyond repair in front of a million people, and this was one of those mornings. The room was still dark, with only a somewhat less dark filling the window. He had no idea where this sorrow came from, especially after such a peaceful night, but by now he knew it well and was learning not to fear it. Maybe it was a matter of the wrong brain chemicals dripping out, a leakage over which he had no control, or maybe the lingering residue of a past life flaring up. Maybe the alignment of the stars and planets had shifted in the night. If the nameless sorrow could be from one of those sources it could be from any of them. What mattered was not that he woke to sorrow but that he did not climb out of bed still wearing it like a lead robe. It had to be left on the bed so that he, disrobed, could tend to the work of the day.

Fortunately he was learning to shrug off the robe by asking himself why he felt so hopeless and heavy and then ticking off the possible reasons and eliminating them one by one. No, he had not lost a fortune. No, he had not humiliated himself in front of a million people or even one person. No, he was not unhealthy nor destitute nor grotesquely and permanently deformed nor a man who corrupted children or abused animals or deliberately hurt others. He was a decent man like billions of others and only wanted to do something useful and good with his life. Yes, he had lost his mother and his son and his never-born daughter, and he had lost a lot of his past to things he wished now he had never done, but loss is the very foundation of life and to surrender to grief is the epitome of failure, and the bad things he had done all seemed at the time the proper things to do and were never done with malice in his heart. Well, maybe there was some malice in his heart for a couple of the bad things but mostly there was love for his mother as the basis for that malice. Besides, all of those incidents occurred long in his past, and for the next thirty years he had been trying his damnedest to be a good person. So damn the sorrow and the lead robe and the debilitating heaviness of life. He wasn't going to let it ruin another day when so few days remained. He figured he had maybe twenty years left on this beautiful planet, maybe twenty-five, and he wasn't going to spend them lying in bed feeling sorry for himself. There was work to do and even if there weren't he was not going to waste another day. There was sunrise and sunset and the gloaming and the cool soft darkness of autumn. There was good food and music and a dog that woke him with its wet nose every morning and a fine, strong, honest and beautiful woman who loved him. There were bison made of hay and colleagues made of the finest virtues and intentions. And there were truly bad people whom he, if he did his job right, could prevent from doing any more harm. So there was no room left in his life for a nameless sorrow. No room left in his closet for a leaden robe that did nothing but weigh him down. There was another day and then maybe twenty more years of days after that, and nothing short of death itself was going to keep him from appreciating every last one of them.

It was not yet 5:30 a.m. when DeMarco finally slipped out of bed after shedding the leaden robe. Today was a Sunday and he wanted to continue the tradition established just the previous Sunday of walking to the local Sheetz for their breakfast, and because he knew that the rest of the day, after their visit to the cemetery, would offer little opportunity for rest, he was looking forward to a silent walk with Hero through the cool clarity of morning. Later he would inform Captain Bowen about Joe Loughner and his incident in Elk County with Thomas Reddick Sr. He would relay his and Jayme's suspicions and allow Bowen to decide how to handle the situation. It was, after all, a state police matter, and he and Jayme were no longer active members of the state police. Bowen would no doubt confer with his own superior, and up the chain of command the matter would go.

DeMarco figured the odds at fifty-fifty that no actions would be taken against Loughner. Too many former arrests would be jeopardized. Maybe Joe suspected that already. Maybe he knew that nothing of consequence would happen to him. Maybe all he wanted was to share his guilt with somebody. Somebody in whom he had sensed an abundance of guilt already.

For now DeMarco wanted to stop thinking about Joe Loughner. He gathered up his khakis and socks and a clean sweatshirt from the dresser, got his cell phone from the bedside table, then tiptoed downstairs with Hero at his heels. Hero waited at the back door while DeMarco dressed and shut off the alarm system. He laid his cell phone on the kitchen counter and used a finger to scrub his teeth with water from the sink. Soon they were outside. The morning smelled like fishing worms after a heavy rain. Like slimy things wriggling up from underground.

Some writer had once made a list of rules about writing fiction and had placed as number one the admonition that no story should start with the weather. DeMarco stood in the dewy yard, holding to the leash while Hero completed his first tinkle of the morning, and thought that rule complete nonsense. The very idea of having a list of rules for writing fiction was nonsense, but the one about avoiding a description of the weather struck him as especially foolish. Every morning started with the weather; why shouldn't a story? Weather was often not only the barometer of his mood but also the progenitor. This morning, for example, while inhaling the scent of damp grass and the light fog that enveloped him in a diaphanous haze, with a pale orange glow just now suffusing the eastern horizon, and his decision made to speak with Captain Bowen, and the image still in his head of Jayme sleeping peacefully in their bed, her breath deep and soft and even, and with the memory still fresh of the softness of her skin and the warmth and pleasant scent of her body under the sheet and cover, the weather had a calming effect on his mood. The air was too cool for just a sweatshirt but he liked the challenge of the chill and felt it strengthen him, liked the friendly competition between himself and the temperature and knew that he could beat it.

With each breath of morning air DeMarco felt better. It had taken them two weeks to identify Reddick as the murderer and to put him behind bars. Despite Reddick's boasts, DeMarco was confident that the man would never again experience a morning like this one. He also felt better about Miller and Flores, and about Georgina in the women's shelter in Washington County. He had been uncomfortable with the thought of being any kind of mentor to them, but now he was feeling differently about it. He would do what he could for each of them. A person did not have to be a perfect human being to be of assistance to others. Kindness was all that was required. Maybe he wasn't the wisest man in the world but he did have a lifetime of hard experience in his back pocket. Maybe making a lot of mistakes and learning from them was a kind of wisdom too.

He and Hero walked in no hurry to the store on the corner across from the courthouse. The red light at the intersection was still blinking yellow. He tied Hero's leash around a table leg on the patio, then went inside. The store was quiet, with only one other customer, a man at least eighty years old coming toward the door with a Payday candy bar in one hand and two Mounds Bars in the other. DeMarco smiled and held the door for him and thought, *When I'm eighty, I will have candy bars for breakfast too.*

A pair of cashiers, neither more than twenty years old, chatted behind the counter while looking at their cell phones; a middle-aged woman was busy filling the coffee decanters. He stepped up to one of the screens and ordered two everything shmagelz and a sausage and cheese biscuit sandwich, then, while the order was being prepared, poured two large cappuccinos from the machine, capped them, and put two apple fritters in a sack.

Out on the patio a few minutes later, he peeled open the wrapper on the sausage and cheese sandwich and laid it on the concrete. Hero picked the sandwich up off the wrapper as delicately as a graceful old woman at morning tea, flipped it into his mouth, chewed it twice, and swallowed. Then, ready for an encore, he looked up at DeMarco.

"Sorry, boy. Only one. Mama's rules."

The streets were brighter on the walk home, the air clearing, more people rising. He could smell the coffee in the bag in his right hand as he walked and the bagel sandwiches in the bag in his left; no aroma rose from the fritters but his mouth watered at the thought of biting through the crisp glaze of sugar and into the yeasty dough and apple filling.

He was already feeling better about the day. When Jayme awoke he would warm up the sandwiches and coffee and the fritters. Then they would go to the cemetery to visit Ryan Jr. and his tiny sister. The visit would sadden them but also bring a measure of peace. Then he would call Bowen and rid himself and Jayme of the day's only unpleasantness. And then they would make plans for the rest of their lives.

He was feeling very good about the future when he unlocked the back door and came into the kitchen and saw the white envelope lying in the center of the little table. He had seen an envelope exactly like it on the floor of his foyer the previous summer. The sight of this one weakened and dizzied him, and for a few moments he could not believe what he was seeing. Then a wave of chilling fear washed over him and he dropped the leash and, already moving, tossed the three sacks of coffee and food toward the counter and raced into the living room and then up the stairs. He stood beside the bed, his breath too quick and shallow at first, his pulse thumping too loudly for him to determine if Jayme was breathing or not. There was something wrong with his vision too; he was seeing her through a gray mist, the rest of the room dark around the edges. But then she said "Mmm" and smiled in her sleep and the wave of relief that swept over him nearly drove him to his knees.

Still unsteady, he retreated from the room and made his way back down the stairs. In the kitchen he saw that the coffee had spilled inside the sack and was dripping off the counter and onto the floor. But now he was getting angry and wanted to see what message Khatri had sent him this time. He used a paper towel to hold the envelope in place while he used a clean fork to lift the unsealed flap and carefully draw the single sheet of paper out onto the table.

He leaned over it, nauseated and chilled but growing hot with rage, and read the typed message:

Dear Sergeant Detective,

Imagine what I might have done to her in your absence.
Imagine what I will do to her if you refuse my invitation.
You will meet me at the old mill on Slippery Rock Creek.
I will wait until 6:30 a.m. There are eyes on you wherever
you go, whatever you do, even now. If you do not come alone,
or if you are late, consider my invitation withdrawn.
No future invitation will be extended.

I am Magus

ONE HUNDRED SIX

There was no time to think about which action was most prudent or to differentiate right from wrong, no time to think about whom to call or what might happen to him. The image of Jayme in their bed flashed across his mind's eye as he lurched toward the counter and was aware of Hero standing there with the leash attached to his collar and dragging limp on the floor but he had no time for that either. The clock on the stove read 6:19. His focus had narrowed into a pinpoint and his movements felt heavy and thick as he yanked open the drawer and grabbed the 9mm and then spun in the opposite direction to yank his car keys off the hook on his way to the back door. With a quick twist he set the lock and pulled the door shut behind him and raced down off the porch with his thumb repeatedly clicking the Unlock button on his car's remote.

Only when he was in his car and moving in reverse with the tires spinning the wet grass into a gel did he remember his cell phone still on the kitchen counter where he had left it forty minutes earlier. Then he slammed the gearshift into Drive and prayed no one would get in his way. He drove bent forward over the steering wheel and calculated the distance to the old mill at six and a half miles. The time was now 6:21 a.m. Nine minutes for six and a half miles. He would need at least three minutes to get out of town if he slowed as usual for all of the turns and paused at the four stop signs and one traffic light. But he would not pause this morning. He would stop for nothing. The seat belt warning kept beeping but he would not take his hands from the steering wheel or look away from the road except for a quick glance at the 9mm sliding back and forth on the passenger seat with every squealing turn.

ONE HUNDRED SEVEN

Twenty yards past a yellow diamond-shaped sign that read Hidden Drive, DeMarco made a hard right onto a long gravel lane and glanced at the clock: 6:28. He took a deep breath and tapped the brakes to slow to twenty miles per hour. Three more deep breaths and then he came to a stop halfway across the old blacktop parking lot where brown weeds now stood up through the cracks and frost heaves. He put the gearshift in Park but left the engine running, then, keeping his movements slow and, he hoped, undetectable from the building a hundred feet away, he covered the 9mm with his right hand, slid it across the seat, leaned forward, and slipped the barrel and the trigger housing into the waistband below the small of his back. He made sure that his sweatshirt concealed the weapon, then leaned forward again and waited.

He had already decided that Khatri would not walk away this time, not even if he was accompanied by two goons carrying assault rifles. If that happened DeMarco would slip the gearshift into Drive, aim the car directly at Khatri, hit the gas and flatten himself across both seats. The bullets would have to rip through a lot of metal to reach him, but steel-jacketed rounds from an L115A3 would pass through a radiator like gamma rays through cardboard. Still, he would take the chance if one were offered.

The old mill had stood empty for most of eighty years. For a long time it had been an important part of the community but now it stood useless and in decay, surrounded by cracked and broken pavement where nothing grew but the toughest of weeds. He sat facing the rear of the building, the eastern side. The sun had only now reached the bottom of the steeply slanting roof and threw a bright red aura all around that side of the building. A wide path had been made over the years by people walking along the side to the front of the mill, where the huge wheel that turned the grindstone inside could be seen, its big paddles slowly rotting above a dry creek bed.

The sandstone blocks of the first four floors of the building were the same light brown as the flattened grass and weeds surrounding the mill. Four rows of six tall windows each, most of the glass broken out, with sheets of weathered plywood on the inside of every window. Only the single window below the peaked roof was not boarded shut. Six glass panels in that attic window, all intact except for the one in the bottom right corner.

The rage still seethed in DeMarco but the tension was slowly slipping out of his body. He had beaten Khatri's deadline. And now he was prepared to die to keep her safe. If it happened this morning, so be it.

But Khatri must not escape. If DeMarco had his phone he would have called Bowen and Brinker but he had been mindless and stupid and maybe that was the last mistake he would ever make. He took a look out of the passenger window, then out of his own. Nobody on either side. Trees and weeds and scrub grass. The morning haze had lifted and now the sky was a perfect, unbroken blue. Not since childhood had he seen so many consecutive skies like that, all unmarked by a single cloud. He watched for movement along the flat front of the building and at both corners and at the uppermost window. Nothing. The sun peeked above the bottom corner of the roof and threw a sharp light into the windshield. He put a hand to his eyes and tried to cut the glare. *Where are you?* he thought.

His hands were shaking a little and he told himself it was because the air was cold and he hadn't paused to grab a jacket before leaving the house. But a wiser part of him knew that his decision to come here had been rash and not a flattering decision for a man his age. His love for Jayme and his desire to protect her had coupled with an old hatred for being told what to do and with the equally fiery anger, seared into him by his days as a soldier, toward all bullies who threaten innocent people.

On the other hand, had he chosen to stay at home with Jayme, to seal them inside their illusory bunker and call the police, what would have happened? Even the township and municipal police would have arrived at the mill after the 6:30 deadline. And Khatri was slippery. Demented but slippery. He would be long gone before any police arrived, and then what? Then DeMarco's and Jayme's lives would be a prison of fear.

He did not believe that Khatri possessed an army of devoted disciples. In each of the security cameras that had caught his image, he had been alone, a scrawny young man grinning at the camera. His only known disciple was awaiting sentencing and would likely grow old behind bars. He had at most one or two malcontents to push around, castoffs like Connor McBride in search of a purpose, any reason to give their life meaning.

But it did not matter to DeMarco if there were one or three or twenty people inside that building with Khatri. He was not built to hide from danger. Was not wired for it. And there had been no time to think. So he was here now whether he should be or not. Waiting. Hands shaking. Alone with the soft rumble of the engine.

He glanced at the clock: 6:34. And when he looked up through the windshield he saw a figure backlit by the sun walking around the side of the building. Tall and slender, all legs and arms. Khatri. He was taking his steps gingerly over the uneven ground, even put his hand out against a skinny tree to steady himself. Something about the prissiness of his movements made DeMarco smile.

Khatri angled toward the center of the building as he moved forward. Held his hands up, palms out and even with his shoulders. He was wearing cream-colored linen trousers baggy around his legs, a blue nylon windbreaker, the hood pulled over his head.

DeMarco placed his left hand on the door handle. *Wisely and slow*, he told himself. *They stumble that run fast.*

Khatri came to a stop thirty feet from the front of DeMarco's car. He called out something, but DeMarco heard only a muffled wave of noise. He briefly considered driving forward, staying inside the car, though he would not run down a lone unarmed man, not even Khatri. Foolish was one thing but cowardice was another. He would rather be considered a fool than a coward.

He opened the car door. Glanced to the unboarded window at the top of the building, saw no shadow, no movement. Then fixed his eyes on Khatri again. And reminded himself, *This is the man who stabbed her. This is the man who killed your baby.* He welcomed the rage as it flowed back into him, filled him with strength and resolve.

He put his feet outside the car door, felt the chill in the air and smelled the dirty scent of broken asphalt and the fumes from his vehicle's exhaust. He stood behind the door, head cocked, waiting.

Khatri pushed back his hood. "I said I am glad you came!" he called.

"I didn't come here to make you happy." He was shivering now and heard the tightness in his voice.

"And yet I *am* happy. I have traveled all this way to see you again."

DeMarco said nothing. Calculated the distance and the likelihood that he could place a shot or two in Khatri's legs. A skinny man running was not an easy target. Beneath the car's window, he let his hand slip along his thigh and toward his back.

Khatri said, his voice sounding almost musical in the stillness of the morning, lilting, "Do you not wish to know, good sir, why I have invited you here?"

DeMarco offered no reply. He could not stop shivering and knew the tightness of his muscles would do him no good, would slow down every movement but he could not make the quivering stop.

Grinning, Khatri lowered his right hand to his side, and then lowered his left, and DeMarco looked beyond him and up at the highest window in the building and saw the flash like a tiny star exploding.

He was aware of the car window shattering before he felt the pain. The glass shattered at the same instant he was thrown backward off his feet. Then came the loud crack and only then did he recognize the blow to his chest and the searing pain. His first thought was, *Please not now, I have too much to do.*

He landed on his left side, still reaching for the gun at his back. Sucked in a breath and heard the whistling in his throat. Tasted blood in his mouth. Heard pigeons burst explosively off the rooftop, wings thrumming.

"That is why!" Khatri called.

DeMarco scraped his head across the cracked asphalt. Tried to find Khatri in the pool of water that had filled his eyes. He fumbled for the gun and finally found it, struggled to free it, and fired blindly. With each of the four shots his arm rose and the aim went higher, so that the barrel was pointed at the sky with the final shot. Two more shots coming from the building struck the pavement near his head and sprayed his face with slivers of asphalt and dirt. His arm dropped and the gun in his hand clattered away.

He heard footsteps running, quickly fading. Then a muted thumping echoing inside the building. *Ba bump ba bump ba bump ba bump ba bump.* Footsteps banging down wooden stairs in a hollow building. Then more silence.

He blinked, felt a piece of grit in his eye. Both eyes watering, vision blurring. He slid his right hand along his body toward the center of the pain, covered the bullet hole with his palm, pressed down with as much pressure as he could muster. His left arm, stretched out at his side, jerked back and forth, fingers scratching at the rough blacktop. His breath was sticking in his throat now, each inhalation a sloppy, rasping gasp.

He thought of Jayme sleeping. Wished he had had a chance to thank her for finding him and loving him and bringing him back to life. Felt that pain too suffuse him. That sweet, sorrowful pain. He closed his eyes and waited.

There was something more than a little bit humorous to the whole situation, he thought. To all of the desperate machinations men and women put themselves through in a lifetime. As if any of it really matters. As if all of the fear and ambition and terror is in any way warranted.

Now that the adrenaline was seeping out of his brain, he knew what he should have done. He should have called out the horse cavalry to surround the old mill with men and armaments three layers deep. A simple 9-1-1 call would have done it. He should have locked the doors and sat tight and enjoyed a nice cup of coffee in the quiet of the morning. But Khatri had played DeMarco's ego like a fiddle. The kid had perfect timing. Don't let DeMarco think. Don't give him two seconds to take a deep breath. That's when mistakes happen. When the brain clouds with rage and you go racing out of the house leaving your phone on the kitchen counter. When a simple phone call, three simple digits, would have changed everything.

Yep, DeMarco thought. He had to smile despite the pain. *He played you like a cheap violin.*

Sometime later, how soon or long he could not say, a sound emerged from the stillness, a softly treading sound of someone approaching in no hurry, rubber heels scuffing the ground. *The shooter*, he thought. DeMarco opened his eyes and moved his head, tucked his chin and blinked to clear his vision. Scratched a quivering hand across the pavement, feeling for the gun.

But no, the man coming toward him was unarmed, a shadow against the sky, arms low at his side, both hands empty. DeMarco wanted to lift a hand to him, call out, but there was no air in his lungs, no strength in his arm.

The figure kept approaching, a silhouette of a man taking long, easy strides. The sun was rising above the roof of the building now, surrounding the man with a brilliant nimbus of golden light so that bit by bit his features came into view, the clean-shaven smiling face and the neatly combed blond hair, the clean firm lines of his face and limbs and the easy, rhythmic gait of his stride. He was a tall man, slender but not thin, dressed in a pair of faded blue jeans, a crisp white shirt untucked, a pair of white Chuck Taylor high-tops. The sudden clarity and keenness of his vision surprised DeMarco. And although he had never before looked at a man and considered him beautiful, he did so now, the most beautiful man he had ever seen.

And that was when DeMarco recognized the man and realized that he had been waiting for him a long time, had been searching for him as a boy escaping into the safety of the woods and in every grain of Iraqi sand and in the flames and screams in Panama. And here he was now, unbidden. Not some comic book character. Not some actor in costume and makeup. He was the real thing. The bona fide. *Imagine that*, DeMarco thought.

The man strode up to him, stopped just short of DeMarco's feet, and smiled down.

Only seconds earlier DeMarco had thought his last breath gone, but he found himself breathing easier now, the air warmer, his body relaxing in the stillness of the new day. To the man smiling down at him, DeMarco said, "You don't look the way I expected." The strength and clarity of his own voice pleased him and he thought that he might be able to stand up soon.

"I am sorry to disappoint you."

"No apology necessary," DeMarco said, and pushed himself up on one elbow and returned the man's smile.

The man said, "'The robbed that smiles steals something from the thief.'"

"But you seem like such a friendly thief," DeMarco said.

The man held his smile as he turned slowly to the side and lifted his gaze to the whitening blue of the sky. "It is a beautiful day, isn't it, Ryan?"

And in that moment every second of DeMarco's life flashed across his mind's eye like images on a movie reel, running in reverse through the horror and dread accompanying Khatri's letter to the tenderness of Jayme smiling in her sleep to his love for Huston and Ryan Jr. and Laraine and the academy, back through the blind unthinking sickness of Iraq and Panama to the relief of his father's death and the comfort of his mother's touch, the healing humbling holiness of the woods and their uplifting elegance, the cleansing wind in his face as he stood high above a silent river, the beautiful black rope of shiny-scaled muscle he found sunning itself on the railroad tracks and the small birds swooping and gliding over the water, and every other moment all the way back to his birth with the chill of the hospital room and the inarticulate wonder and hope of his tiny beating heart, all of it not just witnessed but lived again in its fullness, all in that moment between the man's question and DeMarco's answer, lived first in reverse and then forward again, all while the air chilled his skin and the glow of a tangerine sun warmed it and he recognized that he was yet in his body but never of it.

"Every day is beautiful," he said, and knew that as the truest sentence he had ever spoken.

The man nodded while still gazing at the sky. Then he looked down at DeMarco once more, the beautiful smile widening as he extended his hand.

"And now, my friend," the man told him as their hands came together palm to palm, "I have so many things to show you."

Reading Group Guide

1. At the beginning of this book, DeMarco has officially retired. What is he running away from?

2. How do you feel about Chase Miller's sensationalist style of journalism? In what ways can it help or harm a case?

3. Jayme struggles after her miscarriage, though working the case seems to help her break out of her grief. Why do you think that is?

4. Both Flores and DeMarco get a bad feeling after interviewing Reddick. Why did they suspect him? Did you feel the same?

5. Do you think it was wise for DeMarco and Jayme to let Chase, a civilian, get involved with the case? Why or why not?

6. Discuss Daniella Flores. What motivates her?

7. Throughout the investigation, the serial killer Daksh Khatri stalks and threatens Jayme and DeMarco. Put yourself in their shoes. Would you want to keep working the case, knowing a killer was hot on your heels? Why or why not?

8. How do you feel about Sonny Jakiella, the burnout who worked for Reddick and seemed to genuinely love Amber Sullivan? Do you think he is a good person?

9. Would working an upsetting case like this one make you question the goodness of people? Do you think it's possible to investigate violent crimes without becoming jaded?

10. DeMarco starts having strange dreams. What are they about? What is he questioning?

11. Think about the murder Jack Loughton committed—he killed Reddick Sr., a drug dealer, pedophile, and serial abuser. How does that crime compare with the murders that Reddick Jr. committed—that of vulnerable young women? Are some murders worse than others? Should the punishments be equal?

12. If you were in DeMarco's place, would you choose to tell your superiors about Loughton's crime? Why or why not?

13. What do you think happens to DeMarco at the end of the book?

ACKNOWLEDGMENTS

As always, my deepest thanks to my agent, Sandy Lu, and to my editor, Anna Michels, and to the entire Sourcebooks team, and, of course, to my readers.

ABOUT THE AUTHOR

Randall Silvis is the author of twenty-one critically acclaimed books of fiction and nonfiction. Also a prize-winning playwright, produced screenwriter, and prolific essayist, his literary awards include the Drue Heinz Literature Prize, two NEA Literature Fellowships, a Fulbright Senior Scholar Research Award, and an honorary Doctor of Letters degree for "a sustained record of distinguished literary achievement."